HAWKHURST

29 SEP 2018

20 OCT 2018

28 DEC 2018

-5 MAR 2019

-2 MAY 2019

18 J...

08 ...

2...2019

...2021

10/Nov/22

-3 OCT 2023

KT-434-273

Books should be returned or renewed by the last date above. Renew by phone **03000 41 31 31** or online *www.kent.gov.uk/libs*

Libraries Registration & Archives

CUSTOMER SERVICE EXCELLENCE

Kent County Council
kent.gov.uk

'Truly fine entertainment ... sure to leave you **hungering for more**'
Publishers Weekly

C334259713

'Well written and **keeps you guessing** to the end'
Sun

'I hope Ms Roberts continues to write new
stories for this pair for a long time to come . . .
Long live Eve and Roarke!'
Bella

'This is a series that gets **better and better**
as it continues'
Shots Magazine

'A **perfect balance** of suspense, futuristic police
procedure and steamy romance'
Publishers Weekly

'**Much loved**'
Daily Express

'A **fast-paced, superbly crafted story** that is an
amazing – and possibly unique – combination
of top-notch suspense, detection, and
intensely romantic sensuality'
Library Journal

'**Great fun**'
Cosmopolitan

J.D. Robb's number one bestselling series began with *Naked in Death*, introducing the world to the tough as nails but emotionally damaged homicide cop Eve Dallas and charismatic Irish rogue Roarke. Since then, Robb has become one of the biggest thriller writers on earth, with each novel reaching number one on bestseller charts the world over.

Robb is the pseudonym of Nora Roberts, recently named the third bestselling author in the world, with 500 million books in print.

Become a fan on Facebook at
Nora Roberts and J. D. Robb

J. D. ROBB

DARK IN DEATH

piatkus

PIATKUS

First published in the United States in 2018 by Berkeley,
a division of Penguin Random House LLC
First published in Great Britain in 2018 by Piatkus
This paperback edition published in 2018 by Piatkus

3 5 7 9 10 8 6 4 2

Copyright © 2018 by Nora Roberts

The moral right of the author has been asserted.

*All characters and events in this publication, other than those
clearly in the public domain, are fictitious and any resemblance
to real persons, living or dead, is purely coincidental*

All rights reserved.
No part of this publication may be reproduced, stored in a
retrieval system, or transmitted in any form or by any means, without
the prior permission in writing of the publisher, nor be otherwise circulated
in any form of binding or cover other than that in which it is published
and without a similar condition including this condition
being imposed on the subsequent purchaser.

A CIP catalogue record for this book
is available from the British Library.

ISBN 978-0-349-41787-5

Printed and bound by CPI Group (UK) Ltd, Croydon, CR0 4YY

Papers used by Piatkus are from well-managed forests
and other responsible sources.

Piatkus
An imprint of
Little, Brown Book Group
Carmelite House
50 Victoria Embankment
London EC4Y 0DZ

An Hachette UK Company
www.hachette.co.uk

www.littlebrown.co.uk

Finish, good lady; the bright day is done,
And we are for the dark.

The great art of writing is the art
of making people real to themselves
with words.

LOGAN PEARSALL SMITH

1

On the mega screen bloody murder played out in classic black and white for an audience of one hundred and seven. With the sharp screech of violins, violas, and cellos that number dropped by one.

Unlike the character of Marion Crane, Chanel Rylan didn't scream or flail at the shock of violent death. In row twenty-seven in theater three of Vid Galaxy in New York City's Times Square, she let out little more than a mouse squeak as the ice pick plunged into the back of her neck.

Her body gave one quick jerk; her hands batted at the air and upended the mini bucket of popcorn in her lap. Her last breath escaped like a long sigh.

She died in the dark as blood circled black down the drain on the screen.

No one noticed. With all eyes, all attention riveted to the screen, no one noticed the killer slip into the aisle and walk away from dark deeds.

When Lola Kawaski hurried back in, dropping into her aisle seat, she cursed in a whisper, 'Damn it, I can't believe

I missed the big, classic scene. *And* I'm going to have to miss the rest. I'm kicking myself for agreeing to be on call tonight, but we've got an emergency coming in, so—'

In apology, she patted Chanel's arm. The movement caused her dead friend's body to shift, slumping against Lola. Lola's initial amusement – leave it to an actor to go all dramatic – flipped to alarm.

Then the screaming started.

Lieutenant Eve Dallas stood over the body. Someone had dragged said body into the aisle in a useless attempt at first – or more accurately last – aid. Now the scene was totally fucked.

So was her evening at home. She'd actually walked in the door on time for once, out of the claw swipe of late February wind and into the warmth of a Summerset-free house, as Roarke's majordomo was off on his winter vacation.

She'd even beaten Roarke home and experienced the odd and rare sensation of having the big-ass fancy house all to herself. And the cat.

She'd considered squeezing in a workout – contemplated just jogging from room to room; if she managed to hit them all that would equal a pretty damn serious workout.

Instead, she wandered into the big front parlor with its art, antiques, and rich colors. She decided she deserved a big red circle around the day on the 2061 calendar, and she put on the fire, poured a glass of wine, sat in one of the butt-cuddling chairs.

The cat sat at her feet, eyed her suspiciously.

'I know, weird, right? I'm just sitting here.' Kicking out her legs, she crossed her booted feet at the ankles. 'Maybe I could get used to it,' she said, lifting the wine for the first sip.

Her communicator signaled.

'Or maybe not.'

Two minutes later, she grabbed her coat from the newel post where she'd tossed it. And Roarke walked in.

The wind followed him, tossing his black-as-midnight hair around that remarkable warrior-poet face. His perfectly sculpted mouth curved, those wild blue eyes smiled at her.

Then he noted she shot her arms into the coat rather than stripping it off.

He said, 'Uh-oh.'

'Sorry. Five damn minutes home, and I caught one. DB at a vid palace in Times Square.'

'An unhappy ending for the DB.' Ireland cruised through his voice. And as she wrapped her scarf around her neck, he left the door open to the cold. 'Opening scene for my cop.'

He caught her face in his hands, kissed her – taking his time with it, despite the cold wind and the call of duty.

'I'll see you later,' she told him. 'Maybe even sooner. There's a glass of wine in the parlor. I'd just poured it.'

He gave her another, briefer kiss. 'I'll think of you when I drink it.'

Less than ten minutes after she'd walked in, she started out. 'Don't forget to feed the cat.'

'As if he'd let me.'

Now Eve imagined Galahad's belly was full, and Roarke had enjoyed her wine while she studied a woman identified as Chanel Rylan by her vid-watching friend.

Eve stood alone in the theater, having already taken the report of the first officer on scene. She studied the blood on the back of the chair – first in from the aisle – and the smeared drops helpful civilians had stepped in when moving the body.

Eve opened her field kit and, with her hands and boots sealed, crouched down to do her job.

She pressed the victim's right thumb to her Identi-pad.

'Victim is identified as Chanel Rylan, mixed-race female, age thirty-two. No marriages, no offspring, no current cohab.'

She took out her gauges for time of death.

'TOD eighteen-thirty-one. No defensive wounds visible. ME to confirm.'

Prepared to turn the body, Eve looked up and over at the familiar clomp, and watched her partner start down the slanted aisle.

Pink, fuzzy-topped boots, pink magic coat, and today's scarf a long snake of variegated blues. Peabody wore a matching cap over a flip of dark hair.

'So much for the night off.' Peabody studied the victim. 'Then again, she's got nothing but nights off now.'

'Seal up. I want to turn her. First on scene reports the wound's at the base of her neck.'

Peabody stripped off her outdoor gear, sealed up. 'I'd just

ordered a bowl of minestrone. McNab offered to come with, but I told him to eat, and take mine to go. I figured if you wanted EDD, we'd just tag him.'

Since Eve considered Peabody's skinny, wildly fashionable main man an e-ace, if she did, she would.

Together, they turned the body. Eve parted the victim's blood-matted blond hair.

'Single puncture wound, base of the skull. Not a flat blade. Stiletto maybe, or an ice pick. Hand me microgoggles.'

Eve fit them on, her eyes huge and whiskey brown behind the lenses as she leaned over. 'Smooth, small, and deep. Looks about three inches deep. No hesitation marks visible.'

She rocked back on her heels, still crouched on long legs as she studied the chair.

'The killer had to be sitting right behind her. I can't see any angle to the wound. The theater's dark, people are watching the screen. All he has to do is lean up a little and jam it into her. In and out. A couple of seconds. If this hit the brain stem, she wouldn't even have time to say ouch.'

She stood now, hooked her thumbs in the front pockets of her trousers. A tall woman and lean with it, she took a penlight from the kit to examine the aisle, the seat directly behind the victim's.

'You can call in the sweepers. Long shot he left any trace on the seat – or that we'll be able to separate it from the hundreds of other asses who've sat in it – but maybe we'll get lucky.'

She scanned the space, raking her fingers through her

short chop of brown hair. 'No cams in the theater. I've got a uniform getting security discs from the lobby, the concession area, anywhere there are cams. A place this size . . . '

'Ten theaters, two floors, with the two mega screens upstairs,' Peabody supplied. 'This is one of the smaller theaters in here, mostly for classic vids. Looks like, what, it holds maybe three hundred.'

'Two seventy-five.' Eve had already checked. 'Uniforms have over a hundred people holding in the theater next door. The friend of the vic and three potential wits holding in another. Call the dead wagon, Peabody, and let's get a uniform to sit with her until she's bagged and tagged.'

'She was really pretty.'

'Yeah, I bet that's a comfort to her now.'

She retrieved her coat, scanning, thinking, assessing as she put it on. 'It's cold. Cold and precise. And cowardly. A stab in the back, in the dark. Didn't need to see her face, to watch her die, so some emotional detachment.'

Eve took one last look at the body – objective, but not detached. Chanel Rylan was hers now, and that was as attached as it could get.

'Start with the big group,' she told Peabody as they walked out. 'Hold on to anyone sitting in the vic's section, or directly across the aisle. Anyone who touched the body.'

'The killer could be one of them. Could still be here.'

'Could be,' Eve agreed. 'That would be ballsy. Stab in the back in the dark, not ballsy. But killing in public, even in the dark, takes some balls. We need a search for the weapon.

All bins and recyclers, all areas. If the killer hung in, he had to ditch the weapon.'

Eve paused a moment in the wide, dimly lit corridor that led to the various theaters. 'Me? I'd do the jab, stick the weapon back in my pocket, and slip out.'

Hands on hips, she studied the setup. 'Who's going to notice? Somebody needs a pit stop, wants more popcorn. He wouldn't even have to leave the building. He could just walk into one of the other theaters down here, take a seat in the back.

'We need to check and see what time the other vids let out, which ones ended before the body was discovered. If any did, he could have just walked out like the rest.'

Eve signaled to a uniform. 'Nobody touches or uses any trash bin or recycler. I want the sweepers to do a full search. That includes bathrooms. Which theater houses the audience from the crime scene?'

'That's number one, Lieutenant. *A Dog and His Day*. Kid-friendly early show. It let out at eighteen-thirty-five, so it was between shows when first on scene arrived to secure the scene.'

'That answers that,' Eve murmured. 'Peabody, start in theater one. Where's the friend of the victim?'

'We've got her and three others in separate areas in number five. The three jumped in to try to assist, comprom-ised the body and the scene. All three were seated in the proximity of the victim.'

'Okay. Peabody, go ahead and pull in McNab. We're

going to need more hands anyway, and he's likely to get here and review the security feed before either of us finish with the wits.'

'Will do. Dallas, some of the wits are probably going to need to use the bathroom before we're done.'

'Hell, you're right. Officer, have a team clear the unisex facilities on the second level. Odds are slim the killer went up there to ditch the weapon, if he did ditch it. But clear it first – sealed up and on record. Anyone who needs to go needs to be accompanied by an officer. One at a time, and the facility is subsequently recleared before the next. Got that?'

'Yes, sir.'

'Do employees have facilities, a locker area, break room?'

'Ah . . .'

'Find out, have it closed off. Let's get started, Peabody.'

Eve moved down the long, curving corridor to the double doors of theater five.

She saw the woman seated with a female uniform in the rear row of the far right section. A man and woman together, one man alone, all with two officers, spread out in the far left section.

Nobody looked very happy.

Eve went to the lone woman first, gave the uniform the nod to step out.

'I'm Lieutenant Dallas.'

'Chanel . . . I don't understand.'

Eve sat. The chairs here were wider, deeper than those at the crime scene. 'I'm sorry, Ms . . .'

'Kawaski. Lola Kawaski.'

'I'm sorry, Ms Kawaski. You and Ms Rylan were friends.'

'Besties, roomies. I needed a roomie when I busted up with my boyfriend like, God, like, ten years ago. Chanel had just moved here, and she was one of the aps. We just hit it off straight-out. We've been there for each other through all the thin and thick. And now ...'

Lola pressed fingers to eyes red from weeping.

'I'm very sorry for your loss. I know it's hard right now, but I have questions I need to ask. You may be able to help us find who did this to her and why.'

'There's just no why.' Lola sobbed into her hands. 'No why.'

There was always a why, Eve thought.

'Was Chanel involved with anyone? Maybe she had a bad breakup?'

Lola shook her head, began to wind her long tail of brown hair around her fingers. 'Nobody serious right now, or in the last year or so. She had a serious, back like four or five years ago, but they busted. Not mean or anything. Just busted when he got a break, a part in a home-screen series. But they shot it up in Canada, west Canada. So they busted. Chanel was happy for him, you know, but she was New York. Broadway. She worked plenty in swing, too.'

'Swing.'

'It's like the supporting cast in a play, and you have to learn lots of the parts because you're going to play more than one character. She worked at Broadway Babies, too. It's a restaurant in the theater district where the waitstaff sings and performs while they serve you. She worked really hard.'

'Did she beat someone out for a part, cause resentment there?'

'It happens. People in the business know it happens. I know lots of them through Chanel. They get pissy, maybe, or depressed, but they don't kill each other. She had lots of friends. She dated around, but not serious. She was bi. We didn't . . . I'm just straight, and we were like sisters. She kept it light dating after Damien. She was happy for him. He's still out there – Canada, and New LA – in another series. But it broke her heart a little, too.'

'So she dated a lot of people, competed for a lot of parts.'

'Yeah, that was, like, her life. I'm not going to say everybody loved her, but a lot did, and a lot really liked her or respected her. I don't know anybody who'd do this to her. Who'd just . . . It doesn't feel real.'

'Why don't you tell me what happened tonight? You and Chanel decided to see this vid. Why this vid, at this theater, at this time?'

'That's easy. It's classic, and we're both really into classic vids. We try to come every couple weeks. If Chanel's in a play, we work it around rehearsals or workshops or performances. She was in auditions for one now – second callback – so we came to the six o'clock because she had the night off, and we were going to go out to dinner, then to this club for open mic. She loves to hit open mics. It helps her rev for a big audition. It was just a girl-pal night on the town.'

'So you came here often.'

'At least a couple times a month. Mondays if she didn't have a shift at the restaurant because the theater's dark. Wednesdays if she was between plays. Sometimes we'd hit a matinee on my day off if she wasn't in rehearsal.'

'So coming here was a routine for you. And just the two of you?'

'Mostly. We'd double-dated here a few times, but mostly people aren't as into classic vids as we are. It's, you know, our little thing.'

'Tell me about this evening. Walk me through it.'

'Okay.' Lola took a deep breath, swiped her hands over her face. 'Chanel was juiced up because she thought she nailed the first callback. We met for a drink when I got off work.'

'Where?'

'Toodles, over on Seventh. I work just a couple blocks from there, so she met me. We hit happy hour, split a half carafe of house wine and a plate of mini pierogies. We just talked about stuff, like always. Her callback and, oh, Carmine, this sweet teacup poodle I neutered today. I'm a vet. Then we walked to the theater, talking about the first time each of us saw *Psycho*, and how it freaked me so I didn't take a shower for months, and how she watched it over and over to study Janet Leigh's performance.'

'Did you notice anyone who seemed to be listening to your conversations? Paying too much attention?'

'No. I just didn't.'

11

'Okay, keep going.'

'So we got here early enough to get popcorn and drinks and good seats. The classic theater's never full, especially on a weeknight, but I really like the aisle seat. And I wanted one especially since I was on call. I hate when people pick their way across the aisle in front of you during a vid. We just settled in, hung out for a couple minutes until it started.'

'Did anyone speak to either of you? Out in the lobby, in the theater? Did you notice anyone who made you feel uncomfortable?'

'No, we were talking to each other. I mean, the guy at the concession stand asked if we wanted the special but we didn't.'

'Okay. Your initial statement said you came back to your seat and found Chanel. Why did you leave the theater?'

'I was on call, and my 'link vibrated. Right after Marion had dinner, had the talk with Norman Bates. I had to go out to the lobby to take it. I work at Pet Care, and we run a twenty-four-hour emergency clinic. There's a vet assistant and a couple of support staff in the clinic at all times, but one of the vets is on call for emergencies. Gloria, the assistant on duty, said we had an emergency coming in.'

'What kind of emergency?'

'A dog, struck by a car, and the owner was bringing him right in. I had to go – if the dog needed surgery or had to be put to sleep, they needed a vet. I got some information from Gloria, but she didn't have much because the owner was panicked and running with the dog. I gave her instructions because he'd probably get there before I could, then I went back to tell ... to tell Chanel. I — I sat down for a second, said how I'd missed the big scene. You know, the shower scene, and I was sorry, but I had to go into work. I ...'

Lola covered her face now, rocked. 'I put my hand on her arm, I think. I think. She just sort of tipped against me. I started to laugh, I think. Drama queen. Then I ... there was blood. I could feel it, smell it, and she wasn't moving. I'm a little, ah, not sure exactly then.'

Her hands shook as she lowered them, and her eyes blurred as she tried to focus on Eve. 'I think I started screaming. I think I tried to drag her up, and I was scream-ing for help. I think people were like shut up, sit down. But other people came over, and I think somebody ran for an usher or security or I don't know. The lights came on, and the vid stopped, and Chanel was lying there.'

'Lola, did you see anyone come out when you were in the lobby on your 'link? Did you pass anyone going in or out of the theater?'

'I don't think so. I was kind of annoyed to be called out, then, well, some poor dog's hurt, so I was pretty much focused on talking it through with Gloria.'

'How long do you figure you were out of the theater?'

'I'm not sure. Maybe four or five minutes. I don't think more than that. Well.' She shut her eyes. 'Wait. I saw it was the nine-one-one signal we use for emergencies. I got up, went out. I went all the way out to the lobby because even with the soundproofing you can kind of hear the vids, just enough to be distracting. I still had my drink, so I walked over to the area where you can sit and eat if you want. I guess there were a few people there, waiting for the next show. I tagged Gloria back, talked to her – a couple minutes, maybe three, because she's still a little green and I wanted to be sure she prepped. Then I walked back. So however long that was.'

'Did you see who was sitting in the row behind you?'

'I didn't notice. You mostly notice the people in front of you, if they get in the way. Behind or around, if they're talking or rattling, you know. It was nice and quiet in the vid. People who go to classics are usually really respectful.'

'What about the dog?'

'The dog? Oh, oh, God, the dog. I had to tag Gloria. The officer asked me not to say why, just that I had an emergency of my own, and to pull in Carter or Lori.'

'About how long after you took the emergency tag did you tag them back, tell them to get another vet?'

'I'm not sure, really not. I guess fifteen or twenty minutes. Maybe even longer. I just forgot about that poor dog.'

'Understandable. I'm surprised the clinic didn't tag you again after the owner brought the injured dog in.'

'He hadn't gotten there, Gloria said.'

Eve only nodded. 'He must've been running a long way. Is there someone we can contact for you, Lola? Someone you'd want to stay with you?'

'I don't think I can go back to our apartment yet. I just

don't think I can stand that until I . . . I'm sort of seeing this guy. Maybe I can go to his place for a while. Maybe.'

'Do you want us to contact him for you, have him come and get you?'

Eyes welling again, Lola nodded.

'Give me his contact information. We'll take care of it. I'm going to have the officer take you out to the lobby, stay with you.'

'Will you talk to me again? When you know . . . when you know, will you tell me?'

'Yes. And if you think of anything else, you contact me.' Eve reached into her own pocket – almost surprised to actually produce cards. Gave one to Lola.

Eve called the uniform back, gave her the friend's contact information. Then turned her attention to the three people across the theater.

She chose one at random, sat down beside him. 'I'm Lieutenant Dallas.'

'Um. Mark Snyder.'

'You came to the vid alone, Mr Snyder?'

'Yeah. I wanted to absorb it, without distractions. I'm a film student. I, ah . . . ' He clasped his hands together, stared at the blank screen. 'I'm working on my master's at NYU. Oh boy, this is really, really real.'

Though she'd run him, Eve judged him to be in his early twenties, a young black man with wild and improbably red dreads, a bar stud through his left eyebrow.

'Why this vid?'

'Hitchcock. I'm doing a paper on Hitchcock, and this particular work is a major part of the paper. But I, but I— Sorry.'

He pressed a hand to his stomach, spent a couple of seconds breathing. 'I – I love film. I want to direct. The classics are a particular inspiration to me. I come here a lot. The classics, at least two or three times a month and, in general, probably twice that. It's a different, ah, experience watching in a theater than on a home screen or a mobile.'

'Where were you sitting?'

'In the same row as . . . the same row. In the center seat. We were the only ones in the row. I like to sit alone as much as I can, but I sort of knew them – the women. I mean, I'd seen them here off and on, and I knew they'd be quiet. Not talking during the vid or being distracting, so I sat in the center seat.'

'Tell me what happened.'

'It was – it was right after Bates cleans up the bathroom, after the shower scene. He's going to wrap Marion's body in the shower curtain, put her and her luggage and the money she stole and wrapped in newspaper in her car and sink it in the swamp. Perkins is amazing, he's perfect. You believe him. You believe he's horrified, panicked, protecting his crazy mother. I was studying the work, his expressions, his body language, and she started screaming.'

He took a moment to swallow. 'The woman on the aisle, I mean. It jerked me out, pulled me out of the story. I was annoyed for a second, but then I realized it was one of the women in the row, the ones I sort of knew. So I knew something was really wrong, because they're respectful. And the way she was screaming – I'm sorry, I don't know her name. The one with the darker hair. I stood up. I could see something was wrong with the other woman. The blond woman. I thought she'd gotten sick or something. I started over, and the couple there?'

He gestured to the man and woman seated in another section. 'They started over, too. From the other side. They were together on the other side, so we got there, and ... there was blood, and the screaming, and they said – the other couple – to go for help, to get the lights on while they laid down the one with the blood in the aisle. I ran out, and part of me – in my head – kept running. Like a vid in my head. But I grabbed somebody from the lobby, and told him somebody in number three was hurt really bad. We needed an ambulance. They needed to turn on the houselights. She was bleeding really bad.

'I don't know why I went back in, because in my head I was running away. The woman of the couple – not the one with the, with the one who got hurt, but the couple who tried to help. She's a— God, I can't find my words. A physician assistant. She said that, and she had blood on her, and she told people to stay back. I sat down, I just sat down because I didn't think I could stand up. And then the police came.'

'Did you notice anyone sitting in the row behind you?'

'Not behind me, but behind them. At the end of the

row. I really didn't want anyone in my box, if you know what I mean. Within my area. In front, beside, behind. And there were lots of empty spots. I saw somebody slide into the row behind right after the houselights went down, and would've moved if he'd come toward the center. But he just sat behind them.'

'A man.'

'I . . . I don't know. I didn't look so much as sense. The houselights were down, and the opening credits starting to roll. I hate people who come in late, so I sensed the movement, figured I'd just move if he came into my box, but he didn't. Or she. Honestly, it was dark, and it didn't matter if it was a man or a woman to me. It was a corner-of-the-eye sort of thing.'

'Was he or she there when you heard and reacted to the screams?'

'I don't know.'

'You stood up, started across the row. Was there anyone behind the women?'

'Give me a sec, okay?' He shut his eyes. 'I'm going to visualize it. I don't want to, but I will. I'm watching Anthony Perkins embody Norman Bates, because he does. He becomes and you as the audience believe. And she screams. To my right, she screams. The really, really pretty blonde is slumped over the brunette with the soft eyes. The brunette's screaming, struggling to lift her friend. And I know something's very wrong. Very wrong, so I stand up. Some people are yelling for her to shut up, but I know something's

18

just wrong, so I start over, and see the man and woman start over from the other section. And . . .'

'No.' He opened his eyes. 'Nobody was sitting behind them when I stood up. The whole row behind was empty.'

'Okay, Mark, that's very helpful.' Eve dug in her pocket to give him a card. 'If you think of anything else, if you get a better sense of the person who sat behind them, contact me. Do you need a ride home?'

'I think I want to walk. I think I need to walk.' He got up when Eve did. 'You think the person who sat behind them killed her.'

'I need to find out.'

'I wish I'd looked. I wish I'd just turned my head a couple inches to the right and looked. I have good visual skills. If I'd looked, I'd be able to tell you what the person looked like. But I didn't look. I just thought: Good, not going to push into my box, and the vid's starting. Then I was inside the vid until the screams. Forty-five seconds.'

'What's forty-five seconds?'

'Sorry, the shower scene. It runs for forty-five brilliant, terrifying seconds. I just wonder if the last thing she saw before . . . if the last thing she saw was murder.'

Forty-five seconds, Eve thought when he walked away.

More than enough time to kill.

2

While sweepers in their white suits sucked and brushed and tweezed and collected, Eve sat at the back of the crime scene working on her notes.

The scene itself, the witness statements, the timing, and what she knew about the victim already told her a great deal.

When McNab bounced in on his plaid airboots, the symphony of hoops on his earlobe glinting in the bright houselights, she paused in her work.

'Reviewed the feed straight through from the time the vic came in – that's seventeen-forty-eight – until the first responders entered. Eighteen-thirty-nine. Nobody left through the lobby or using emergency exits from your TOD until the show let out in number one at eighteen-thirty-five. Then you've got maybe a hundred and fifty, and at least forty percent of them under twelve, streaming out.'

'Odds are he walked out with that group.' Eve looked down to row twenty-eight. 'He kills her, slips out of here, walks down to the other theater. Just has to hang there for a few minutes, then stroll out with a bunch of kids.

'We need to look for people coming in earlier, hanging out in the lobby. Anyone who moved toward the theaters when the vic did. And anyone who came in directly after her. Most probably solos. See who we can match with the group leaving from one.'

'I can cover that.' He slipped his hands into two of the half dozen pockets in his atomic-blue baggies. 'You ever see it? *Psycho*?'

'Yeah. It's in Roarke's collection. He's a fan of the Hitchdick.'

'The what?'

'The director guy.'

'Is that really his name?'

'Something like that.'

'Huh. So really creepy vid. Seriously old and creepy. Maybe it's not just chance, right? Maybe some psycho picked *Psycho*, and the vic? Wrong place, wrong time.'

'Nope. Specific target.' Eve rose as Peabody came in. 'The vic's friend and vid mate's a vet. On call for emergency detail tonight. And she happens to get a nine-one-one from the clinic that takes her out of the theater right before the vic's jabbed. Plus it's looking bogus.'

'The friend didn't get the tag?' Peabody asked.

'No, she got it. The clinic got it. Some guy claiming his dog got run over and—'

'Oh, poor doggie!'

Eve sent Peabody a sour look. 'There was no dog. The dog was bullshit, a ploy to remove Lola Kawaski and give the killer a clear shot at Chanel Rylan.

'Timed it,' Eve continued. 'The timing's perfect. And so's the research. The killer knew Rylan would be here, knew Kawaski was on call, knew when the big shower scene would hit, and anybody who'd shelled out to see this vid would be focused on the screen.'

'Or covering their eyes.' McNab wagged his thumb at Peabody.

'I did ... so,' Peabody admitted. 'None of the people I talked to saw anything. One guy thinks maybe he noticed somebody leaving, but it's an indefinite maybe. He was in the back, watching the slice and dice with his date's face buried in his shoulder.'

'Timing,' Eve repeated. 'He had it worked out.'

'And he knew her,' Peabody put in.

'Yeah, knew her, chose her, stalked her, studied her. The question is why. The vic was an actress who supplemented that income working at someplace called Broadway Babies.'

'I love that place! We love that place.'

McNab grinned at Peabody. 'Dorky fun.'

'I like dorky fun. Jeez, she might've waited on us.'

'The friend says the vic was up for a part. Maybe somebody didn't want her to get it. Killed in a theater.' Eve shrugged. 'It could play. No current relationship, no recent breakups, but maybe she brushed off somebody who didn't like being brushed. She was a switch-hitter, so we look at both teams.'

'It feels a little impersonal for relationship revenge,' Peabody pointed out.

'Agreed, but we look so we can close that line off. Plus there's enough personal in it for that look. This night, this theater, the bogus dog emergency. McNab, copy the security feed to my home unit. I want to take a look. And why don't you give whoever's in charge here the bad news that this theater will be sealed off and shut down until further notice.'

'No prob.'

'I got one more.'

'I'm here to serve, LT.'

'The animal clinic. Pet Care on Seventh. Hit that on your way home, will you? See if you can tap where that emergency call came from. If you need to take the e-toys in, tag me, and I'll get the clearance.'

'All over it and back again.'

'Peabody, since you like the Babies place, let's go swing by there, see what we see.'

'Yay!'

Eve saw her partner and the e-ace bump wiggling fingers – their strange little gesture of affection – before McNab pulled a bright purple earflap hat over his head and long blond ponytail.

Since they didn't mortify her by locking lips, she ignored it.

Outside, she and Peabody hiked the two blocks to the overpriced underground lot through the unrelenting insanity of Times Square.

They wound through the drunks, the revelers, the gawking

tourists, the hustlers, and the street-level licensed companions while lights flashed and mega screens hawked designer fashion worn by pouty and sexually ambiguous models.

Eve caught the eye of a street thief, watched him wisely turn on his heel and head fast in the opposite direction. His coat – likely with several of the loot pockets already holding wallets and wrist units – flapped around his legs.

Eve skirted around construction barriers. If it wasn't drunks, thieves, and tourists, it was some guy in a hard hat jacking a hole in the street.

She went into the relative quiet of the lot, opted to take the stairs down.

'Are we going to do notification after the restaurant?'

'I did it.' Boots clanged on the metal steps. 'Just the parents, and they live in Wisconsin.'

Shocked faces, glazed eyes, choked voices.

'I talked to a couple people who work the concession. They knew her. Not personally,' Peabody added. 'But they knew her face, said she was always friendly. She sang "Happy Birthday" to one of them a couple months ago. Small popcorn, medium Diet Coke, and for a comedy, she added gummy bears.'

'Creature of habit,' Eve said when they reached the car. 'It makes it easy to stalk and study and plan. We need to run the staff. Even the ones not on tonight. People who saw her regularly, got to know her habits.'

'How'd he make the tag to the vet place, make it so close to the murder?'

'A good question, and one I hope McNab finds the answer to.'

'A partner? A partner makes the tag.'

'Maybe.'

'It's more logistical than the killer making it: Have to do it outside the theater – then come in again, sit down again, kill her, get up, walk out again. More likely someone notices that. The in, sit, stand, out, in, and all that.'

Eve didn't disagree – up and down, in and out brought attention. But she wanted verification.

She parked again, a half block from where her navigation system put the restaurant. This time she copped a street-level spot. In a loading zone, but flipping on her On Duty light covered that.

'I know I told you what a mag time we had in Mexico, and thanked you about a zillion times.'

'So don't do it again.'

'What I didn't say,' Peabody continued, 'mostly because I wanted to see if the results stuck, was how McNab conked on the shuttle on the way to the villa. Just dropped out, and he extremely loves flying. And after we got there and basked, had a couple of birdbath margaritas, took a swim, he conked again – even before we continued to bask with sex – and slept dead out for twelve solid.'

'Like you said, he needed a break.'

'And he got one. You and Roarke made it so he got one. I'd've been okay if he'd slept the entire time we were there, but the twelve solid really helped. So we had lots of sex.'

'This is how you say thank you?'

'We had lots and *lots* of sex,' Peabody said, unabashed. 'Lots of drinks, lots of sitting around doing nothing, lots of everything that wasn't work. And it's stuck. He's got his bounce back.'

'McNab always bounces.'

'But it's the real deal again. The natural bounce. It's a load off, Dallas. I just wanted to say.'

'Good. Good,' she repeated when she reached for the door of the restaurant.

She opened it to a blast of voices raised in song, and the smell of Italian cooking that made her stomach yearn.

Eve stepped to the hostess podium, where the woman behind it beamed a smile, held up a finger, then joined her rather stupendous soprano on the chorus.

People at tables, in booths stopped twirling pasta, stabbing meatballs, forking up chicken piccata to applaud.

The music dropped away into the clatter of dishes, the hum and buzz of conversation. And the waitstaff, all clad in sleek black, continued to serve and clear as if belting out some Broadway standard just came with the field greens salad.

'Welcome to Broadway Babies. Do you have a reservation?'

'I have this.' Eve palmed her badge, tipped it up.

'Oh! Oh dear, is there a problem, Officer?'

'Lieutenant. I need to speak to whoever's in charge.'

'Of course. That would be Annalisa. If you'd wait here, I'll get her.'

As she scurried away, the party at a long table in the center of the room burst into mad laughter all at once. As if taking his cue, one of the bartenders began to sing as he poured wine.

Across the room, a waitress did a hands-on-hips dance toward him, made it a duet.

'I love this place! It's just so much fun.'

Fun, Eve thought, if your idea of same equaled waitstaff singing and dancing around your table while you were trying to eat. Or, Jesus, actually pulling you up from your seat, spinning you around while singing in your face.

Then again, the man currently being spun and sung to and, good God, the woman the bartender grabbed up – after actually leaping over the damn bar – both appeared to enjoy it all just fine.

It took all kinds.

The hostess hurried back, accompanied by a woman with whipped-cream-white hair, tiger-gold eyes, and a statuesque body tucked into a bold blue dress.

'Good evening, I'm Annalisa Bacardo,' she said, with the faintest accent that went with the scents of Italian food. 'How can I help?'

'Is there somewhere more private where we can talk?'

'Of course.' The polite smile never wavered. 'I would like to ask what we might be discussing.'

'Chanel Rylan.'

'Chanel?' The smile only widened. 'Surely Chanel couldn't be in any trouble with the police. She's ...'

Something in Eve's flat, direct gaze caused the smile to fade. 'Yes, of course. If you'll come with me.'

Annalisa led them back, through the swinging kitchen doors, into the heat and chaos of the heart of a busy restaurant.

'My office is through here – I need to be close. Giavanni!' She called out, then rattled off a spate of Italian before she opened a door, waved Eve and Peabody through.

The office largely consisted of a desk, a couple of chairs, and walls covered with photos.

'Our staff, over the years – twenty-two years – performing all over the world. Off-planet as well. Here, Chanel.'

She tapped a photo of the doomed actress, spotlighted, arms outstretched, face lifted.

'What's happened to her? She's been hurt?'

'I'm sorry to inform you Chanel Rylan was killed tonight.'

'But no.' Going as pale as her hair, Annalisa braced a hand on the desk, slowly lowered into a folding chair. 'No, she's . . . An accident?'

'No, not an accident.'

'I . . . A moment, please.' She clasped her hands in her lap, shut her eyes. 'I'm rude,' she managed. 'Please sit down. Please sit.'

'Could I get you some water, Ms Bacardo?'

'Annalisa,' she murmured, eyes still closed. 'I'm Annalisa. There is wine over there. I would very much thank you for bringing me a glass of wine.'

She sat in silence until Peabody touched her hand, put a glass of wine in it.

'Thank you.' She sipped, sipped again. 'They're my children, my family. Some will only perform here, in this happy place. Some will go on to more, to much more. They're my family. Please tell me what happened to her.'

'She was killed tonight at the Vid Galaxy, Times Square.'

'You have the murderer?'

'Not at this time.'

'You must.' Those tiger eyes went bright and hard. 'You must find and punish who did this. She was sweet and smart and talented. She brought joy. Those who would kill one who brings joy have no place in the world. What can I do to help you put him away from the world?'

'Do you know anyone who'd want to hurt her?'

'I promise you I don't.'

'Someone she was involved with, romantically, sexually?'

'She had many romances. She brought joy there, too. Lightly,' Annalisa added. 'Her work was first. No one serious, no one angry.'

'Competitors, in her work.'

'Ah, there is drama and strife and camaraderie and even a little madness in such work. But I know of no one. She was talented and worked hard, but not destined to be a star. That takes more. She was happy to have what she had, to do work that satisfied and fed her, to make a living doing what brought her joy and gave it. Some are more ruthless, yes? Some don't have a care for bruising feelings or crushing opportunities. She didn't have that quality. I think this must have been a madman, and someone who didn't know her.'

'Maybe you noticed someone who paid too much attention to her, who came in, watched her.'

'The tourists come and go, though some come back when they visit New York again. We have regulars, and family groups who often come to celebrate a birthday or anniversary. I noticed nothing like this. If one of the others had, I would have been told. Family,' she reminded Eve. 'And family looks out for each other. I want to help, but there's no one I know who would have hurt her.'

'That helps.'

'How?'

'It tells me you feel it's very unlikely someone who works here or comes in on a regular basis would have done this.'

'I believe it absolutely.'

'Who on your staff was she most friendly with?'

'Ah, we all work together, perform together. We are a company, too. But I would say Micha – on the bar. They sometimes . . . dated. Lightly, for both. And Teresa, one of our sous chefs. They were friendly, and also dated lightly. And Eliza, a waitress. Sometimes they were up for the same part, and would support each other. Often they would run lines together.

'You will need to speak to them?'

'Yes.'

'I will arrange it. But Teresa? She has this night off.'

'If you'd give us her contact information, we'll take care of that.'

'I will. I will tell you as well both Eliza and Micha have

been here since four-thirty. We have a short rehearsal before we open, and there is restaurant business as well.'

'That's also helpful, thank you.'

'I'll bring Eliza back first. I have to arrange for someone to take the bar for Micha. May I bring you wine?'

'Appreciate it, but we're not allowed. On duty.'

'That's very much too bad, but I'll bring you cappuccino. We make very excellent cappuccino.'

Eve drummed her fingers on her thigh when Annalisa stepped out. 'I think, if her killer stalked her here, he was subtle about it, careful about it. That's a woman who'd notice, or would be told if anybody gave the wrong vibe. Both she and the roommate insist the vic had no angry or disgruntled exes. But some can play that game and seethe inside.'

Rising, Eve wandered the little room. 'But it strikes as less personal than an ex or a rival. We'll talk to these two, just to wind it up, then unless something pops out, call it. I'll put together the book and board at home. We'll hit the morgue first thing in the morning, see if there's anything we missed about the body.'

'Homicide,' Peabody intoned. 'Our day starts and ends with death.'

'That's why we get the shitty bucks, Peabody.'

Eve drove through the gates of home for the second time that night. She wanted that glass of wine Annalisa had offered – though the cappuccino hadn't sucked. And she wanted something, anything, that tasted even half as good as the air in Broadway Babies.

But wants took second place to needs, she thought. She needed to set up her murder board and book, and to think about Chanel Rylan.

Lights sparkled in the windows of the big house, lending it that castle-in-a-fairy-tale air. Low-lying clouds, shadows in the night sky, floated over turrets and towers. She caught a hint, just a hint, of the moon behind those blanketing clouds.

The wind, quieter than it had been, still bit, so little felt better than escaping it and letting the warmth inside envelop.

Once again, she tossed her coat and scarf on the newel post. This time no cat waited. She'd find him, she knew, with the master of the house.

Book and board first, she thought, then she'd catch up with them. But when she walked into her office, she found them both stretched out on a sofa, the fire snapping. The man held a book in his hand, had a glass of wine on the table. The fat lump of a cat sprawled across Roarke's knees.

'And there she is.'

'I figured you'd be in your office, or watching a vid.'

'Work's done for the day – for me, in any case. And watching a vid's more fun with you. Reading's a nice solitary choice.'

He gave the cat a nudge that had Galahad rolling over on his back. 'You've work yet.'

'Yeah. Sorry.'

He got up, setting the book aside, walked to her. 'You'll tell me about it.'

She moved into him, wrapped her arms around him, just held there. 'Sometimes it hits me especially.'

'What does?'

'That I have this to come home to.'

She'd tell him about it, she thought, knowing from experience that it would help line up her thoughts.

'I'll wager you haven't eaten.'

'You'd win that bet. It has to be Italian. The last interviews were in an Italian restaurant and it smelled like heaven coated in red sauce.'

'I can take care of that. Pour yourself a glass of that wine,' he advised as he eased back. 'It's exceptional. Then you can tell me about it while we eat.'

'"We"? Didn't you eat already?'

'I did some work, I did some reading. It's not that late,' he added and started toward the kitchen. 'Especially for an Italian meal.'

She poured the wine. He was right, as usual. Exceptional. And while he programmed the meal, she started on her murder board.

'Your victim?' He glanced at the ID shot on the board as he carried domed plates to the table by the window. 'She was lovely.'

'Yeah. An actress – theater – doubled as a waitress at Broadway Babies.'

'Ah, the place where they sing while they dish up the

pasta.' He went back into the kitchen, came out with salad, bread.

'That's the one. Weird, but people sure looked happy.'

He glanced back at the board after he set the rest on the table. '*Psycho*? Was she hacked to death in the shower?'

'No, but that's what she was watching when somebody jabbed a thin, sharp blade into the base of her skull. That smells really good.'

She stepped over. She could work her way through a salad if the reward was pasta.

'One of the vid palaces in Times Square,' she said as she sat. 'Early evening show in the classic vid theater. Her name was Chanel Rylan.'

And she told him of murder and misery while they ate.

He listened, with little comment, until Eve cleared the salad bowls and he lifted the domes on one of his wife's personal favorites. Spaghetti and meatballs.

As he knew her body language intimately, he noted she relaxed by a few degrees even before she wound the first forkful of pasta.

'Your conclusion would be a target-specific victim, with the emergency call to the friend the cap on that stone.'

'Bogus emergency,' Eve said with a mouthful of pasta. 'Pretty exquisite timing.'

'It is.' Watching her relax with the meal made him glad he'd waited for her. 'And the choice of that timing. The shower scene – the shocker, the murder of what the unsuspecting audience believes is the central character – thirty minutes into the vid. That forty-five seconds of stunning violence.'

'How do you know that?' She poked her fork in the air before stabbing a meatball. 'Thirty minutes in, forty-five seconds.'

'It's one of those things you pick up. I have no doubt that in the single viewing you had of the vid with me a year or so ago, your cop brain would have estimated that timing very precisely.'

'You're not a cop, as you like to remind me.'

'Happily. But I live with one, and would make another wager. She's already concluding the purpose of that exquisite timing.'

'Rich guy always making sure bets.' She ate more pasta. 'Forty-five seconds, during which anybody who had an ass in a chair would be completely focused on the screen. Or have their hand slapped over their eyes, like Peabody on her first viewing. The timing, the method say target specific. The victim herself . . . ' With a shake of her head, Eve picked up her wine.

'Tell me about her.'

'Happy, hardworking, talented. Three of the top words her friend, her parents, her employer, her coworkers all used to describe her. Sexually she batted for both teams, but didn't take the game too seriously. The only long-term ex moved to Canada years ago – career deal. No big drama, according to her friend, and he'd have no motive to come back and stab her to death.'

'But you'll look at him.'

'You've got to look. She was up for a part – a bigger one than usual – so I'll look at whoever else is up for it.'

He knew her – the tone, the body language, the look in those cop's eyes. 'But?'

'Okay, it's target specific. You can't discount that bullshit dog emergency that had the person sitting beside her leaving the theater for several minutes. The timing of that, the fact the killer sat right behind her, which indicates he either followed her there or knew she'd be there. That's no random stab in the dark. Literally.'

He nodded as he ate. 'And again, but?'

'There had to be countless, less risky ways to kill her. She's a night creature, right? Either coming out of the theater after a performance at night, or from the restaurant. Walking home from the restaurant after shift, from the theater after a show. Grab her, stab her, and book it. But this was dramatic, right? And really risky. And it depended on everything falling into place.'

'Which it seems to have done.'

'Yeah.' She stabbed at another meatball. 'But. What if somebody decides to sit beside the killer? What if the friend decides to ignore the call, even for a few minutes? What if somebody else walks out at the same time as the killer? If you're going to plan as well as he or she did, those are risks that have to be weighed in. So why go to all that trouble, take all that time to find that moment, when there are easier ways?'

'The killer enjoys or craves the risk and the drama?'

36

'Maybe, yeah, and I've got to tug on that. And maybe the method, the precision of it, the moment of it, were all as specific as the victim. Maybe, shit, maybe they had sex during that scene sometime in the past. And it meant more to him or her than it did to the victim. Maybe he'd seen her in that theater before, and something she said, did, the way she looked triggered something.'

'How long before the showing are the layout of vids announced?'

Sitting back for a moment, she picked up her wine, lifted the glass toward him. 'That's a good question, Mister Civilian. Three months. They set the classic vids up three months ahead, advertise them in-theater and online. And before you ask, the victim and her friend had a routine, and going to that vid, on that night fell right into it. Plus both of them blasted it on their social media feeds. "Going to *Psycho* with my bestie." "Girls' night at the Bates Motel." I'll never understand why people do that stupid shit, but they do.'

Eve paused, ate a little more. 'She's coming across as a decent human being, one who enjoyed her life, her work, had a nice circle of casual friends – and that bestie. He ended that, and so far, while the method says she was a target, nothing's popping to show why.'

'What can I do to help?'

'I'm not sure there's much at this stage with this one.'

'Throw me a bone.'

She sat back with her wine again, studied him as she sipped. 'You could just go back to your book.'

'Or?'

On a half laugh she sipped again. 'Okay, or. You could run the background on the ex, check any travel over the last couple days. Eliminate him or nudge him onto the list. Damien Forsythe, currently living and working in the Calgary area of Canada. He's a regular on some series. *The Enduring.*'

'That's simple enough. What's on your agenda?'

'A deeper look into the vic. So far she's not telling me much. Some basic checking on her friend, the pet clinic and staff, a few runs on staff at the restaurant, and the play, the other contenders, she was auditioning for.'

'That's quite a bit.'

'Mostly just routine.'

'Well then, I'll see to my assignment.' Rising, he looked back at the board. 'Sometimes there's just no logical reason.'

'But there's always a reason.'

3

With a pot of black coffee, Eve settled into the work. Routine, yes, and some of it tedious. But routine mattered, demanded structure and direction, and tedium could lead to rewards.

Not so much this time, she thought as she worked her way through the life of Chanel Rylan.

Nothing stood out, nothing rang a bell. Other than a handful of traffic violations, including a minor accident, no injuries, prior to moving to New York, she had no bumps.

Slightly above average student – with stellar marks in drama, theater, dance, music. Starring roles in school plays, some community theater.

No medical issues that showed up on a standard run. No pregnancies, no rehab.

Financially, Eve mused, she'd done okay, and obviously wasn't in it for the dough. Her outlay for clothes, rent, the voice, acting, and dancing lessons she continued ate up most of her income.

Eve shifted to Lola Kawaski.

Lola had two bumps – two arrests for protesting for animal rights. Currently, and for the past three years, she'd worked as one of the three rotating vets at Pet Care. Previously, she'd studied for her license and worked as a veterinary assistant at Pet Care.

So that showed either loyalty or an appreciation for routine.

Eve finished it out – financially the vet did better than the actress/waitress, but the vet sure wasn't rolling in it – as Roarke came in.

He poured himself a mug of Eve's coffee. 'I sent the details on the ex to your file.'

'Give me a roundup.'

'His only bump – from your standpoint – along the way was a charge of drunk and disorderly. This after a bachelor party. He's had a couple of high-profile romances since moving to Calgary – and also keeps a residence in New L.A. The romances might be quite sincere or the result of a publicity campaign. His star seems to be rising. He gets good reviews, gives clever interviews, and appears to have the respect of his current cast and crew.'

Roarke eased a hip onto a leg of her command center. 'Not only hasn't he traveled out of Canada in the last week or so, he was, at the time of your murder, in front of cameras, shooting a scene.'

'You didn't get that from a run.'

'I didn't, no. I got that when I noticed I'm acquainted with one of the producers on the series.'

'Aren't you acquainted with everybody?'

'At times it seems as though. In any case,' he continued, 'I tagged him up, chatted a bit. And was able to wind it around to how things were going on the set and so on.'

Eve nodded approval. 'Better that way than direct. The ex is going to hear about it before much longer, but better to ease the info out without adding murder to it.'

'So I thought. When I asked, he mentioned they'd just wrapped a key scene only an hour before, one they'd worked on most of the day. I was treated to nearly a bloody play-by-play of the shoot, the setup, the technical challenges, and so on. And to the characters therein. Damien Forsythe's character played an integral part in it.'

'He didn't make sense anyway. We'll cross him off. Thanks.'

With a shake of his head, Roarke drank more coffee. 'You owe me thanks, as the man blathered on for twenty minutes.'

Eve shot a finger at him. 'You asked for it.'

'I did. I can't deny it. I'll be a glutton for punishment and say give me someone else to run.'

Eve glanced down at her notes. 'Annalisa Bacardo.'

On a frown, Roarke lowered his mug. 'That name seems familiar.'

'You're probably acquainted. She owns the restaurant where the vic worked. The singing waiter place.'

'Hmm, something. I can't quite snag it up.' He rose, walked around to sit at her auxiliary unit. Seconds later, he leaned back. 'Yes, of course.'

Eve picked up her coffee, smirked. 'She's a little old for you, ace.'

'Age means nothing to the heart.'

'Or the dick.'

'I'd be insulted for my dick if that weren't completely true. However, in this case, I've never met the woman, much less had any part of my anatomy involved with her. I have heard of her.'

He swiveled his chair toward Eve, sat back a bit. 'About thirty years ago, Annalisa Bacardo lit up Broadway. A genuine diva, multiple Tony Awards. Her name alone could make or break a play. Musicals were her forte, and she translated that talent to the screen a time or two, to exceptional reviews.'

'How come she's not still lighting things up instead of running a restaurant?'

'She was involved personally and professionally with Justin Jackson, another towering talent. They didn't always perform together, but when they did? Magic.' Roarke flicked his fingers in the air. 'You can read about it if you like.'

'Just keep going.'

'They didn't marry, but lived together, had a child together. A daughter,' he said, glancing at the screen to corroborate his memory. 'When the child was about three, and Annalisa was in rehearsals for a new production, Justin walked the girl to the park. On the way, a car jumped the curb, struck both of them. Killed both of them.'

'Ah, Jesus.'

'She hasn't performed since, that I know of. I didn't

realize she owned Broadway Babies.' Curious, he did another search. 'She owns it under the name Lost Angels.'

'She said the staff were her children,' Eve remembered, 'her family, and I guess they are. I've confirmed she was in the restaurant at the time of the murder, but this gives me a better sense of her.'

Sitting back, Eve scanned the screen, picked up her coffee. Then with a hiss, swiveled to face Roarke. 'I'm getting nothing from any connections, from anybody who'd be connected to a connection. Target specific.'

Eve pushed up and away to pace, to think on her feet. 'All current evidence points there, and target specific generally equals personal. But it doesn't feel personal. Not in method, not in background of vic. So, potentially, the victim represents a type, or was a surrogate. Mira territory.'

She paused by the board. 'I need to talk to her. The vid. Was that just luck of the draw, or also specific? The research into the victim could have started back when the schedule of vids was announced. The vid becomes the trigger, but then, if so, how does the killer latch onto Rylan in the first place?'

Roarke waited a beat to determine if she had asked the question to herself or to him. Decided it was both. 'I imagine there's a subscription service.'

'A what?'

'Like a season buy – so many tickets purchased in advance – and a sign-up for tickets to ones slated to show.'

'Like season tickets for baseball. Shit.' She double-timed it back to her comp to run a search. Roarke beat her to it.

'Rylan belonged to the theater's Golden Ticket rewards program.'

'Show-off.'

'We do what we do. Buy a package of twenty-five tickets per year, get one free, an automatic ten percent discount at concessions, a monthly newsletter, an assortment of benefits,' Roarke added.

'They probably split it, Rylan and Kawaski. I can verify that, but that's what they did. So, the killer maybe buys the same package – I'm going to want to see the subscription list. Sees her there often enough to focus in on her. Maybe he makes a pass she deflects. But ...' Tapping her fist on the workstation, she shook her head. 'It wasn't sexual. The killing wasn't sexual so that doesn't hold for me. The on-screen killing, that's sexual. Killer spies on victim through peephole, enters when vic's naked and vulnerable in the shower. Knife penetrates. A lot.'

'The on-screen murder provides the sexual component?'

'I don't know. I don't think so, but I'll talk with Mira. To me, this was quick, nasty business. In the dark. The vic's facing away, not toward. She's fully dressed. The killer penetrates, yeah, but it's one jab. On-screen it's ...'

Eve made a decent mimic of the shower scene's repeated shriek while she mimed jabbing repeatedly with a knife.

'Murder usually makes sense,' she continued, 'even if it turns out to be crazy, shit-house-rat sense. So far I've got a victim with no known enemies or bitter, even mildly annoyed exes, no big potful of money or influence, no apparent knowledge of some dastardly deed or connection thereto. No sexual component. But at the same time, the killer knew her or took the time, made the effort to learn her routine and habits, as well as the routine and habits of her roommate.

'She stands for something, someone,' Eve finished. 'It's all that makes crazy, shit-house-rat sense.'

'Then it seems to me you've shaken out quite a bit in a few hours.'

'Maybe. Or maybe I'm off base and the killer jerked off while anticipating the shower scene and the murder, then shot his wad of sexual component in his boxers when he jabbed the sharp into the base of Rylan's skull.'

'That's a visual I'd just as soon not have playing in my head.'

'Or' – Eve rose, circled the board again – 'she's up for a part. She's beaten out others for parts before.'

'And lost out to others, I assume.'

'Yeah, but we'll stick with beating out. It's a circle, a community – though some likely come in, others likely give up – but you'd get to know each other. If you're up for the same part, odds are you've been up against each other before. Her coworkers at the restaurant didn't ring for me, at all, but they've been up for the same part over the years. Maybe someone had enough, or someone went desperate. Have to have this one or I'm finished. Have to have it or I can't pay the rent, whatever. Have to have it. Not so much time or effort needed to learn the victim's routine and habits, to get information on the roommate. You're in the same club already.'

'Wouldn't it make more sense to wait and see who got the part?'

Eyes on the board, on Chanel Rylan, Eve fisted her hands on her hips. 'Desperate makes for crazy, shit-house-rat sense.'

'It's impossible to disagree.'

'So I talk to her agent. I talk to whoever's in charge of the auditions. And we see where there's overlap. It wasn't sex, a twisted version of love; it wasn't rage; it wasn't for financial gain, revenge, or, as far as it shows, to preserve a secret. It sure as hell wasn't random. That leaves jealousy as the most likely motive.'

'What part was she up for?' Roarke wondered.

'Some new play. Second lead. Not even the headliner.'

Roarke rose, drew her in against him. 'You'll just keep circling the board and the same thought pattern. You can't talk to anyone else until tomorrow, dig into it until. Let's shut it down for the night.'

'Everyone I talked to who knew her liked her. But they're actors, so they all know how to put on a show.'

He tapped a finger to the dent in her chin. 'You're a cop, and you excel at seeing through a show.'

'Yeah, and what I saw came off as real. People liked her. Still, somebody killed her – specifically – and more, did it in a way that involved unnecessary risks. Something's missing.'

'If there is, you'll find it. But not tonight.'

'No, not tonight.' She drew back to shut down, and abruptly remembered. 'We're Summerset-free.'

'And, since I'm sure you're interested, he's very much enjoying his winter break.'

'Yeah, great. We have to have sex.'

'Well now, if you insist.'

When he reached for her, she gave him a light shove back. 'Not so fast, pal. I've got logistics to consider.'

'It's all right. I remember how it's done very well, and can walk you through it.'

'We'll see who walks who where. I've got it. Count to thirty.'

He let out a laugh. 'Seriously?'

'You want sex or not?'

Arching his eyebrows, his gaze locked on hers, he said, 'One.'

She gave him a hot, noisy kiss, then jogged out of the room.

He counted it off as he shut down her machine, the fireplace, the lights, strolled into his own office to do the same.

When he hit thirty, he stepped into the hall, spotted one of her boots.

'Ha.' He walked to it, picked it up, continued in that direction. He found the second boot after a turn to the right.

Amused, he picked that up as well. 'So she's after a game.'

He'd play. He could, of course, simply ask the house system where she was, or call up the monitors and see for himself.

But that would be cheating.

He followed the trail, found her jacket on a doorknob. Though he recognized a ploy, he also understood the double bluff, so opened the door, ordered the lights.

No, they wouldn't be making good use of the big gel bed in that particular guest room.

He put her jacket and the boots on a bench in the hall, continued on.

When he'd worked with architects and engineers on the design of the house, when he'd watched it built layer by layer, he hadn't imagined himself wandering through it some night, following the trail of his wife's stripped-off clothing.

And there a sock.

He paused to study a painting he'd stolen, oh, six or seven years before. A lonely hooded figure crossing a windswept moor under brooding skies. He'd taken it for his own collection, as it had pulled at him, that resolve, the loneliness, while his primary target of a small, exquisite Corot he'd sold for a very tidy fee.

Then he'd met his cop, his mate, the love of his life, and he'd arranged for the painting of the lonely figure to be 'found' and returned to its owner.

Then he'd bought it, legitimately.

He'd done the same with the other bits and bites he'd still had inside the plump pies baked on the shady side of the line. Divested of them, given up those dark little thrills.

A small price to pay, he thought as he moved on, found

the second sock, for the woman now leading him through the maze of his own home.

She never failed to fascinate, frustrate, and fulfill.

Doubling back, was she, he mused, spotting some loose credits she'd likely pulled out of her pocket. And he spotted a door open an inch or so, to lure him.

Sliding the credits into his own pocket, he moved on, as he knew the room to be linen storage for that section of the house.

Then doubled back himself, as he wouldn't put it past her to decide they'd have sex in a bloody linen closet.

Apparently not, he thought, when all he found inside were linens.

The game took on fresh interest when he found her trousers tossed over the banister of a stairway leading up to the next floor.

Intrigued, he started up, mentally going over the floor plan.

Ballroom level. Sitting rooms, baths, a staging area for catering, storage, a small, efficient kitchen and butler's pantry – again for catering – another separate area for any staff hired for a party to break or gather, another storage area, a game room.

The ballroom, of course.

He found her shirt hanging over the door of one of the sitting rooms, considered, and decided that after the hunt, a sitting room ranked very low on the scale.

Then turned the other way.

He found her pocket debris – the lockpicks he'd given her, her pocketknife, her communicator, her 'link, even her badge – all together on the hunt table outside the wide doorway, and stepped inside the ballroom.

She sat in the shadowy light, perched on the arm of one of the sofas.

'I wasn't wearing enough to cover the house,' she said. 'Next time I'll have to gear up.'

'You managed to cover considerable ground, nonetheless. Lights on, ten percent.'

The grand chandeliers overhead flickered on, soft, quiet light.

She wore her white support tank, her simple white panties. And her weapon harness. Long, long legs, tousled hair, a smug, smug smile. Was it a wonder he went hard as rock instantly?

'I've never been up here when there hasn't been a party or the prep for one. How come you have furniture in here when nothing's going on?'

'Something's about to.'

She grinned at him. 'That's a point, a good point.'

'And so you come to the only area of the house without an actual bed.'

'Anybody can have sex on a bed,' she pointed out. 'How many have sex in the middle of a big-ass ballroom?' She rose, walked to the center of the room.

She pointed at the floor. 'Right in the damn middle.'

'We might as well do it right then.' He moved to a panel, flipped it open, danced his fingers over the controls within.

The enormous fireplace flared on, blazed. Music, something low with a lot of bass, streamed on.

She grinned again. 'Not bad. That's not bad.'

He crossed to her, hooked an arm around her waist, yanked her against him. When she linked hers around him, prepared to drop to the floor with him, he circled her into a dance.

'Damn it.' She let out a sigh. 'That's really not bad at all.'

It might have been dreamy – the music, the lights, the man – then she remembered she was dancing in her underwear, while wearing her weapon.

She tipped her head back, started to make some snarky comment about just that. He stopped the words with his mouth.

Circling, swaying, with a long, long kiss, deep and lush with body pressed to body in a perfect fit. It topped dreamy by several points. What he brought her in a room built for glamour, for crowds? The simple and the intimate.

He felt her slide into the moment with him, the just us, anytime and anywhere. And always. He couldn't say why the fun and the foolishness she'd begun had struck such a strong, clear romantic chord in him.

Now he could take that moment, this moment, their moment, to show her both.

'I like your dress,' he murmured.

'Oh, it's just a really little something I pulled on.'

His lips curved against her hair. 'It suits you. Not everyone wears white so well, or with such powerful accessories.'

'Yeah, it's a stunner,' she said, making him laugh.

'So's my wife.'

Again, she angled her head back. 'So you're married?'

'I am, yes. Right down to the marrow. You?'

'I got talked into it. It's working out pretty well.' She laid a hand on his cheek. 'He's got this way of making me feel I'm the only person in the world.'

'When I'm with my wife, when I'm holding her, she is.'

She pressed her cheek against his, closed her eyes as they danced. 'No one ever made me the reason before him. No one else ever made me the one.'

'She changed my life the moment she walked into it. She's the reason, and the one.'

'I don't know if I believed in love before, but I know I didn't understand it. And now . . .'

'And now.'

This time, she tipped back her head, took his lips. And gave herself to the now.

He hit the release on her weapon harness, slipped it off, letting it slide to the floor before he circled her back to the center of the room, of the moment.

Together, they lowered to the floor while the music beat, the lights shimmered, the fire snapped.

He let his hands roam – that long back, the narrow torso – over smooth skin under thin white cotton. The tough, disciplined muscles never failed to arouse. His woman was a fighter, a brawler, a tireless warrior, and still could offer him the soft and the sweet.

Her hands roamed as his did, the short, unpainted nails digging in, letting him know his body, his touch, his needs pleased her.

She smelled of soap and winter wind, tasted of woman and warmth.

He tugged the tank away to cup her breast – small, firm, lovely – in his hand. Her heart bumped beneath his fingers.

She tangled her legs with his, let herself float on the gentle surf of rising senses. The feel of his hands – always clever, now patient – on her skin, his scent, one she'd recognize among thousands, the taste of him as her lips skimmed along his jaw.

All coalesced into one, into him, while the fire sizzled and snapped, while the music drifted through the air.

She slipped his sweater up and away, wanting skin to skin now, craving heart to heart. Used hands and mouth to saturate herself with him, to indulge herself, to take what was only hers.

When he pressed her back, she flowed with it. When he gripped her hands, she linked her fingers with his and held on. Held on as with mouth alone he turned her body into fire. One quick gasp escaped her, a gasp that shuddered into a moan as he churned her system into glorious chaos. Feasting on her breasts – his teeth adding a tiny, exquisite pain – he made her tremble.

He wanted her to quake, wanted to feel her quake and break beneath him. He needed to drive her into helplessness before her power whipped back and conquered him.

She would give, he knew, he knew, as his mouth played over that lean torso, she would cry out in surrender and yield all.

So her hips pumped up, body arched, breath sobbed, as his tongue slid over her, into her.

Hot, impossible pleasure broke over her, swamped her. Helpless, yes. Helplessly she rode the torrent to its dizzying peak, trapped there in a kind of glorious madness before tumbling down, weak and dazed.

He exploited, he plundered, and she, still wrecked, could only writhe under the assault. The next orgasm ripped through her, velvet claws. And still.

And still.

She tried to say his name as her mind whimpered: too much. It's too much.

But when the word slipped from her, the word was 'More.'

So he used his hands on her, and gave her more.

Half-crazed now, he moved up her body, his only clear thought to take, to have.

'Wait.' Her heavy eyes met his. 'Wait.'

'Eve.' He pressed his lips to her throat, prepared to beg if he must.

She gathered what little strength and sanity she had left, rolled. Simply laying her head on his chest while she found her breath.

'Eve.' Fighting the animal clawing inside him, he gripped her hips. 'I need you.'

'I know.' She rose up, looking into his eyes as she

54

straddled him. 'I know.' Letting out a long sigh as she took him in. 'I know.' Pressing one of his hands to her heart, she began to move. 'I know.'

So her power whipped back, built, built. She surrounded him, accepted him. Conquered him.

When she melted, heated honey, against him, they lay together, tangled, dazed, in the center of the ballroom.

Fleetingly, he wondered if he'd ever not think of this when they had the room full of people, food, lights, and music. He also wondered how he'd find the energy to carry her to their actual bed if – as he thought she might – she fell asleep on top of him.

Then she stirred, let out a long, low sound of satisfaction.

'Well, that's another checked off the list.'

Adoring her, he laughed. 'You have a list?'

'It's just a mental list, for now. How many rooms do you figure we have yet to hit?'

Adore her, hell. He bloody well worshipped her. 'I'll have to do a count.'

'Do that.' She pushed up enough to look down at him. 'Because we have to hit them all. Big house, so it'll take awhile. But we have to hit them all, even if we hit the last one when we're old and creaky.'

He skimmed a finger down her chin. 'We might save one for when we are. As a kind of incentive and reward.'

'That's a good idea. I like it. I think I can get up now, especially since I don't have to worry about the clothes I left scattered around out there because, hey, Summerset-free.'

She rolled off. 'I've got to get my stuff, though. Badge, 'link, like that.'

'You get that, I'll get what's in here – including your weapon.'

'Deal.' Eyes still heavy, face still flushed, she got to her feet. 'It's a good deal,' she said when he got to his. 'All around.'

He took her hand, kissed her fingers. 'The best of deals.'

'Now I'm walking in a ballroom naked,' she said as she crossed the gleaming floor. 'How many people can say that?'

4

Eve woke in the predawn dark with a weight on her chest. When she opened her sleep-blurred eyes she made out a silhouette that had her reaching for her weapon with one hand, balling the other into a fist. Before she punched the shadow, as her brain cleared enough to remember she wasn't wearing her weapon or anything else, the shadow let out a familiar, growly sort of sound.

'Jesus Christ, what's wrong with you? Lights on, ten percent.'

In the low light, Galahad's bicolored eyes stared, hard and steely, into hers. 'What's your problem?' She hauled him up, dumped him on the bed beside her.

Those odd feline eyes only narrowed. The growly sound clicked up to an actual growl.

'Watch it, pal. I'm bigger than you.'

Eve scrubbed her hands over her face, called for the time.

The time is five-thirty-three. Current temperature is nineteen degrees.

Eve shot a finger at the cat. 'I had another thirty coming to me.'

Galahad's response was a snarl.

Since she didn't have Roarke as backup – already up and buying a solar system or selling a small country, Eve imagined – she rolled out of bed, snagged the robe her husband, who inexplicably thought of every damn thing, must have tossed on the foot of the bed.

As she pulled the robe on, the cat stalked to the edge of the bed. Sat. Stared.

'Look, you're creeping me, okay? Knock it off.'

She walked to the wall panel, opened it to the AutoChef, programmed the first cup of life-sustaining coffee.

And got it.

No Summerset, and Roarke in one of his emperor-of-the-business-world meetings. Still, the man who thought of every damn thing usually fed the cat when the house was Summerset-free.

Turning, taking that first gulp of good, strong black coffee, Eve eyed the cat.

'Are you bullshitting me, tubby?'

He jumped off the bed – a definite *thud*. Sat. Stared.

His bullshit generally took the tack of sucking up, rubbing that pudgy body against legs, looking sad or appealing.

Now he just looked pissed. Righteously.

'Okay, I'm buying it.'

She programmed kibble, and though he didn't deserve it after costing her a half hour down, she added some salmon.

When she set it down, he strolled over, tail swishing. His body language clearly stated: It's about damn time.

'Yeah, you're freaking welcome.'

Eve took the coffee with her into the shower.

Fully awake, considerably less grumpy, she came out to see Roarke standing in the bedroom. Dressed in one of his impeccable suits, he gestured at the empty bowl across the room while the cat wound between his legs and sang his sad song in pathetic meows.

'I can see the bloody empty bowl right there. I've eyes. And no doubt if I lowered myself to take a whiff, I'd smell tuna or salmon on your breath.'

'Salmon,' Eve confirmed.

The cat glanced over, obviously concluded the jig was up. He strolled toward the fire, sat, and began to wash.

'You didn't feed him before, right?'

'I didn't,' Roarke confirmed, 'as he was both sprawled out and snoring, and I knew I wouldn't be more than forty minutes or so.'

'He woke me up, sitting his tonnage on my chest and staring holes through my brain.'

'If we put a micro AC on his level, he might learn to operate it.'

'He doesn't have to,' Eve pointed out. 'He operates us.'

'Entirely too true.'

Eve went back to the AutoChef, put herself in charge of breakfast. Which meant a Summerset- *and* oatmeal-free day.

While she contemplated her choices, Roarke switched on

the financial reports, muted the sound. He stood a moment, studying what would always remain incomprehensible to her, while she settled on berries, bacon, and *mmm* pancakes.

She topped it off with a pot of coffee.

'Did you add a planet to your collection?' she asked as she carried plates to the table of the sitting area.

'Not this morning. I'll get the rest.'

She sat, drenching her pancakes with syrup while he brought over the berries and coffee. 'So, what's on your plate today?' she asked him. 'Besides breakfast.'

'As it happens, I just agreed to pay a quick visit to an ag complex I have an interest in. In Bristol.'

'Where's Bristol?'

'England. Since that requires considerable shuffling of the day's schedule in any case, I'll likely check on the rehab in Italy before heading back. A pity you have a case,' he added as he poured coffee for both of them. 'Or we could take a day or two.'

To the bone, Eve knew she'd never take to the idea of casually shuttling off to Europe. 'Do you need a day or two? For the work, I mean.'

'No, a few hours. It's more for public relations than work in Bristol. For Italy, I think it's time for an unexpected drop-in. I expect you'll be in the field quite a bit today.'

'Starting with the morgue.'

'Lovely. My best to Morris, of course.'

Considering, Eve ate more pancakes. 'You go to Europe, I go to the morgue. That about sums it, right?'

'And yet here we are.' Roarke patted her leg. 'Sitting here having breakfast while our cat calculates if he can manage to snag some bacon.'

'He can't.' Lifting a slice, Eve gave the cat the same quality of stare he'd given her. And crunched in.

Once she'd hit her limit on pancakes, she went to her closet to dress, and to line up her morning agenda.

Morgue, then Cop Central to put her board together there, check any reports, update. Schedule a consult with Mira – get Mira the data. A visit to the victim's apartment, Eve added. See how she lived, fill in some blanks. A talk with the people in charge of the auditions, the casting. Another talk with the vet assistant who took the bogus emergency.

As she planned it out, she pulled on black trousers, a white shirt, yanked a gray V-neck sweater over that when she remembered the temperature. Shifted to grab a black jacket at random, but Roarke beat her to it.

He stepped in, took another – a sort of tweed, maybe – of deep forest green with touches of gray and black woven through.

'There's an undertone of green in the sweater,' he pointed out.

She frowned down at it. 'It's gray.'

'With a green undertone.'

She shrugged, took the jacket from him, then deliberately grabbed brown boots.

'You'd be breaking my heart if I didn't know you're winding me up.'

'Serve you right if I wore them anyway.' She switched them for black.

'I need to go deal with the schedule changes, which will likely have Caro set her hair – or maybe mine – on fire.'

Eve sat to pull on the boots, imagined Roarke's steady-as-a-rock admin would handle it all, without flames. 'I'll see you when we're both back.'

'Meanwhile, take care of my cop.' He bent over to kiss her.

'I will if you take care of my traveling gazillionaire.'

'That's a deal.'

Alone, she strapped on her weapon, filled her pockets. She gave Galahad a quick scratch and rub – no point holding grudges – then jogged downstairs.

Coat, scarf, snowflake cap, then out into the cold where her car sat, engine and heater already running thanks to the man who thought of everything.

And, thanks to the cat, she ran thirty ahead of schedule. No ad blimps blasting yet, she noted, and traffic at the edge of insane rather than fully over the line.

Some commuter trams, overhead and on the street, carted the night shift one way, the early shift another.

Eve used her wrist unit, dictated a text to Peabody.

Skip the morgue, go straight to Central. Get me a consult with Mira, and clear the way for us to go through the vic's apartment.

More time saved, she thought as she played weave and dodge on her route downtown. Time she'd spend getting that subscription list for the vid palace, running down the names.

Somebody knew you, Chanel, knew a lot about you, Eve thought. Coworkers aren't ringing so far. Exes aren't ringing.

A neighbor maybe, somebody who belonged to the same gym, or shopped at the same market.

A friendly woman, everybody said. A happy one. Friendly and happy tend to talk to people.

Neighbors, she thought again. Markets, a gym if she used one, bank, beauty salon. And the vid palace.

Somebody you see regularly, but more important, who sees you.

Before you know it, you've got a target on your back.

Or on the base of your skull.

Those angles played in her head all the way downtown.

When she walked through the white tunnel of the morgue, her boot steps echoed. She heard muted voices behind a set of doors, smelled bad coffee, something fried. Hash brown cake, she decided, which somehow managed to be both disgusting and delicious.

She stepped into Morris's theater and a chorus of voices singing about ... making the match.

'Early and bright,' Morris commented, turning the music down to a murmur.

He stood beside Rylan's body in a navy suit with thread-like stripes of maroon. His shirt matched the stripes and the tie played both colors together in a pattern she thought they called – for whatever reason – paisley. He'd braided his long, dark hair, then twined it with maroon cord.

His eyes, exotic, sort of beautiful, smiled at her from behind his safety goggles.

Rylan's chest, already spread, lay open to him.

'The cat woke me up, so I got an early start.'

'Our Galahad's not ill, I hope.'

'No, fat and healthy. He wanted breakfast, and apparently we're there to serve. Anything I can use yet?'

'As you see, I haven't gotten far, but I can tell you that at this point, I see a healthy, well-proportioned female who took care of her body. Though slightly underweight – as many are in her profession – she has exceptional muscle tone. A lovely face as well, and no signs I've found thus far of any surgical enhancements.

'Your TOD concurs with mine,' he added. 'She was enjoying some lightly salted popcorn and Diet Coke when she died.'

'I don't get how anybody enjoys popcorn if it's only lightly salted, but it takes all kinds. COD?'

'I'd suspect the ice pick plunged into her brain stem.'

'Ice pick.' Eve nodded.

'You're looking for one with a spike about three inches long, with a diameter of three millimeters. It has a wooden sheath, as I found microscopic traces of wood in the wound.'

'That's good, that's helpful.'

He ordered his work screen on. Eve watched a spine, and

what she assumed was the brain stem attached, revolve in bright yellow and blue.

'The spike entered between the first and second vertebrae, penetrated the brain stem, disrupting the central nervous system in a slightly upward angle. With that penetration, the brain ceased to transmit orders to breathe, to regulate body temperature and blood pressure, heart rate. That cessation would result in, most likely, a short seizure as the body – cut off from the brain – objected, you could say. Death followed quickly, a matter of seconds.'

'How good would you have to be to make that shot, in that spot?'

'A bit of practice.' Morris lifted his shoulders. 'From reasonably close range on a sitting target, you wouldn't need more than a rudimentary search to know where to aim, and your aim could be off a bit and produce the same results. If you're thinking the killer needed medical training or expertise, I have to say no. May have had, certainly, but wouldn't need it.'

'Okay.' Hands in pockets, she wandered. 'Okay. Ice picks are easy to come by. They use them in bars, commercial kitchens. She worked in a place that has a bar and a commercial kitchen.'

'I thought she worked in the theater. That's a cast recording playing now, from one of the plays she worked in.'

'She did, and doubled as a waitress. Broadway Babies.'

'Ah, a very entertaining place, if you're in the mood for it.'

'Home bars and kitchens, too,' Eve mused. 'You can pick one up at a hardware or home store, no problem.'

'I have one myself,' Morris told her. 'I'll send her tox off, but from what I'm seeing she lived clean. No signs of chemical abuse, addictions. No recent sexual activity. She never had a child and, though the blood work will confirm, I don't see any signs of pregnancy.'

'That fits with what I know about her. So ice pick, specific kill spot for fast, quiet work. I don't think she's going to give us much more.'

'The dead only know what they know.'

'Yeah. And this one? She never saw it coming.'

With the rest of her morning's agenda in place in her mental file, Eve pulled into Central. She'd juggle whatever she had to for the Mira consult, she thought as she wound her way up, shifting from elevator to glide, but she had a reasonably clear picture of the victim.

Talented, friendly, happy, unencumbered sexually or romantically with no hard-edged breakups. Financially steady, as long as she kept the second job, which by all accounts she enjoyed anyway.

Take away the method, Eve thought, and she'd have pegged Rylan as a random.

She jumped off the glide on her level as Peabody popped out of a viciously crowded elevator.

'Hey, good timing. Anything from Morris?'

'Confirmation of on-scene conclusions. The vic lived a clean and healthy life, up until an ice pick severed her brain stem.'

'Ice pick. They just look mean.'

'I'd say Rylan agrees with you.'

She swung into Homicide, stared for the three seconds she calculated she had before Jenkinson's virulent blue tie with its hard-candy pink – were those elephants parading over it? – seared her corneas.

Reineke, Jenkinson's partner, had one foot propped on his desk as he worked his 'link. A tough-soled cop shoe clad the foot, and the positioning allowed a peek of the multicolored puppies – she thought they were puppies – frolicking against the screaming green background of his sock.

They were solid cops, she thought, solid, sensible cops she'd go through any door with. And yet they insisted on assaulting the senses of all in their viewing area with their insane choices of accessories.

She had to stop asking herself why.

Instead, she turned and headed straight to her office, and the coffee in her AutoChef.

'Maybe I could get one.' Unwinding the boa constrictor of her scarf – pink, blue, and white today – Peabody followed Eve in. 'Because I scored you a consult with Mira. Nine-thirty.'

Eve programmed a coffee regular in addition to her own preferred black.

'We can follow that with interviews with the director and producer of the play Rylan was up for,' Peabody added. 'They have the other callback – Jessilyn Brooke – scheduled for eleven.'

'That'll work.' Eve passed Peabody the coffee. 'Contact Kawaski. I want a look at the apartment, and the victim's room. We'll slide that between Mira and the theater. And put in a visit to the vet. I want to talk to the one who took the bogus emergency.'

'On it. You've probably got a report from McNab in your inbox. He went by the vet's after he left the scene last night, as requested, since they're open twenty-four. He took a look at the 'link transmission on that. He determined on site the tag came from a drop 'link, but since they cooperated, he brought the desk 'link in to triangulate location at the time of the tag.'

'Good. I'll get up to EDD if I can, check his progress on that.'

Peabody went out; Eve settled in.

Once she'd set up her board, updated her book, she did deeper runs on the victim's coworkers, the roommate, and added one for the competitor – Jessilyn Brooke.

Nothing and no one popped.

She sat back, put her boots on the desk, studied the board.

Point one: Whoever committed this murder was a planner. Detail-oriented, someone who knew how to schedule.

Point two: The killer was someone willing to take risks to achieve the goal.

Question: What was the goal beyond Rylan's death? What was the purpose or gain?

Point three: no sexual component. Ice pick penetrates, but the weapon, as she saw it, had been chosen for speed and silence, not to simulate sex.

Question: How to resolve the personal nature of the planning, the target specificity, the intimate knowledge of the victim's habits with the impersonal nature of the murder?

She got up, walked to her narrow window.

I see you, she thought. I watch you. Study you. I know what you like, where you go, who you sleep with, what you want.

Was it just that? she wondered. Just the thrill of taking a life. Of plucking someone – at random – studying them like some bug under a scope. Then crushing them.

That's how it played for her. Rylan might not have known her killer. Maybe she'd have recognized the face. Someone she'd seen in the restaurant, at the vid palace, at the theater. But the connection, on her part, remained just that loose.

On the killer's? One-sided intimacy and knowledge. The thrill of that. The goal? Maybe nothing more than taking it from selection to study to planning to conclusion.

If so, Rylan wouldn't be the last, the only. In fact, she may not have been the first.

She turned back to her desk, intending to bring up unsolved homicides from the past year that contained at least one of the elements of her case.

And heard Peabody's pink winter boots clomping toward the office.

'Hey, Dallas, Nadine's here.'

'I don't have anything for Nadine.' The on-air reporter and bestselling writer was a friend – and often useful on an investigation – but this one didn't call for Nadine Furst and her crack skills.

'It's more like she's got something for you.'

Eve's eyes narrowed because Peabody's totally sparkled. 'Am I going to smell double fudge brownie on your breath?'

'No, and I'd be sad about that, except for what she did bring. She's got Blaine DeLano with her!'

'Okay.'

Peabody's sparkling eyes rolled in disbelief. 'Blaine DeLano, Dallas. She's a really famous novelist. The Hightower Chronicles, the Dark novels. She writes about cops. She writes really solid cop stories. I've been a fan for, like, a decade.'

'So get her autograph if that blows up your skirt, and send them both on their way. I'm just a little busy with, you know, murder.'

'That's the thing. Jeez, I got so flustered.' As if it cured the flusters, Peabody patted a hand on her chest. 'Ms DeLano says she might have some information on the investigation.'

'You didn't think to mention that first?'

'I got really flustered. I started seriously thinking about being a cop after I read *Devil's Due*. But she says – and Nadine backs her up – she thinks she has relevant information.'

Eve considered her office and the logistics of fitting four people inside the deliberately limited space – as she'd probably have to knock Peabody unconscious and drag her out to bar her from the interview.

'Have them go to the lounge. I'll be there in a minute.'

'Um, I think it might be better if I tried to grab an

interview or conference room. Santiago's a big fan, too, and Trueheart. Lots of cops are. So you may want to limit the access to her.'

Even as she spoke, Peabody pulled out her PPC, did a quick check. 'Interview B's open.'

'Bag it, and I'll be there in a minute.'

She pulled up an incoming on her computer, noted that McNab worked fast. And had interesting data.

Not only a drop phone, she read, but he'd narrowed the location of the transmission to the crime scene. Inside the theater, in the section where Rylan had been seated.

And while he couldn't confirm it as a timed auto-send, he could and had confirmed it as a recording.

Since he'd attached it, Eve ran it.

Street noises, traffic, horns.

Oh God, oh God, Prince broke the leash, he ran out, into the street. Oh God, he got hit by a car. He's bleeding. He's hurt, he's really hurt.

Eve heard the vet assistant try to interrupt, to calm, to ask questions, but the voice just rolled over her, spiked with panic.

I'm bringing him. I'm running. Please, Prince. Hold on.

Eve listened to it a second time. The killer had done a good job projecting fear and panic in a high register that might have been female or might have been a male feigning hysteria. The video portion only showed a blur of lights, pedestrians, all in the jumpy, jumbled stream of someone running.

'Damn good job,' she murmured. 'More than enough to have the assistant on duty call the vet on the slate. You go out some night, push record, run and babble for a minute or so, and done. Last night, you wait for your moment, send it. Wait again until Kawaski leaves her seat. Do the deed, walk out.'

She rose, and went to see what some cop writer thought she knew.

Inside Interview B, Nadine Furst sat at the scarred table as camera ready as she would have been at the Chanel Seventy-Five anchor desk. Her streaky blond hair waved perfectly around her foxy face. A red top with a hint of lace played off her slim and severely cut gray suit.

She lifted her brows over cat-green eyes.

'Lieutenant Dallas, Blaine DeLano.'

'Thanks so much for making the time.'

The woman Eve judged as early forties rose, extended a hand.

About five-five, by Eve's gauge, a good, probably gym-fit build in narrow black pants, a casual black sweater. She wore her hair short, a sleek cap of brown with hints of red around a quietly attractive face. Eyes, deeply brown, met and held Eve's.

Her low-register voice held a smoothness along with the faint remnant of a Brooklyn upbringing.

72

'Have a seat,' Eve told her. 'Peabody?'

'She went to grab us some water. No point being annoyed,' Nadine added, as she knew Eve well. 'I think you're going to want to hear what Blaine has to say.'

'If you know what she has to say, why are you here?'

'She came to me, I brought her to you. I've already agreed to be off the record because Blaine asked, so chill it down.'

'I should have come directly to you,' DeLano said quickly, 'but I wanted the opinion of someone I trust and respect. And, frankly, I wanted the conduit. I'm aware you also trust and respect Nadine.'

'So far.'

Eve glanced over when Peabody came in with tubes of water. She sat, waited while DeLano cracked a tube.

'Okay, Ms DeLano, what do you want to say?'

'I want to say – need to say – I think I might be responsible for Chanel Rylan's murder.'

5

The woman seemed steady and sane enough, Eve thought, though distress eked through.

'If you're going to confess to murder, I should read you your rights.'

'Don't be such a bitch,' Nadine snapped.

'I have to be true to myself.'

DeLano let out a breathless half laugh. 'I appreciate the mild kick in the ass. When I killed her in *Dark Days*, her name was Amelia Benson.'

'You're talking about a book? About a fictional character.'

'Yes. Amelia Benson was a young actress who held a series of jobs, as her acting income didn't pay the rent. She had ambitions, some talent, and considerable energy. Every week she went to a classic vid, to study, as she hoped, one day, to be a star of stage and screen.

'One rainy Wednesday, in a nearly empty theater while she watched Grace Kelly thwart an attempt on her life, Amelia's ended. An ice pick through the base of the skull.'

It rang, Eve realized, loud and clear. 'Why an ice pick?' Eve asked.

'Such a mean and common tool. And effective, I thought. Sharp.' DeLano spread her hands. 'Small. Easy to come by. They found her body when they brought the houselights up after the credits. The killer, of course, had long since left the building.'

'Okay. And you believe this applies to Chanel Rylan's murder.'

'I do. I'm sick because I do. The bulletin I heard this morning said an actress, a young actress, and the vid – a classic Hitchcock vid like the one my fictional victim watched. *Dial M for Murder* in my book, same director. And that she'd been stabbed during the vid – the shower scene, a compelling scene like the one I used for my book. The bulletin didn't identify the weapon.'

'So you wrote a book with a murder victim, an actress who's killed during a vid by stabbing, and you figure it's connected to an actual case.'

'I do. I do, and, worse ... I think it's the second one.' Now DeLano gripped her hands together on the table, knuckles whitening. 'I think it's the second.'

'Why?'

When DeLano brought her joined hands up to press between her breasts, Nadine started to speak.

'Let her tell it.'

Nadine hissed out a breath, but didn't speak.

'This was easier in my head.'

75

'Drink some water, Ms DeLano,' Peabody advised. 'Take a breath.'

'Okay. Yes.' She obeyed, cleared her throat. 'I think I'd have been struck by the similar elements. A young actress stabbed while watching a Hitchcock vid. If subsequent reports had termed the weapon an ice pick, I'd have been more than struck. I was only somewhat intrigued by what I now think was the first. About a month ago, a young street-level LC, only a few weeks into the job, was strangled in a flop many use for their work. Her body showed no sign of recent sexual activity, no other injuries. The killer used a white scarf.'

She paused, drank more water.

'In my book *Dark Falls*, a young street-level LC, only a few weeks into the job, was strangled in a flop many use for their work. Her body showed no signs of recent sexual activity, and wouldn't, as this was her first client of the night. No other injuries. A sedative mixed with wine – a cheap Chianti – was discovered in her system during the autopsy. The killer used a white scarf, left in place and tied into a bow at the side of her neck.'

DeLano cleared her throat again. 'At the time, as I said, I was mildly intrigued. The young licensed companion, no sex, the white scarf. But it's a dangerous line of work, especially at that level. If you tell me the case is closed, that there was no bow, no sedative found, if you tell me Chanel Rylan was killed with a steak knife, I'll mark this all up to coincidence and paranoia. I'd like to be able to do just that, more than I can tell you.'

Eve leaned back in the chair. 'You write cop books?'

'Police thrillers, yes.'

'Maybe you know what cops say about coincidence.'

Deliberately DeLano picked up her water, drank. 'There aren't any. God.'

'Peabody, get the file on the LC. Jenkinson and Reineke caught it, but I don't remember all the details.'

'Yes, sir.'

DeLano closed her eyes as Peabody left the room. 'It was an ice pick, there was a bow. You don't have to tell me for me to know it. I don't know what to do, what to think.'

'How long ago did you write the LC one?'

'*Dark Falls*, the first book of the spin-off Dark series. Deann Dark, former police detective – still one in that book – who turns in her badge at the end of the book and turns to private investigation. Eight years ago. That was a spring release as part of the Hightower series. They were partners. The second, *Dark Days*, with the ice pick, came out that fall. I've done eleven Hightowers and eight Darks. Eight, and now two ... I feel sick.'

'This isn't your fault or your responsibility.' Nadine turned to Eve. 'She could use hearing that from you.'

'I don't know either way yet. Has anyone contacted you suggesting turning your fiction into reality?'

'No, no, nothing like that. I've had readers who want to give me plotlines or ideas, and murder techniques might come into it. I've had readers upset or disappointed – even angry – that a romantic relationship hasn't developed between Deann and Hightower. I don't know why anyone would do this, or pick my books specifically.'

'Anybody too obsessed or pissed?'

'Nothing raises a flag. These characters – Hightower and Dark – have been around for eleven years. They've gone through changes, growth, personal tragedies and triumphs. Not all readers want the changes, others want more. You can't let that influence the story or the characters.'

Watching DeLano, Eve shifted angles. 'How about personally obsessed or pissed? With you, not the characters or the books.'

DeLano swept her hands up over her face, into her hair. 'I lead a quiet life, Lieutenant Dallas. A deliberately quiet and simple life. I have two teenage girls, and raising my girls, building my career takes about all I've got. I don't even date. I tried it a couple times, at Heather's and Piper's urging. My girls,' she explained. 'But I'm just not at a place in my life where I have the interest or the energy. I have friends, mostly other mothers or, like Nadine, someone in the business. I have my family, my mother, my girls. And I have my work. I stay home more than I go out.'

'You're not married to or cohabbing with the father of your daughters? Or one of the fathers.'

'Just one, and no, I'm divorced.'

'How long?'

'Twelve years.'

'But you have contact?'

'Not really, no. Craig rarely sees the girls. He's not that

interested. He's remarried, and has a son, which is what he wanted.'

'Acrimonious divorce?'

DeLano offered a thin smile. 'Is there any other kind?'

'There wouldn't be in my world, but some people claim it.'

'I don't. But if you think, after all these years, Craig would kill two women to make me suffer, I'd have to say that stretches credulity.'

'Was he or is he ever violent?'

'Once.' More nerves showed as DeLano shifted in the chair, linked her hands together, pulled them apart. 'Do you really need this information?' she asked as Peabody came back in with a file.

'I don't know what I need until I know.'

'Briefly then, I married Craig when I was twenty-four, and had my two girls before I was thirty. I was a teacher, and had been working on my doctorate, but when we married I gave that up, as Craig wanted me to stay at home, keep the home, and tend to the children.'

'He wanted?' Eve repeated.

'Yes. And while I was content being a professional mother, I did begin to feel the squeeze with the limitations of my social activities, my outlets. I accepted that Craig was a very old-fashioned, traditional man, and he provided for us. I accepted that he wanted a son and didn't interact as much as I expected or would have liked with the girls. I accepted that he wanted things done a certain way, and his response when I didn't reach that level was subtle insults, coldness. I accepted. You may not understand—'

'Just because I haven't been there doesn't mean I can't understand.'

'All right.' Again DeLano linked her hands together, but this time it seemed like a reset rather than nerves.

'I had a lovely home, was expected to make myself and that home attractive, to be a charming hostess, to be a fully involved mother. I enjoyed all that, but I wanted something for myself. I started to write. I'd always had an interest, and I had the time when the girls napped or on the rare occasions I was allowed – though I didn't see it then as being allowed – to let my mother take them for an afternoon. I told no one. It was just for me, and over the course of a year, I'd written a book.'

She smiled now, quick and easy. 'It thrilled me, thrilled me enough I took a chance and contacted a college friend who worked in publishing. She agreed to read it, and she liked it.'

Now DeLano let out a sigh. 'What a moment that was. She had a few editorial suggestions, and I worked on those in secret. And when I had, when she read it again, she bought the manuscript. It was, and is, one of the biggest moments of my life.'

DeLano glanced at Nadine. 'You understand.'

'I do, absolutely.'

'I contacted my mother,' DeLano continued. 'I didn't tell her, but asked if she'd like to have the girls, an overnight. Of course she did, so I arranged that. I spent the day shopping for candles, flowers, what I needed at the market to prepare Craig's favorite meal. I did all this with such excitement, such joy. I was a writer. I'd written a book. It would be published. People would read it.

'When Craig came home, I had the scene set. An elegant, intimate dinner for two. I had champagne. He questioned why I'd let my mother take the girls – without clearing it with him – but I told him I wanted a special evening for the two of us.'

She looked down at her linked hands. 'He thought I was pregnant. He didn't know, as I also kept that to myself, that I was on birth control because I wasn't ready to have another child so quickly. I wanted another year first so, rather than argue, I'd lied. I'm not proud of that.'

'Your body,' Eve pointed out. 'Your choice.'

'Yes, but he wouldn't have agreed, so I took the coward's way. In any case, I told him no, not yet, but I had, in a way, given birth.

'That night, I poured the champagne, and I told him about the book, how I'd written it in my free time over the last year or so, how much fun it had been for me, how satisfying. And best of all I'd sold it. He listened to all this, and I should've known, I should've seen it, but I was so happy, so inside my own excitement, I didn't see what was coming. Free time? he asked me. Wasn't that interesting? I had so much free time. I had free time because he did all the work, and I'd used what he'd given me to lie and deceive, to hide my ingratitude.'

She took a long breath. 'I tried to defend myself, to tell him I hadn't neglected anything. Him, the girls, the house. But . . . He took my plate, dumped the food on the floor – to remind me I only had food and shelter because he provided them. When I objected, he hit me. When I objected to that, he hit me again, and again. He ordered me to destroy the manuscript, tell this friend he suspected I'd had sex with I'd made a mistake. He ordered me to clean up the mess I'd made, then come upstairs and do what his wife was obligated to do.'

Eve gave it a moment while DeLano visibly composed herself. 'And did you?'

'A stronger woman would have told him to go to hell, but, yes, I cleaned up the mess, put the kitchen to rights. I locked myself in the powder room long enough to take a picture of my face, the bruises, the blackening eye. Then I went upstairs. It was rape, but I didn't fight. I didn't protest. In fact, I pretended to enjoy it. In the morning, I fixed his breakfast, apologized again when he demanded it. When he left for work, when I was sure it was safe, I packed what I needed, I packed what the girls needed, and I left. I went to my mother's. She called a friend, a lawyer. I arranged for a neighbor of my mother's to keep the girls while the three of us went to the police and filed charges. I also filed for divorce.'

'What did he do?' Eve asked.

'He objected. He claimed I'd committed adultery, had been an abusive wife and mother. But he couldn't prove any of it, as it simply wasn't true. He threatened, and he made the next several months very hard. But I knew he didn't want the girls, and I would not, I would not have them live under a man like Craig. I went to therapy, I wrote another book – and lived with the girls, with my mother.'

'What about the assault? Did he get dinged for it?'

'His lawyer suggested that the divorce would go smoother if I withdrew the charges. I wouldn't. I'd had smooth, accepted smooth, and it made me a doormat. What would being a doormat, what would allowing myself to be physically attacked teach my daughters? He eventually pled it down, did community service, had to agree to rehab for domestic abuse, and two years' probation.'

'A ding. Not enough of one, but a ding.'

'He remains bitter, and I think sincerely believes he was wronged, that he was an ideal husband to me. But he never laid a hand on me again. As I said, he remarried, he has the son he wanted, and – from what I can glean – a biddable wife.'

'Maybe tuning her up is part of the biddable.'

DeLano shut her eyes again. 'I don't know. I hope not, but I don't know.'

'He resents your work – I bet part of the bitter is lodged in your success with that work.'

'Yes. And I'll admit to feeling some ugly little satisfaction from that.'

'Using your work to kill could be some serious payback.'

'I can't see it. Believe me, that's not defending him. He's

a small man, Lieutenant. And a man who prides himself on image and status. If he wanted payback, if he needed it, he'd try to smear my reputation. But to do that would smear his own. So he leaves me and mine alone, and I do the same for him.'

'Okay.' Eve let it drop, fully intending to see for herself.

She opened the file, studied the crime scene photos of the street LC, the white scarf with the perfectly tied side bow around her neck.

'Who killed the LC in the book, and why?'

'I had a female killer, a fairly traditional wife and mother, I later realized I based in part on myself. She had a psychotic break when she realized her husband used LCs – very young LCs – and murdered three before they caught her. The white scarf and bow symbolized the sash and bow from her wedding gown.'

'A female serial. Any connection to the killer and motive from the second book?'

'None, except the characters of Dark and Hightower, and some of the other cast I developed in the first series. In that second case, the killer was male, paid to kill the actress by the lover of an actress up for the same part.'

'A pro?'

'No. A failing screenwriter trying to get backing for his script. A friend of the lover was a producer. The agreement is: Kill this woman and I'll produce your script. The killer had no connection to the victim. They'd never met. The screenwriter and the producer have a falling out when the producer goes low budget and the screenwriter wants more. The producer kills the screenwriter.'

'How?'

'God, do you think … He sets it up to look like a suicide. Gets the screenwriter drunk – while agreeing to the high budget treatment. When he's drunk enough, the producer hangs him, types a suicide note on the computer. It's bungled, and Dark is already looking at the producer. More, the screenwriter left the outline of a new script on the same computer. One that mirrors the deal made, the killing done.'

'The third book. The main murder if there's more than one.'

'I'm going to need stronger than water before this is over. Poisoning, in an edgy, popular club, a crowded dance club. Cyanide added to a pomtini.'

'A what?'

'A martini flavored with pomegranate. They're popular. The victim is a minor celebrity. She was the girlfriend of a trash rock musician – that's what launched her celebrity. Bad girl, wild child, lives on the edge, and often over it. She uses people as freely and carelessly as she uses illegals.'

'Nice. Okay, we're going to want to see your reader communications. Start with the last year.'

'All right. I'll have my mother put it together. She handles that end of things, and the social media.'

'You say you don't date. Is there anyone you've brushed off in the last year or so?'

'I don't really put myself in that situation.' With a half smile, DeLano lifted her shoulders. 'I'm a forty-three-year-old single mother and introvert.'

'You look good, you've got a brain, notoriety, and you've got money.'

DeLano opened her mouth, closed it, considered. 'Well, yes.'

'Think about it. You may want to talk to your mother about this, since it would give her more of a sense of what to look for, or it might spark a memory of a communication that applies. Otherwise, don't talk about this.'

'I need to tell my girls.'

'Teenage girls tend to blab to other teenage girls.'

'Not if I put it under the dome. The Family Only Dome. It's a sacred trust in our house. My mother's the same, Lieutenant. If it's put under the dome, it stays under the dome.'

'You can consider all this under the dome,' Eve said to Nadine.

'Understood and agreed in advance. It'll break eventually, Blaine. You should work on a statement, have it ready when it blows.'

'Right, yes. You're right. If you need me for anything, Lieutenant, anything, I'll be available. I'll get out of your way.' She rose. 'Thanks, Nadine, for coming in with me.'

'If you need anything, tag me,' Nadine replied.

'I will, and I'm not going to be shy about it. I love my work. The good guys win. Terrible things happen, ugly things, but the good guys win. I'm going to count on that.'

'I'm going to show you out, Ms DeLano.'

When Peabody took DeLano out, Eve stayed where she was.

'How well do you know her?' she asked Nadine.

'I'd call us casual friends. She's been on *Now* a few times, gives a good interview. She's not bullshitting about not socializing much. I did meet her kids and her mother – they all came to the studio once. Tight unit. What was your impression of her?'

'Smart and steady.'

'That would be correct. The kids strike me as the same, and I'd say the smart and steady comes down from Blaine's mother. They'll hold it together.'

'What do you know about the ex-husband?'

'More now than I did. I poked around a bit pre-interview, but she's kept a lid on it. And casual friends don't push that line much in a nonprofessional arena. My impression there was controlling jerk, but the smacking around? She's kept that under wraps.'

'But you knew about it.'

Nadine's lips curved. 'It might be that in the act of poking I unearthed some documentation buried under layers of time, privacy, and discretion.'

'You didn't hit her with it during the interviews?'

'What would be the point?' Nadine jerked a shoulder. 'She could've ridden that train herself, probably sold more books on that track, but she didn't – likely to shield her kids. I slap it out on-air, I get that momentary reaction, some buzz after, and I humiliate a couple of kids, and a woman who rebuilt her life. What's the point?'

'The point is you'll dig, but you understand and respect the line between petty gossip for ratings and real juice. It's why she tagged you,' Eve said. 'It's why I'm telling you I have no doubt we'll be investigating a cyanide poisoning at a dance club in fairly short order if we don't get lucky first.'

'Why not a bogus hanging suicide? That's the next murder in the series.'

'The second murder in the second book? First, the killer's likely done with the second book. And it was bungled. This killer isn't looking to replicate a bungle.'

'But they all get caught in the end,' Nadine argued. 'It's just as she said. The good guys win.'

'Not in the book the killer's writing. Now beat it.'

'It was great seeing you, too,' Nadine said dryly as she rose. 'Since we're on books, I've got *The Red Horse Chronicles* about ready to submit. I want you to see it first. And there's no point in giving me a pained look – the book's happening. I'd like you to read the manuscript before I send it off. Just like *The Icove Agenda*, it was your case.'

'Yeah, yeah.'

'Your enthusiasm and support sings in my writer's soul. Meanwhile, since I'm getting an early start, I think I'll visit a couple journalism departments, start dealing with getting myself an intern.'

'I've got a candidate for that.'

'So you mentioned before,' Nadine remembered. 'Where does he or she go to school?'

'She. I'd call it The School of Hard Knocks. She's smart, annoying, relentless – relentless and sly. She's like you, basically.'

'How old is she?'

'I don't know. About fifteen.'

'I'm looking for a college student.'

Eve just shrugged. 'It's your deal. If you decide to take a look at her, it's Quilla Magnum. She's at Harbor House now, but she'll be transitioning to Roarke's An Didean when it's ready in the spring.'

'She's in a shelter? I'm not looking to take on a troubled youth. I'm after an intern, someone I can mentor.'

'Your deal,' Eve said easily. She gathered up the file, got to her feet.

'Did she know any of the dead girls you found in the building Roarke's rehabbing?'

'Ask her. I've got a fresh dead girl to deal with.' Opening the door, Eve jerked her thumb in a get-out gesture.

Nadine narrowed those feline eyes. 'You threw that at me on purpose, but I'm not taking on a teenager.'

'Whatever.'

Satisfied, Eve turned toward Homicide, and went straight to Jenkinson's desk. She curled a come-ahead finger at Reineke.

'What's shaking, boss?' Jenkinson shifted in his seat. 'You've got something fresh on the Kent case?'

'Might. I've got the file, and I've got a consult coming up, but run it through.'

'Reineke took primary.'

'Yep,' Reineke agreed. 'Eighteen-year-old Caucasian female. Rosie Kent. Kid had barely started in the life. Her family didn't like it – parents divorced, both remarried, had a civil but distant deal going. Kent had one full sib – older sister – two younger half sibs, one from each parent. Older sib, high achiever, going to Florida State on scholarship.'

'Vic's a little bit of a screwup,' Jenkinson continued. 'Got through high school, flunked out of community college the first semester. Started the LC training. She figured it was an easy way to make money, and kind of a middle finger to her family.'

'They couldn't stop her,' Reineke put in, 'so decided to wait it out, figuring she'd get tired of trolling the streets to make a score, get tired of being pawed for a fee, and dealing with all the restrictions, the regular testing, and all that.'

'She didn't have a chance to get tired of it.' With a head shake, Jenkinson's chair squeaked when he leaned back. 'She was just a couple months in when she bought it.'

'Nobody saw the john. It's frigging cold, right?' Reineke eased a hip onto his partner's desk. 'It's dark. She hasn't been around long enough to make friends with the other LCs, and it comes out she's standoffish anyhow. Acts superior, so nobody hangs with her. The way it plays is she comes out of the SRO where she's living and gets picked up straight off. That's how the timing played. She used one of those flops where the LCs check themselves in if the desk guy isn't on duty, which he ain't most of the time. It's like a time clock, and it auto-charges by the quarter hour. John or Jane pays upfront. LC takes the key to the room on the tab, does the job, tosses the key back after, and the room goes back in rotation.'

'No security?'

'Nada,' Jenkinson confirmed. 'As low-rent as low gets. So she ran up three hours before the clerk – who was watching porn in the back room – saw it on his tote board. He went up to haul her out, figuring she was using it to sleep in the warm, found her.'

'No sex, no DNA, no trace.' Reineke lifted empty hands. 'Vic had an OTC sedative mixed with cheap wine in her system. No sign of restraints or struggle. She logged in for thirty minutes. TOD came in about ten minutes after the log-in. The murder weapon more of a sash than a scarf. White, tied in a fancy bow.'

Reineke tapped the left side of his throat.

'We ran like crimes, followed a few similar to nowhere.' Jenkinson shrugged. 'Nothing special about the sash, the sedative, the wine. The vic didn't have a regular boyfriend or fuck buddy. You had to figure the killer intended to do what he did, maybe targeted her because she was new at it, and that made her an easier mark.'

'Was she registered for men and women?'

'Yeah, and the ME cited – especially with the vic being unconscious at the time – it didn't take a lot of strength to strangle her. We looked at the female angle,' Reineke added. 'But hit the wall there, too. We've been waiting for the next shoe to drop. You know, the bow, a symbol maybe. But so far, nothing.'

'You hate seeing one open this long.' Jenkinson glanced at the case board. 'A month goes by, five weeks, it stays this cold, the odds just get longer. Either a break falls in your lap, or you get another one. You got another one, LT?'

'I think she was another one.'

'Nothing popped out of IRCCA with the white sash and bow. We got scarves and bows and sashes,' Reineke said, easing to his feet again. 'But not with all the elements.'

'We've got all of them, just not in reality. In fiction.'

'Fiction? Is that why that writer was here with Nadine?' Reineke asked. 'The one Peabody was all about? Santiago's a big fan. Talked me into reading one. I don't much like cop books. They end up pissing me off, but this one was pretty solid. I keep meaning to try another.'

'Never read a cop book that didn't blow. You want fiction?' Jenkinson said. 'Go with science fiction. You know it's bullshit going in.'

'This one didn't blow,' Reineke insisted. 'You're saying the Hightower writer wrote about a killing like ours?'

'She says exactly like, and the way she ran it down, she's right about that. She also wrote one that plays like the one Peabody and I caught yesterday. Too many mirroring elements to be coincidence. Take a fresh look with this in the mix.

'Your victim wasn't just plucked off the street,' Eve told them. 'She was target specific to mimic the victim in the book. The killer had to stalk and research. The motive arrows back to the books, and the books come from the writer.'

'Which book was it?' Reineke demanded. 'Santiago'll have it. It'll help to take a look at it.'

'*Dark Falls*. It's the connected series ... Hightower, and launches the Dark series. The second's my case. The third's going to be a poisoning in a dance club. Female vic. Anybody gets a dispatch on that, I hear about it. I take it. Spread that word. I've got a consult.'

She looked over as Peabody came in.

'Did you get the fangirl out of your system?'

'Born a fangirl, die a fangirl.'

Eve smiled, very, very pleasantly. 'You might just, and sooner than you expect.'

'I wasn't just fangirling.' Peabody kept herself beyond boot-kicking distance when she joined them. 'I escorted her out, and fangirled just the proper amount so she wouldn't freak any over the line of questioning I worked out while you were handling the more personal in interview.'

'What line was that?'

'How some writers use readers to beta test a story. She doesn't. I figured if she did, we'd want to look there, but it goes straight from her to her agent and editor. Nobody, not even her mom or her kids – and they're tight – see any of it. And some writers use researchers to dig up especially obscure or highly detailed information. She doesn't, so no go on that, either. She's a little superstitious about the process, like, if she lets too much of what she's working on or thinking up out there, it, like, diffuses or something. But she has talked to our own Morris a few times, and she sometimes asks Detective Olivia Diaz – retired – some procedural questions. That's one of the detectives she went to when her ex tuned her up. She was out of the eight-three in Brooklyn. They keep in touch.'

'Diaz still in Brooklyn?'

'She moved to Cape May about three years ago when she put in her papers. I did a quick run on her on the way back up. She looks solid.'

'Reach out, talk to her while I'm with Mira. You've avoided unexpected death.'

'Always a good day.'

'The day's not over,' Eve commented, and walked out.

6

Eve grabbed a glide, then wove her way through people who obviously weren't in any damn hurry. She quick-walked the rest of the way to Mira's outer office, where the dragon admin guarded the gates.

She said, 'You're late, Lieutenant.'

Damn it. Deliberately, Eve looked at her wrist unit. Two fricking minutes. Two. 'Sorry. I was detained by a little something we call *murder*.'

The admin simply smiled her thin, humorless smile and tapped her earpiece. 'Dr Mira, Lieutenant Dallas is here. Of course. You can go right in,' she told Eve.

Eve breezed by the dragon's lair and opened the door to Mira's sanctum.

At her desk, perfectly presented in an ice-blue suit, the department's top profiler and headshrinker raised a finger in a one-minute signal as she finished a conversation on her 'link.

'She just walked in. Yes, I'll tell her, and yes, it is very interesting. Thanks, Dennis. I'll see you at home.'

Mira clicked off, brushed an absent hand at her mink-brown wave of hair. 'Sorry, have a seat. Dennis thinks he might have some information relevant to your case.'

Eve thought of the dreamy-eyed, absentminded Mr Mira, a man she had a helpless, harmless crush on. And made the connection.

'He reads Blaine DeLano.'

Mira sat back, eyebrows arching over soft blue eyes. 'Wind. Sails.' She flicked her fingers in the air. 'Poof. I'm not about to tell you anything you don't know.'

'She came in. Nadine brought her in. I just finished interviewing her.'

With a nod, Mira rose, walked on ice-blue heels to her office AutoChef. Eve accepted she was in for a dainty cup of flowery tea. 'And with the number of mirrored elements, you believe the killer used DeLano's book as a template.'

'I do. And not for the first time.'

Mira paused in her programming, glanced back. 'There are more?'

'One we know of, for now. The book in the same series just prior to this one. The Dark series. You're not familiar?'

'I've read several of the Hightower books, but I haven't started the other series. I keep meaning to. Dennis devours both, and when he heard the report, he thought of the book.'

She gestured Eve to one of her pretty scoop chairs, brought over the dainty cups, sat. Crossed her excellent legs while she balanced her own cup with a careless grace that continually baffled Eve.

'He actually pulled the book up on his reader, checked the scene, and made notes on the repeated elements. Before we discuss that: What other murder, other book?'

'Jenkinson and Reineke caught one last month. A new-to-the-life street-level LC: strangled, no sexual activity, left in a time-flop. The killer used a white sash, tied a fancy bow on the left side of the throat.'

'I'm not familiar with the case.'

'They didn't come to you. They did consult with . . . ' She flipped back through the file in her mind. 'Strighter. But with the – for now, anyway – one-shot, no wits, no history, the profile was pretty loose. No like crimes that hit the main notes. The book's the one DeLano used to – what's it – spin off the Dark character into another series.'

'Wait, wait.' Mira closed her eyes a moment. 'I read that. Years ago, but it's coming back. It was a serial case, and the Detective Dark character knew this particular victim.'

'In both the book and the case, the vic was tranq'd. An over-the-counter sedative mixed in Chianti. No signs of struggle or other injuries. No clerk on the desk, no security. Both vics are in the same age range, same race, both were new to the life.'

'So repeated elements again,' Mira observed. 'In the book, if I'm remembering correctly, it was a female killer, and the victims represented the LCs she learned her husband engaged.'

'Your memory's on target. I don't think that's what we're dealing with in reality.'

Thinking it through, Mira lifted her tea. 'No, given this second killing, it would be the books, the author, as motive.'

'DeLano was up front in the interview.'

Though she'd send Mira a copy of her refined notes, she relayed the salient points now. Mira nodded, sipped her tea.

'You'll have to look at the ex-husband, of course, but my conclusion, with what you now have, is these killings are too tied to her work, too indirect a strike at her. And too intellectual. You've described a spousal abuser who relies heavily on manipulation and intimidation, and only broke into violent rage when crossed, when he felt his authority and status threatened. His wife – whom he'd view as his property – challenged his authority, moreover, usurped that authority and status by reaching a level of success – writing and selling a book – completely on her own terms.

'The killer is detail oriented,' Mira continued, 'very controlled. The killing is an act, a reproduction of something he – or she – envies. Or admires. Perhaps both.'

'She can write about it,' Eve suggested, 'but I can make it real.'

'Yes.'

'Her killers get caught. I won't.'

'Exactly,' Mira agreed. 'Because he's smarter – than the character and the creator. The victims are simply characters. They aren't real, they have no personal connection to him. They're avatars, until he makes them real.'

'Clearly, he's read the books. More, he must have studied them. So an obsessed reader?'

'Would fit, yes. The books become real, and the need to re-create grows. That need may come from an obsessed reader or a frustrated writer. A killer with both qualities is a very high probability. He puts himself in the story, writes it from his own point of view. He admires and resents DeLano, professionally. Another reason I think the ex-husband falls outside the profile.'

'He didn't start with her first book.'

'That's interesting, isn't it?' Mira considered as she enjoyed her tea. 'The Hightower books launched her career.'

'Another reason the ex-asshole is low on the list.'

'Yes. As I said, I haven't read the Dark series, but I did read the one where she turned in her badge, separated from Hightower – as official partners. I need to reread that now. It may be that the separation plays a part in the killer's mind-set. The fact that the female detective struck out on her own, rebelled against the badge and the limits of it.'

'Which would bump the ex up the list,' Eve commented.

'Yes, it's a factor. The Dark series, from what Dennis told me, is centered on a strong, somewhat reckless woman. Female empowerment. She chose another path, even if parallel. She stills seeks justice, but often breaks rules to find it.

'Your killer is, obviously, a reader, one who enjoys police procedurals, detective novels, murder mysteries. Entirely too much. They become a world he inhabits. Very likely he believes he has the talent and intellect to create those worlds, and better than DeLano. He – or again she – is mature, controlled, patient enough to select the victim that fits the needs of the story he stars in. To study and plan. A risk taker – it's worth it, the risk. Nothing great is achieved without risk.'

'With Rylan, a lot of easier ways to kill. But if he needed to follow a script ... It's not Rylan so much as the re-creation.'

'I'd agree at this point. I wouldn't profile him as less than thirty. If he's male, sex isn't of great import. Male or female, the killer likely lives alone or in a situation where he or she has considerable time alone, or privacy. He lives in books. He may work with them. Selling them, or at a low-level position in publishing. Nothing with any power. His power's inside the books, and now manifesting with the actions he takes.'

'Eventually, he'll run out of books. I'll damn well bag him before he gets to eight, but he's a planner, so he has a plan for when he finishes the last book in the series.'

'I agree. When the series is done, the only thing left is the creator.'

'Yeah.' Eve had thought of it while listening to DeLano. 'He writes that one. Maybe he already has, right?'

'It would certainly be a work-in-progress.'

'Got it.' Eve pushed to her feet. 'The third vic's already selected, studied, and marked.'

'Who?'

'It'll be a half-assed celebrity, self-made badass who used to bang a rock star – I don't know if it has to be trash rock like in the book. Poison this time, dropped into her fruity martini. Crowded dance club.'

'Another female victim.'

'Yeah. Huh. Yeah, that's three for three.'

'Give me a second.' Mira pulled out her pocket 'link, said, 'Dennis.' A moment later Eve heard his voice – warm, distracted.

'Charlie.'

'I know you're on your way to class, but I have a quick question. In the Dark series, are the murder victims primarily female?'

'It's her specialty, you could say. You see, after her friend's sister was killed in *Dark Falls*, and Deann becomes embittered by the restrictions on police work, she devotes herself to female victims. There are male victims throughout, of course, but—'

'The primary victims are female.'

'That's the framework of the series. This becomes her mission, her raison d'être. You must read them, Charlie. They're very cleverly done.'

'I will. In fact, I'm going to reread *Dark Falls* tonight.'

'We'll snuggle up together. You look so pretty.'

'Dennis, I adore you. I'll see you later. Have a good day.'

Still smiling, Mira slipped the 'link back in her jacket pocket. 'It's nice when the man you've been married to for decades still thinks you're pretty.'

'You are pretty.'

'Thank you. It takes considerably more work than it once did. I know you have to get back, and I have another consult, but I think this is another key factor. Female victims.

It may be yet another reason the killer focused on this series – and one written by a female. Women may be seen as weak or competition. He may be impotent. She, if it's a she, may be jealous of what she sees as female power. But female victims, female protagonist, female creator. I doubt that's insignificant.'

'It won't be. I appreciate the time. And I'd appreciate hearing about it if Mr Mira has any more insights.'

'He'll be thrilled.' Mira rose, walked Eve to the door. 'Good luck. I'll send you a formal profile.' Then she turned to her admin as Eve left. 'Would you download the novel *Dark Falls* by Blaine DeLano? And the book that follows in the series. To my tablet, please.'

Eve contacted Peabody. 'Grab my coat and stuff, meet me in the garage. We'll take the victim's residence, then the theater.'

She aimed for an elevator, jabbed the call button as she calculated working in a visit to DeLano's ex, work or home. The door opened to reveal a pair of uniforms struggling with a guy with mad tufts of hair, unlaced knee boots, and a flapping topcoat covered in what appeared to be weird symbols drawn on with some sort of metallic marker.

He actually had tinfoil capped and peaked on his head.

'They're coming!' He screamed it, eyes bulging in Eve's direction. 'They eat your brains while you sleep. They look like us, but they're not. Only the Sign of Umberto can protect you. Don't sleep! Don't sleep!'

Eve opted for the stairs.

She still beat Peabody and had time to lean against her car, check the victim's address, the theater's, check Craig Jefferson's home and work on his official ID.

She took a minute to study him. What most would call good-looking – a good head of styled hair, a smooth face. And a smug look in his eyes she'd have noticed even without knowing he was an asshole.

A marketing executive for some company that made health food, vitamins, supplements.

For the hell of it, she looked up his current wife. Younger than DeLano, she noted, by six years, but the man had a type. Same coloring as wife number one, same build. First marriage for her, and a listing as professional mother.

She put her PPC away when she heard Peabody's boots.

Eve swung on her coat, stuffed the scarf and hat in pockets for later, and got behind the wheel. 'Diaz?'

'Was happy to help. She comes off genuinely fond of DeLano, and rates the ex as low on the murdering bastard list. She pegs him as more of a sniveling, abusive coward with a massive ego and a hard-on – in the nonsexual way – for women. Unless they're, in Diaz's term, of the Breed and Bake category. Outside that, they're bitches. She's happy to put the word in with her former LT, ask him to share her case file on the Jefferson arrest. She says he broke pretty fast once they put him in the box – hence the sniveling. But coated it with badass attitude.'

'I lean toward her take, but we'll look at him because the killer likely has that same hard-on for women.'

She filled Peabody in on the consult with Mira as they shoved their way to the victim's theater district apartment.

'I should've flipped to it,' Peabody said. 'The female angle. The writer, the central character, the primary vics throughout the series. I think it's a solid angle. And you can take it further. The writer lives in a female household. Her mother and two daughters.'

Peabody glanced over. 'You've already gone there.'

'It's in the mix. We can look at it two ways: either the killer's male with that hard-on for women, or the killer's female to keep it consistent. That doesn't narrow it down.'

When Eve spotted a street slot within a block of her target, she considered it her lucky day. She hit vertical, ignored Peabody's muffled squeal, zipped over traffic, and dropped between a bunged-up rattletrap and a filthy sedan, with a couple inches to spare.

'I would've been all right with walking,' Peabody managed. 'I would've been all right with it.'

'Good, because you score a slot like this, you keep it. We'll hike it to the theater from here after we check out the apartment.'

'It's because I bought that Danish on the way into Central. I wasn't going to, I told myself not to. But it was right there, all glossy and full of the gooey yumness. McNab ate two, but does his skinny ass care? No, it does not.'

'I thought you had loose pants.'

'I took them in as an incentive.' Peabody checked her waistband as they hoofed to the building. 'Maybe I should've left them loose as a reminder.'

'Your ass is smaller.'

Peabody stopped dead, jaw dropping. 'What did you say?'

'I've got eyes.' Eve kept walking, forcing Peabody to jog to catch up. 'They don't latch themselves onto your ass, but I've got eyes.'

'I want to kiss you on the mouth. With tongue.'

'Try it and your marginally smaller ass will have my boot marks imprinted thereon.'

'It could be worth it.'

Eve pressed the buzzer on the narrow door between a store called Center Stage and a tat and piercing parlor.

Lola's voice came tinny through the speaker. 'Yes?'

'Lieutenant Dallas, Detective Peabody.'

'Okay.' The door buzzed, clicked.

Eve took one look at the skinny elevator with its dented door in the tiny lobby and took the stairs.

'Fourth floor.' Peabody sighed. 'It's definitely the fault of the Danish.'

'We play the angles with her. She's had some time to settle. Did she notice anybody she saw repeatedly at the vids, especially over the last couple of months? Somebody she saw in the neighborhood, somebody Rylan commented on. You talk to her while I take a look at the vic's bedroom.'

'Got it.'

Lola stood in the doorway, nibbling on a thumbnail.

She'd had time to settle, Eve thought, and had spent a lot of it weeping.

'Chanel. Do you know who . . . '

'Not yet, but finding who is our top priority. Can we come in?'

'Yeah, sure. Ah, this is DeVon.'

The tall, skinny black man with wild, red-tipped dreads appeared to have done some weeping of his own. He offered a hand.

'I live across the hall. I can go. I just didn't want Lola to be alone.'

'Can he stay? Please? Is that all right?'

'You know Chanel, Mr . . . ?'

'It's Monrow, but it's just DeVon. I knew our Chanel. I'm a costume designer. Chanel and I worked on the same play a couple of times.'

His huge dark eyes teared up, but when Lola let out a broken sob, he put an arm around her shoulders, blinked away threatening tears. 'Come on now, my baby girl, you sit down. I'm going to make you some more tea. Can I make some for both of you?'

'I'm good, thanks. I'd like to see Chanel's room.'

'I'll show you. No, you sit down, baby.' He nudged her into a chair with a colorful print, tucked a bright blue throw around her legs. 'I'll be right back. It's just over here, ma'am.'

'Lieutenant,' Eve said, and followed him to the right.

DeVon stepped into the room with Eve, lowered his voice. 'She hasn't slept all night. She came home early this morning after trying to settle herself down with this guy she's seeing. Just needed to come home, and came over to get me. I didn't want to leave her alone. I can step out until you're done, if you'd rather.'

'She'd tell you everything we did or said anyway, and it's clear she needs someone. You make her the tea. But let me ask you if you noticed anyone in the neighborhood, anyone who looked like they might be watching the building, anyone hanging around the theater, the market Chanel used, the vids – if you ever went with them.'

'I'd go sometimes, but I don't remember anybody who stood out. We haven't – hadn't – worked at the same theater in about seven months. I do the market more than Chanel did. Lola'd do most of that, I guess. I wish I'd noticed somebody. Anybody. She was just a sweetheart. When the man I thought was the love of my life dumped me eight weeks and three days ago? Chanel and Lola were right there, right there for me. I don't want Lola to be alone.'

'Go ahead and be with her.'

He nodded, took a damp-eyed look around the room, managed a smile. 'She liked happy, Chanel did. She liked pretty, bright, and happy.'

When he stepped out, Eve took her own look around.

Bright and happy covered it. The tiny room all but glowed with bright pink walls – what was it with pink? – and the cheerful art covering them. Mostly flowers and butterflies, Eve noted, and all, to her eye, little originals likely done by friends or bought on the street.

A candy-striped duvet flowed, just a bit carelessly, over the bed under a mountain range of pillows. More flowers and butterflies, she noted, along with a dancer in one of those ballerina skirts, a unicorn.

Clothes, just as colorful and bright, tumbled over a chair. Over the single window a half dozen suncatchers were draped from fishing wire. A curlicue mirror over a three-drawer bureau held a collection of photos tucked into its white frame. Bottles, pots, a bouquet of paper flowers in a thin vase, costume jewelry – earrings, bracelets, and pendants in a multicolored bowl – jumbled together on top of the bureau.

The lone bedside table held a lamp with a frilly white shade, a tablet, a candle that smelled like sugared cookies. In its drawer Eve found tubes of hand cream, face cream, lube, a vibrator, a lighter – likely for the candle – a nail file, little clippers, and basic female paraphernalia.

She tried the tablet – not passcoded – and skimmed through with the vague hope for a diary or journal. She found what she realized were plays, some with parts highlighted, a calendar and schedule, a lot of bookmarks for stores, theaters, music, emails – plenty of them junk and spam – more photos.

She'd leave the deeper search for EDD, she decided, and turned to the closet.

If she'd spread her arms, she'd have rapped her elbows on the sides. While she didn't really appreciate the size of her own closet, studying the complete chaos here made her grateful that hers, through little effort on her part, somehow remained organized.

Everything jumbled and tumbled – dresses, pants, jackets, shirts – in cheerful disarray. Dozens of scarves and belts hung over the rods. Boots, shoes, skids tumbled together in skinny cubbies, and out of them like a footwear river. A pair of battered toe shoes hung on a hook by their pale pink ribbons. Worn ballet slippers, shoes with straps and low heels Eve took for dance shoes – and a couple had those metal tap things on the bottoms – crowded onto a shelf above the rods.

Getting dressed every day must've been a frigging opera, she thought as she reached up for a box that bore Chanel's name in big, bold letters among the glitter of stars.

Inside, Eve found playbills, old programs from school plays, dance recitals. The playbills had been signed by fellow cast members, some with inscriptions. Inside each, Chanel had tucked photos. Of herself, of other cast members – rehearsals, costume fittings, makeup sessions.

She'd saved some menus from the restaurant, had her coworkers sign them, attached photos.

No journal, no diary, Eve thought. Chanel had recorded her life as she lived it. In theater.

Eve replaced the box, stepped out of the closet. She wouldn't find the killer here, or any trace of him. Chanel's life hadn't mattered to him. She'd only been a character in his world.

She went back out.

Lola remained tucked up, DeVon beside her. Peabody sat across from them, talking in low, soothing tones.

'Did you find anything that helps?' Lola leaned into DeVon as she spoke. 'I didn't touch anything in her room. I couldn't even go in.'

'I'd like to take her tablet in, go through it more thoroughly.'

'You can take anything you need, anything.'

'Did she have other electronics?'

'Just the tablet. And the 'link in her purse – you already have that. Do you want mine? You can take mine.'

'That's all right.'

'Should I . . . should I go see her? Her parents are coming in, and they're going to see her. Should I?'

Eve read dread, guilt, fear, grief.

'I imagine her parents are going to want to have a memorial for her. Maybe you could help them with that. I think that would be more important.'

'I could help.' She pressed her face to DeVon's shoulder. 'I could.'

'We'll help. I bet Annalisa would let us hold one in the restaurant. Music, dancing. That's Chanel, right?'

Lola nodded. 'Would it be all right if I cleaned up her room some, before her parents come? And maybe, ah, take out a couple of things Chanel would be embarrassed for them to see?'

'I think Chanel would appreciate that,' Peabody said as she rose. 'You're good friends, both of you.'

When they trooped back down the stairs, Peabody sighed. 'They don't know anything, Dallas. They want to know something, they'd turn themselves inside out to find something that would help.'

'There isn't anything for them to know. We'll finish it out, hit the vet office, the theater, but it's long odds. If she knew her killer, it was casually, more like peripherally. Someone who came into the restaurant or to a performance, to the vids, all to observe her. She didn't keep a diary, but she posted every damn thing on social media. Where she had dinner – while she was having it. Her classes, rehearsals, something that happened at the restaurant, a date, a shopping trip. It's all there, so he could follow her tracks, pick just the right moment. The one that mirrored the scene in the book.'

They stopped at the pet clinic on the way to the theater. Eve had Peabody interview the distraught assistant while she herself warily eyed the waiting room full of cats, dogs, and what appeared to be large, furry rodents. One of the cats hissed like a snake inside its carrier, but the rest, as cats often did, simply looked bored or superior.

Dogs, in Eve's mind, had three basic modes: dangerous, insanely happy, or just insane.

She caught the crazy-eyed look in one about the size of a small horse, wondered vaguely why anyone would want a dog they could essentially ride around the house.

When she made the mistake of meeting those crazy eyes for a split second, it danced its great gray bulk in place, then charged, dragging its squeaking owner out of her chair.

In defense, Eve slapped a hand to her weapon, but the horse-dog covered the ground like a sprinter, heaved itself up, planted its enormous front paws on her shoulders. And lapped its wide, wet tongue from her chin to her hairline in one noisy *slurp*.

'Sampson!' Uselessly, the woman tugged on the leash, pulled at the thick collar. 'Down, Sampson, down! He doesn't bite!'

If he bit, Eve thought, she would no longer have a face.

'He likes you.' Breathless, the owner pulled and tugged. 'Sometimes something just clicks with someone he sees. He's still a puppy.'

Eve looked into eyes shining with a terrifying, crazy love. 'A puppy.'

'He wouldn't hurt a fly. Sampson, down! He's gentle as a lamb.'

'Step on his back foot,' the assistant advised.

Willing to try anything, Eve put her boot on one of the enormous paws. Sampson dropped down, wagged, leaned his considerable weight lovingly against Eve's legs.

'Mrs Pinksy, you have to be the alpha.'

'I know, I know. I'm sorry. I do apologize,' she said to Eve.

'Uh-huh. Peabody?'

'Yes, sir, we're done.'

Relieved, Eve sidestepped, turned for the door. Sampson blithely galloped with her, dragging his owner behind as she begged him to stop, sit, heel, behave.

Once again, Eve looked down into the eyes gleaming with mad love.

She pointed, said, 'Sit!'

He dropped his huge ass onto the floor, slapped his axe of a tail. 'Stay,' she ordered.

As she escaped, she heard the assistant say, 'That's an alpha, Mrs Pinksy.'

'He was sweet,' Peabody began. 'Big and sloppy and sweet.'

'He licked my entire face.' Eve ran her hands over it, grateful her skin appeared to be intact. 'I think he might have licked my eyeballs.'

She shuddered it away as they walked. 'I lost track in there, but from what I heard, she couldn't add anything.'

'Nothing. She bought the emergency, and why wouldn't she? She tried to get more information, but he broke the call. She followed protocol, contacted Lola, then went in to set up an exam room, and possibly surgery.

'She also checked their records. They have two patients named Prince, but one's a cat, the other's a ferret. No canine patients by that name.'

'We tie it up, then we layer over Jenkinson and Reineke's work on Rosie Kent. The killer crossed both vics' paths, and DeLano's. We find the intersections.'

The wind blew and with it brought the scents of soy dogs, hot pretzels, roasted chestnuts. The urban street banquet. She caught Peabody's head swivel toward a smoking glide-cart.

'After,' Eve said.

She badged the guard at the theater door, crossed the empty lobby. She paused at the back of the house as music swelled and the woman onstage finished up a number in a belting Broadway voice.

She ended it with her arms raised high, her head flung back.

Then she dropped her arms, shot out a megawatt smile as one of the three seated in the center of the house applauded.

'Thank you!'

'Thank you, Jessilyn. Or should we say Sadie.'

'Oh God.' She clasped her hands together. 'I got it? I got it?' On a throaty laugh she circled the stage in pirouettes. 'Oh my God.'

'She looks enough like Rylan to be her sister,' Peabody commented.

'Yeah. Take the three, and I'll start with her. Let's see what we get.'

7

With her high, sunny ponytail swaying, the actress bounced offstage toward the three in the seats. Eve started down the sloping center aisle.

She heard the woman bubbling, saw her shaking hands, or in one case, hugging the one she called David.

Eve gave it a moment to play out.

'Sorry to interrupt. Lieutenant Dallas, Detective Peabody.'

She watched the amused pleasure in David's eyes fade away. 'Yes, of course. David Reingold. We're running just a little behind.'

'Are you being arrested at last, David?' Still flying, Jessilyn Brooke beamed at him. 'For being criminally talented.'

He shot her a quick smile, took Eve's arm. 'Give me a minute,' he said as he led her a few paces off. 'We haven't told Jessilyn yet, about Chanel. Mitzie and George agreed we should wait until after this callback, rather than have Jessilyn carry that through it, or postpone it. If you'd give me a few minutes to speak with her, tell her what happened.'

'I'll take care of that.' Eve turned. 'Miss Brooke, if you'd come with me.'

'Sorry, what?'

'Go ahead, Jess. I'll be right here.'

'All right, David. You're the boss. What's this about?' she asked as she walked up to Eve. 'Are you really the police?'

'Let's sit back here.' Eve gestured to Peabody so her partner would take the group to the front while she took the actress to the back.

'Can we make it fast? I'm really on a high, and I need to contact my agent. My mother. My ex-boyfriend.'

Eve pointed to a chair in the last row, sat on the armrest of the one beside it so she could face the woman.

'Can you describe your relationship with Chanel Rylan?'

'Chanel?' Jessilyn glanced around the theater as if expecting to see her competitor. 'Look, I know she got the callback, too, but ... Is this some David way of telling me we're sharing the part? That we're going into rehearsals co-owning it?' Some of the shine faded, but Jessilyn shrugged. 'I can live with that. I still got it. I *nailed* that number.'

'I take it you haven't listened to or read any media this morning?'

'On the morning of the biggest callback of my career? You're joking, right? I spent the morning sacrificing black-feathered chickens to the primeval theater gods. In my brain,' she added when Eve didn't smile. 'No chickens were actually harmed.'

'Miss Brooke, I'm sorry to inform you Chanel Rylan was killed last night.'

'That's not funny.' All the shine dropped now, and angry insult took its place. 'That's an ugly thing to say. David!'

Eve continued to face Jessilyn, just held up a hand to stop David if he tried to come back.

'It's not meant to be funny, and murder is usually ugly.'

'Stop it. Just stop it.'

'You and Chanel were competing for this part.'

'Stop it. I want you to stop this right now.'

Eve took out her badge. 'Look at this. I'm with the NYPSD. I'm investigating the murder of Chanel Rylan. I need you to answer some questions.'

'This isn't— I can't— But . . .' She pressed a hand to her mouth, sucked air through her fingers. 'They knew. They knew, and didn't tell me. They . . . I get it.' Closing her eyes, she rocked in her chair. 'I get it. The show must go on. I get it. Chanel gets it. We all get it. Oh God, what happened to her? What happened?'

'She was stabbed.'

Tears glimmered, shimmered, spilled. 'A mugging?'

'If you'd answer the questions. Tell me where you were last night, from five to seven.'

'Where I . . . I'd kill her for a part? Is that what you think?'

'Can you tell me?'

'God. God. I . . . I went to my friend's dance studio after work. Wait.'

117

As tears continued to leak, she pressed her fingers to her eyes, took several hitching breaths.

Lowering her hands, she gripped them tightly in her lap.

'I worked from eleven to six – I bartend at Sylvia's. I went to Missy's studio. I – I picked up some Chinese on the way, at ah, oh Jesus, at the Brass Gong. I waited until she'd finished her last class. She ran lines with me for today, and I rehearsed the number, she helped me with the dance. We went out for one drink after, then I went home to get a solid eight hours – to be fresh for today.'

She paused again, struggling. 'To be fresh, to be my best because I was going up against Chanel. I was with Missy – and Hank came into the studio for about an hour. I was there from like, six-fifteen, six-thirty until ten, I guess. And we had a drink back at Sylvia's before I went home.'

'All right. I'd like the contact information for your friends.'

'Chanel was my friend, too.' The words blurred on a sob. 'Not like Missy and Hank, but a friend. We were up for this part, and we've been up against each other for others. Sometimes I got it, sometimes she got it. Sometimes we both washed out. I wanted this one bad, that's no secret. It would've crushed me to lose out, but you get used to being crushed or you go back to Wisconsin and do community theater.

'Lola! Her roommate, her *person* is Lola, like Missy's mine, and I can't remember her last name. Does Lola know?'

'Yes. Did you socialize with Chanel?'

'Sure. Sure, we hung plenty.' She swiped at tears with

her hands. 'We're theater people. You hang together or you hang separately. I've got better pipes, she has better pins. If one of us had a part, the other sometimes helped in practice – voice for me, dance for her. She dated my ex-boyfriend before he was my boyfriend.'

She stared up at the empty stage.

'When we got this callback, we made a pact. It wasn't easy because we both really wanted it, but we made a pact. Whichever of us got it, the other would pitch in. I'd work with her on the songs, she'd work with me on the choreography.'

Eve guided her through a few more questions, took the contact information.

'Do you think I should get in touch with Lola? I don't know if she'd want to talk to me. I got the part.'

'Would you have kept the pact?'

'Yeah, sure. Chanel would have kept it, too. It wasn't our first pact.'

'That's your answer, isn't it?'

She bought Peabody a glide-cart lunch, indulged in her own loaded dog washed down with Pepsi. You might as well drink battery acid as cart coffee, in her opinion.

From there they headed back downtown to talk to the street hookers, the beat cops, the LC trainers and certifiers, the useless desk clerk at the flop. They spent two hours recrossing her detectives' boot prints, and couldn't shake out anything fresh.

Still Eve circled back again to the sad little room where Rosie Kent died.

A single bed with a lumpy mattress covered with questionable sheets. It wasn't meant for sleeping, after all. A closet-size bathroom with a pitted wall-hung sink, a toilet no one in their right mind would plop their ass on, a spotty mirror.

Ceiling light in the bedroom, no lamp. A small table that wobbled, no dresser. Bare floors, a window that leaked in cold air and walls of sickly gray. A key-operated time clock hung beside the door. The LC keyed in the time allotted, and when it ran out, the clock buzzed.

The hall door locked from the inside, but could be bypassed with a standard master.

'They may have settled on the deal, the details, on the street, but it's January, it's cold. It's time to party, so she says let's go. Details are worked out as they head to the flop. How much time, the standard fee.

'With this settled, she logs in downstairs, takes the key. They walk up. She brings him/her in, locks the door, keys in the time. Puts the key on the table there. She's new, maybe she gives him some sex talk, puts on some moves. It's an adventure, and she's in charge. She thinks she's in charge.'

But she's not, Eve thought. It's a scene that's played out countless times in this sad room. But this time, the killer had written a lethal ending.

'He's brought a bottle with him, wants to have a drink, relax first. Fine with her, she gets paid whatever they do.

Can't drink out of the bottle, can't drink from the same bottle or they'd both pass out. So he has to have a glass for her. At least one glass, maybe two. A case? A briefcase? A purse?'

Eve circled the room. 'Go freshen up a little for me – that's one way to get her into the bathroom so he can add the tranq to her glass. He's got both glasses when she comes back, hands her the doctored one. Maybe he pretends he's nervous, maybe he asks her to start to undress while they have the wine.'

Easy to imagine it, Eve mused, easy to see it. Unless you're inside the scene, and think you're in charge.

'She's the center of attention. She likes it. Does her little striptease, tries to do the sexy while she drinks. It takes a few minutes for the tranq to start to kick in. A little dizzy, a little off. Sweepers didn't find any wine spilled in here, so he doesn't let her drop the glass. Maybe he gets a little more in her before he puts her down.'

'She's new at it,' Peabody added. 'Anyone experienced would have tried to bolt, would have struggled the minute she felt off. But there wasn't any sign of a struggle.'

'No, she was easy pickings. He just led her to the bed. Time to lie down, sure, lie down, and let me do what I do. Take the rest of her clothes off, watch her go under. Get the sash out of that briefcase or purse or bag. Here's the moment. Does he call her by the character's name? I bet he does. *She* does, because whatever gender the killer is, for this scene it's a woman who wraps the sash around Pryor's neck. A woman

121

who pulls it tight, tighter, watches the eyes flutter and roll, the struggle of the body for air, hears that last choked breath expel. A woman who tests the pulse to be sure the heart's stopped beating, then ties the pretty bow, angles it.

'Then it's just get the glasses, cap the bottle, fold the clothes neat just like in the book. Unlock the door, peek out to be sure no one's around. Walk out, walk away.'

'And scene,' Peabody murmured.

'What?'

'It's what they say.'

'It's all about the scene. He might have been a man under it, but for this scene, for this killing, he posed as female. Rosie, like Pryor in the book, was certified for either, so the killer dressed as a woman, either way. The killer bought her as a woman, and killed her as a woman. That's the fresh here. That's the new angle.'

'If that's true, the killer came to the vids as a man.'

'That's right. It's what plays through. It's the scene reenacted.'

A scene, she thought as she circled the room, reenacted on a sad, ugly stage.

Maybe that made it more real to the killer.

'It's not that hard to pose either way,' Eve continued, 'but it's unlikely we're talking about a big guy. Even world-weary LCs are likely to notice an unusually large woman trolling for action. Average to small build likely as a male killer, average to tall build as a female. That's basic probability. Maybe a wig for this. The sweepers didn't find any fibers or hair, but maybe.'

'A female dressed as a male for the vids is also possible,' Peabody put in. 'If so, she's unlikely to be busty, curvy. Could've kept outdoor gear on, but it's still noticeable if you're, you know, zaftig. Anyway, it's generally easier for a woman to pass as a man than the other way. And for the vids, you could just wear regular unisex clothes. The man's in your head, right?'

'That's just right. The point is the killer has to, and is capable of, sliding into the role. But it's not theater. It's his or her personal reality.'

Eve turned one more circle. 'Let's get out of this dump. I want to write this up, send it to Mira. And we're going to start looking at DeLano's communications with an eye for one person who can play a lot of parts.'

Back at Central, Eve called Jenkinson and Reineke into her office to update them.

'What'd we miss?' Reineke asked her.

'You didn't miss anything. We've got new information, new lines, and a new theory. Rosie Kent wasn't a one-shot or the start of a serial in the traditional sense.'

She ran it through for them as she added Kent to her board.

'So we're after a whacko who's living inside a book?' Jenkinson frowned over it. 'Maybe a tranny, a cross-dresser.'

'Possible, but it's not about the lifestyle. It's about the scene, and re-creating it as closely as possible. So for Kent's murder, we're looking for a female – for Rylan's, a man.

123

That's how the killer saw himself, that's how he approached it, and how he presented.'

'What's the why?' Reineke muttered. 'What's the frigging point?'

'DeLano's going to be the point, or the books, or a combination. The vics – including the one coming up next in the books – are female. The creator of the scenes is female, the detective in the books is female. That's going to play in. When DeLano divorced, she moved in with her mother. She has two daughters. That's a lot of females, and it has to factor in.'

'How about DeLano's ex?'

Eve nodded at Reineke. 'I'm going to take a hard look there, but he doesn't fit the profile – I'll send that to you. Add that these are complex, detail-oriented killings, and he's mostly a domineering asshole with violent spurts. My sense, at this point, is his dick's too important for him to pose as female.'

'He timed it good, with Kent.' Jenkinson studied the board. 'Picked her up right after she came out for the night. We figured either he got real lucky, and luck's mostly bullshit, or he'd scoped her out before, maybe even bought her before. Now you've gotta figure it didn't have jack to do with luck. We can go back, talk to the working girls and boys again. Any of them been on the stroll awhile would spot a cross-dresser or tranny, even somebody pretending to be.'

'It wouldn't hurt, but it's possible – and how I'd play it – the killer did the scoping as whatever the hell sex he was born with. And if that's male, geared up for the kill, not before.'

'We'll play it out anyway. It's pissing me off now.' Jenkinson took one last hard look at the board. 'Yeah, it's pissing me off. Let's hit the streets, partner.'

Alone, Eve grabbed coffee, sat, wrote up a report for Mira.

She took time to run some probabilities, chewed them over. Dissatisfied, she brought the security footage from the vid palace up on her screen, ran through it. Slowed the speed, picked through it.

She watched Chanel and Lola cross to the concession stand, chatting, chatting. Chanel pulled off her hat, shook out her hair, laughed at something Lola said.

Eve studied people who filed into line behind them, a couple of teenage boys, another couple she judged to be on a date.

She toggled to the snack area, the tables, studied every face. Toggled back, followed Chanel's progress toward the theaters, with her popcorn and soft drink.

The teenage boys headed in the same direction – two jumbo corns, two jumbo drinks, assorted candy. She spotted the student she'd interviewed on scene, watched a few others – no solos.

Sat back, drummed her fingers. Then ordered the feed to start thirty minutes earlier.

People coming and going, a matinee letting out – kids show, she had to figure by the number of children and exhausted-looking adults herding them.

A full twenty minutes before the victim and her room-mate entered, Eve felt a little buzz.

A solo, wearing sunshades, and something about the way he — the stride, the boots, the long, bulky coat read male — checked his wrist unit, turned his head as if checking the lobby area for someone, seemed studied to her.

No hair showing with the thick, dark cap pulled low on the forehead. No clear view of the face, with the cap, the shades, and the scarf bundled around the neck, skimming over the chin.

No bag, she noted, but deep pockets in the coat.

Another check of the wrist unit — a chunky, mannish one. Gloves on the hands. An impatient shrug before he marched across the lobby, head down, face averted, and disappeared into the corridor that led to the theaters.

She ran it back, stopped on the best angle of the face, zoomed. Caucasian, she determined. Hard to judge the age, she thought, but if she had to guess, between thirty and fifty. About five feet, seven inches in height, and no way of knowing if there were lifts in the boots. Medium build, say a hundred-fifty — but, again, no way to know what was under the coat.

She zipped it forward to TOD, slowed it again. When the first show let out, she slowed it more, worked her way through the crowd looking for the dark coat, the cap, the body type.

She kept it running after the first responders arrived, after alarm spread on faces and body language in the lobby.

Ran it back again, picked through again.

And there, she thought. There you are.

Still studying, she hit her interoffice comm, snapped, 'Peabody!'

Changed the coat, she thought. It's reversible – that's thinking of the details. Pale gray now with weird little penguins all over it. And the cap, changed to an earflap with pom-poms on dangles at the sides.

Same boots, same trousers – can't change everything.

Playing it up, Eve observed. You know where the cameras are, so you keep your face angled just enough. And you're laughing, like you're with the people around you, while you pull on those stupid pink-lensed wind goggles.

'Sir!' Peabody rushed in.

'What do you see?' Eve tapped her screen.

'Ah, female, Caucasian, probably. About, um, five-six. Maybe five-seven, on the heavy side at like, a buck-sixty. Long winter coat, gray with black-and-white penguins. Winter cap, earflaps, long ties with pom-poms. Dark scarf, wind goggles with pink lenses.'

Eve ordered the feed to cue to the first stop point.

'What do you see?' she repeated.

'Okay, male, Caucasian. Like, ah, five-seven, five-eight? Medium build. Long, dark winter coat, dark cap and scarf, sunshades, dark lenses.'

'Split screen,' Eve ordered. 'Now?'

'Well, they ...' Peabody jerked back, then leaned in. 'The same damn boots. The same pants. There's a height

127

difference, maybe. I don't think that's cam angle, but ...
The cut of the coat, that's the same, too. Reversible. Take a minute, turn it inside out, retie the scarf. The cap, it could be the same one, too, turn it inside out, pull down the flaps and ties. Yank out the lifts. Switch the shades for the goggles.'

'What do you conclude?'

'I conclude I'm looking at the killer, and the killer's female. You can get more height with lifts, but you can't shrink – without removing lifts. The coat adds bulk, and she could easily add more under it, so she may not be as heavy as she looks here. No hair showing, no eye color, and we can only get a partial on the face. Hell, we can't get a clear view of the ears or eyebrows, but I see a woman.'

Eve pushed up, gestured. 'Get me hard copies, full body, close-up on the faces.'

She stalked over to her window, scowled out. 'Send them to Reineke and Jenkinson. They can show them around. She didn't look like that for the Kent murder, but you've got to try. I looked at the feed last night. I didn't catch it.'

'You weren't looking for the transformation. McNab and I looked at it, too.'

'I didn't go back far enough. She came in a solid twenty minutes before the victim. Came in, settled in while they were still having a pre-vid drink. Then she just had to shift her seat when they came in, sit down behind Rylan. Sit in the back until, that's what I'd do. Sit, wait, watch. Maybe slip in behind Rylan after the movie starts.'

She turned back. 'Why bother to change the look to leave? Is it, what, a flourish? For fun?'

'Plot twist? It's a story for her. Her story, but a story. So, come in as a man, kill the character as a man, leave as a woman. Plot twist.'

'Plot twist.' Eve grabbed her coat. 'Let's go see the writer.'

Blaine DeLano lived with her family in a settled Brooklyn neighborhood with rejuvenated old houses, heavy on the brick. A place of sidewalks, financial security, good schools and restaurants.

DeLano's corner-lot three story had a narrow garden area in the front and a covered portico over the front entrance, with a small, attached garage on the side-street end.

Window boxes holding some sort of purplish cabbagey-looking plants added a female sensibility.

Top-flight security, Eve noticed, which showed the females inside had sense as well.

Eve pressed the buzzer expecting the security comp to quiz her. But the door opened in seconds.

DeLano's mother, Eve concluded, as the resemblance, despite the age difference, was strong. The mother might have gone boldly red with a short, sculpted cap of hair, but the eyes, the shape of the mouth, the line of the chin, she'd passed down to her daughter.

'Lieutenant Dallas, Detective Peabody.' Brooklyn rang in her cheerful voice. 'I recognized you.' She grabbed Eve's hand to shake, used it to pull her inside while she gestured

Peabody in. 'I've seen the *Icove* vid three times. I'm really rooting for it next month.'

'Next month?'

'The Oscars. You're going, aren't you? I hope you're going. What an experience. And listen to me, blathering on when you must be here to see Blaine. I talked her into going up to her office to write, take her mind off things. She's so upset about that poor girl. Come in, sit. I've got the fire on. Spring can't come soon enough.'

She led them out of the wide foyer with its vase of fragrant lilies on a glossy table, its big oval mirror and pretty, girlie chairs, into a spacious living area where a fire snapped in a hearth of dark gray brick flanked by tall white cabinets. On the mantel over the hearth stood more flowers, candles, and a large painting of what Eve thought might be tulips.

Lacy curtains fussed at the windows that let winter light slide inside in frilly patterns. Soft throws draped artistically over the backs of facing sofas, while the pillows Eve assumed women loved simply because lined the seats.

'Let me take your coats, and you make yourselves at home while I get Blaine.'

'Thanks. We'd like to speak with you, too, Mrs DeLano.'

'Audrey, please. And I'll confess, I'd be thrilled to be interviewed by Dallas and Peabody. I know it's a terrible situation, but if there's a silver lining, you should find it. I'll go get Blaine.'

She carted off the coats, steps brisk in her house skids.

'This is a really nice house,' Peabody commented as she

wandered around. 'I really like this room. It's girlie, but it's comfortable girlie.'

She sat in one of the occasional chairs, snugged her butt in. 'Really comfortable, and it smells really good.'

Eve scanned the photos on the cabinet shelves. Family shots, generational. Baby pictures, little girls, young women, mothers and daughters – some men sprinkled in. One of Audrey, Blaine, and two teenage girls – Heather and Piper, Eve remembered.

Photos, some books, lots of pretty, useless things.

She turned when she heard footsteps.

DeLano had changed since her morning visit to Central and now wore baggy gray pants, a hip-length blue sweater with a kangaroo pocket, and house booties designed to keep the feet warm.

'I didn't expect to hear from you so soon,' she began, 'or see you. I hope it means you've broken the case, or that, at least, found some way I can help.'

'We have some angles.'

'My mother said you wanted to speak with her as well. She's excited about that.' DeLano let out a short laugh, sat on one of the sofas. 'She's followed your work closely since Nadine's book. She's just getting coffee – she likes to fuss, as we don't get many visitors during the workweek. At least not until the girls, and often some of their friends, charge in from school.'

'How soon will that be?'

'The coffee?'

'Your daughters. When do you expect them home?'

'Oh, I . . .' She looked at her wrist, laughed. 'No wrist unit. I don't pay attention to the time when I'm working. What time is it?'

'Three-ten,' Peabody told her.

'Really? I lose track. Shortly then. If you want them out of the way, I can just—'

'Actually, we'd like to speak with them. With all of you.'

'Oh.' A worry line dug in between her eyebrows. 'I haven't spoken to them yet about any of this. They've been in school.'

'If you'd like time for that, we can wait.'

'No, I . . . No,' DeLano said more firmly. 'They're tough and they're sensible. We can explain it all to them together. Just, can you tell me, should I be concerned for their safety?'

'I don't think there's any cause to be overly concerned at this time. But we'll talk about that.'

Audrey carried in a loaded tray. Peabody jumped up to take it.

'Let me help you.'

'I'm strong as an ox, but you're a good girl. Just on the table there. Sweetie, the girls will be home in a few minutes. Do you want me to steer them off?'

'The lieutenant wants to talk to them, too.'

Mother and daughter exchanged a look. Audrey sat, patted DeLano's knee. 'Well, we're in this, and everything else, together.'

DeLano tipped her head to her mother's shoulder. 'Always.'

8

Audrey gave her daughter a quick pat on the leg, then shifted to pour the coffee. 'Two black – that's Lieutenant Dallas and me. Two coffee regulars for Detective Peabody and Blaine. And I hope you'll try my sugar and spice cookies. They're a favorite around here.'

After she passed around coffee and cookies, Audrey sat back. 'Now, what do you need from us?'

'Peabody, photos. I'd like you to look at the photos,' Eve told them.

Mother and daughter huddled together, studied the photos.

'The same person?' DeLano asked. 'Brother and sister? It's hard to see much of either face.'

'Same person,' Eve confirmed. 'And at this time the prime suspect in Chanel Rylan's murder.'

'You can't see the eyes,' DeLano murmured. 'Or the features very clearly. Still, I think if this was someone I knew well, it would click. But it doesn't. I'm sorry.'

'It's a woman, isn't it? At first glance – well, even at a

second good look – you assume this one here is a man. But when you see them together like this … You're looking for a woman?'

'We believe the unsub is female,' Eve said. 'And presents herself as the character in the specific murder scene, as written. A woman for the first, a man in this case. This individual clearly selected, studied, and stalked both victims. Very likely selected them from others considered and settled on them because they best represented the victims in the books.'

'It's more about the books, that's what you're saying, than about the women who were killed.'

'It's more about the books,' Eve agreed. 'Which means it's more about you.'

Eve heard the voices – female – the clatter of footsteps coming from the back of the house.

'The girls.' DeLano squeezed her mother's hand, got to her feet as the voices – obviously in the heated rush of an argument – ebbed and flowed.

DeLano walked to the foyer. 'Heather, Piper! Grand and I are in the living room.'

The voices continued.

'I so did *not* give Brady Mishner the sexy eyes.'

'You so did. With the hair-flip combo!'

'Cut it out!'

'Brady, Brady!' Kissy noises followed.

'You're such a wheeze, Piper.' Sounds of a scuffle followed. Two voices, as one, whined: 'Mom!'

'Girls, we have company. Pretend to be civilized.'

As the girls stepped up, DeLano hooked an arm around each of their necks – a kind of affectionate double head-lock – and drew them into the room.

The one on the right topped her mother's height by about an inch, had a long mane of dark blond hair with a couple of bright blue braids worked through it. Startlingly pretty, she wore skinny pants that swirled with color, a sweater that matched the braids, and may or may not have given some boy named Brady the sexy eye–hair flip combo.

The one on the left had the look of a clever, potentially devious elf. The top of her head came to her mother's cheekbone, and she studied Eve out of long green eyes that tipped up at the corners. She wore her brown, streaked-with-pink hair pixie short, and had on baggies with a sweatshirt that claimed GIRLS ROCK AND RULE on a compact frame.

She may or may not have been a wheeze.

'I know who you are,' Piper said, and looked up at her mother. 'Who got killed?'

'No one you know. Lieutenant Dallas, Detective Peabody, my daughters, Heather and Piper. Sit down, girls.'

They sat on the sofa, immediately went from squabbling siblings to a unit. All four females ranged themselves together.

'I went to see the lieutenant and the detective this morning because a woman was killed last night. She was stabbed with an ice pick while watching a vid in a theater in Times Square.'

'Like in your book,' Piper said, those odd elf eyes direct on Eve's face.

'Yes, and there was a murder last month of a licensed companion, and it was like one of my books.'

'That's awful.' Heather snuggled closer to her mother. 'Mom, that's awful.'

'It's sick plagiarism.'

'Piper.' Heather shot out an elbow, slickly evaded by its target. 'It's not a joke.'

'I'm not joking. Somebody's copying Mom's books to kill people. Sick plagiarism. Do you have a suspect?'

Does the kid ever blink? Eve wondered.

'I'm here to ask the questions. Has anyone approached either of you asking questions about your mother or her work?'

'Just the usual.' Heather took the lead. 'Sometimes one of the teachers or one of the other parents asks when a new book's coming out, or they want us to ask Mom to come talk to a class or their group. She doesn't much do that.'

'Because she's working,' Piper ... piped up. 'And some people just don't get it.'

Closed ranks, Eve observed.

Girls rock and rule.

'Have you noticed anyone around the neighborhood you felt didn't belong?'

The sisters looked at each other, shook their heads.

'Peabody.'

Peabody pulled out the photos again. 'Have you seen this person?'

'You can't see the faces, really. Are they the suspects?' Heather asked.

'Not *they*,' Piper corrected. '*Her*. I've seen her.'

'Don't make things up.' Elbow jab.

'I'm not.' Return jab. 'She was wearing those dopey goggles and the lame-o hat from the other picture. And that coat. The goofy one.' Piper closed those eerie eyes. 'She had a scarf, too, but not the one in the picture. I think it was black-and-white. I think.'

'Where did you see her?'

'It was before Christmas. Remember we went on the stocking-stuffer hunt, then had dinner at Angelo's? We walked.' She shifted to look directly at Eve. 'The shops are only a few blocks away, and with the stocking-stuffer hunt, everything's small, so no prob with big, heavy bags. And we kind of spread out so everybody doesn't see what everybody else is buying. I saw her in City Kitchen when I was buying those spice bags for Grand, and I found those sugar spoons, too, for Mom's coffee.'

'Did she approach you?' Eve demanded.

'Nuh-uh. Then we went into … At Your Leisure, and I got Heather those frilly socks, and I spotted Mom going gooey over this robe with blue checks, but she didn't buy it. So I told Heather and we went back and bought it for her for Christmas.'

Piper looked up at her mother. 'That was a good surprise.'

'It was a really good surprise.'

'Anyway. She — the woman in the goofy coat — was poking around in there, too. I didn't pay much attention because a lot of people were shopping like we were.'

'It was like, two months ago,' Heather began. 'You can't be sure you remember, especially since you can hardly see anything in these pictures.'

'I see what I see.' Piper gave her sister – yeah, that could be termed a sexy eye – and mimed a hair flip.

She earned an elbow jab, but it was half-hearted, and Heather snickered with it.

'Do you remember the date?' Eve asked.

'It would've been the Saturday before Christmas,' Blaine supplied. 'We always bake cookies in the morning and afternoon, then do the shopping hunt, end the day with pizza at Angelo's.'

'You and Grand split a bottle of wine,' Piper added. 'And got giggly on the walk home.'

'Our family elephant,' Audrey commented. 'She never forgets.'

'Have you seen her since?'

'I don't think so. The goggles are mega lame-o, so I'd remember them. Britta Gleason has a pair almost like them, and she gets pissy when I tell her they make her look goon.'

'Piper!'

'Sorry.' She hunched her shoulders at her grandmother's rebuke. 'She gets annoyed when I tell her she looks goon.'

'She does look goon,' Heather agreed. 'Piper does notice things.'

'I observe. I'm going to be a writer like Mom, so I observe. She had a shopping bag! She had a shopping bag from Artie's. We were in there, too, so that's three places we were she was – that I noticed.'

'Is she going to try to hurt Mom?'

'Heather, sweetie.' DeLano cuddled her daughter closer. 'Of course not.'

'I'm going to be straight. You've got good security. Use it. You've got good eyes,' Eve said to Piper. 'Keep using them. If you see this person again, do not approach. Don't screw around. Contact the police – local, then me.'

'You don't . . . You don't think she'd go after my children.'

'I think this woman has an unhealthy obsession with you and your books. I think through that obsession she's killed two people, and I'm damn sure she plans to follow that up by re-creating the scene from your next book. She's focused on the scenes, the characters, but she's been close enough for your daughter to identify her as trailing you through local shops.'

'Should I keep them home from school?'

Eve dampened Piper's instant grin with a head shake. 'Not necessary. How do they get to and from school?'

'It's walking distance. In bad weather we have a car-pool system.'

'Talk to the car pool participants, talk to the school. They should be aware. I'm going to speak to your local police, request regular drive-bys, and make sure they're aware of the situation. Use common sense. Don't let anyone into the house you don't know. If somebody comes to the door saying you've got a gas leak – verify with the gas company.

If somebody claims they've had an accident or uses any ploy to try to get you to open the door, it's nine-one-one.'

'I've reached third kup in tae kwon do.'

Eve gave Piper a respectful nod. 'Blue belt, red tag. Nice. I'm fifth dan, currently studying with a grand master, and I'm telling you: Don't screw around.'

'She won't.' The steel in Audrey's voice resonated. 'None of us will.'

'Good. Peabody, cards.'

Rising, Peabody took out contact cards, handed them out. 'It's good you know how to defend yourself,' she said to Piper. 'And your family. Contacting the police is another form of defense.'

'I got it. Heather's fast. Really fast. She's lettered in track and field, and cross-country. Running's a defense, too.'

'That's exactly right.'

'We'll stick together, right, Mom? Right, Grand?' Heather took her mother's hand, her sister's. 'It's what we do.'

'Meanwhile, I want your fan mail as soon as possible.'

'Oh, I've got that for you.' Audrey stood up. 'I've got all the email on a disc – most comes that way. But I made copies of everything else. I'll get it for you now.'

Outside, Peabody glanced back at the house as they walked to the car. 'It's a solid family. Serious girl power.'

'Not a pushover among them. Contact local PSD, walk them through it. We'll go show the photos through these shops the kid talked about. Not much chance anybody's going to remember like she did, but we could hit a streak of luck.'

Eve got behind the wheel. 'That's not the household of a woman who let herself be bullied, let herself be subjugated.'

'I guess sometimes it takes a punch in the face to shake out the inner strength.'

'I guess it does. After the shops, I'm going to dump you at Central. You can take the photos to Yancy, though I don't know what even the genius of police artists can do with them. There's no point in you going all the way to Queens to interview Jefferson, and I'll work at home after that.'

They not only didn't have a streak of luck, they didn't manage so much as a sputter – and no store security that kept the feed longer than forty-eight hours.

As traffic thickened on the drive back to Manhattan, Eve braced herself for a long, ugly slog to Queens.

She passed the disc from Audrey to Peabody, ordered her partner to copy and send to her home unit, and started the slog.

Blasting ad blimps, farting maxibuses, a bike messenger with an obvious death wish, cross streets clogged with delivery vans, crosswalks clogged with pedestrians who appeared oblivious to the meaning of Walk/Don't Walk signals, cabs, cars, blaring horns, and an underlying rumble of simmering anger slapped together to form New York at rush hour.

Though why some idiot termed it rush hour when it was crawl hour, Eve would never know.

A waste of time talking to Craig Jefferson, she knew it in her bones, but it had to be done. And though she was tempted to wait – to just go home to the quiet – and come up with a ploy to get him into Central the next day, she wanted to see him at home. She wanted to observe his dynamic with his wife.

She soothed herself with coffee from the in-dash AC, and finished the slog.

Another decent neighborhood, she noted, maybe glossier than Blaine's, but Jefferson's house couldn't boast a corner lot. A newer structure, she noticed. Smaller, but ... shinier, a two-story painted sleek white, with a short, one-story leg of nearly all glass.

Decent security, she judged, and this time the computer answered her buzz.

Good evening. Please state your name and the purpose of your visit.

'Dallas, Lieutenant Eve, NYPSD.' She held up her badge for scanning and verification. 'I need to speak with Craig Jefferson.'

One moment please ...

It took more than a moment – long enough Eve considered buzzing again. Then the door opened.

She recognized Jefferson's wife from her ID shot, just as she recognized the anxious look in her eyes. She wore a dark blue sweater with subtle swirls of silver threads worked through and pants that matched the threading. She'd swept her hair back with some sort of blue and silver clips. Maybe to show off the silver studs in her ears.

The coordinated outfit – down to the short silver boots with the little navy heels – the carefully made-up face, the perfectly groomed hair made Eve think: Camera ready.

142

Or demanding, overbearing-husband ready.

'Mrs Jefferson.'

'Yes, I'm Mattie Jefferson. How can I help you?'

'Lieutenant Dallas, NYPSD. I'd like to speak with Craig Jefferson.'

'My husband's only just gotten home from work,' Mattie began.

'That's good timing, isn't it? Can I come in? You're letting in a lot of cold air.'

Obviously flustered, Mattie stepped back. Eve used the fluster and the space to step in, shut the door at her back. A movement had her glancing up.

A boy – Craig Junior, age eight, according to his official records – stood at the top of the stairs, arms folded. Like his mother, he wore a coordinated outfit. In his case, a navy-and-red-striped shirt with a navy sweater vest over it, navy pants.

And a glowering expression.

Eve hadn't known an eight-year-old could pull off that expert a glower. He must have practiced.

'Mummy,' he said in affected, superior tones, 'who's at the door?'

'Someone to see Papa. You should finish your home-work, C.J.'

'I *have* finished it.' His snarly tone clearly implied: You idiot. 'Papa doesn't like strangers in the house.'

'I'm a cop, kid.'

He came down two steps, used his superior elevation

to look down his snotty little nose at her. 'Do you have a warrant to enter?'

Eve gave him a hard, thin smile. 'Want me to get one?'

'C.J., just wait in your room, please.'

The kid barely suffered her a glance, and didn't budge.

'If you'll wait here, I'll get my husband.'

She hurried off.

'My papa can make you leave. This is *his* house.'

Intimidating kids wasn't her usual course of action, but for this one, she made an exception. She took out her badge again, in a way that shifted her coat and jacket back enough to give the little shithead a glimpse of her weapon.

'This is my badge. That means, if your father doesn't want to talk to me here, I'll leave. And get a warrant that obliges him to talk to me in my house. That would be Cop Central. I wonder which he'd rather.'

An angry flush rose up on the boy's face. He fisted his hands at his sides, came down two more steps. 'He doesn't have to do *anything* he doesn't want. You can't make him. You're just a girl.'

'So's more than half the world's population. You're outnumbered.'

She shifted, looked down the hall as Craig Jefferson strode toward her wearing a gray business suit and an annoyed expression.

'Just what's this about?' he demanded.

'She called me a bad name!' The kid raced to his father. 'And she said she was going to stun me with her weapon.'

'Seriously?' Eve might have laughed, but Jefferson took a menacing step forward. 'If you lay hands on me, sir, I'll have to take you in for assaulting an officer.'

'You threatened my son!'

'I did no such thing. Recorder.' She tapped her lapel. 'Engaged. Would you like me to order a replay?'

'I don't like her! Make her go away!'

Ignoring the boy, Eve kept focused on Jefferson. 'I expect to take up about ten minutes of your time here and now. If you refuse to speak to me, here and now, I will make arrangements for you to be brought into Cop Central. My questioning there is likely to take longer than ten minutes. So now or later, simple or complicated, Mr Jefferson. It's up to you.'

'I demand to know what this is about.'

'It involves your ex-wife.'

'I should have known.' Disgust echoed through his voice. 'C.J., go upstairs.'

'I want to stay with you, Papa.'

'Upstairs,' Jefferson repeated, but patted the top of the boy's head.

The kid took two steps, and Eve read his intent in his eyes. She danced back, avoiding an angry kick in the shins. The miss and momentum had the boy skidding back. He'd have fallen on his ass – a moment Eve would have enjoyed – but his father reached out, steadied him.

'Upstairs,' Jefferson repeated, adding a light ass swat. One that Eve interpreted as a congratulatory ass pat.

The boy stomped up the steps, pausing only to shoot Eve his middle finger behind his father's back.

'Mattie!' Jefferson bellowed. 'I left my drink in my den!' Then he turned into the living area.

The furnishings coordinated as meticulously as the outfits of the residents, and every inch shined clean and stood ruthlessly organized.

Eve imagined if a dust mote tried to sneak in for a visit, it would be eradicated in seconds.

'Ten minutes.' Jefferson sat in a chair with wide, masculine arms. Eve chose the (pillow-free) sofa. 'What has Blaine done?'

'Ms DeLano's done nothing. However, two people have been killed in the last month. This individual is replicating scenes from Ms DeLano's books.'

His eyebrows rose, indicating surprise, before he let out a snorting, derisive laugh.

'It amuses you, Mr Jefferson, that two people are dead?'

'It amuses me that anyone reads that dreck Blaine churns out, and that the police would have any trouble finding the lowbrow reader of second-rate potboilers who'd use their simplistic plots to kill.'

'You must have read them yourself to have such a strong opinion on their content.'

'I have not. I don't need to read them to know they're dreck.'

Mattie hurried in, carrying a lowball glass of amber liquid with a twist of orange on a small tray. Like a skilled waitress she set a cocktail napkin on the table beside Jefferson, put the glass on it.

'Is there anything else I can get you, Craig?'

'No. This won't take long.'

When Mattie turned to go, Eve spoke up. 'Mrs Jefferson, if you could stay for a moment.'

'My wife is preparing dinner.'

'It won't take long,' Eve repeated.

On a sigh, Jefferson waved at a chair as if giving his wife permission to sit. She did, on the edge of the chair, back straight, knees pressed together, ankles crossed.

'Apparently one of Blaine's readers – and I use the term loosely – is copying murders from her books. Turning low-rent fiction into reality.'

'I . . . Killing people? Murdering people?'

'Isn't that what I said?' Jefferson snapped. 'What do you expect me to do about it?' he asked Eve.

'You can start by telling me where you were last night between five and seven P.M.'

Face flushed as red as his son's had been, that same ugly heat burning in his eyes, Jefferson pushed halfway out of his chair.

'You would dare accuse me? Mattie, get my lawyer on the line.'

'You can do that.' Eve held up a hand, watched the woman struggle over who to obey. 'You're absolutely entitled to that, but it's a simple, straightforward, and routine question. Getting it out of the way saves everyone time. Let's be clear. I'm not accusing you of anything. I'm establishing your whereabouts so we can move on, and so I can tie this up and leave you to enjoy the rest of your evening.'

'Craig, I don't have Stan Grotti's contact number.'

At his wife's apologetic tone, Jefferson flicked his wrist at her. 'I don't like the question, your tone, or your attitude.'

'I get that a lot, but answering the question gets me out of your hair faster.'

'I arrived home at five-twenty. I unwound from my workday in my den until Mattie served dinner at six-thirty. At seven-fifteen, while Mattie cleared and ordered the kitchen and dining room, I spent thirty minutes with my son in the family room. I believe that more than covers it.'

'It does. Mrs Jefferson, can you corroborate that?'

'I – yes, yes, of course.'

'Thank you. Has anyone contacted either of you asking questions about Ms DeLano?'

'Why would they?' Jefferson shot back.

'She is the mother of your two oldest children.'

'Blaine lives her life, such as it is. We live ours.'

'Could you tell me the last time you had contact with her?'

Jefferson shrugged, picked up his drink. 'I live my life,' he repeated.

'Mrs Jefferson?'

'Ah, I – that is, we – sent the girls gifts for Christmas. They sent us thank-you notes.' When this earned her a cold stare from her husband, Mattie returned it with a quiet smile. 'You said it was fine as long as I paid for them myself.'

'If you want to throw your ... "professional mother" salary away.' He tapped fingers in the air, making air quotes around the term.

'The long and short, this is none of our concern. If some moron decides to pattern murders after Blaine's ridiculous excuse for novels, it has nothing to do with me. And if the blowback throws her silly career in the ditch, it was always going to end there. Now, is that all?'

'I think that covers it.' Eve rose. 'Thanks for your time.'

'Mattie will show you out.'

When she reached the door, Eve dug out a card, handed it over. 'In case you remember something. Or have any issues that require police assistance or intervention.'

'I don't see how I can be of any help to you.'

Eve glanced up where the kid sat at the top of the steps, watching, listening.

'You never know where help might come from.'

She thought about it on the drive home, concluded she wouldn't hear from Mattie Jefferson. Eventually she, or another badge, would end up sitting across from Craig Jefferson Junior in the box.

She knew a violent offender in the making when he tried to kick her in the shins.

But for now, she could cross them off her list. No question in her mind Jefferson loathed his ex-wife, but he also believed her unworthy of his attention. That bled over to his daughters.

He didn't think of them, didn't care about them.

Whoever murdered Rosie Kent and Chanel Rylan cared a great deal about Blaine DeLano.

From what Eve could see, the ex-husband made sure he knew no one who cared about his first wife.

Too bad, she thought. She'd have gained great satisfaction from making the asshole's life a living hell, even just for a few days. She'd have enjoyed screwing with his regimented life where he reigned as a god the moment he walked in the door.

Since the possibility of that remained slim to zip, she'd just have to settle for catching a killer, and making her life a living hell. For a couple of life sentences.

Bolstered by that, she drove through the gates of home, saw lights gleaming in the windows, and the sweep of outdoor lights illuminating the grounds, tossing the glamour of the house into relief against a moody sky.

She thought of Roarke, a man with the money and power to reign as a god if he'd chosen. And she decided he probably did in areas of his business – or at least gave that impression to any who tried to cross him.

Inside that castle of a house no rigid schedules were made or even suggested. No dismissive wrist flicks on either side. Pissy behavior on both sides? Sure, now and then.

If he'd wanted a woman who'd have a hot meal on the table at six-thirty sharp, or who scurried to make him some stupid cocktail when he walked in the door, he sure as hell wouldn't have married a cop.

She pulled up, got out to leave her car where it sat, and decided if the murky sky had opened up to show even a single lucky star, she'd have thanked it.

9

She walked into an empty foyer, just stood there a moment to breathe it in. Stripping off her coat, she tossed it and the rest of her cold-weather gear over the newel post.

She looked around, taking stock. She couldn't compare it to DeLano's, or Jefferson's. It was uniquely Roarke's, and now hers.

Full of art and antiques, rich colors and fabrics, gleaming wood. Lush and plush, rich and privileged. Warm and welcoming.

And, she was pretty sure, empty except for the cat.

She went to the house comp. 'Where's Roarke?'

Good evening, Darling Eve. Roarke is not currently in residence.

'Okay.' She started upstairs, intending to head to her office, dig into work.

Then detoured to the library.

Roarke loved books, and had the space and means to create a small cathedral for them inside his home. Shelves, full of them, lined the walls. And not for looks, though she had to admit they added a distinct style. He read them, enjoyed them, preferred the weight of a physical book in his hands, she knew, to the same words on a screen.

It occurred to her he might have some of DeLano's books.

Though she hadn't spent much time in the room – big enough to earn the term *house* in some circles – she knew the books ranged in a kind of order.

He had shelves of the classic literature the state school had tried to pump into her brain. She'd been okay with some of it.

He owned prose and poetry, plays and philosophies. Religious texts, art books, histories, biographies, books on mechanics and mathematics – that would no doubt make her brain bleed.

She circled the two-level room, marveling at Roarke's capacity and interest in collecting. Books, weapons, properties, vehicles. Clothes.

But she knew, with books, whatever he collected, he preferred novels and poetry for pleasure reading. She paused, slipped out the book she'd given him their first Christmas together.

Yeats. An old copy because he valued the old, the history of what lasted. And Yeats because as a young boy in Dublin, living in hell, he'd found a discarded copy of Yeats. And had taught himself to read from it.

So he loved poetry and great literature and . . .

Yeah, a good, solid murder mystery.

Skimming those shelves she found not just a couple of DeLano's books, but several.

She pulled out the two that currently applied, added the one she feared would before this was done. She carried them to one of the long, low leather sofas and, what the hell, ordered the fire to light as she hunted through *Dark Falls* for the murder of Pryor Carridine.

The cat found her while she read, jumped up. Galahad started to cozy right in beside her, then froze. Every hair on his pudgy body stood up. He hissed.

'What? What?'

His eyes, feral in their light, fired at her before he sniffed her arm. His back arched like a Halloween cat.

'What the hell ... Jesus, the dog? Are you kidding me? It was hours ago. I was wearing my coat. You can't possibly ...' She sniffed her own arm. 'I absolutely do not smell like big, sloppy dog. Besides, it wasn't my fault. He had the crazy eyes.'

Galahad snarled, sniffed her leg. Let out a bitter, throaty sound.

'He leaned on me. It was line of duty, so get over it.'

He turned his back on her, tubby body rigid, angry eyes focused on a wall of books.

'How come you don't act this way when I come home with blood on me, or street thief stench?'

She could ignore his jealous ass, she thought, but ...

It was, in its weird way, sort of flattering.

So, reaching over, she stroked a hand from his head to his tail. Twice. 'Don't be an asshole.'

She went back to the book, to the scene. The cat held out

for nearly two minutes, then curled up against her. Absently, she scratched between his ears as she backtracked to study the plot, and tried to put herself in the mind of the killer.

Fictional and real.

Deciding she needed a more solid sense of the characters, she went back to the beginning, pulled out her notebook. Made notes as she read, and wished she'd hunted up the AutoChef — there had to be one in here — before she'd settled in. Before she'd ended up with a cat sprawled over her lap.

A little annoyed, somewhat frustrated, Roarke walked into the foyer. Unlike Eve — or what Eve wouldn't admit even under threat of death — he actually enjoyed being met by Summerset and the cat after a workday.

Especially a workday that had been largely a pisser.

He'd spent far too much of it untangling a snafu before it could roll into a full-blown clusterfuck. And the fact that he'd eventually tracked the initial mistake back to one of his most valuable and reliable people in R&D only added to it.

A tiny miscalculation, really, he thought as he tossed his coat over Eve's because he just didn't feel like hanging it up. And that tiny miscalculation had led to another, and another, building like a bloody snowball rolling downhill.

He'd caught it, so a stroke of luck there, before it cost serious money or damaging PR. And his valued and reliable mechanical engineer had been so appalled and apologetic, had offered no excuses, Roarke hadn't been able to relieve frustration with a verbal ass-kicking.

He considered heading down to the gym, taking Eve's tack and ass-kicking the sparring droid.

Maybe Eve was down there, he thought. Or maybe he could talk her into going a round or two in the dojo. And capping it off with sex.

There's a room we haven't hit yet, he thought as he went to the house comm. She'd appreciate the thought.

'Where is Eve?'

Good evening, Roarke. Darling Eve is in the library.

'What? Where? Dallas, Lieutenant Eve, is in the library?'

Affirmative, that is her current location.

Baffled, fascinated, he wound his way through the house, came to the open doors of one of his favorite rooms.

There sat his wife, her boots up on the long bench table, the cat lengthwise across her lap, and a book in her hand.

A fire snapped and sizzled cheerfully. The cat snored.

'Well now, this looks cozy.'

She looked up – hard, flat cop's eyes clearing slowly. She said, 'Hey.'

'And what might you be reading on this cold winter's night?'

'More reviewing. Or studying. You read Blaine DeLano.'

'I have.' He walked over, angling his head to read the titles of the books she'd taken off the shelf. 'Is she victim or suspect?'

'Neither. Did you read this one?' She tapped *Dark Days*.

'I haven't as yet. I've been through most of the Hightower series – and they're quite good. I haven't dived in to the series with his former partner. That one.' He gestured to the book in her hands. 'I've read that one. *Dark Falls*, where she quits the force.'

'LC strangulations.'

'Ah, yes.' He flipped back in his mind, dropped down beside her. And God, it did feel marvelous to sit. 'Serial killings. A white scarf.'

'Sash.'

'Six of one, but yes, sash. And a fancy bow. As I recall, the first victim was a friend, or the ... sister of a friend of Dark's, and it proved a breaking point for the detective.'

'It also inspired the actual murder of an LC – young and new like in the book. Last month. And the *Dark Days* follow-up? My vic. Vid theater, ice pick, Hitchcock vid, young actress.'

'And DeLano's not a suspect?'

'She came to me with it this morning. Nadine brought her in – they're friendly. DeLano's clean.'

'So you're pursuing a case of lethal plagiarism.'

'Funny, that's how her kid put it, more or less. She's got two, teenage daughters. Add an asshole ex, who's also unfortunately clear.'

'I believe I need to catch up, and I'd say we should have some wine.' He rose. 'I tend toward brandy or whiskey in here, but I think wine.'

She started to say she'd take coffee, then he distracted her. Just loosening his tie as he walked across the room to a fancy cabinet. Why was that sexy? she wondered. She didn't even get why men insisted on wearing ties – and don't get her started on Jenkinson. But the way Roarke loosened that knot, flipped open a couple buttons on the shirt?

It was kick-in-the-guts sexy.

'A full-bodied red, I think.' He glanced back, caught her look. 'And what's that about?'

'I spent about ten, fifteen minutes with the asshole ex before I came home. And it just struck me, you could toss away all your money—'

'Then how would we afford this very nice wine?'

'I mean without the money, or being so damn pretty, you're everything he's not.'

He opened the wine, brought it and two glasses back to the sofa. 'I assume that's a compliment.'

'You can bank on it, ace.'

He sat, leaned over, kissed her lightly. 'Thanks for that then. And is that where you want to begin? With the asshole ex?'

'It sort of starts there, with DeLano and the books.'

While she talked, he poured the wine, sat back with her. Galahad rearranged his bulk, stretching out so he took up part of both laps.

'She could have destroyed him,' Roarke commented. 'She's a popular writer – add single mother supporting her two daughters, her own mother. She could have destroyed him by using the media. But she didn't.'

'She built a good life for herself, for her family. They're tight. It's kind of admirable. A lot of – you know – estrogen in the house. It sort of simmers in the air.'

'Simmering estrogen.' Roarke sipped his wine. 'Sounds bloody dangerous.'

'It's plenty girlie, but not weak.'

'Too many regard the female circle as weak.' He stroked a hand over Eve's hair – much as she'd stroked the cat. 'To their peril.'

'The killer's female.'

'You have a witness? That's burying the lede, darling.'

'Process, not a wit. She killed the first victim as a woman, killed the second in the guise – and mind-set – of a man.'

She told him of the security video, moved through to the conversation at the DeLano house.

'The younger kid – Piper – strikes me as scary smart. Not just with the school stuff and math and whatever. Just ... canny. That's one of your words.'

'Is it?'

'It even sounds Irish. Anyway, she makes this woman from the printouts – no hesitation. Describes what she's wearing, and it was two months ago. DeLano's nervous because the suspect was that close to her family, obviously following them around, but she's not surprised the kid remembers. Apparently she remembers shit.'

'How old is she?'

'Fourteen – sister's got a couple years on her. But here's the thing, and something I didn't say to any of them. I think, yeah, maybe the kid observes and remembers, but I don't think a fourteen-year-old girl pays that much attention

158

to some random woman, not when she's juiced about Christmas, in the shopping mode.'

'You think something about the woman had her paying more attention.'

'Probably subconscious. Just an instinct. She might have seen her otherwise – looking different – but something triggered something.'

'Are you concerned for DeLano and her family?'

'Not yet.' But she'd fully apprised Brooklyn PSD. 'Eight books in the series, and she's going to want at least a couple more. She's planning on all of them, but she might snap before eight.'

Because she worried about that snap, Eve frowned into her wine.

'Then she'll go for DeLano. Or one of the kids, the mother, to make her suffer first. I've got Brooklyn keeping an eye on things, and I gave the family the precautions to take. Mira thinks the killer'll turn on what she calls the creator at some point, but not yet. She's having too much fun to eliminate the source.'

'What do you hope to find in the books?'

'DeLano's not a cop or a killer, but she has to try to think like one. And she taps a retired cop for some research when she needs to. I've got three detectives I know of who say she hits the mark.'

'Add an expert consultant, civilian.'

'Okay. But in a story, there's got to be a trail or a screwup, or some luck, right? It seems to me our killer's real familiar with the books, and she'd avoid that trail, screwup, try to block the luck.'

'Ah.' Understanding her, Roarke managed to top off their wineglasses without disturbing the snoring lump of cat. 'She'll need to do some editing.'

'You could say. The first's a serial, but she's not going to go after another LC. That's not the point. Did that, move on. In the second, the killer – male – was connected to a competitor of the victim. She won't have a connection.'

'So you're looking for what not to look for.'

'Sort of. You've still got to cover the ground, but I have to figure she's copying the book, so she thinks: Doing this led to Killer A's downfall. So I'm going to do this instead. The other thing is, for the first book the killer's just targeting street-level LCs between eighteen and twenty-two, because that's what her husband goes for, for sideline fucks. Our killer needed to find a more specific type, one that matched the first victim. Eighteen, in her first two months in the life, who used a time-in-and-out flop.'

'Writing it's one thing, a blank page. Re-creating is more limiting.'

'Bang. And still, with street-level LCs it's not hard. You troll around some, you cull out the ones who fit the age bracket. Maybe you take some pictures on the sly, find a way to get info on them. It's going to take a little time, but you're a planner, and planning well takes time.'

Understanding where she was going, Roarke nodded. 'The second's more difficult. A young actress with a vid habit. A classic vid habit. The Hitchcock vid – was it the same vid in the book?'

'DeLano said it was the Bitchcock—'

'Funny.'

'It's got a ring. It was him, but another vid. Ah, shit, *M Stands for Murder* – I need my notes, because that's not it.'

'*Dial M for Murder.*'

'That's the one, and the killing's during a big scene where the main female character fights off a killer.'

'Grace Kelly. Ray Milland's her husband who's hired – more blackmailed – someone to strangle his very wealthy wife, while he's at another location, but on the phone – it's mid-twentieth century – with her.'

'Solid alibi.'

'Exactly so. He rings her up – the husband does – to get her on the line, the killer attacks. And she struggles while the husband listens.'

'Cold.'

'But she manages to get her hand on the scissors she was using earlier, still on the table, and she kills the killer.'

'And in the theater, everyone's focused on the screen, like with Chanel Rylan's murder. The killer stabs her in the back of the neck, walks out. I haven't read it yet to see where it diverges. Has to be some.'

'I'll take that one. And this?' He tapped another book.

'*Dark Deeds* – third book. She's already working on it, already selected the vic. I have to read it, find out more about the book vic, then start looking for potential targets.'

'Well then.' Roarke picked up the second book. 'What do you say we settle in for an hour or so, then we can have our own murder book club over dinner?'

'Okay, but we're looking for—'

He patted her hand. 'I've got it.'

He put his feet up on the bench table beside hers, opened the book. Smiled at his wife. 'It's nice.'

'It's work.'

'It's nice work.'

With the cat spread over both of them like a furry blanket, the fire simmering, their bodies hip-to-hip on the sofa, she couldn't deny it.

She dug into it, into the dynamics between the partners. A good balance and contrast, as far as Eve could tell, with Hightower's more straight-arrow leveling out Dark's instinctive moves and gut plays. And vice versa.

She reread a section from the victim's point of view, clearly saw the similarities to Rosie Kent. The youth, the recklessness, the inexperience.

And both from solid, suburban, edging toward conservative backgrounds.

The murder itself where the author kept the killer's gender neutral. To keep the reader guessing, Eve supposed. The meet when the killer approached Pryor/Rosie just as the young LC strolled onto the street to start the night's work.

The killer showed – more likely faked – nerves to give the victim the false confidence of being in charge. And yeah, yeah, just as Eve had imagined it, the killer requests her 'date' freshen up. More vic point of view, washing up a little, thinking smugly how this one should be easy money, thinking about a pair of mag shoes she'd be able to buy. How her lame sister just doesn't get how much *fun* this is.

Steps out, finds wine on the table. Sure, sugarplum, let's have a drink and relax. Followed by the shy request for the LC to undress first.

As she drinks, Pryor/Rosie does a little striptease, something she's practiced in front of the mirror. Her date for the evening looks like money, and sometimes money added a nice tip, so she played it up.

Starts to feel a little dizzy, laughs it off, and keeps rolling her hips, doesn't argue when her date insists she finish the wine.

Doesn't hesitate when she's told to lie down. So sleepy. She wonders vaguely why her date takes the time to pick up the clothes, to fold them neatly, like her own mother used to.

It's the last thing she thinks – the last thought of the dead girl is about her mother.

The killer studies the girl on the bed, the firm, perfect breasts and the smooth, perfect skin. The young face under the whore's makeup, the nails – fingers and toes – inexpertly polished a glittery pink.

Takes out the sash, lifts the head to wind it, winds it around the neck. Thinks of punishment come due because she'd had no right to flaunt those breasts, that skin, that face.

Nerves, fears, doubts – can I actually do this? – fade away in cold rage.

Tightening, tightening the sash, heart drumming, drumming.

The eyes flutter open, blind, bulging. The whore-dyed lips open, like a fish gulping. The body shakes.

It's like sex, yes, like the sex the little whore sold. Tightening, tightening as tears of grief and betrayal gather. No more, no more selling sex, no more tempting, no more taking. Then it all dies away. It dies. It's done.

Relief makes the killer almost tender. Patient fingers tie the bow, adjust it, perfect it, study it, approve it.

And with it makes death a gift.

Eve closed the book, stared at the fire as she let it roll around in her head. Moments later, Roarke closed his.

'No question about it,' he said. 'Lethal plagiarism. Why don't we eat in here and talk about it?'

'In here?'

'What better place to discuss books? Computer, open drapes.'

The heavy drapes parted on the window between sections of shelves.

'Ah, it's snowing.'

Eve scowled at the windows. 'Crap.'

'It's lovely from in here.' Rising, Roarke walked to another cabinet, opened it to an AutoChef. He called up the menu, perused it a moment. 'Well now, Summerset said we wouldn't starve while he was away, and he certainly saw to it. I think a snowy night in the library calls for shepherd's pie.'

'Why is it "pie" when it's not?'

'I think before potatoes came around England and Ireland, it was made with a pastry crust. But as we won't be tending sheep, Summerset does his up pub style.'

He programmed two servings before she could wheedle him into pizza. 'The Deann Dark character's fascinating. I'll definitely read more of the series. But as to the relevant book, I see your point. The killer followed the book when it came to victim and method, but shifted other things about – as plagiarists are wont to do – trying, often succeeding at least for a time, in getting away with it.'

'What changes?'

He brought two personal casseroles to the library table, gestured for her to bring the wine. 'No reversible coat or changing from male to female. The killer walked in and out as himself, but made a point of asking for the vid in the theater two down from where the victim would be.'

He walked to another table, took the two heavy candlesticks, and carried them to the library table. Lit them.

'How did he know the victim would be there?'

'Amelia Benson – the character – talked about it in dance class, in the workshop she was part of, and on her social media. She admired Grace Kelly particularly, and had never seen the vid. She had a friend planning to attend with her, but said friend received a text minutes before the show's start, purportedly from the restaurant where she worked as a line cook, citing a staff emergency and instructing her to come in and cover.'

'"Purportedly"?' Eve sat, studied the pie that wasn't pie.

'Yes. When the friend arrived at work some twenty minutes later, no one knew what she was talking about. No one had texted her, but it was too late for her to go back, as the vid had already started.'

Once again, he topped off their wine. 'Meanwhile, the killer slipped from one theater to the other, and there we have your mirror scenes. With the deed done, he slipped out again, back into the other theater. In this case, the killing wasn't discovered until the houselights came up, and by then he'd left with the crowd exiting the other theater.'

'How did they identify him and wrap him up?'

'Haven't gotten there yet.' Roarke dug into the pie. 'But I have gotten to the point where he raises the suspicions of the clever and intrepid Deann Dark. The victim's mother hired her, by the way, as she believes her daughter's former lover did the deed, despite being cleared by the police – Hightower specifically – as he has a solid alibi for the time in question.'

'Okay, the mother hires the PI because she thinks the cops are idiots, and the PI ends up proving the cops aren't idiots. Back in reality, the killer reads the book, concludes strolling in and out, letting the security cams track her may lead to trouble. Because if the cops, and the PI, don't review the feed, eventually pinning the killer as connected to the victim, they're all idiots.'

'I suspect you're right, and am now invested – fiction and non – in discovering for myself. And yours?'

It wasn't pie, and it had a hell of a lot of vegetables, but they were all inside a meaty stew that had just enough kick, and mushed up with mashed potatoes that weren't exactly mashed potatoes.

So it all went down easy.

'If I didn't know the fictional killer to be female, I'd know after reading the killing scene.'

'Easy to say.'

'Mmm.' Mouth full, she shook her head. 'It's the way the killer looks at the vic's body when the vic's unconscious, before the kill. It's not with lust or disgust, not with admiration or perversion. It's with envy. The firmness, the smoothness, the youth. It's an older woman envying the young. You could twist it, sure, make it play the other way, but the killer's thoughts and sensibilities at that moment are female and envious.'

'Interesting. I don't know if I caught that when I read it.'

'She's resentful. The fictional killer, she's snapped. She's not planning things out step-by-step like the real one. She's on a mission. It's revenge and it's – in her mind – protecting her family, her home, her way of life. It doesn't matter to her that the vics are new and inexperienced, and therefore easier prey. It matters that her cheating husband bought them, that he sneaks off to buy sex from barely legal LCs. And she's stupid because the LCs are just doing their jobs, so if she wants to punish somebody, she ought to tie a damn bow on the husband's dick before she lops it off.'

Roarke held up a finger as he swallowed. 'Or perhaps

have a firm and reasoned discussion with him on why he solicits those barely legal LCs.'

'"Reasoned discussion" my ass. Next time after he gets home late – telling her he had to work – she waits until he's asleep, and whacks it off. Think you can go out and stick that in some teenage working girl, then try to stick it in me? Think again, asshole. Then maybe while he's still screaming, she grinds up his cheating, dismembered member in that kitchen thing she likes so much, cooks it up in a pie, and force-feeds him his own cock.'

She pointed at him with her fork. 'Let that be a lesson to you, pal, or a dire warning.'

'I require neither, and you're putting me off my dinner.'

Eve shrugged that off, kept eating. 'But does she go after the real problem, with that discussion or the whack? No. She kills three women. And would've gotten a fourth if Dark hadn't tromped all over the law and the rules, stolen and hacked into the killer's pocket 'link and found the first three victims and their data listed, along with three more.'

'How do you know that? You couldn't have finished the book.'

'I skipped to the end.'

'You ...' He closed his eyes as he drank more wine. 'Some things are unforgivable.'

'It's work, ace. I need to know what the killer knows, and how she uses it. They were closing in. Hightower was building a case, had a plan for drawing the killer in. But Dark jumped over the line, and if Hightower hadn't covered her, would've lost her badge, likely soiled the case against a serial killer. She was right to turn in her badge at the end.'

'She'd known the first victim since childhood. That family was more family to her than her own. She was in emotional turmoil.'

'She was a cop,' Eve countered. 'And if Hightower hadn't caught up with her in that flop, she might have killed the killer. She wanted to, recognized that in herself. Recognized she'd warped the badge.'

'She saved a life.'

'And still. Justice first – I get that. And Hightower's along those lines, but he stays on the right side of it, or bends it a little. She – Dark – snapped it.'

'He reminds me of you a bit. Hightower. An excellent cop, with good instincts – maybe not as deep as yours,' Roarke commented, 'but good. And becoming, being a cop? A goal he never deviated from. He's by the book, but understands the book isn't only the law, the rules, but people and justice.'

'And she – Dark – tends to find the book a limitation, becomes frustrated by procedure. Maybe it's growing up rough, learning how to slip and slide early, but ... Hey, she's a little like you, now that I think about it.' She shot him a grin. 'You're the girl in this one.'

'Now you're metaphorically whacking off my dick.'

Amused, she shoved in more pie. 'Just saying. Anyway, the killer changes scenes, enacts them differently, as the ones in the book get caught. She doesn't intend to get caught.'

'So you'd look at the books as not only a blueprint, but a kind of dry run?'

'Yeah. The killer knows the books inside and out. Who knows the books as well as the writer?'

'I suppose, first, the editor.'

'Yeah, looked there. DeLano's editor's a guy, in his sixties, married, two offspring, and offspring from offspring. Not only doesn't he fit the profile, but on the night of Rylan's murder he was in his office – confirmed – until eighteen hundred, then met – also confirmed – one of his other writers for drinks at your Palace Hotel bar. And, just to be thorough, I also confirmed that on the night of Kent's murder he was in Chicago speaking at a conference.

'He does, however, have a female editorial assistant, and there are proofers and other people who work in the publishing house who could – and do – access books even before they're published.'

'Another however,' Roarke commented. 'For the price of the download or hard copy, anyone can own the book and read it countless times.'

'Yeah, and that's where I'm actually leaning. It seems to me, as tight as the DeLano family is, she'd have taken her kids to the publishing house. The canny one would likely have met a lot of the people there, and if – as advertised – she doesn't forget stuff, she'd have recognized the woman shadowing them on the shopping trip. So I'll be shifting my reading agenda for the rest of the night to fan mail. Anybody this obsessed with books, character, author – or all three – would have contacted DeLano, and probably more than once.'

'I lean with you there. I can also shift my reading to mail.'

'I'm tossing some to Peabody, but depending on how much there is, and if your slate's clear, I could toss some at you.'

'Who doesn't enjoy reading other people's mail? And my slate's clear enough. An hour with a good book, prying into someone else's mail, comfort food? All a good antidote, as I came home irritated.'

'Irritated? You didn't seem irritated.'

'Likely because I found my wife reading in the library with the cat on her lap. The lovely homeyness of the picture collapsed irritation.'

'So if I'd been huddled at my command center you'd still be irritated?'

'Potentially.' He shrugged it off. 'I'd thought to beat up a sparring droid, as that works so well for you, or talk you into a bout.'

'Sparring or sex?'

'I like the combination of both.'

She sat back, nudged the nearly empty casserole away. 'Now I'm too full of the pie that isn't pie for either.'

'The night's young yet.'

'If you tell me why you were irritated, is it going to irritate you?'

'I'm over it, so no. Just a very, very slight miscalculation in R&D that formed the basis of a series of miscalculations and bollocksed up an entire project until I happened to catch it. And then spending a large portion of my day working with the team to unbollocks it.'

'Did heads roll?'

'At a few points I might've pulled out the axe, but this particular head is known for the meticulous, the deadly accurate, and the innovative. A mistake,' he said with a slight shrug. 'They happen.'

'You probably scared the crap out of him.'

'I may have, but he was so busy flagellating himself I'm not sure he'd have noticed. And a good book, a glass of wine – you and the cat – spared me the trouble of replacing yet another sparring droid.'

'We could go down and take turns beating hell out of it before bed, but I like to save doing that for when I'm really pissed off.' She downed the last swallow of her wine. 'Have we ever had sex in here?'

'I'm sure I'd remember if we had, so no.'

'We need to come back, definitely need to come back before the Return of Summerset, take care of that.' She made a check mark in the air with her finger.

'Consider it on the schedule.'

Now she frowned, looked around. 'It's a really good room, but it just hit me there's no kitchen. We're going to have to haul the dishes up or down.'

He rose, took her hand. 'I'll activate a droid to deal with it – a domestic one.'

'I forget you've got any around here.'

'Domestically, you and I are failures. Something has to deal with such matters when Summerset's gone.'

'I used to do my own,' she said as they started out. Thought back to it. 'I sucked at it.' She gave him a hip bump. 'Makes me smart for hooking the rich guy.'

'Makes the rich guy smarter for not having a cop wash his underwear.'

'When I was actually washing my own underwear, the machines always ate a sock. Just one sock. Every frigging time. Why is that?'

'We'll ask a droid.'

'But he's not back for another week.'

With a half laugh, Roarke hooked his arm around her neck, reminding her of Blaine DeLano's headlock of affection that afternoon.

It made her smile.

10

Roarke checked his incoming and found he had a couple of things to attend to after all. Eve programmed coffee, updated her board and book.

Took a few minutes to study Jefferson's ID shot.

If life ran to the fair and the just, he'd be guilty of the murders, and she'd put him in a cage. But though he was, undoubtedly, guilty of being a bullying, abusive asshole currently training his son to be the same, if not worse, life didn't run to the fair and just.

Without a lot of work.

Maybe one day he'd cross a line, and she'd have a shot at him. But for now his picture graced her board only because she'd eliminated him as a suspect.

She went to her command center, poured coffee, checked her own incoming.

The report from Jenkinson and Reineke held a faint glimmer.

One of the LCs they'd reinterviewed remembered – maybe – she'd noticed a woman hanging around a time or two during Christmas week.

Remembered, she said, because it was damn fucking cold and pickings were slim. The penguin coat had sparked the possible memory more than the person inside it.

It looked warm, the statement read, but tragic lame, so she'd recognized it when she'd seen it again a few days later. And had called out to ask if the woman was looking to hustle or to party. If it was hustle, to get the fuck off her turf.

Both detectives deemed the sightings real, as they'd pinned down a bouncer at a sex club half a block away who'd noticed the same 'ugly, dumpy coat'.

Neither disinterested witness could verify race, build, coloring.

Still, probability put the penguin coat stalking Rosie Kent since the end of December. The timing worked.

She plugged in the fan mail disc, winced at the number of communications calibrated. She did the math, dumped a third on Peabody, another third on Roarke, then settled down with her own.

She considered doing the first run on multiples, calculated the potential for any communication from the killer – if so – to have been sent under various names.

Very possible, and still, you had to start somewhere.

'Computer, calibrate and organize any and all multiple communications from the same individual.'

Acknowledged. Working . . .

In a fraction of the time it would have taken her clunker at Central, the computer finished the task.

'Okay, that's not small potatoes, either. Why potatoes?

Why not elephants or trucks? Computer, prioritize any and all communications from the same individual numbering five or more instances.'

She waited, nodded, then tackled the smaller batch.

In the middle of it, Roarke came in, ordered the fire on, as she'd forgotten.

'Sorry, just a little of this and a bit of that.'

'No problem.' She stopped long enough to look up when he poured his own coffee from the pot. 'Not the irritating stuff?'

'No, that's all well in hand again. And so now is the this and the that. You now own a small, ramshackle farm of just over sixteen acres in Nebraska.'

'Huh? What?'

'Have you forgotten our wager?'

'Wager on . . . ' She cast her mind back, a couple of weeks, vaguely remembered some silly talk about him buying crap property and turning it into gold. And betting he couldn't do the same out in some area of Bumfuck.

'You actually . . . '

'The terms you set – rural area in Nebraska. I sent the details to you in a file – with photos.' He shot her a smile. 'It should be fun.'

'Have you ever actually been to Nebraska?'

'A time or two, yes.'

Since he'd distracted her, she called up the file, studied photos of a dilapidated house, dilapidated outbuildings – the purpose of which remained a mystery to her – and some overgrown fields. Piles of rusted, toothy-looking equipment heaped up like dinosaur bones.

'So you're going to set fire to it?'

'Not at all. Wait and see.'

'You're going to lose at least a cuff of one of your tailored shirts on this one.'

He smiled again. 'Wait and see.'

He'd taken off his suit jacket, rolled up his sleeves, and tied back his hair in his office. So he sat at her auxiliary in full work mode.

'And so?'

She shifted back to work mode herself. 'I dumped a third on you. I've started with multiple communications from the same person, and am now sort of amazed at how many people write again and again. Like, what are they called – pen friends.'

'Pals. Pen pals.'

'Pen friend rhymes.'

'And so it does.'

'Plus a lot of them who write multiple times talk about the make-believe people like they're actually people. Some of them get a little pissy when those make-believe people don't do just what they figure those make-believe people should do. Some get more than a little pissy. A lot of the pissy is because the characters haven't banged.'

Roarke worked his way through Eve's roundup. 'I assume you're talking about Hightower and Dark.'

'Yeah, them. Some are getting a little pissy they're not banging, others can wait for the banging but want them to exchange some sloppy kisses and express their feelings of love and devotion. Others don't want either to happen ever. There's a subset who seriously objects to the language. Like real people never say fuck you. Especially real people who're cops.'

Eve blew out a breath. 'There are some threats, but they run to the: If you do this/don't do this, I'll never read you again. It makes me wonder why DeLano doesn't write back and say: Thanks for your interest. Now fuck off.'

He laughed at her over the rim of his mug. 'It's likely why you're a cop and not a writer. I expect the complaints, as well as the kudos, are just part of it all. It does indicate an interest and attachment to the work, which would relate to how said writer earns a living.'

'I'd rather be a cop. The mother, Audrey DeLano, is really efficient. She's attached the response to each communication to said communication. She's also really patient and diplomatic, as she's the one responding to the bulk, which bumps her up on the potential target list.'

'Because she's the one who says no, however diplomatically.'

'Yeah. She's the daughter's voice when she responds with the Gee, thanks for your interest and whatever, but. A lot of people send in ideas, suggestions, and straight demands. This is what needs to happen. Some even wheel out elaborate story lines, to which Audrey has a kind of standard response that's basically the Thanks, but. Most accept this, but some get puffed up or insistent, so let's highlight that sort.'

'All right then.'

'One more thing. We're looking for a planner, detail-oriented. It's probable that she used different names, at least once she started thinking about that lethal plagiarizing. Once I finish my section, I'm going to run a comparison on language, syntax.'

'Writing style,' Roarke commented.

'Yeah. But that's the next step, and means running the whole batch.'

'Then we'd best get to it.'

Less than fifteen minutes later, Roarke interrupted.

'I think you'll want to take note of this one. Letters, all by post, from an A. E. Strongbow, the first dated March of '58. This first is quite polite and complimentary, detailed as well on what Strongbow finds appealing in the books – and particularly the Dark series. Strongbow considers DeLano brilliant and admirable, like the character of Deann Dark, and feels DeLano has put much of herself into the character, as the best writers do.'

'Doesn't sound too wacky.'

'Not yet. Strongbow – and there's no indication of male or female here – states he or she is also a writer, though as yet unpublished. Much humility, and hopes to one day be as good a writer as DeLano. Requests advice on how to hone the craft toward publication.'

'I've got a number of that sort in my share, too. And Audrey's general advice.'

'There's a second letter, posted in May of '58, thanking

DeLano for the response, continuing with specifics on the latest entry in the series, again very complimentary. Near to gushing thanks for the advice and encouragement. "Your support has changed my life," it reads. "You've given me the courage to move forward, to stop making excuses, and dedicate myself to my craft, my art. You are my inspiration, my muse, my mentor. One day I hope to meet you in person, writer to writer, and thank you for all you've given me.""

'A little over-the-top, but—'

'Not done. Strongbow asks, humbly again, if it's possible to take DeLano to lunch, to discuss writing and perhaps to brainstorm over the manuscript Strongbow is working on.'

Yeah, Eve thought, she'd definitely rather be a cop.

'How'd Strongbow take the no? DeLano gets invites from professional organizations to speak, attend events, give workshops – and plenty from readers to weddings, bar mitzvahs, birthday parties, and memorials. The answer is invariably a polite, gracious no.'

'In the letter responding to that polite, gracious no, dated June of '58, Strongbow expressed understanding, hoped DeLano would consider it an open invitation, anytime, anyplace. More gratitude, more admiration. Then nothing until the next spring – May of the following year. I'm sending this to your comp so you can read it yourself.'

'Okay.'

Eve shuffled her share aside, waited for the transfer.

She poured more coffee, read.

Dear Blaine,

I hope you and your family are well. It's a credit to your incomparable skill and your ceaseless dedication that you can raise two daughters as a single mother and create such memorable characters, such intricate and entertaining stories, and with such consistency!

I enjoyed your latest Hightower book, With Prejudice, *tremendously, and have already read it a second time, doing so with a writer's eye. You have such talent, like a magician, you bring your characters to full, fascinating life. Even though I knew Hightower and justice would prevail, my heart beat faster through the last climatic chapter.*

Of course, as Deann is a particular favorite of mine, I was very happy to see her make appearances in this installment. I'm already eagerly anticipating the release of Sudden Dark *this fall.*

Meanwhile, I'm thrilled to send you my completed manuscript of Hot Blood, Cold Mind, *which your invaluable support helped bring to life. Knowing I can, at last, repay that support in a tangible way brings me great, personal pleasure. I can only hope you'll enjoy my work as I do yours.*

Please! Settle down in your favorite chair with the beverage of your choice. You're in for a long, entertaining night of reading!

Of course, I welcome your thoughts, your suggestions, and any recommendations you may have on how I might improve the work.

I understand now, with your help, that the art of writing, of birthing a story takes real sacrifice. I've made the sacrifice and, thanks to you, know who I am, and what I was meant to be.

As you'll see, I've taken a risk, as art also requires risk, and made the killer the central character, the protagonist, telling the story through his eyes. It is his blood that is hot, his mind that is cold. And yet . . . Well, you'll see!

You are the first to read this labor of love, of sweat and tears. I could not have written it without you, would never have found the courage inside me to make the sacrifices necessary to become what I'd only dreamed of becoming.

Believe me, I will take any and all of your constructive criticism to heart, and do my best to implement your suggestions before I submit Hot Blood, Cold Mind *for publication.*

I hope, when that time comes, you will take my trembling hand and be my stalwart guide through that exciting process.

With gratitude, admiration, and joy,

A. E. Strongbow

Eve sat back with her coffee. 'Okay, more than over-the-top. There's obsession here, and the illusion of a relationship that doesn't exist and expectations on a personal and professional level that weren't in any way offered. Return address is a post office box in Brooklyn. We'll check it out. Are there more?'

'There are, yes, but you should know the first letters were from a post office box in Delaware.'

'Indicating this Strongbow moved to Brooklyn – closer to DeLano. That's edging over the scary fan line.'

'In the follow-ups, it goes to a giant leap over that line. You'll see the response from DeLano's mother there as well.'

'Yeah, I'm looking at it. Quick response this time, coming less than ten after Strongbow's. Sending the manuscript back, unopened and unread, as DeLano has a firm policy, on advice of her agent and lawyers, not to read unpublished work. Lots of encouragement and congrats on completing the book, blah blah. Lots of good-luck wishes, but a little more careful, just a little distant. Audrey's no idiot and obviously saw this had crossed that line. And Strongbow responded?'

'Crushed, disappointed. Understood the policy, but believed the connection to DeLano meant they trusted and valued each other as writers. It's sad, actually, and you'll read it for yourself, see how the edges start to fray. Audrey didn't respond.'

'Smart. Cut the cord.'

'Strongbow wrote back at the end of September, shortly after the publication of *Sudden Dark*. And dark's the tone.'

'You read it.'

As he did, Eve pushed up to pace.

'"Blaine,"' Roarke read,

I opened Sudden Dark *with a sense of anticipation.*

Imagine my shock, imagine the depth of my sense of betrayal as I read your twisted bastardization of my own work. Did you think I wouldn't see? Did you think I wouldn't know you'd torn the guts out of Hot Blood, Cold Mind *and used its bloody flesh to cover your own inferior work?*

How could you? How dare you?

Your thin and pathetically drawn character of Lucius Osgood is so obviously your feeble attempt to make my Evan Quint your own creation. You fool no one!

Do you think making Osgood a struggling artist rather than a successful businessman gives you cover? Do you think giving Osgood a beard disguises him?

I see him, Blaine, and I see you. I see you for what you are. A thief, a liar. How many other far superior writers have you betrayed in this way to build your fame, your fortune?

I trusted you. I believed in you. I sacrificed everything to emulate you.

In the end, you're nothing. Your work is nothing.

Anyone can copy, Blaine, anyone can cheat. You stole my soul when you stole Hot Blood, Cold Mind. *And you murdered it when you tore it to pieces and called it* Sudden Dark.

Yes, anyone can copy, and you've proven I was right. Sometimes the villain wins.

It's past time you, Hightower, and Dark learned that.

I will never forgive you,

A. E. Strongbow

'That book's in the library, right? *Sudden Dark*?'

'Yes. I can get it for you.'

'Later.' Eve waved that off for now. 'If Strongbow's the killer, she doesn't start with *Sudden Dark*, the book that snapped her. She goes back to the beginning. Because that's orderly and organized. It's linear. Are there any more communications from her?'

'There aren't, no. At least not under this name. You could be right about her using other names. Don't you think she'd need to keep the connection?'

'Yeah, I do. I haven't hit on anybody sending a manuscript to DeLano in my batch, but there's got to be a few here and there. The response had that sense of ready statement. Policy, agent, lawyers, blah blah. We'll check out the post office boxes, see what we find. She'd have shut the one in Delaware down when she moved here, shut the Brooklyn one down, at least under the Strongbow name, when she turned on DeLano. But we may get data to follow.'

'You think she's smarter than that.'

'I think she's plenty smart. Being delusional doesn't mean she can't be plenty smart. She took a long time to stew, to think, to work it all out before the first kill. I'm going to bet she doesn't just have the next target selected, researched, worked out, but every one of them, down the line.'

'Sacrificing for craft, for art, that's a common theme – and very often true. Obviously, she sees her sacrifice as great and courageous.'

Eve nodded slowly. 'Moving to New York – inspired by

DeLano, maybe thinking something in the air in Brooklyn sparked creativity or some shit. If she had a job in Delaware, she probably had to quit if she couldn't do it long-distance. If she had a family, she either left them or convinced them to relocate. And I'm going with left them, if she had one, because she's completely self-involved. So unless she had a pot of money, leaving to move here equaled a financial sacrifice. Leaving the familiar, a sacrifice.'

'Reading her letters, I'd say the writing isn't merely a career hope, even a calling or an aspiration. It's a kind of religion to her.'

Eve pointed a finger at him, then dropped back down into her chair. 'I'm not going to diss writers. I like stories, too. Maybe I mostly like them in vid form, but somebody has to write the story. I know Nadine works hard. I got the clear sense DeLano does. It's not like they sit there and the words just . . .'

Eve waved her fingers at the screen.

'I have to write reports, evals, and it can be a pain in the ass to put the data together so it reads clear, so it lines up. But it's not fucking holy, and you're right. This one makes it out to be something beyond, above. So she decided DeLano stole her book – which is bogus – which means DeLano committed a big-ass sin. Punishment must follow.'

'Smart she may be. But a sensible person would know several simple facts going in,' Roarke added. 'One, Strongbow mentions looking forward to *Sudden Dark* when she writes DeLano in May of '59, meaning the book was already titled, certainly already written, as it takes more than the four months between May and its September publication to edit, produce, print, promote, and so on. Yet Strongbow concludes DeLano read her manuscript in May, was so impressed she cobbled together a book using pieces of it, tossed it to her publisher, and everyone managed to get it on the shelves four months later.'

'You're right. More delusion.'

'And more, I'll wager the publisher produced advance copies for reviewers and accounts at least three or four months before the on-sale, which would have the book written before Strongbow sent DeLano the manuscript. It would be a major publication,' Roarke explained. 'The advance copies are SOP.'

'So Strongbow knows squat about how publishing works.'

'Which anyone so invested in becoming published should know a bit about. My take? If you want it.'

'I'm sitting here.'

'She dismissed it because it doesn't fit her story line. It doesn't make her the victim and heroine, and DeLano – who rejected her manuscript – the villain.'

'Okay.' Eve considered, nodded. 'I can go with that. Alternately, she doesn't know squat because the business part of it isn't holy. It's the writing, the creating, and the being published. But the business of publishing doesn't apply.'

'Also a valid theory.'

'Still, I'd say we could eliminate anyone who works in publishing, anyone who works in DeLano's publishing house. You can't dismiss what you absolutely know. And that's all saying Strongbow is the killer, which we can't know. She tops the list, no question. But where there's one loony, there's usually more. We have to keep going.'

'Understood. It's all there, though, isn't it?'

'Yeah, it is. Let's run A. E. Strongbow, which is going to dead-end because if that's not an alias, I've never heard one.'

'Pseudonym.'

'Same damn thing.' She ran it, got a list of Strongbows with first and middle names matching the initials. 'More than I figured, but only a handful in New York, most male. Still, I'm going to run these through if you can keep going with your share.'

'I can and will. Strongbow sounds Native American, doesn't it?'

'It sounds made-up – but apparently it isn't for everybody.'

Before they began again, Roarke angled his chair toward her. 'Wouldn't you think if writing, if creating a book equaled a kind of religion, then the name you chose to write under would have some deep, personal meaning?'

Eve stopped, turned her head to look at him. 'Maybe it just sounds literary or mysterious. But ... The initials, deliberately non–gender specific. Doesn't want to be boxed? Male writer, female? Just writer?'

'It's my turn to—' He pointed a finger at her.

'People take an alias because they want to hide – or because they want to be somebody else. And yeah, maybe she takes one – if it's not her legal name – because it's a family name, from some ancestor she admired. Or, or, or, and crap.'

She shoved both hands through her hair.

'More work then,' she concluded. 'Aaron Edward Strongbow, Bronx address, is six years old. But that doesn't mean he doesn't have a third cousin twice removed who's a homicidal writer wannabe.'

She worked her way through the new list, highlighting a few names for a deeper look, shifted back to the communications to at least make a solid dent in her share.

Roarke interrupted again. 'I think I may have found her, April of '60, under the name of Chris Bundy. Chris,' he commented, 'could be male or female, and the writer – email this time – doesn't say. I'm going with *she* for consistency. What she does say is she once admired DeLano's work, as a reader and a writer. But with *Sudden Dark*, while portions of it were some of the finest writing DeLano had done, the story didn't hold, and the voice throughout wasn't consistent. It read as though someone else had written it.'

He paused, glanced at Eve. 'She demands DeLano reveal the name of her ghostwriter.'

'Let's flag that one.'

'There's more – it's a fairly lengthy rant. She asks: Isn't it past time to add some realism? For both Dark and Hightower to fail, and the villain to triumph? To have real impact, to gain immortality, fiction has to reflect life, the writer must make sacrifices and take risks to achieve greatness.'

'Okay, androgynous first name, claims to be a writer,

some key words, and a pretty steady series of bitch slaps. It rings.'

Roarke wound his finger at Eve for another hit of coffee. 'And on the next with this name – coming in July – a different email address. The first – I checked – opened and closed the day the email was written. I'll run that down in a bit,' he said as Eve dumped more coffee into both of their mugs. 'This one did the same, and claims to have it from very reliable sources that DeLano uses ghosts and gullible, even desperate, aspiring writers to do the bulk of the writing, and cheats the public. Again demands DeLano admit this and reveal the names of the ghosts. Even with them, DeLano is incapable of creating a villain who doesn't make sloppy mistakes that lead the somewhat inept protagonists to his doorstep.'

He glanced over at Eve. 'It ends with: You, Blaine, are a thief and a liar as well as a panderer to your undemanding and unsuspecting fans. Remember, sometimes the villain wins.'

Eve drummed her fingers on her knee, frowned. 'You're hogging all the luck tonight. Let's run them with Strongbow's for syntax and style.'

'Done,' he said with a faint smile. 'Eighty-three-point-four probability they were all written by the same person.'

'Yeah, hogging the luck. Can you use what you're hogging to get me anything from the accounts?'

'We'll see what we can do.'

If there was something to find, she thought, he'd find it.

She opted to multitask, increase her odds of snagging some of that luck. She ran the Strongbow names on auto while she ordered a search for any communication matching syntax and style with the two Roarke found with an above fifty percent probability.

'Hit. Another eighty percent plus probability. Letter, not email, no return address. Jesse Oaks. Wait.' Eve closed her eyes a moment. 'Bundy – Ted Bundy, twentieth-century serial killer. Oaks – Stan K. Oaks, twenty-first-century serial killer.'

'I sense a theme,' Roarke murmured.

'Yeah. Killing's part of that religion now. Still harping on *Sudden Dark*. Going on about inconsistency of voice in the book, and claiming it as proof DeLano doesn't write solo. Demands she reveals the name of her cowriter. Pushes harder on the Dark character here, saying the character is obviously an extension of DeLano's own ego, and thereby unrealistic. And a reprise of the villain as superior theme. "Realism demands Deann Dark/your ego face an adversary who triumphs. Only then will the character created from your limited understanding and need to inflate your own vanity truly comprehend the complexities of the killer, and embrace the villain within and without."'

'That's the next step, isn't it?' Roarke commented. 'Conflating Dark and DeLano. DeLano is now the character, Strongbow the adversary.'

'Rewrite the scenes, book by book. I need to send these to Mira. She's got one bat-shit crazy head to shrink.'

'Crazy it may be, but, as you said, it's sharp as well. The emails came from a mobile device, and my conclusion is a clone. Unregistered, but no flag by CompuGuard, which tells me she cloned it. Most likely picked up a couple of drop 'links on the street, cloned one to the other, which takes some skill. Opened the account, sent the email, closed the account, and shut down the 'link – most likely to rework it so the second email appears to be sent not only from another account, but from another 'link.'

'That's a lot of trouble,' Eve mused. 'If she bought two unregistered, why not just use each one, toss it after use?'

'Cheaper this way, if you've got the patience and the savvy. You could, potentially, rework the two endlessly. If one's flagged, you've altered it before it can be traced. But you have to be good, and fast, to do that. Easier to shut it down, wipe it, then you've time to switch components. And if you're very clever, you've picked up a couple of universal repair kits and you work in those parts.'

'Sounds like experience talking.'

Comfortable, he sipped his coffee. 'Well now, there was a time when I had to watch my pennies, so to speak, so the time and effort were easier to come by than the scratch. There are far easier ways to avoid a flag or a trace, but this would be the most economical.'

'Which indicates she needs to economize. A couple of decent drop 'links? It's an investment.'

'It is, which is why I, watching those pennies, preferred stealing them.'

She let out a sound between a laugh and a snort. 'You just liked stealing.'

'Ah, so I did. Very much.'

'The last thing you stole, and when.'

'Other than your heart?'

Rolling her eyes, she poured more coffee. 'Professionally. For profit.'

'That would be a strange and fascinating little still life by an underrated painter named Andre Mendini who, in despair at being underrated, leaped into the Seine and drowned in 2027 or '28 – I'm not quite sure now. In any case his fame subsequently rocketed, and his paintings became of great interest to collectors in the decades following. *Persimmons by Candlelight*—'

'Now you're just bullshitting.'

Roarke tapped a hand to his heart. 'Absolutely not. The strange and fascinating *Persimmons by Candlelight* was generously lent in 2056 for an exhibition in the d'Orsay. From there, it was stolen on behest of a collector who coveted it for his private collection, where it remained until 2057, when it mysteriously reappeared at another exhibition of Mendini's works at the Smithsonian.'

'You stole it twice?'

'Well, the first was for a fee as well as the fun, but I found myself regretting the job when I read about the daughter of the original donor who, at only eleven, had a deep attachment to that particular painting.'

'The kid liked persimmons?'

'Apparently as painted by Mendini. It had, in fact, been loaned out in her name. My client simply coveted it, and kept it for his own pleasure. The young girl loved it, and mourned the loss. So I returned it to her.'

'Softy.'

'Guilty. Plus stealing it back, then breaking in to the museum to return it? Vastly entertaining.'

He sighed it away.

'And a handful of months later, while I was contemplating the Baroness of Mallow's emeralds, and whether I should vastly entertain myself by relieving her of them, I met a cop who interested me a great deal more than emeralds.'

Shaking her head, she drank more coffee. 'By the time you stole that painting the first time, you didn't need a fee. You sure as hell weren't economizing. Maybe Strongbow just likes to fiddle with tech.'

'If so, and in her place, I'd have purchased higher-end 'links and had a fine time playing with them. You'd still need skill and patience, but you'd have more flexible results and more options.'

'All right, if it's economy, she probably has to work to pay the rent, and she'd need to keep the rent low. I haven't been able to trace the coat. Lots of reversibles, but nothing that matches. Nothing close to matching, so far anyway.'

'Perhaps she made it.'

Eve's gaze narrowed. 'Made it. Maybe she made it. Maybe she knows how to make clothes. A seamstress, a tailor. A seamstress or tailor with some good e-skills who lived in

Delaware who might have a family connection with the surname Strongbow and aspires to write.'

'To be published,' Roarke corrected. 'She writes, and surely continues to do so. But, like Mendini, yearned to be recognized for her art. When that recognition eluded him, he killed himself. As it eludes her, she kills.'

'You're right, and the persimmon guy's a good comparison because I'm not going to be surprised if Mira concludes that doing the equivalent of jumping in the Seine becomes the endgame here – whether Strongbow knows it now or not.'

'I'll live forever, immortalized by my words and deeds.'

'The question is: How many will she manage to take with her before she jumps?'

11

Eve sent the communications and a detailed report to Mira. She sent an update to Peabody and, since between the two of them only Peabody actually knew how to sew, instructed her partner to push that angle.

Because Jenkinson and Reineke had an investment, she copied them.

She widened the search on the Strongbow name, but found no connection in Delaware.

Rising, she walked to the board.

'She's got no real connection to anyone up here. It's all illusion. She's put them all into her story, one where she's the writer, the main character, the victorious villain. She makes herself into the killer in the individual books, the sex, the weapon, the method, the crime scene – close as she can get. Kent and Rylan, they're surrogates, and as close to the fictional victims as she could manage – and it's damn close in both cases. But DeLano blends into this Deann Dark, and that's delusion. DeLano's nothing like this character, not in looks, lifestyle, personality, or experience.'

'The antagonist must have a protagonist,' Roarke pointed out.

'In this case, she's flipped them, right, from the traditional roles. That's where she's living. She's got to move to the next book. Hell, she's got the next six picked out and ready. Look at the timeline of the communications. She used those lags to start her research, to select and study and plan. That way she can move from book to book. A month between the first two.'

Stepping back, she took a hard look at both victims. 'Some of that's recovery time. First kill's big. Time to settle down again, to wait and see if you made any mistakes. And part of it's just opportunity. She wanted the vid to mirror the one in the book as closely as possible. It's on the schedule, so she just had to wait until that scene's set. But the next?'

Eve rubbed her hands over her face. 'Could be tonight, could be six months from tonight. If it's the six months, she'll move on someone else, or rush it, because she's in it now, and the need escalates.'

'Who's the third?'

Moving to it, Eve rolled the stiffness out of her shoulders. 'Ex-girlfriend of a trash rocker. Edgy lifestyle, mid-twenties. Lots of illegals and easy sex. Poisoned in a club – high-end sex club pretending to be a dance club. Cyanide in some fancy martini.'

'And the killer?'

'Obsessed fan of the rocker, female, same age group. Rumor is the vic and the rocker may be getting back together. Rocker's out of rehab, clean, and obsessed fan kills his ex to protect him from her. I need to read it,' she muttered as she came back to her desk. 'But I really need to find the victim before she is one. How many badass ex-girlfriends of trash rockers are going to be living in New York? Maybe don't narrow it to trash rock. Successful rock-ers, any subset thereof, to start. All the killings are in New York, killer lives in New York, so it has to be ... Christ.'

'More than you thought?' Roarke asked when her search results came up.

Her eyes wanted to bleed. 'I can narrow it,' she mumbled. 'I will narrow it.' But she felt obliged to skim through first. 'Double Christ! Nadine's on here.'

'Nadine?' Roarke stopped his work. 'Our Nadine?'

'Wait. Wait. There are a couple articles on gossip sites. Blah, blah, Jesus. Photos, too. Stuff about her having dinner or going to a concert with Jake Kincade. That's that guy in that band.'

'I know who he is, and Avenue A as well. Strong, innova-tive rock musicians. Strong and innovative enough they've stayed at the top of their game over two decades. And Nadine's seeing him?'

'Yeah, she is – according to this stuff. He was performing, like Mavis, at Madison Square the night of the massacre. He was backstage, hanging with Nadine when I got back there. He called her Lois.'

'Lois?' It only took a moment. 'Ah, as in Lane. Clever. And if you're worried, I wouldn't be. Kincade has a reputation for being a hardworking musician, and one with a reasonably clean lifestyle. Nadine doesn't fit the victim here.'

'No, they don't fit the characters, and Nadine's not going to hang out in a sex club ... Well, the Down and Dirty, but that's different. She never mentioned she was banging a rocker.'

'And dinner, a concert, equal banging?'

'They're grown-ups. Unattached grown-ups. Banging ensues. Anyway.' She narrowed her search parameters. 'Younger, toss in the rehab ... '

She looked at the notes she'd written earlier.

'Victim made her living charging for interviews, taking kickbacks from clubs, selling data to gossip reporters and blogs. And brokering illegals. Consumed same.'

Bit by bit Eve fed it in until she got down to a half dozen potentials.

'Better, I can work with that.'

'I'm through this,' Roarke told her. 'Do you want me to take some of those?'

'No, I'm going to run them on auto for now. I need the books. This one, and the *Sudden Dark* one. Hell, I need them all.'

'Two library visits in one evening. Why, it could become a habit.'

He went with her. 'I'll take one, you the other?' he suggested as they walked through the house.

'You take the, what is it, *Dark Deeds* – with the rocker. I skimmed the murder scene, but you may catch something I missed. I want to see what the hell there was in *Sudden Dark* that snapped this woman, get a better sense of it before I talk to DeLano again. And her mother,' Eve said. 'The mother's probably got a better sense of the communications.'

She stepped into the library, unsurprised to find it ordered. Dishes cleared, wineglasses whisked away, books they'd been reading neatly stacked on the bench table.

Because he knew her, Roarke headed to the cabinet first. 'Coffee time's passed at this point. I believe I'll have a brandy.'

Knowing her opinion on brandy, he brought her water.

She considered arguing, then considered if she won said argument – doubtful – she'd probably be awake until it was time to get up again.

She took the water, pulled *Sudden Dark* off the shelf.

Once again she sat beside Roarke with a book, with the fire simmering. The only thing missing was the cat, and she imagined they'd find Galahad sprawled over the bed when they got there.

She didn't have to hunt up the first murder, as the book opened with it, from the killer's point of view. Male, a sexual predator who abducted women – first victim age twenty-four – kept her for three days, raping, torturing, and eventually drowning her in a bubble bath. After which he applied makeup to her face, styled her hair, and dressed her in a business suit.

He added pearl studs to her earlobes, kissed her tenderly, and called her Britina. Then, in the early hours of the morning, he transported the body to a location in Little Italy and dumped it on the sidewalk in front of a restaurant called Lucia's.

She skimmed through to the first Dark scene, then skimmed until she found the killer again. His thoughts as he stalked and captured his next victim.

She set the book aside, got up to prowl and pace.

'I think you summed up the victim here in *Dark Deeds* well enough,' Roarke told her. 'I'd add it may apply that the only reason Dark took the case was because the victim's mother – a friend of a friend's mother – came to Dark and pleaded with her. The victim's painted as careless, selfish, even a bit vicious. But the mother never gave up on her.'

'So see if there's one on my list of rocker girlfriends who has a mother who hasn't given up. It could apply.'

Roarke set his book aside. 'You're frustrated because you find yourself investigating on two fronts. Fiction and reality.'

'Fiction is reality to this bitch.'

'It is. And for you fiction is an occasional form of entertainment, and for you again, primarily through vids. A book's a different thing.'

'Made-up stuff is made-up stuff.'

Roarke shook his head. 'A vid comes to you, even at you. It's visual, it's auditory, and can, of course, pull you in. Its purpose is to do just that, draw you into the world you see and hear. But a book? You go into it. There's no visual or auditory other than what forms in your own mind. You visualize the characters, the scene, through the words. You, as reader, interpret the tone of voice, the colors, the movement as you physically turn the pages. Now you have a killer not just experiencing the story, not just replicating it, but living it. So you have to do the same, and that's frustrating for a woman as reality-based as you.

'And more,' he added, 'with each killing she becomes a different character with a different motive, a different psyche.'

'But under it, she's just one sick, twisted – and you know what? – whiny bitch. Whoever she puts on?' Eve waved her hands around her face. 'She's still under it.' Then she sighed. 'And the sick and twisted is, I don't need Mira to tell me this one is likely to end up in a facility for the sick and twisted instead of an off-planet cage when I find her.'

'Yet another frustration.'

'It's how it is.'

'Still, a part of you will think, however damaged she is, she still took the lives of the people on your board, she still shattered the lives of those who loved them.'

'I'll worry about that later. Worry about catching her now.' She paced a little more, and circled a finger in the air. 'This,' she said, indicating the books surrounding them. 'They're different kinds of fantasy.'

'You could say.'

'And she's zeroed in – reader and writer – on murder fantasies, crime fantasies. That's what – like you said – pulled her in, and enough for her to spend time writing to DeLano, enough for her to spring off another fantasy of being a writer, of that kind of fiction. Why read murder mystery type books?'

'Entertainment,' he began, but Eve cut him off.

'No, you. You're the reader here. Why do you read them?'

'Ah well.' Swirling brandy, he thought it over. 'I enjoy a puzzle, I suppose, and playing along with it. Certainly since I married a cop I get more entertainment and satisfaction at experiencing the villain's ultimate failure. Good overcomes evil in the end, and that makes them a kind of morality play.'

'Okay, but that's not what she's after. She wants to flip that. She wants evil to overcome good. She wrote a book she claims makes the killer – the villain – the star, right?'

'And claims that that's what makes it innovative and brilliant,' Roarke added. 'When it's certainly been done before.'

'She's self-absorbed. Nobody's done what she's done, not in her mind. In this *Sudden Dark* one? DeLano writes stuff from the bad guy's perspective so you see him plotting and thinking and doing stuff, but just bits and pieces, right? It's not his book, it's Deann Dark's book. But Strongbow's rewriting it, all of them, and making herself the star. She's in charge. What if—'

'It's the only way she can be,' Roarke finished. 'The only time she's ever been in charge.'

'Bang. It's not, for her, the puzzle, the entertainment, even the temporary escape from reality, it's the only way she's in charge, that she's important. The only way she wins.'

'What does that tell you about her?'

'It tells me the probability's high that whatever job she

has – or did in Delaware – is low-rung. Likely she's been overlooked and, at least to her mind, undervalued. And, I think, she's had little interaction with males. I'm betting female-centric profession, maybe comes from a female-centric background. Female authority figure or figures, because she sure latched on to female-centric books.'

'Yet she wrote her protagonist as a male,' Roarke pointed out, 'who kills women. That may stem – edging into Mira territory – because she's never had any real power as a woman.'

'Could play in. Most likely she lives alone, no real connections to pull her into the real world. Possible, always possible, she's got a big shit pile of money, but most likely she's living on a budget, and since a roommate or partner is unlikely, I'd look for her in a small, cheap apartment. And likely in Brooklyn. Likely she works there, too. Maybe has a job where she can work out of her own place. I like that one. Limited contact with actual people, that's how I see her.

'She's ordinary,' Eve added. 'She's not particularly attractive because attractive people tend to make connections if they want them. And she does. She wants people to see her, they just don't. So no sparkling personality, no charm. She doesn't stand out, never been popular, never been *somebody*. She's kind of invisible, and that enables her to become whoever she wants to become.'

'A. E. Strongbow was her chance, to be someone, to become visible and important, and DeLano stole it. Killing DeLano wasn't, isn't, enough. Before it comes to that,' Roarke said, 'she has to steal DeLano's work, flip the theme of the morality play, and rewrite it with herself as the center.'

'That's the circle,' Eve agreed, 'and around it are plenty of angles to work. Okay. Okay.' She had them lined up in order of priority in her head, and now she looked at Roarke.

'Well, strip it off, pal, and let's get this done.'

His eyebrows winged up as she hit the release on her weapon harness. 'That's quite the pivot.'

'Summerset-free house, library not yet checked off. It's a straight line, not a pivot.' After laying her weapon on the bench table, she pulled off a boot. 'That's a good couch.' She tossed the boot aside, pulled off the other. 'It'll work.'

'I don't believe I had that purpose in mind when I bought it. Then again, that was before you.'

'I'm here now.' She pulled off her belt. 'You, too.'

'I am, yes, and currently watching my wife strip in the most practical and efficient way. And wondering just why that only makes her more alluring.'

'"Alluring," right.'

She stripped off her sweater and shirt to the tank beneath. And he timed it well, he thought, waiting until her trousers dropped to her ankles.

Before she could fully step out, he grabbed her – quick and sharp as a whip – so she tumbled on top of him.

'You're still dressed,' she pointed out.

'Not for long.' And rolled her under him.

Since she seemed in the mood for heat and speed, and he

felt the same, he took her mouth, ravished it with his. Her hips pumped up, circled in grinding invitation even as her hands wedged between them to make quick work of the buttons of his shirt.

He dragged her tank down to her waist so flesh pressed to flesh.

'Two more minutes, we'd have been naked.' Her voice came breathless; her teeth nipped. 'But this way works.'

While her mouth warred with his, she unhooked his trousers, freed him. He rolled her panties down to her knees.

When he thrust into her, she rose up to meet him, to take him.

'Yeah, yeah.' Her fingers dug into his hips; her breath went ragged. 'This works.'

He let himself go. It was what she wanted, what he needed, so he took, took. Found himself taken. Pistoning hips, muffled gasps, hot bodies, hot minds merging into one frantic unit.

Mating, he would think later when capable of thought again, at its most elemental.

No frills, no sweet words, no seductions needed here and now, not for two people who knew love spread under and over and through all.

To be needed always struck her as elemental. To be needed by him added miraculous to the basic.

So she, too, let herself go, to take and be taken hard and fast until pleasure, already keen, sharpened blade bright.

In those last seconds, on that thin, edgy point of release,

her eyes met the wild blue of his. She said, as that blade slashed them both, 'I love you.'

Elemental.

Later in the night, curled up against him in bed, Eve dreamed strange dreams.

She walked through the pages of a book until the words blurred under her feet and became the cheap, scarred floor of the flop where Rosie Kent died.

She saw two bodies, two beds, two white sashes tied into bows. As if, she realized, on facing pages of a book.

Rosie Kent on one side just as she'd been in the crime scene photos from the file. Pryor Carridine on the other, as described in the book.

Close, she thought. Not exact, not like twins or clones, but close.

'That one's mine.'

Eve glanced over. She'd read the description of Deann Dark enough times now to recognize her. The dark hair drawn back in a short tail to leave the face unframed. A pretty face, deceptively soft, as the woman inside it, behind it, knew how to be hard.

'I know which is which.'

Even as she spoke, the pages turned. Now she stood in the theater, a body slumped in a seat on either side of the aisle.

No, of the page, Eve corrected. Again, they were close but not exact.

'I know which is which here, too, but they're the same to her.'

'Him,' Dark corrected.

'That's the fiction. They're the same.'

'We're not.'

'I'm not in the books.' Still, Eve crossed over to examine the fictional body as she would any victim. 'Strongbow had to change some things around so it worked for her. She'd call it rewriting, but really, it's just cheating.'

She straightened, gestured. 'This one came in alone because the friend got the bogus tag before showtime. But the real murder? Strongbow had to wait until both the vic and her friend were in place, because a real person doesn't have to follow the book, right? Rylan could have decided to skip it if her roommate got the emergency tag before the vid started.'

'That's not how it was,' Dark insisted.

'It's not how it was because the killer changed it. Benson came in alone because that's how DeLano wrote it. Rylan came in with a friend because the killer couldn't risk her changing her mind. She wrote it different, just different enough.'

Eve turned back. 'Benson has to do what's written, no choice. Same for you. I'm not in the books,' Eve said again. 'How does the killer account for that?'

'You don't exist,' Dark told her. 'You're not real until you're on the page.'

Eve smiled, cool and thin. 'That's exactly right.'

*

She awoke to morning's reality. Roarke sat on the couch in the sitting area, drinking coffee, the morning stock reports scrolling on the muted screen, the cat sprawled beside him.

She stayed in the warmth of the big, fancy bed another moment, studying the man who'd banged her like a drum the night before. The business suit radiated the elegant power of the man wearing it, and she had no doubt he'd already wielded that power in the predawn hours.

The cat showed a man content in his home, and the coffee? Well, a man who understood priorities.

She sat up, said, 'I'm not in the books,' and rolled out of bed.

'You're not, no, and good morning to you as well.'

'Coffee. Shower. Think.' After programming coffee – hot, black – she stumbled off to the shower with it.

Roarke reached down, scratched Galahad between the ears. 'Another cold one for those of us who have to venture out of the house today. What do you say we get a bit of oatmeal in our favorite cop, and help it go down easier with a ham and cheese omelet?'

When Eve came out the cat was sprawled in front of the fire, no doubt where he'd been banished, as two domed plates sat on the table. Along with a pot of coffee.

She hit the coffee first. Priorities. And sat.

'I'm not in the books.'

'So you said.'

'How does she deal with that? I don't know anything about writing a book, but it seems to me it's got to be a problem to add an entire character to the mix, right? And not just one,' she continued as Roarke removed the domes. 'There's you, there's Peabody. You've got McNab and, for this at least, Reineke and Jenkinson. Mira, Morris. It's a frigging cast of characters.'

As she spoke, she added brown sugar, berries to the small bowl of oatmeal. Her mind definitely elsewhere, Roarke noted, as the look that clearly said, *Crap, oatmeal*, didn't appear.

'Your subconscious must have been busy in the night.'

'Maybe, but I'm right, aren't I? She can replicate, with some creative fiddling, the murders. But she can't replicate the investigation. She can't rewrite me or the investigative team, because we're not in the books.'

'She's delusional, Eve.'

'Yeah, but that could work for us. I bet she follows the crime beat. If she didn't before, she's following it now. And I happen to know the reigning queen of the crime beat, and just how much she loves an exclusive.'

'Which you'd give her.'

'I put it out there we've connected these two murders, and we're looking for a single individual, one suspect. Then I spin the whole following leads, unable to divulge. I can play that out.'

'Writing yourself into the book?'

'No, no, just the opposite. I'm outside it. I'm the reality, but now I'm a face, a voice – visual and auditory, right? And she has to figure out what to do about it.'

'You'll try to shift her focus to you.'

Her back went up, instantly. 'If you don't think I can handle some whiny wannabe—'

'I don't doubt you can, but I'd hardly be as I'm written, would I, if I didn't have some concerns.'

'Okay, and anyway, it's not about shifting her focus to me. Going after me? That's a whole new book, and she's got to finish what she's already lined up. It's about shaking things up, giving her something to worry about in the real world. It's a slap on her writing on one level. She wasn't good enough to convince me two different people committed two murders.'

'It's a bad review,' Roarke added, finding the angle inspired. 'And quite a bit brilliant. Wear black.'

'You're telling me to wear black?'

'Suggesting,' he corrected. 'And, though I enjoy you in strong colors, you'll be projecting that visual. Dangerous black. Uncompromising. In fact, I have something in mind.'

When it came to projecting an image, she thought, who had a better handle? 'Have at it,' she invited.

Roarke rubbed a hand on her leg, rose, then wandered off into her closet.

As he did, the cat began a slow, silky bellying toward the table.

Eve forked up a bite of omelet. 'Do you really think because he went in there, I'd let you get away with it?'

Galahad blinked at her, rolled over, and went back to his sprawl in front of the fire.

Roarke came back with a mock turtleneck, body-hugging pants in a combination of leather and some sort of stretchy material, and a leather jacket with dull silver zippers on slash pockets on the sleeves.

He'd added a pair of chunky boots that would hit well above the ankle and had that same dull silver in buckles over a series of tough-looking straps.

All in dangerous black.

With a nod, Eve polished off her eggs. 'I'm good with that.'

She rose to dress as he sat again – noting he'd brought her underwear, too. Black.

Not just the man who had everything, she thought as she started to dress, but the man who thought of everything.

'I'm going to work here for an hour,' Eve told him. 'Get that list of potential third victims hashed out. I want to talk to DeLano again, and her mother, and I'd rather do that in my house this time. And Nadine. I need to see if Mira's on board with my assessment. Or ours,' she corrected, 'as you've had a lot of insight on this.'

'I wouldn't wish for another murder,' he said as she crossed over to hitch on her weapon harness. 'But I did enjoy the time with you in the library. All of it.'

'I'm pretty fond of that room now myself.' She shrugged into her jacket. 'Dangerous?'

'Very. Add lip dye and mascara.'

Her back didn't go up this time, but her body sagged. 'Come on.'

'Consider it insight. Just add that. For the visual.'

'Crap. Bullshit crap.' She mumbled it, but strode off to the bathroom to push through the limited supplies Trina forced on her.

She came out. 'Now?'

'Now? Lethal. You'll worry her, darling Eve. I have no doubt. See that you, at some point, slip a hand into your pocket in a way that shows the camera a hint of your weapon.'

'That's good. That's a good one. I'm going to get started.'

He rose, walked to her. Skimmed a finger down the dent in her chin. 'Take care of my lethal cop.'

'Count on it.' She kissed him, walked out.

'I do,' he murmured, slipping a hand into his own pocket to rub his fingers over the button he carried there. 'I do count on it.'

12

In her home office, Eve read the list of names from her search list. Potential third victims, and some, she thought, hit close to the fictional character's careless, reckless, selfish description.

More than a few of them had a sheet – assaults, illegals, destruction of property, shoplifting, DUI, disorderly conduct, public nudity. Some charges dismissed, some community service, some cage time, and a lot of court-ordered rehab.

As far as she could discern not one of them contributed in any way to society. And not one of them deserved to end up on her board as a victim.

She sent them to Peabody with instructions to set up interviews – and to twist arms where necessary to get said individuals into Central.

As she'd likely be talking to people most of the day, she didn't want to start now. She sent Nadine a text telling her to come in to Central, with a camera.

She sent a message to Blaine DeLano requesting that

she and her mother come in to Central at their convenience, advising them to contact Peabody with the time they expected to arrive.

After one more message, this to Mira asking for another consult, she sat back a moment to review her notes, then her board.

Shake things up, she thought again. Change the angles and give the crazy bitch something to think about.

She looked forward to giving Strongbow a dose of the real.

She headed downstairs, saw her coat, a scarf — not the one she'd unwound the night before but a long black cloud — along with black gloves probably lined with some ridiculously expensive fur, and her oddly beloved snowflake cap.

She lifted the memo cube topping the pile, engaged.

After a brief, sort of jazzy instrumental, voices — male and female — sang in harmony.

Baby, it's coooold ouuutside!

She snickered, wondered how he managed to think of the silly. After gearing up, she slipped the memo cube into the pocket of her coat.

She walked into the cold outside.

Something fell from the sky that wasn't quite snow, wasn't quite ice, but took elements from both to create the altogether nasty. The thin skin of it over the streets boosted traffic from annoying to insane.

She cursed it. Cursing it didn't make anyone move faster or with more skill or sense, but she felt better after venting.

By the time she pulled into the garage at Central, she wished the entire driving population of New York City into the fiery flames of hell.

She made her way up to Homicide, and as she swung in noted Santiago sat at his desk. He wore a cowboy hat and a sulky expression.

She said, 'You're wearing the hat.'

'I know, boss. It's on my head.'

'Why are you wearing the hat?'

He shifted to aim his sulky look at his partner. Detective Carmichael smiled her most serene smile. 'A little bet,' she said, 'on the Knicks game. Chicago wins, I spring for lunch for a week. Knicks win, he wears the hat for a week.'

'You bet against the Knicks? You deserve the hat.'

'I grew up in Chicago,' Santiago protested. 'That's gotta count.'

'The people of New York pay your freight, Santiago. That's what counts.'

The sulk deepened. 'Don't you own the Celtics?'

'Roarke owns the Celtics,' she corrected. 'And when they play the Knicks, they're the enemy. We have standards in this division. Mets, Knicks, Giants, Rollers, Rangers. Get on board, Detective, or you may wear that hat permanently.'

'What about the Yankees, the Jets?'

Eve stared coldly. 'Don't make me write you up.'

She turned to Peabody as her partner clicked off her 'link.

'Got some of it lined up,' Peabody told her.

'My office.'

Eve walked straight to it, dumped the outdoor gear as Peabody followed.

'The DeLanos are coming in as soon as the girls leave for school. On the skank list . . . It's heavy in skank, Dallas,' she said when Eve aimed a fresh stare. 'On that I'm mostly getting machines. Your average skank's not an early riser. I did tag one who hadn't been to bed yet. She told me to fuck off, but since she's currently on parole – jumped another skank in a club, attempted to shove second skank off the balcony. Both were intoxicated at the time. Also stoned. And as one Loxie Flash – legal name change from Marianna Beliski – is on parole, and in court-ordered rehab – which ingesting illegals and/or alcohol would break – and since she appeared to be under the influence of both, my suggestion that she come in or have her parole officer advised of this violation was met with a "Fuck you, I'll be there."'

Peabody's rundown gave Eve a fairly clear picture. However. 'I think we'll refrain from referring to potential targets of a murderer as skanks.'

'Let's see what you say after you deal with her, and the others once I run them down. I predict a skank parade. Anyway, I read your report. This Strongbow looks like a viable suspect. Obsessed.' Peabody ticked them off a list with her finger. 'Pissed off. Threatening. Irrational.'

'Now we have to find her. I didn't find a single Strongbow in Delaware after casting the net over the last five years. And the ones I've found in New York don't fit.'

'It's her nom de plume.'

'It's her nom de bullshit, but we need to keep pushing on it. There's probably some sort of connection. Going with the odds again, she's in Brooklyn, low-rent digs, low-level job. We can start running females who relocated to Brooklyn around the date Strongbow wrote DeLano she'd taken the risk – so May '58. Females living alone, no spouse, no cohab. No criminal,' Eve considered. 'She never took a risk before, stayed in the background. We can flag any seamstresses, tailors – though that might just be a hobby.'

'You really think she made that coat? If she did, that takes real talent.'

'I've exhausted the search, and that sort of reversible wouldn't be hard to pin down if it's retail. You're going to run that down. You've got to get the material, right, whether she made it or had it made? If we continue with the living-on-a-budget line, having it made is less likely. If she made it, that dopey penguin material came from somewhere. Let's find out where.'

'I've got some sources there that might be able to help. If she's a serious craftsman, she wouldn't order material online. You want to see it, feel it. And I'd guess she'd need a professional machine.'

'Tap the sources.'

'Will do. I want to study the security feed again, get a good zoom of the material. I bet my eyes would be sharper if I had coffee.'

Eve just jerked a thumb at the AC. 'If you tap out with local sources, try Delaware. Maybe she brought it with her, the material. If she's that good, she must've had specific venues for buying her supplies.'

'If she actually made it, she might be in the business. If she's in the business, she probably gets her supplies wholesale.'

Frowning, Eve took the coffee Peabody handed her. 'That's a point. If you wash out with your suppliers, tag Leonardo.'

'He's a high-end designer,' Peabody pointed out. 'Did he design those pants you're wearing, because they're abso-mag. If I had yard-long legs toned like steel, I could wear those pants.'

'I don't know who the hell made them, and Leonardo wasn't always high-end. He'd still know people.'

And her oldest friend Mavis's 'honey bear' had the sort of sweet, open nature that drew people.

'Get on it, stay on it. Pull in help if you need it, but let's track those stupid penguins. I'll take the DeLanos when they get here.'

'Already booked A. Dallas, we could pass the run on Strongbow – hunt for single female in Brooklyn – to EDD. They'd cut through it faster.'

'Do that. And . . . ' She trailed off when she heard foot-steps coming their way. Female.

Hell, all she had today was female.

Mira, looking very female in her soft blue winter coat, some sort of fuzzy white beret angled over her dark sweep of hair, stepped to the doorway.

'I'm interrupting.'

'No, your timing's great.'

'I'll get on this. I love the hat,' Peabody said to Mira with a grin, getting one in return.

'It's a new favorite. You do such pretty work, Delia.'

'It's not work if you love it.'

Peabody clomped out; Mira swept in.

The thin, short heels on the rose-colored booties made no concession to whatever fell out of the sky. But they matched the pretty suit under the coat to an exact shade.

Mira set down her suitcase-size handbag – shades of blue and rose in a wavy pattern – unwound her white scarf.

'You want some coffee? Or that tea stuff?'

'The tea, thanks. I had coffee this morning.'

Though Eve couldn't say what having had coffee had to do with *having* coffee, she programmed the tea.

'I appreciate you getting to me so fast.'

'I read your reports, last night and this morning.' Mira sat in the desk chair after Eve pulled it out for her, crossed her legs. 'I wanted to get to you before my day started, as it's very full. From the data and evidence you've gathered, Strongbow is the prime suspect. This person – and I agree with your conclusion, she's a woman – exhibits signs of obsession and delusion.'

'And then some,' Eve agreed.

'She's clearly obsessed with DeLano, with the books, with her own desire to publish. She's moved from fan to fanatic. The accusations – her absolute conviction that

DeLano plagiarized her work – is part of the delusion. And that delusion and obsession has its roots in her conviction that DeLano was not just the author of a series of books she enjoyed, but her personal friend, her mentor and advisor.'

'She saw what she wanted/needed to see, and made that her reality.'

'Yes. There is nothing, absolutely nothing in DeLano's responses – though they are warm and friendly, even helpful – to warrant these conclusions.

'This is a woman who creates situations, imagines actions, reactions, connections, and turns them, as you said, into her reality. She wishes something was so, and it becomes so. She has no one to talk to, no one to ground her to reality. She lives in the books – ones she reads, ones she writes.'

Mira sipped some tea while Eve edged a hip onto the desk.

'She kills in the books, and now in reality.'

'Taking her power. I'd say she's felt powerless,' Mira continued. 'She's watched those who break the rules, who do what society considers wrong, profit and thrive. Likely she's experienced being treated unfairly though she, at least in her mind, did her very best, though she followed those rules.'

'Bad guys win.'

'They often do in reality,' Mira agreed. 'Reading a series like Hightower, or like Dark, there's a comfort. Terrible things happen, and they happen often to good people, to the innocent. But evil is overcome and punished by good. Balance is restored. At some point, this wasn't enough. If those who do evil win, why not write about that, why not show that? And eventually, why not be that?'

'You agree she's living in the books, as she's writing them.'

'Her improved version of them, yes, exactly. The version where she, as creator and as the dark protagonist, has the power. The longer she does, the harder it will be for her to come back to reality, the shorter the time she'll be able to hold that reality. If, as you believe and I agree, she's already selected the third victim from *Dark Deeds*, she is living as the character of the killer in the book. Whatever job she might have, whatever other tasks she needs to perform, they're becoming the illusion. Eventually the illusion she creates will become too strong, and far too appealing. Without medication and treatment, reality will cease to exist.'

'You're saying she's not legally sane, but she plans, she edits, she's choosing to kill, to become the killer.'

'I don't want to diagnose without examining her, but it's the killer choosing. A part of her writes – whether literally or in her head. The writing is so consuming – the betrayal by DeLano, as she sees it, so abhorrent – she becomes the character, but her more finely crafted version. One who punishes, who seeks to harm, seeks to win by any means. Who, in her version, defeats Dark, thereby vanquishes DeLano.'

'And right now, she's some jealous, vengeful ... skank, plotting to kill the woman she feels is ruining the man she wants, the man she needs. She has to troll the clubs,' Eve continued. 'She has to spend some time living the life to inhabit that character.'

'She'll kill again.'

'She'll sure try. If she gets in deep enough, wouldn't she get stuck? Wouldn't she stick inside the same character?'

'It's a series, and Dark is her adversary each time. She follows Dark. I think she needs the books, the stories, the continuation, and, oddly, the thrill of becoming someone else, someone new.'

Mira set her teacup aside, rose. 'This is a clever woman, one who thinks everything through, step-by-step, but that thinking is limited to the story she lives in. I think a large part of her life has been lived that way, and the world outside's thin and inconvenient to her. She'll do whatever she needs to do to stay inside the story where she's strong and triumphant, and out of the world where she fades into the ordinary.'

'She'll like my world, where she ends up in a high-security facility for violent mental defectives, even less.'

As Mira went out, Peabody came in. 'The DeLanos are here.'

'On my way.'

'I got one of the other ... potentials. She bitched and moaned, but she's coming in.'

'Keep at it,' Eve told her, and made her way to Interview A.

The DeLanos sat beside each other at the interview table, and both looked over at Eve as she came in with nearly identical expressions of anxiety.

'Has someone else been killed?' Blaine asked.

223

'No.'

'Thank God. Detective Peabody said no, but . . .'

'We worked ourselves up,' Audrey admitted. 'Convinced ourselves you wanted to tell us in person.'

'I appreciate you coming in. I did want to talk to you in person, but about some specific correspondence.' Eve sat with the file she'd brought in. 'A. E. Strongbow.'

This time she got nearly identical blank looks.

'Neither of you recognize the name?'

Blaine shook her head. 'Sorry.'

'Maybe this'll help.'

Eve pulled out the first letter, watched it click for Audrey almost immediately.

'I do remember. Of course. He sent a manuscript – after a couple of letters, he sent a manuscript. We have a post office box, as some people like to write letters rather than emails. He sent his book. Not merely a disc copy or download, which is more usual, but an actual physical copy of the manuscript. It happens, rarely, and when it does I send them back unopened with a letter explaining Blaine can't read it. And I try to offer a lot of encouragement, maybe some advice on how to find an agent or publisher.'

Audrey nudged the letter away. 'I remember this because when he wrote after *Sudden Dark* came out, he was furious, and accused Blaine of plagiarizing his manuscript.'

'Oh, for—' Blaine stopped, held up a hand. 'Wait, I remember that, you told me about that. I didn't remember the name.'

'I probably didn't mention his name. It was an ugly letter, and ridiculous on top of it. Not only didn't Blaine see the manuscript, which I sent straight back unopened, but she'd already written *Sudden Dark* before he sent his stupid book – without asking, I'll add. Damn it, we got the ARCs – the advance reader copies – at the end of May, just days after he sent the manuscript. It was so insulting I nearly—'

'It's all right, Mom.' Blaine reached over, rubbed her mother's arm. 'When she told me, I let my editor know – just in case. But as far as I know that was the end of it. Do you think he's involved in this?'

'She,' Eve corrected. 'And I think she's killed two people.'

'Oh my God. I didn't handle it right. I didn't follow through the right way,' Audrey began.

'You handled it right,' Eve told her. 'This has nothing to do with you. This woman is delusional, psychotic. She contacted you again.'

'No.' Firmly Audrey shook her head. 'I would have flagged any more correspondence from that name.'

'Twice more I found, different names. Harsh letters.' Eve took them out. 'Accusatory.'

'You get that sometimes,' Blaine murmured as she picked up a copy, read it. 'You take the good with the bad. Are you sure these are from the same person?'

'I'm confident. I believe this woman relocated from Delaware to Brooklyn.'

'Brooklyn?' Blaine went sheet white. 'My girls.'

'Local police have an eye. And they're not in this. They're not in the books. Are there any coordinating characters with them in the series?'

'No. I don't understand. If she's this angry with me, what better way to strike at me than through my girls?'

'She's angry with you, but you've blended, at least in part, with the character of Dark.'

'That's just crazy. Dark is fifteen years younger than I am, in better shape and a lot better-looking.' She said it with a half smile, but her eyes stayed full of fear. 'She's never been married, has no children, eats fast-food, and drinks scotch when she can get it. Her relationship with her mother is strained at best, and for good reason, as Maggie Dark's a user of people. She likes loud music and bars, breaks rules as much for the fun of it as expediency.'

Eve listened to the rundown until Blaine stopped herself. 'Sorry, none of that matters.'

'Actually, it applies. You talk about her like she's an actual person.'

'She has to be real for me. I have to be invested in her, attached. I have to *know* her. She's fictional, of course, but she exists inside my head.'

'She's real for Strongbow, and she's lost or is at least losing her grip on the fictional part. You created Dark, she's inside you. You represent her, or she you. Strongbow's rewriting your books so the killer wins, because she's the killer, and it's her story now.'

'That was her thing, I remember.' Audrey gripped her

daughter's hand. 'The killer's book, with the killer as the main character, as the protagonist.'

'She's connected her book with my Dark series. She's what, showing me she's a better writer?'

'That's part of it, and it may be the foundation. We've got angles on her now, and we're pursuing them all.'

DeLano lifted a hand to her heart, rubbed lightly. 'You think she's lives in Brooklyn.'

'Not in your neighborhood. I don't think she could afford it. Do you have any tailoring done, any sewing?'

'Not really. I've had – we've all had – things altered in the shop we use for the less casual wear.'

'Do you know the seamstress?'

'Gia? Yes. For years. When I had my first signing, Mom insisted I get a nice suit, have Gia fit it. That's been over a decade.'

Unlikely, Eve thought.

'Have you had anyone come in and do the curtain things, drapes, whatever?'

Blaine smiled again. 'We're just not that fancy. Do you think she's a seamstress?'

'We believe she may have those skills, whether it's a job or a hobby. If she submitted her book, she likely did it at your publisher.'

'I don't think that happened. They'd have notified me after Mom sent them the letter if they'd gotten a manuscript from that name.'

'Okay. We're reading through the books, getting a sense

of the story, and particularly of the first victim and killer in each. But it would be helpful if you could send me, we'll say, a kind of profile on those characters, a basic outline of the crime scenes.'

'I can and will. I know what you mean.'

'Good. I'm going to give you the same instructions I did yesterday: Don't open the door to anyone you don't know. Nobody comes in the house you don't know. If you see anything or anyone that makes you uncomfortable, contact your local police, then me.'

She paused, studying DeLano's face. 'I'm going to add: If beefing up your personal security makes you feel safer, then do that.'

'I'm going to. My mother, my girls aren't in the books, but they're part of me.'

'We'll get us some bodyguards.' Audrey added a little shoulder shake to try to lighten her daughter's worry. 'Good-looking ones.'

'Mom.' DeLano laughed a little, then sighed. 'You'll stop her,' she said to Eve.

'Let's say I intend to write the ending.'

Eve showed them out, went back to her office to add to her notes.

Minutes later, her interoffice signaled.

'I've got Loxie Flash in A,' Peabody told her. 'Do you want me in there?'

'Keep at what you're doing. I'll take her.'

She wound her way back.

Loxie Flash fit the physical description of the third victim well enough. Had a few more pounds on her, wore her hair longer, but gave off the same vibe.

The fuckhead vibe.

In the book, Bliss Cather had – in the last hours of her life – spiky hair of the palest blond tipped with black. Plenty of piercings on both, though Cather had gone for an eyebrow bar and the live-and-in-person Loxie chose what Eve thought of as a bull ring, a hoop studded through the tender dividing line of the nostrils.

A lot of tats, plenty of heavy makeup. The skin shirt proclaimed BALL BUSTER over a pair of impressive, unharnessed breasts. Jeans, held together with lacing at the hips, showed a lot of skin.

Loxie curled her lip, spoke with a raspy verbal sneer. 'What the fuck's your damage, bitch?'

'Lieutenant bitch.' Eve sat. 'And I'm here to tell you a story that might save your life. There's a woman out there who may be thinking about killing you.'

'Shit. Bitches don't want to kill me, assa-hola. Bitches want to *be* me.'

'Not this one, maybe because she's crazy.'

Loxie curled her lip in an arrogant sneer. 'Crazy don't stop my sleep none.'

'This one's about five-six, white. Red hair with blue side dreads. She'll have a tat of an orange dragon on the inside of her right wrist. She'll try to look about twenty-five but she's older.'

'Old bitches are boring.'

'She's not. You've seen her around, places you hang out, places you party.'

'I see a lot of people.'

'Any of those people look like the person I just described?'

Loxie shrugged. 'If they ain't on my team, I don't pay them much mind. Look, Bitch Badge, I gotta sleep. Had a big night.'

'You had a big night breaking your parole. If you don't want a big night in a cage, lose the bullshit.'

Eve shoved the stills from the surveillance feed across the table. 'Have you seen her?'

'Jesus, what is that clucker-fucker wearing? Looks like she got swallowed by ugly. I don't know people who wear dumb-ass coats covered in lame-ass birds.'

'You haven't seen the coat before?'

'If I'd seen that coat, I'da lit it on fire.'

'Look at her face, take a good look.'

'I'm telling you I don't know this bitch. You think I hang with losers like this?'

'I'm telling you, if you do see her, keep away from her and contact me. If you see her – white, red hair with blue side dreads, orange dragon tat inside her right wrist – she's there to kill you.'

'Bull.' Loxie shot up her index finger. 'And shit.' Then her middle.

'You'd be her third, so she's had experience. Two people are in the morgue who might've claimed bull and shit. Do yourself a favor and stay out of the clubs for a couple weeks, and don't drink any martinis.'

'I'm in rehab, bitch. No drinking, no clubbing, no party time.'

Eve looked into the bloodshot eyes, still glassy from breaking parole. 'I don't give a rat's ass if you drink yourself into a coma or pop enough Erotica to bang your way from dusk to dawn. Just stay out of the clubs. Stay out of the clubs if you want to live.'

Leaning forward Eve pushed the photo under Loxie's nose. 'Look at her. Remember her. She's crazy,' Eve said, 'and if she's fixed on you, she'll hit you in a club, that's her plan. She'll poison you with a martini – pomegranate. Because she's got the jumps for your ex.'

'Glaze?' Loxie flicked her fingers in the air – but bright green jealousy flicked in her eyes at the same time. 'All hers. I'm done with that fuckhead.'

'She wants to make sure of it. She doesn't like you, Loxie. She blames you. Glaze, he doesn't even know she exists, but she'll kill you to save him from you, to have him for herself. Get this point: She's crazy.'

'Crazy enough to wear that fugly coat.'

'She won't be wearing it the next time you see her. Get this in your head. White, red hair with blue side dreads, orange dragon tat on the inside of her right wrist. It'll be loud, it'll be crowded when she puts that martini down in front of you. The house band's going to be playing one of Glaze's numbers – her request. It's the last thing you hear before you drink that idiot martini with the cyanide she dropped in it.'

For the first time Loxie looked worried. Her eyebrows knitted; she gnawed on a thumbnail painted glittery black. 'You're talking about the future, man, and that's bullshit. How come you know all this?'

'I read the book.'

13

Eve stopped off at Vending. She wanted something cold, and if the machine gave her grief, well, she'd kick its ass the way regulations had prevented her from kicking Loxie Flash's.

She plugged in for a tube of Pepsi. Snagged what it shat out.

'This is a damn diet cream soda, you fuck.'

Inappropriate language noted. Fester's Diet Cream Soda offers classic taste guilt free! There is no nutritional value, and certain additives – listed on request – may pose health risks including—

'Shut up. Just shut the fuck up and give me my damn Pepsi.'

Second incident of inappropriate language noted. Warning! A third incident will result in suspension of Vending privileges.

'Note this. I will rip your circuits out with my bare hands, blast them to oblivion with my police issue if you don't give me my damn Pepsi.'

Threats of vandalism will be reported, Harcove, Detective Clint. Acts of vandalism will result in suspension of Vending

privileges and a two-thousand-dollar fine, plus cost of damages.

Eve started to tell the idiot, computerized pain in her ass she wasn't Harcove, Detective Clint, then reconsidered.

'Give me the tube of Pepsi I ordered.'

It shat one out.

Your account has been charged for one tube of Pepsi. Pepsi, the choice of generations!

That would be Harcove's account, Eve thought as the machine spouted off its hype and warnings.

Two notations of inappropriate language and one threat of vandalism have been added to your file.

'Yeah.' Eve cracked the tube. 'Add this: You can bite me.'

Eve walked into Homicide. 'Peabody!'

When Peabody looked up, Eve tossed the tube of cream soda.

'Hey, thanks.'

'Thank Detective Clint Harcove.'

'Who's that?'

'I have no idea. Progress?'

'I washed out on my usual shops, but I got some direction from the manager of one I use a lot. How'd it go with Flash?'

Eve took a moment to drink some Harcove Pepsi. 'Skank.'

'Told you.'

'Bad-attitude skank with a heavy side of asshole, but I got under her skin by the end of it. She's warned, she has the description of the unsub, and claims she's going home

234

to sleep. As she hadn't yet reached the hungover, strung-out stage of her night's binge, that I believe.'

'You've got another coming in. At least she said she'd give us five on her way to a recording session. She claims she's putting a band together that blows your skin off. Shanna K. Just the initial for the last name because, she says, labels limit expression.'

'Can't wait.'

'And Nadine's on her way.'

'Good.'

Eve wrote up the interview with Loxie. Went out again to repeat the routine with Shanna K.

Shanna didn't call her a bitch, listened with wide eyes heavily lashed in magenta, smiled with lips outlined in tiny, tiny sparkles.

And dismissed everything Eve told her, as she claimed people only killed other people when they'd run afoul of each other in a past life. As she herself had undergone reincarnate cleansing, she was therefore absolved of all past-life transgressions.

Still Eve pressed, pushed, went so far as to wipe the sparkle smile away by shoving photos of the DBs across the table.

By the end she figured if she hadn't put the fear of reincarnated gods into Shanna K, she'd put the fear of Dallas into her.

That would have to do.

On the way back she caught it. The siren's perfume. The aroma of sin.

Chocolate.

Nadine stood in her bullpen, laughing with Santiago as every cop in the place scarfed down brownies. Any cop currently in the field, using the john, or doing their damn job trying to save some reincarnated skank's life would be dead out of luck, brownie-wise.

She noted Nadine had, as instructed, brought a camera, and the woman appeared to be reading the division motto posted over the break-room door with interest.

She noted, too, Nadine had brought along her new intern.

Quilla perched on the corner of Peabody's desk, chattering away and eating a brownie. She'd whacked her hair short, with sharp points over both ears, a trio of them at the neck, a grouping of narrower ones over the forehead.

Some of them were the blue you might get if you lit gas on fire, then tossed in some napalm.

Eve had stopped wondering why people insisted on adding colors not seen in nature to various parts of their bodies.

The kid spotted her, grinned.

She'd added that blue to her lash tips, too, Eve observed. She wore ear hoops and a red sweater with black baggies and chunky, lace-up-to-the-knee boots.

Quilla said, 'Hey.'

'Hey. Aren't you supposed to be in school or something?'

'I got a waiver for the day. Educational career training. Thanks for the recommend.'

'Yeah. Don't blow it.'

'I'm gonna rock it so solid.' Quilla looked around as she

236

spoke. 'Been in the cops, but never in Homicide before. I figured it would look more chill and spill.'

'We mop up the blood and gore every morning.'

Quilla snickered, and spoke again before Eve could turn to Nadine.

'They took us on a field trip last month.'

'Great. Peabody, find someplace to plant the kid while we—'

'They took us to An Didean. It's a whack name, but frosty whack. So, they let us go through and look at the plans, and a couple of people who're going to work there talked to us about what's the what and all that.'

'Okay.'

'It's going to be sweet, you know? It's going to be solid sweet. We even went up to the roof, and they talked about the memorial for the girls who got killed, and how we're going to have a garden up there. I hung back when everybody went down. We weren't supposed to, but—'

'You don't always do what you're supposed to.'

Quilla mated a grin with an exaggerated shrug. 'What's the fun in that? Anyway, I did it because I wanted a minute up there by myself to think what I've been thinking since it all went down. One of those girls could've been me. I mean, the crazy guy was gone and all, but that's just timing, right? It could've been any of the girls who're going to live in the new digs. They said maybe it'll be ready in May, and that's not long to wait.'

'Are things okay where you are?'

'They don't all the way suck.' Quilla shrugged it off, then glanced at Nadine with a gleam in her eyes. 'They're going to get better.'

Eve moved closer. 'She's no pushover, kid.'

'Why would I want, like, career training from a push-over? If I'm gonna rock it solid, I need a solid to show me the ropes, right?'

'Good thinking. Nadine, my office. Just you right now.'

Nadine signaled to her camera to wait, turned to Quilla. 'Observe,' she instructed. 'I want a thirty-second report on the Homicide bullpen, any aspect thereof, when I'm done.'

'Can't I observe the one-on-one? You know, observe you work?'

'Observe here,' Nadine ordered and followed Eve. 'I've either made a brilliant stroke or a terrible mistake.'

'You're taking her on?'

'God, she's smart. I figured that out in one quick minute. Sly, too, and I admire sly. She's also going to be a pain in my ass, I know it. Just like I know the sensible thing would be to go to Columbia or NYU and interview solid journalism students. I'm not altogether sure whether I took her on or she took me, but I've got myself a teenage intern. And now I have to file weekly reports on her with Child Services, with copies to my own boss and to the head of the shelter.'

'She will be a pain in your ass, but you'll probably like it. Lois.'

Nadine's eyebrows lifted.

'I figure that's what the rocker calls you when you're banging.'

Smoothly, Nadine reached into a handbag the size of a semi, pulled out a compact, and checked her face. 'When you're banged well, it doesn't matter what they call you. However, I'm just seeing Jake casually. Now and again.'

'Right.'

'He's busy, I'm busy. And he travels quite a bit. Our life-styles are very different, though he's certainly more stable and steady than most expect from a rocker.'

Eve said nothing for a moment. Then blew out a breath. 'Jesus, you're serious about him.'

'I don't know that I am. Or he is. We are.' Nadine tossed her compact back in the enormous bowels of her bag. 'We only started seeing each other a few weeks ago, and I'm not looking for serious anyway. We're not even exclusive. Not that I'm seeing anybody else right now, because I'm busy. God, I really like him. I need coffee, since you won't have any booze in here.'

Eve turned to the AutoChef, and Nadine dropped down in the desk chair.

'You know, I have my own show, and *Now*'s ratings are solid. They're rock solid. I have the desk at Seventy-Five. I have one bestseller under my belt, and I'm up for a goddamn Oscar for the screenplay adaptation. I've written another book, and it's damn well going to be a bestseller. I have an amazing new apartment, and I'm actually thinking about buying a vacation home in Aruba or somewhere, though when the hell am I going to actually use it for more than a blink of time because I'm busy.'

'Yeah, you said.' Eve handed Nadine coffee.

'So why did I get it into my head to take on this teenager?'

'I think you said something about mentoring and molding.'

'Yeah, yeah, and I wasn't even drunk at the time. I'm taking on this smart, sly kid because I lost my mind. Why the hell am I getting tangled up on the personal side with a rock star?'

'He bangs right?'

'Funny. And that would be one thing, that's the okay, this is fun, no worries. But there are so many aspects to him. The music, and that's core to him. The audience, and they matter to him. His bandmates, they're like family. And he's interesting and aware. He's not an asshole.'

'Not being an asshole's important.'

'It *is*!'

'Who's arguing?'

Nadine sighed. 'I am.'

'Do we have to go have ice cream now or something?'

Nadine's sigh turned into the gimlet eye. 'No.'

'Are you going to give me the brownie you've got stashed in that blimp you haul around?'

'How do you know I have a brownie in my purse?'

'I can smell it. Give.'

Nadine took it out, held it out. Eve unwrapped it, bit in.

'Do you want to know the actual reason you're here?'

'Yes.' Nadine swiped her hands in the air, made a shoving motion. 'The other is now outside the door.' She gestured to the board. 'And, as I'm telling my young apprentice, reporters observe. You've got a suspect. Two. Working together?'

'Observe more closely.'

Obliging, Nadine rose, walked to the board, studied the shots from the vid palace's feed. 'One. That's the same person? Entering a male,' she noted. 'Sunshades, watch cap, bulky coat. Leaving as female. Truly horrible coat, pom-pom earflap hat, those ridiculous wind goggles. But . . . same boots, same pants. Wait, wait – that's . . . that's *Dark Days*, that killing. The actress, the vid. And the killer was male.'

Eyes sparking, Nadine turned back. 'Not just killing someone representing a character, but killing *as* a character.'

'We're not going public with that.'

'Ouch.'

'I've got a line on her, Nadine: wannabe writer, obsessed with DeLano. I've got correspondence.'

Eve summed it up quickly.

'How is Blaine dealing?'

'She's hiring security. She'll be smart.'

'I'm going to talk to her about this. I'll keep her name out of it as long as possible. What are you looking for with the one-on-one?'

'We've linked two cases, and are investigating them as connected. We believe we're looking for one suspect. I'm primary on both cases. I'm heading a team focused on bringing this individual to justice. You'll ask what you ask. I'll give you the "can't comment" when I can't, give you a few juicy bits when I can. She needs to see me as an adversary. I don't think it'll take her off DeLano, she's too dug in. But it will give her something to worry about. It'll shake the bubble she's living in. It may damn well pop it.'

Jiggling a foot, Nadine nodded. 'You're changing the plot on her, writing yourself in. I can tell you that introducing a major element, like a new antagonist, changes everything.'

'I'm counting on it. Let's get it done.' Eve hit the inter-office. 'Peabody, send Nadine's camera in.'

Nadine took out the compact again, and this time actually did check her face, dusted her nose, then glanced over as not only the camerawoman but Quilla came to the door.

'You're on bullpen observation.'

Quilla stood very straight, turned to the camerawoman, who grinned back at her. 'The detectives and uniformed officers who inhabit the Homicide bullpen at NYPSD's Cop Central may spend some parts of their shifts at desks, talking on 'links, writing reports, meticulously gathering data on investigations. But these often tedious tasks are as essential a part of the job they perform as confronting suspects and apprehending killers. They perform these duties with dedication and with a kind of intricate camaraderie, like soldiers during a battle lull. Their standards, their duty, their ethics are encapsulated in the motto they've posted in the bullpen to remind them what it is to carry a badge and work for the victim.

'It reads: "No matter your race, creed, sexual orientation, or political affiliation, we protect and serve, because you could get dead. Even if you were an asshole."

'These are the words the brave men and women of the NYPSD, Homicide Division, live by.'

Nadine touched up her lip dye. 'You ran over the thirty, so you'd need some editing. And you've fallen back on passive voice here and there. Example: "The motto in their bullpen speaks for itself." Then you quote it. Active voice, fewer words.'

'Got it. Can I observe the one-on-one?'

'Stay off-camera, and keep it zipped.'

As Quilla pumped a fist at her side, Nadine saw her eyes track to Eve's board. It made her proud. 'That's off the record,' she said briskly. 'Any journalist who doesn't respect off the record has no ethics, and doesn't deserve to be a journalist.'

'I've got that, too. Can I ask you questions later?'

'Why would I want an intern who didn't ask questions?' Nadine returned. 'But right now, zipped. No visual of the board,' she added to the camerawoman as she rose. 'Let's see how it looks by that sorry excuse for a window. A little slice of the city outside, the murder cop all in fuck-you black, the hard-driving crime beat reporter in her serious, if elegant, plum. How's the light?'

'Second,' the camerawoman muttered as she made adjustments. 'Good. Good light.'

'Content's the big guns,' Nadine told Quilla as she took her angle. 'But on air, if you want those bullets to penetrate, visuals matter. We'll do the intro back at the station, so a straight-on two-shot. In three, two . . . Lieutenant Dallas,' she began.

Nadine hit all the points. Eve kept it short and pithy, and tossed in a touch of arrogance with one viewer in mind. She judged it a satisfying use of her time, and calculated Nadine would have it on air within an hour – with repeat showings through the evening.

Before she could get back to her desk, Peabody came in. 'Got you another skank, in fact, two for one. Turns out they're frenemies and came in together.'

Eve considered. 'I'll take them together then. It may have more impact that way.'

'I'll set them up. Oh, and I may have a line on the fabric – and now I'm pretty sure you're right about her making that coat. I'm waiting for a tag back. How about that Quilla?'

'How about her?'

'Seriously, Dallas, she's really excited about working with Nadine. Talk about impact. It's the kind of opportunity that can change the direction of a life. She told me she binge-watched, like, six hours of Nadine's reports and some of *Now*, and she put in a request to read *The Icove Agenda*. She really wants to learn.'

Peabody pulled out her signaling 'link. 'That's my tag-back.'

'Take it. I'll set up the skanks.'

'They're right outside the bullpen.'

Eve went out, studied the pair of them. Decided they'd entered a contest on who could present a skankier appearance.

She judged it a tie.

'I'm Lieutenant Dallas.'

The one on the left rolled her thickly kohled eyes at the one on the right with the tattoo on the vast landscape revealed by the low scoop of her skin top that read: SEXY BITCH

Sexy Bitch said, 'B to the FD.'

Her companion laughed so hard it made the cock-and-balls earrings hanging from her lobes dance and spin.

Eve led them to Interview, spent nearly thirty minutes delivering the warning. Cock and Balls seemed genuinely frightened, enough she ignored Sexy Bitch's derision, and stated she intended to go stay with her mother in New Jersey for a few days.

Sexy Bitch claimed no crazy cunt scared her, and nobody messed with her good time. But Eve read fear in her eyes.

When she released them, Eve sat in the relative peace of the box and wondered what set a life in the direction of sporting genitalia as an accessory, or having somebody carve 'Sexy Bitch' into your flesh.

Peabody gave the door a quick rap, opened it. 'Dallas, I hit two outlets that carry the fabric. And the fact the fabric exists makes it a damn sure bet that coat was handmade. I think the outlet on the Lower East Side's the best shot. I talked the manager into looking up sales of three yards or more prior to Christmas. She's got one for five yards, logged in on Black Friday. The day after Thanksgiving. It's the only sale of enough yardage to make that coat.'

Eve rose. 'Good work.'

'The clerk who logged it's on a break, but she's due back in twenty.'

'Let's go talk to her.'

'We can do a skank run while we're at it. One on the list lives a couple blocks from the outlet.'

Eve thought of the four women she'd already dealt with. 'I'm going to need more coffee.'

Peabody worked her 'link as they made their way to the garage.

'Another outlet – Brooklyn. It's the first I found in Brooklyn.' Peabody slid into the car, strapped in. 'I hit there first, figuring if she lives there, she'd go for fabric stores there, but this is the first I've found that confirms that fabric. Still, they don't have a record of a sale over two yards.'

'Maybe she works at a fabric store.'

'Even employees have to log the yardage. Otherwise, the manager or owner doesn't know what's selling for inventory and reorders. Or what's low on yardage and maybe going on remnants or clearance. You can get some really nice remnants for small projects and crafts. And the fact is, the people I've talked to all say the same thing. That particular fabric sells primarily one to two yards. Something for kids, for a craft. A lot of one-yard sales for winter and holiday crafty gifts and decorations.'

'Whether or not she lives in Brooklyn, she has to come over the bridge to study and stalk her targets. No reason she can't shop while she's over here.'

'That's what I thought, and I think this place is where

she shopped. It's not that popular a fabric. I only found four places, all boroughs, that carried it at all, and only this one with the right yardage.

'She might've bought it online.' But Peabody shook her head even as she considered it. 'I've bought fabric – more like a sample of it – that way if I really know what I want and can't find it in my usual spots. But that fabric? How could she decide she had to have penguins all over the coat? What she'd want is something easy to work with. Why would she care about pattern?'

'I think, considering the pattern she used, she didn't.'

'Exactly, and Black Friday. It was on sale.'

Watching the budget, Eve thought. Shop the big sale, buy the cheap. 'Look for a silly pattern – who thinks stone killer when they look at a bunch of penguins? Girlie pattern. Come in as a guy, leave as a girl. Again, who's going to look twice?'

'We are!'

'That's not how she wrote it. She's going to think about that when she catches Nadine's report.'

She found a parking spot that required a two-block walk. What fell out of the sky now was a cold and bitter rain, the sort that made her hate February with every cell in her body.

And still she found that icy wet less of a chore than time spent in the bright, patterned, swirling world of the Sewing Basket.

Big bolts of fabric rose in stacks on tables, hanks and

balls of yarn hung from walls. Spools of thread – huge to tiny – formed pyramids or towers. Buttons – also huge to tiny – glinted and glowed.

Why had she never noticed that buttons with two holes looked like faces with empty eyes? Why had she never considered that?

Big, cheerful signs marked sections: BUTTON WORLD, YARN CITY, ON NEEDLES AND PINS.

But the worst of it, the part that made her back itch, were the fake people – men, women, children, even household pets – suspended from the ceiling.

And they all smiled.

Peabody pressed both hands to her chest. 'Oh my God!'

'I know. They dress fake people, they give them fake dogs and cats wearing coats and vests and, Jesus, little hats, then they hang them. It's just sick.'

'How have I missed this place? Oh, look at the colors on that Egyptian cotton! It would make a mag duvet cover. Maybe it'll go on sale. Oh, and those yarns, the pastels look like Easter eggs! Spring sweaters!'

The voice, the eyes, sparkled, and had Eve taking a hard grip on Peabody's arm. 'No.'

'If I could just—'

'No. Ride your hobbyhorse off duty.'

Music played. Not loudly, but it hit the obsessively chirpy level on Eve's personal gauge. The way customers – men, women, children, and household pets – packed the place told her Peabody had a lot of company on that hobbyhorse.

A woman scurried by hauling a bolt of something pink and shiny topped by a bolt of something white and frothy.

Eve risked releasing Peabody to snag her.

'We need the manager.'

'Oh, um ...' Obviously distracted, the woman glanced around. 'She was just here.'

'That pink shantung is gorgeous,' Peabody commented.

'Isn't it? And perfect for a girl's ballet recital, with this tulle?'

'So sweet!'

'Manager,' Eve repeated.

'Oh, yes, Karleen ... There she is! In the midnight mohair gradated tunic and ebony velvet slimmers. I'd take you back to her, but the young diva and her mother are waiting for these fabrics.'

'What the hell is a gradated tunic?'

'It's the mohair yarn that's gradated. I see her.'

All the way back through the maze of tables, the towers, the stacks, Peabody made yummy noises and wistful sighs.

14

They found the manager – long sweater in varying blended blues – in an intense discussion with a man in a fitted vest, a precisely knotted tie, and a topcoat over his arm.

The tone reminded her of people whose views closely aligned discussing some political event. Apparently this had to do with the weight of yarn and the size of hooks.

They both appeared to be very passionate.

'Excuse me.' Eve held up her badge. 'Lieutenant Dallas, Detective Peabody. We contacted you earlier.'

The woman who looked like someone's sensible grand-mother, despite the bun on the top of her head wrapped up in some sort of yarny thing that matched the sweater, patted a hand on the man's arm.

'Give me a minute, Sherwood.'

'Of course, Karleen. I'll be over with the alpaca. Lovely scarves, ladies. Your own handiwork?'

Eve just pointed at Peabody.

'I used Angel brand Black Knight, medium weight, number nine needles for the main body and seven for the thin stripe. For mine, it's In the Pink alternating every six rows with White Knight then Sing the Blues, using a seventeen because I wanted it really chunky.'

'May I?' He took the end of Peabody's scarf, examined it – one side, the other. 'Lark's head knot for the fringe?'

'Yeah.'

'Really exceptional work.'

'Thank you. I've worked with alpaca a couple times for special projects, but it's usually out of my range. It's just a fabulous store, and I'm coming back on my day off. I could spend hours.'

Eve's patience frayed like a sloppily sewed seam. 'Yeah, it's great, but we really need to speak with the clerk about that fabric.'

'Of course, of course. That was Lydia. Let's go hunt her down. I'll be back with you shortly, Sherwood.'

'Take your time, dear.'

'Lydia should be . . . Yes, yes, there she is. In silks. Lydia?'

The clerk set a bolt of red on a stack of jewel tones, and turned.

Mid-twenties, Eve judged, in a short green dress with brass buttons running down the front and back, green tights with colorful socks topping a pair of short boots.

'These are police officers.'

'Oh, well, jeez.'

'It's about some fabric you sold.'

'Was something wrong with it?'

'We're interested in who bought it.' Eve pulled out the photo. 'This fabric, this woman.'

'That's Playful Penguins. Look, Karleen, she made a coat with it.'

'Yes, I see. Interesting choice. Apparently she bought five yards, Lydia, in the Black Friday sale.'

'Oh man, that was a crazy day. I mean ca-ra-zee!'

'Do you remember the sale?' Eve pressed.

'Honestly, after a couple of hours, I barely remembered my name. We sold this mostly for craft projects, right, Karleen?'

'That's right. Take a moment, think back. I'm just going to go get what we have left of the bolt. We opened at eight,' Karleen reminded her as she hurried off.

'How could I forget?' The clerk's eyes shot to the heavens. 'We had regulars waiting for us to open the doors. A lot of them brought friends. Plus we had specials for the first fifty customers – and those were gone in about twenty minutes.'

'The penguin fabric,' Eve reminded her.

'Yeah, I was in fabrics all day. Yarns and tools got hit even harder, but we sold miles. A lot of holiday-theme fabric for crafts, and batting. I had to break up what looked like it was going to be a fight over the last three yards of Peace on Earth, which is kind of ironic, and luckily we had another bolt in the back, but . . . five yards of Playful Penguins.'

Karleen came back with the bolt. Eve decided it was just as ugly in person.

'This is the last of it. It looks like about two yards. You can certainly take it with you if you need it. It's fifty-four inches wide, and it was marked down to twelve-ninety-nine a yard on Black Friday. Another twenty-five percent discount for any purchase of five yards or more from the same bolt.'

'That's right!' Lydia shot a finger in the air. 'I forgot that. Five yards, five.' Lydia closed her eyes, put her hands over her face, ticked her head right and left. 'I think I remember, a little. It's the five yards, the extra discount. Wanted four? She said four yards, and I said if you buy five, you get another twenty-five percent off – so under ten a yard.'

She dropped her hands. 'It's what I said to anybody who wanted three to four yards, so it's pretty blurry. And like I said, we were just slammed. But I sort of remember.'

'Can you describe her?'

'I couldn't even start to, I'm really sorry. She wasn't a regular. I'd remember a regular.'

'Take a look at her picture again.' Eve held it out. 'It might help bring it back.'

'You can't really see her. Did she do something really wrong?'

'Yes.'

'She wasn't mean or rude or loud or pushy. You remember the ones who are, and I don't. I'd have asked if she needed anything else, like you do. Thread or buttons and so on. Maybe somebody else helped her and would remember.'

'She only bought the five yards,' Karleen said. 'Cash sale. Lydia says she wasn't a regular, but if she made that coat she's no novice. I'm sorry we can't be of more help.'

'It was a long shot,' Eve admitted. 'If she comes back in,

contact me immediately. Don't confront her, but stall if possible.'

Karleen took the card Peabody offered. 'If she comes in wearing the coat, we won't miss her. I'll let the rest of the staff know. Officer Peabody—'

'Ah, Detective.'

'Detective, Sherwood wants you to have this.' She offered Peabody a shopping bag.

'Oh, that's really nice, but we're not supposed to . . . '

She peeked in, all but moaned. 'It's alpaca,' she murmured, as if to a lover as she drew out skeins of soft blue, tender rose, cloudy white, and fine sand.

'Sherwood said an artist deserves good, fresh paint.'

'It's so thoughtful, so . . . nice. But I really can't.'

'I should add Sherwood owns the store – and the alpacas. He'd be very disappointed if you didn't accept.'

'I . . . '

'I'm looking the other way,' Eve grumbled.

'Really?'

'I'm walking out. If you see her,' Eve repeated, 'contact me.'

Peabody gathered the bag to her breasts. 'Please thank him for me. I can't wait to . . . I can't wait! And I'll be back – off duty.'

She rushed after Eve, too thrilled to remember to linger over the Egyptian cotton. 'Thanks.'

'I didn't give you anything, and I didn't see anything. And I don't want to hear about your new boyfriend.'

'He can be my yarn boyfriend. McNab will understand.'

'Where's the skank's apartment, and pull your damn nose out of the bag I don't see.'

'A block past where we parked.'

'Good, then you can put that bag I don't see and you're not carrying in the car before you fall into an alpaca coma.'

'I think I've had a couple of alpaca orgasms, but no coma.'

'Keep your weird wool orgasms to yourself.'

'Actually, it's hair – alpaca hair into fiber into—'

'Shut up, and put that damn bag I don't see in the car. She bought an extra yard,' Eve continued, 'because of the discount. So she falls for sales. Or she figured she'd use the other yard for something. She's not a regular, but she knew the place, heard about it, saw an ad, whatever, and hit it on a major sale day.'

Peabody secured the bag. 'It's covering her tracks. She doesn't think the cops are going to put it together, but just in case we do, she buys the material in a place where she's not familiar, and on a day not only for bargains, but crowds. When the clerks are slammed. The odds are, if we got this far, we'd dead-end. And that's where we are.'

'But smarter to buy something plain, something unre-markable we'd never have been able to trace to a vendor. She buys something unique, noticeable. Because under it all, she craves just that. Being noticed.

'It's a weakness. It'll break her down in the end.'

'If her next target's on the list of people we've notified, and if they actually listen, we'll have more time.' Peabody gestured toward a building.

'Working the names, I narrowed the clubs, too. They do club crawls and hit off-places, but mostly all of them stick to the hot spots.'

'Narrow those down by the book.' Eve opted to master her way into the building. 'It'll be licensed for consensual sex and have privacy rooms. Licensed for performance nudity – live performances, not holos. Add the high-dollar drinks, celebrity sightings, VIP sections.'

'I'll whittle it down.'

Considering the brownie she'd devoured, Peabody didn't complain even in her head about using the stairs. Plus Yola Bloomfield lived on the second floor.

Yola had decorated her door with a hex sign and an artful little drawing of two scaly skinned demons copulating.

'She paints,' Peabody explained. 'Calls her work Op-X-Art, as in the opposite of the expected.'

'On the other hand, that's just what I expect demons to do when they're not munching human intestines,' Eve pointed out. 'Unexpected would be to have them dancing under a rainbow in a meadow.'

She hit the buzzer.

'It could be a series,' Peabody considered. 'First they munch, then they dance, then they have demon sex.'

'Expected again. Standard date, any species.'

'I'm probably going to have nightmares.'

Eve buzzed again, longer.

On the second, she got a 'What the *fuck* do you *want*?' from the speaker.

'NYPSD.' She held up her badge. 'We need to speak with Yola Bloomfield.'

She heard the snick of locks, the rattle of chains, the slide of bolts.

If you dismissed the orange and black hair tied with some sort of rag on top of her head, the woman who opened the door didn't look like a skank.

She wore a shapeless, paint-splattered shirt over ragged jeans and ratty house skids. Other than the trio of hoops through her right eyebrow, her face was unadorned and unpainted.

She smelled of paint and soap.

'What the hell? I'm clean for four months, just had my regular test two days ago.'

'We're not here about illegals.'

'Good, because I haven't had so much as a puff of Zoner for four months. What do you want? I'm working.'

'If we can come in, we'll tell you, and get out of your way.'

'Fine. Fuck.'

She waved a hand, left the door open as she stalked away into a room she obviously used as her studio.

Rather than a sofa, a chair, a screen, or anything usually found in a living space, she had a long, burly workbench and a big shelf crowded with painting supplies. Easels, canvases, something green and cloudy in a tall, clear cup Eve took for solvent until Yola picked it up, gulped some down.

On the walls paintings and drawings of various forms of violence and misery crowded together. More demons (no rainbows), an enormous bat with the head of a man, a woman in a pool of blood at the feet of a hooded man, a winged woman running a forked tongue down the torso of a screaming woman in chains.

The one on the easel centered at the window still gleamed wet. A variety of crawling, flying, slithering things came out of a wide, jagged chasm in what appeared to be Times Square. The sky swirled red. People ran screaming while others were consumed.

'You can sit on the floor.'

'We'll stand.'

Yola shrugged, plopped on the single stool in the room. 'Look, I'm not so pissed off at the rehab shit. I did my ninety, and I'm not bitching about the unscheduled tests. I'm clean, and I'm working better because I'm clean. Clear mind. I'm drinking veg smoothies. Clean out the toxins, get healthy. I'm chilled.'

'Good for you. We're here because your name came up during the course of our investigation into two murders.'

'Fuck that!'

'You're not a suspect, Ms Bloomfield, but a potential target.'

'Fuck that squared.'

Peabody walked the photo over. 'Do you know or have you seen this woman?'

'Can't see her anyway, and does she look like somebody I'd hook with? I've got standards, and she's below the line.'

'She's already killed twice.'

258

'What's she got against me?'

'She's delusional, Ms Bloomfield.'

Eve held back, let Peabody take point.

'She's reenacting murder scenes from books.'

'No shit? Now that's iced.' Yola toasted with her veg smoothie. 'Serious performance art.'

'You won't admire the concept if you end up in the morgue.'

'Harsh.' Considering, Yola drank again. 'So what's my scene, what's my part? Death's the ultimate, sure, but I'm not going there yet.'

'The killer will be obsessed with your ex.'

'Which ex?'

'Stone Bailey.'

'The Stoner?' Yola let out a hard laugh. 'I haven't bumped uglies with him since I got busted. He's the reason I did, the asshole. And now that I'm clean, I got the big fuck-off from him. How about I tell this whack job she can have him. Not that she'll get the chance. He can't lay off the Zeus, can't lay off the tits and ass.' She gestured to the bat painting.

'I did that one to remind me. He's a fucking vampire.'

'In her mind you're preventing him from reaching his potential as a musician, as a man.'

'Bogus.'

'It won't matter. The character in the book poisons the victim in a club. She puts cyanide in a martini – a pomtini.'

Yola made gagging noises. 'I wouldn't drink that shit if I

was still using and stoned stupid. You're running the wrong way. I want to get back to work.'

'She won't look like she does in the picture,' Eve put in. 'When she moves on the person she's chosen to represent the character, she'll blend into the club scene. She's white, about five-six. She'll have red hair with blue side dreads. She'll have an orange dragon on the inside of her right wrist.'

'I don't care how she looks, she won't be looking at me.'

Yola started to drink again, stopped, slowly lowered the glass. 'Orange dragon?'

'That's right. You've seen her.'

'Orange dragon. It was fierce. I did some sketches.'

She hopped up, grabbed a couple of sketchbooks, pawed through. 'Yeah, yeah. Fierce. See?'

Eve looked down at the sketch of a dragon, keen teeth bared, lethal tail coiled to strike.

'Where did you see her?'

'I don't know. Maybe Hellfire, maybe Screw U. It could've been Dive Down. Look, I hit the clubs now and then. I don't use, and I've been keeping it to a couple brews. I go for inspiration, take my sketchbook. Yeah, I connect with people, and I've gotten a ram-bam. Nobody said I couldn't have sex, right? I hit one of the clubs two, three times a week, maybe bounce between. I'm going to say I saw Orange Dragon a couple weeks back, maybe.'

'Did you talk to her, go up to her?'

'No, I just sketched the tat. Only got a quick look, it seems to me. Any hot club's going to be jammed and canned. It could've been Styx. I mostly stick with those four, unless I hear there's going to be action somewhere else.'

'You're an artist,' Eve began.

'An Op-X-Artist.'

'Whatever, you notice details, faces, body types.'

'I look at the overview, see? Maybe you zoom in on something – like the tat – but mostly it's the blur and whirl, and you fill in the details from your mind, your guts.'

'Maybe you zoomed in on her around here, in the neighborhood, on the street.'

'The neighborhood's a false front.' Dismissing it, Yola flicked a hand at the window. 'I need something, I get it delivered. I got no reason to go out there until the sun's down. That's when the real world starts to live. I saw the tat. Orange tat, white skin. That's it.'

'Stay out of the clubs for a few weeks.'

'I tell you, I wouldn't drink her sick-ass pomtini.'

'She could find another way. Stay clean, stay away from the clubs, stay alive.'

Eve turned toward the door, stopped. 'You got a mother?'

'Sure I've got a mother. What the fuck?'

'Where's she stand with you?'

'My mom? Well, she was smart enough to tell me the Stoner was wrong, but hell, why would I listen? We've gone at it plenty, but she's proud I've got my four months in. Tags me every damn day. She doesn't give up.'

'In the book, the dead woman had a mother who didn't give up. Be smart, Yola. Stay out of the clubs.'

'Do you think she will?' Peabody asked as they walked downstairs.

'She's clean. She may stay clean, may not, but she's clean now, so her brain's clear enough to let her think twice. It all depends on where she ends up after she thinks twice.'

'I'm going to have nightmares for sure now, with all those paintings. She's good enough to make them really, really disturbing.'

'Death's the ultimate experience.' Hissing out a breath, Eve walked back into the bitter rain. 'What makes some people so damn interested in death?'

'Well, we are.'

Eve frowned as she walked. 'You've got a point. Look up the clubs she listed. See if any of them are open, or if you can tag a manager, an owner.'

They hit two clubs, three more skanks, one club manager, and two bartenders. They didn't get a nibble until the second bartender.

Brad Smithers tended bar at Screw U to finance his pursuit of his masters in political science. Twenty-three, buff, and black, he earned extra pay taking deliveries, stocking the shelves, and doing setups three afternoons a week.

'Plus it's a quiet space until about five and the crew starts rolling in. We open at five-thirty for the happy hour crowd, but things don't start hopping till after nine, and don't really heat up until more like eleven most nights.

'Hey, how about I fix you guys a fancy coffee? It's nasty out there.'

'Black works,' Eve said, but he winced.

'You want to trust me here, you don't want the java straight, not what we've got. But it works fine as a base when I fancy it up.'

'I wouldn't mind it,' Peabody said. 'It is nasty out there.'

'I like to talk while I work anyway.' He went behind the long, stylized U of the bar, began to program an AutoChef.

The lights, on full now, consisted of trios of screws with tips that appeared lethal should they fall and impale a customer.

The walls carried a dull shine and numerous photos of naked or mostly naked people in creative poses of debauchery. Booths and tables crowded in together, some with privacy domes, some with filmy curtains. The dance floor spread, another dull sheen in front of a currently empty stage.

Stairs corkscrewed up to the open second level where Eve could see some lounging sofas, sleep chairs, and doors to what would be the privacy rooms.

'Place shows better at night,' he commented as he took some bottles from under the bar, began to doctor up the coffee. 'For what it is. The lights start pumping, music starts grinding. We get some colorful characters, and they're part of the show.'

Eve laid the photo on the bar. 'Is she one of the colorful?'

He glanced at it while he sprinkled something onto the

thin froth topping the coffee. 'Going by the outfit, as that's about all you can go by, that's not the sort who patronizes this establishment.' He smiled when he said it. 'You might see her wander in during happy hour, look lost, and head out again.'

He set the coffee on coasters sporting a drawing of a screw and a large U.

Eve rattled off names of the women on her list.

'Those are the sort who patronize this establishment. Shanna was in last night. Yola earlier in the week. You never know when the Flash is going to show. Pops in and out or settles in and closes the place down. Are they in trouble?'

'Maybe. How about a woman, more thirties or even forties, white, red hair, blue side dreads, orange—'

'Dragon tat,' he finished.

'You've seen her.'

'Sits at the end of the bar.' He wagged his finger toward the other end of the bar. 'Drinks ... wait, I've got it.' He shut his eyes, hummed a moment. 'Virgin Moscow Mule. She makes one last.'

'The women I named? Does she interact with any of them?'

'I don't think she interacts much. Sits alone. I tried chatting her up once, like you do. She told me to fuck off. I fucked off. Now she sits at the other end of the bar, so I figure she's not here to chat.'

'How often does she come in?'

'Like I said, I've seen her a few times, and she might come

in on my nights off. I wouldn't even call her a semi-regular, but often enough I remember the hair, the tat.'

'Describe her otherwise.'

'Hell. I'd know her if she walked in, but . . . A white girl, like you said. Maybe on the thin side? A lot of skin showing, a lot of face paint. That's like a uniform in here.'

'She blends.'

'Yeah. Except most come in to hang out, to get trashed, to dance, to hook up. She sits by herself, so that stands out. It's why I got her when you started asking.'

'Would you work with a police artist?'

'Ah, sure, but I don't really have a picture in my head.'

'You'd be surprised. Peabody, get Yancy on this.'

'Got it. Can I just say, this is seriously mag coffee. Those touches of caramel and vanilla.'

He smiled, wide and pleased. 'Glad you like it. I did the barista thing as an undergrad. Tips here are way better.'

'Brad – and it is good coffee – if you see her in here, contact me. If she's in here and any of the women I named are in here, see if you can move them to a private space.'

'A lot of times they're here at the same time. Especially if we've got a headliner playing, you'll see most if not all of the regular rock chicks come in to hang.'

'Move them if you can. If the redhead orders a pom-tini, stall.'

Deep, dark eyes showed worry now, and a few nerves. 'You think she's going to hurt one of them? Which one?'

'It'd be easier if I knew. She's dangerous. Don't confront

her, tag me and pull in whatever security you've got. Are they any good?'

'I guess. They handle shit when shit comes down.'

'Let them handle her. I'm going to talk to your manager about passing the word on her, but you pass it to the other bartenders and waitstaff.'

'Yancy can be here in about an hour,' Peabody announced.

'We're going to be open by then. I'm supposed to—'

'This is important,' Eve told him. 'She's already killed two people.'

'Holy fuck.' He rubbed a hand over his hair. 'Holy fuck. I'll make it work.'

'I'm going to clear it with your manager. What do you do if she comes in?'

'Tag you, get security, try to move any of the rock chicks in here to . . . the kitchen's back there. The kitchen would be good, right?'

'It would.'

'And stall if she orders a pomtini – tell the rest of the crew. Don't fucking panic.'

'You've got it.'

Eve worked her way back to Central through the bitter insistence of the rain. She updated board, book, notes, pushed through some standard paperwork.

Then sat, coffee in hand, boots on desk.

Which one, she wondered. Which one of the women she'd spent a big chunk of her day talking to was the target? All of them fit the basic outline of the book's victim.

'How do you pick, Strongbow? Or does it even matter? Is this opportunity mixed in? Who's available when it's time to make your move?'

No, she thought, and got up to pace. That didn't fit the pathology. It would be more specific.

'She weeded it down, weeded all but one or two out. And one – maybe two – through the culling, the research, the opportunity, becomes Bliss Cather. One of them has to die.'

They'd caught a break with the bartender, but it was a damn sure bet she'd trolled other clubs. Watching, observing the one or two she'd picked out.

Eve went back to the board, studied the faces of the women Brad called rocker chicks. It wasn't looks, she thought, not when they were all so much of a type.

Behavior? They all lived on the edge, all actively pursued and embraced the same sort of lifestyle. Illegals, booze, indiscriminate sex, no healthy friendships or relationships, no actual jobs. Lives lived at night, reflected celebrity.

So what . . .

She stopped.

'The ex. It's the ex. He's the determining factor. To kill she has to love. Who does she love?'

She dived back to her desk, called up the names of the lovers, ex-lovers.

Which one? Which one most closely matched the one in the book?

On the first pass, she dropped two names down to low probability. One was firmly hooked with an actress and spending a lot of time in New L.A., the other on tour in Europe.

You had to see what you loved, Eve thought.

She studied the others, found them much the same, like their female counterparts.

She needed the book again, she decided. Something might pop for her – just as it had for Strongbow.

She grabbed her things, stopped by Peabody's desk on the way out.

'I'm working from home – you can do the same. You've got a copy of *Dark Deeds*?'

'Yeah.'

'Go through it, make notes on the ex – on the motive. What is it about him? Compare with the list we have from the women we've talked to. Something had to click with Strongbow. Something about him. Let's find it.'

'Not the victim, the motive. I'll start on it here, take it home when McNab gets off. I've got the audio function. You know, I'll program it for his scenes, listen to it. Listening might make something jump.'

'Try it. She fell in love with one of them. That's her reality now, especially now that she's living in that book. The others are over. It's time for *Dark Deeds*.'

15

Little pellets of ice *ping*ed on the windshield as Eve pushed through skittish, sliding, angry traffic. She spotted a couple of pedestrians with tiny icicles dripping from umbrellas and decided as bad as it was, at least she was traveling in a heated car.

Stopped at a light, she watched a pair of beat cops in pursuit of some guy — early twenties, mixed race, flapping brown overcoat — who loped like a gazelle down the sidewalk.

Until he hit a slick spot, went airborne. His feet flew up, his ass crashed down. Before he could scramble up again, the beat boys had him.

Score one for Team Blue, she thought as the light changed.

Once she drove through the gates, she could appreciate the fanfare of icicles shimmering on the bare branches of trees, enclosing the shrubbery in glitter and gleam, all forming a fairy-tale foreground for the stone, the towers, the turrets, the glass all spreading and rising under that angry bruise of a sky.

She appreciated more actually getting in the house

without falling on her own ass. The cat rose from his perch at the base of the steps, stretched from head to tail, then padded over to wind and snake between her legs like a well-fed boa constrictor.

'Did I beat him home again?' She tossed her coat, hat, and scarf over the newel post, crouched down to give Galahad a scratch and rub.

'Straight to work mode, pal.'

With the cat trailing her, she walked to the library first. She considered the appeal of sitting on the sofa, feet up, fire going, then accepted she'd work faster in her office.

She took a stack of books, hauled them with her.

After setting them on her command center, she updated her board. Then she expanded it, used the new section for ID shots of what she termed 'Motive – *Dark Deeds*.'

As the ice *ping*ed and sizzled against the windows, she ordered the fire on, programmed a pot of coffee.

She settled in, read an early scene between the future victim and the motive, made notes.

Public fight, club/crime scene. Victim trashed/motive half-trashed. Ugly words, threats on both sides. Public fight reported on gossip channels, with video.

She searched the real rockers' gossip history. Rubbed her eyes when she found every single one had a reflective incident.

She moved to the murder scene, also early in the book. Same club, different night, but many of the same characters.

Victim trashed again, and bad-mouthing motive, who

sits in another section pretending to ignore her. Victim hits the dance floor – so does motive. Victim rubs suggestively against several available men – and a couple women – all while watching motive. Victim and motive dance, simulating sex. Victim goes back to her table, pops a little Erotica, brags that she'll have motive up in a privacy room, how she can lead him by the cock wherever she wants him.

Lots of bodies, lots of noise, flashing lights, pounding music. Victim picks up the fresh, blood-hued martini, takes a couple of big gulps. Continues to brag – lots of laughing from her little group of sycophants.

Trouble breathing, drinks more. Gales of laughter as victim starts to lose consciousness. Screams and scrambling when she vomits. Motive tries to push through crowd to get to victim. Seizures, skin turns cherry-red.

Chaos, confusion. One figure back in the shadows observes, then slips out of the club and away.

Will the killer – in real life – need to find a way to have the motive present?

Eve went back to her list, checked residency, band schedule. She found four slated to be in New York over the next few weeks. And yet, she thought as she read a few follow-up scenes with the motive . . .

Having him there, making him a part of the death of the ex-lover triggered emotions in him. Seeing her die shattered him, pushed him into grief and depression. Rather than giving the killer what she wanted – his attention and love, his salvation – it built a wall around him.

Would Strongbow edit that *mistake*? Eve wondered.

She rose to pace, to give her eyes a break, to work her way into thinking like a killer whose entire being sprang from the pages of a book.

By having him in the club, the killer – in the book – failed to achieve her primary goal. The motive didn't come to her, love her, throw off what she saw as the chains the victim had around him, dragging him down into the abyss. In fact, rather than weaning him off illegals, he used them to block the grief, and missed recording sessions and canceled a swath of tours.

Until the cat ran out of the room, until she heard Roarke's voice answer the cat's greeting, she hadn't realized the low-level stress inside her.

She'd wanted him home, off those icy roads. Safe and with her.

She didn't run out of the room like the cat, but she did walk out and wrap her arms around Roarke. 'It's bad out there.'

'It's bloody vicious out there.' He tipped her head back for a kiss, skimming his thumb over the dent in her chin. 'And now we're all in here. And in this world, at this moment, I want nothing more than my cop, my cat, to get out of his shagging suit, and have a very large drink.'

'A hard one?'

'Not particularly, no. Well, but for the bleeding weather. A quick trip to Chicago, or what would've been quick but for the bleeding weather.'

'You went to Chicago?'

'Should've handled it by holo, and that'll teach me. Getting there, simple enough. Getting back? Not altogether pleasant.'

And, she thought, he'd have stayed over in Chicago if not for her. She considered her own skidding ride home in the ice storm, and didn't want to imagine flying through it in a shuttle.

'I'll deal with dinner while you change.'

'Will you?'

She heard the world of suspicion in his voice.

'It won't be pizza. But this is the last time it won't be pizza.'

'What will it be then?'

'I'll figure it out.'

Easing back, he rubbed his hands down her arms. 'A hard one?'

'I'll tell you about it over that big drink.'

'That sounds exactly right. I won't be long.'

She turned back to her board, conceded she'd done little to narrow the field. Then again, the weather — 'bloody vicious' nailed it — lowered the chances of her potential victims braving it for a club night. It seemed to her the killer would conclude the same.

They should all have a little more time, she decided, and went into the kitchen to consider dinner choices.

By the time he came back in black pants and a blue sweater, she had the meal under warming domes and a bottle of wine opened.

'Now this is our version of cozy on a cold and filthy night. I'm grateful for it,' he added as he took the wine.

'Why Chicago?'

'Hmm? Ah, we've just finished up a major rehab to one of the hotels, and I'd scheduled the visit, some media and so forth, before this front moved in.'

'You could've stayed in the major rehab overnight.'

He danced those clever fingers down her arm. 'Then I wouldn't have my cop and my cat. Unless you're starved, why don't we just sit in front of that very nice fire for a bit?'

'I was worried,' she confessed. 'I didn't know I was worried until I wasn't, but I was.'

'Well, I'm sorry for that. I'm not late home,' he added as they sat on the sofa.

'The weather, I guess. The day.' She shrugged it off.

'And what was the day?'

'It was the Day of the Skanks and the Strange Interlude of the Crafts.'

'Obviously, I want to hear about the skanks, at the very least.'

'What perv wouldn't?'

So she told him, punched in what she'd learned at the craft store, from the bartender, and ended with the morbid artist.

'But it's not about them — the possible victims. Not as much about them as the rocker guy. The motive. The killer's obsessive love — and it's not really love — is what drives her.'

'Which is why you have all those new faces on the board.'

'The trouble is, they're not much different from one

another. Physical appearance, sure, but they're a type. The image, the lifestyle. In the book, she kills the obstacle while he's present. But that's just one of the ways she went wrong, so I don't think that's going to be a factor for Strongbow. Unless . . . '

'Unless some part of her maintains enough reality to know the obsession ends for her after the murder. The murder is the goal.'

'Yeah. Trying to think like her gives me a damn headache. Add the fact that she's certainly laid the groundwork for the book after this one, so she has to shift those realities. From this obsessed skanky fan type to the saintly, obedient son – who's really a greedy bastard – who kills his wealthy mother and pins it on his screwup of a sister. And how does she pull that off anyway?'

'It's no wonder it gives you a headache.'

'Under it all, whoever she coats herself in, she's one woman. And that woman knows how to sew, watches her pennies, came from Delaware. Lives alone. Is likely in her forties. If I get a sketch out of that bartender, it's going to turn this around. Whatever mask she puts on to haunt the clubs, she's going to show through.'

'You said the bartender described her as a loner, and not very friendly. But in the book, as I recall those scenes, people knew her by name.'

'Yeah, she was part of that scene in the book. I figure either Strongbow couldn't pull that off, or she saw it as a mistake in the plot. The killer blends, but goes unnoticed.

Except the bartender noticed and remembered her, because she didn't really blend.'

'Or can't,' Roarke suggested. 'Think of the woman you described. She sews, watches her pennies, is likely twenty years older than many in the club, she lives through books. The writing and the reading.'

'She doesn't know how,' Eve mused. 'It's not hard to figure out how to book a street-level LC. You can be nervous, look out of place. They don't care, and they get all kinds. Anybody can sit in the dark at a vid.'

'But weaving yourself into a club scene, and these particular kinds of clubs?' As she did, Roarke studied the board. 'It's more than being able to craft a reversible coat or doctor a drink. It's attitude, it's vernacular.'

'A woman sitting alone at the bar at that kind of place, she's going to get hit on by somebody who figured to get laid up in a privacy room. She can't do that, not even living inside the character. Not just because she needs to observe, but she can't get that personal and stay unnoticed.'

'The fuck-off tends to discourage most.'

'Yeah, especially since there are plenty in there who'll give you a roll with less effort. She's already altered the character there.'

Rising, Eve walked back to her board. 'Still, one of these has to be the object. The vic is the obstacle. It's not going to matter if he's on scene at the killing, but *he* matters. Until he doesn't.'

'Why don't we eat, then I'll see if I can help you find him?'

'Yeah. I've got Peabody on it, too.'

Roarke lifted the domes. 'This looks dead perfect. What is it?'

'It said pork and beer stew. I figured if there's beer it'd neutralize the vegetables.' And she'd programmed a single bowl first, prepared to ditch it if it looked awful. It hadn't, and the smell had done the rest.

'I fed the cat while I was in there,' she added, which explained why Galahad was currently sprawled in her sleep chair in a kibble-with-tuna-chaser coma.

She sampled some stew, decided the beer did help the healthy parts go down easy.

'You know, Nadine's hooked with that rock guy. Maybe he knows some of those guys.'

'Possibly, though I don't think Kincade or the band's played the small club scene in more than a decade. Big venues, major tours. "Hooked with"?' he asked. 'Going out a time or two doesn't necessarily lead to the "hooked with", does it?'

'I had her come in for a one-on-one today, and I poked her a little about him. She got flustered and ... girl-like. Maybe I'm not supposed to say how she was and what she said about it. She didn't say, "Don't say how I was or what I said," but maybe it's supposed to be understood.'

Trying to walk that minefield gave Eve another headache.

'One of those stupid unwritten rules,' she complained, 'which make them impossible to keep track of.'

Because he knew her, Roarke followed the convoluted

logic. 'Before you tangle yourself up in the invisible, I have to say it's already too late. So, she fancies him then?'

'I guess – if that means she's got some hots going for him, in American.'

'It does. We could have them to dinner sometime. And you could grill him like a trout.'

Maybe she'd enjoy that, maybe she would. But . . . 'She's all grown up and capable of making her own decisions on who she's banging and hooked with. Besides . . . ' Eve ate more stew.

'You ran him, didn't you now?'

'Yeah, sure. So?'

He laughed, grabbed her hand to kiss it. 'I'd say having a man you may be or become serious about run by a cop when that cop is your friend is one of those unwritten rules.'

'It ought to be actually written down somewhere, if you ask me.'

'Either way. Well then, let's have it. Do we have to worry about our Nadine being hooked with a scoundrel?'

She pointed at him with her spoon. 'That's a fancy word, and it comes off like a compliment. Jake Kincade was arrested about fifteen years ago for assault, disturbing the peace, and destruction of property. All charges were dropped, as numerous witness statements, and three videos – as some people in the bar where this occurred got right on that – clearly showed the drunk asshole he eventually ass-kicked dogging him, then taking a couple of swings. Which Kincade avoided. It also showed Kincade turning his back on said drunk asshole, walking away, just as it showed the asshole jumping him from behind, and getting in a couple of rabbit punches before Kincade shoved him off. At which time the asshole grabbed a chair, threw it at Kincade, went back for more. Then, and only then, did Kincade kick his ass, which thoroughly deserved it.'

He caught the admiration in her tone, understood it. Agreed with it. 'So, he can handle himself.'

'Sounds like. Other than that, no arrests. A lot of speeding tickets. A serious lot of speeding tickets – all over hell and back. He bought his mother a house.'

'Is that so?'

'When their first recording hit pretty big, he bought his mother a house. All five original band members are still with it, and two of them have been pals with him – and each other – since they were kids. One of them's done a couple of stints in rehab, had some bumps, but not Kincade. He's never been married, but he did cohab with a woman – same woman – for about six years. That's been off for almost as long. He owns a converted warehouse downtown – I bet it's not bollocks coincidence that it's on Avenue A – and outfitted it into a recording studio. He lives there, too.'

She shrugged. Roarke smiled.

'You're all right with it then?'

'It's not for me to be all right with it or not. And if Nadine didn't check him out, I'll eat raw turnips for a week.'

'I think you and turnips are safe there, as I agree with you.'

'Back to the point, he might know something about these guys that doesn't show on a run. The attitude, the personal choices that don't rise up to data. I could tap Nadine about tapping him on it, so it's not weird.'

'Is she happy?'

'I guess. Off her stride some, but she still landed the one-on-one where we aimed it. And I'm hoping that throws Strongbow off stride some. She's – shit, I forgot – she took Quilla on. Quilla, the kid from Higher Power.'

'She . . . ' Obviously surprised, he sat back a moment with his wine. 'Nadine's fostering a teenage girl? That's considerably more than off her stride.'

'No, no, hired her. Or whatever it's called. As an intern. She wanted to mentor somebody, so—'

'I recall that now, remember her saying something about that. And you telling her you might have someone in mind. You had Quilla in mind.'

'Struck me, that's all. Smart kid, pushy but smart – and so's Nadine. Smart and pushy. Anyway, she brought the kid with her to my office. Quilla said they had a tour of the new shelter.'

'There's been enough progress for it, and we've the core of the staff hired.'

'She was juiced about it, about it being ready in a couple months. But the memorial on the roof, that meant a lot. She snuck away from the group – no surprise there. But she did it to stay up there awhile because it meant a lot.'

'That's good to know. You may have changed her life by pointing her at Nadine.'

'That's up to them.'

'It is, yes, but you did the pointing. You gave them both the choice. Summerset changed my life, then you turned it yet again. The badge changed yours.'

'Yeah, then you turned it again. Pretty much upside down.'

'We've righted ourselves, darling Eve. Won't it be interesting to see where these new connections, relationships, take Nadine?'

She started to speak, then turned around in her chair to look at the board. 'The skank list – they tend to know each other, compete or hang. Go to the same clubs, shop in the same shops, frequent the same restaurants or events. It's like that with the motive list. They're all in the same business, more the same subset of that business. There's going to be overlap on who's laying who. In the book, the victim and the motive had – or had had – a serious, if twisted and unhealthy, relationship. At the same time . . .'

She got up, walked to the board. 'The killer – our killer – isn't a part of that world like the character of the killer in the book. She's absorbed the role, but her experience is limited. Peabody called this group skanks because they basically are. They dress like it, act like it, fuck around like it. Peabody – Free-Ager, cop, monogamous relationship. Sews, crafts, bakes. She's a cop, a good one, and she knows how the world works, knows what's in it, but still, she's outside this particular world. So when she looked at a group like this, she puts them together in one lump of skank.'

'Interchangeable, you're saying.'

281

'Yeah. She knows better, and she knows how to separate them into individuals. But Strongbow? They're all the same.'

'You think it won't matter which? She'd kill any of them?'

'I think I was off figuring she focused on one here, two at the most. I think we find out which ones have had a thing – even just a quick bang-in-the-dark thing – with more than one of the motives. Crossover. It's still the motive who matters. But maybe, maybe any one of these who present the opportunity would do.'

'How would you begin to find out how many of these wankers – because Christ, they all look at least a bit like wankers – each individual woman has shagged?'

'I start by asking them. They'll brag about it. It's a badge of honor in Skankdom.'

'Visited Skankdom, have you?'

'With a badge and in the line. I'm going to contact them, start working on a cross-reference. You could take a look at the wankers, dig down a bit. Give me your take on which ones have the most potential. Musically, creatively. The guy in the book has some actual charm, talent, and that potential. Unless he's too busy smoking, swallowing, guzzling, or popping whatever illegals come to hand – and chasing them down with a whole bunch of alcohol. Then he's a dick.'

'So – to clarify,' Roarke said. 'I'm rating the wankers on their level of potential as musicians and human beings if and when they cease the smoking, swallowing, guzzling, popping, and chasing themselves into a dick?'

'Yeah. Oh, and sex. Another addiction.'

On that, Roarke pushed up from the table. 'Sex, drugs, and rock and roll. What an interesting way to spend our evening.'

Eve sat down and started at the top of her list by contacting Loxie Flash.

About ten minutes after Eve got a bang-brag list from Loxie and moved on to the next on the list, Loxie lit up a joint of Zoner, poured a glass from the bottle of top-shelf vodka she'd stolen at a party, and switched on the porn channel.

She hated winter in New York and wondered why the hell she wasn't in St Barts. The fact that her finances were, at the moment, a little squeezed added to her foul mood.

So fuck it, she'd head out to naked beaches in the morning. She could always hitch a ride on a private shuttle, talk Petra at the Beach House into a suite in exchange for some publicity.

Bored, irritated by the skinny cop, and since she'd reeled off all those sex partners, itchy, she reached for her 'link to start wrangling a ride and some digs in sunnier climes.

It *ping*ed in her hand with an incoming text.

Hey bitch where u at? Got r jam going @ Screw U. Place is banging & I scored some prime. Guess who just walked in with a couple hos? G-man, u guessed it. Come on slut time 2 party.

Loxie took another pull of Zoner, drew deep as she considered. If Janis was there, probably most of the usual crew was, too, because Janis was too lame to party without the usual.

Still, she thought of the cold, the ice, the effort of pulling herself away from Zoner, vodka, and porn, getting herself dressed and sexed – mega-style, since her ex turned up.

A lot of work.

The warning about staying out of clubs, about poison and all that bullshit played through her mind. But the idea of pumping Janis – the bitch had the rich – for that private ride trumped all.

She left the porn running on-screen because now that itch felt real good, now she'd pick some lucky bitch or bastard to scratch it.

She answered the text.

B there in an hour. Save me a party favor.

Yola Bloomfield tossed her 'link aside and brooded. She wasn't going to feel guilty for confessing – that's what you did to cops – she'd cheated on the Stoner a few times.

Not all of it was cheating anyway. Sometimes they'd been on a break, and once they'd gotten trashed at some after-party and had had a free-for-all.

Besides, the Stoner had cheated right back.

And she was clean now, and mostly sober.

She studied the painting she'd just finished, decided it spoke to the inevitability of death, and the suffering that preceded it. The dark choices that made the suffering and the inevitability worthwhile.

She decided she really wanted a beer. Even if a lone beer in her empty apartment often made everything echo inside her head.

She shuffled in to check the friggie, cursed. She'd meant to get some brew delivered, but she'd gotten caught up in her work. And now that she didn't have a single brew in the place, she wanted one even more.

She could go out – screw the weather – get that brew, hear some noise, some music, do some sketching, and maybe inspire her next piece.

Stay out of the clubs, the hard-eyed cop had ordered. Well, screw that, too. She did what she wanted when she wanted.

When her 'link signaled, she walked back, checked the text.

From that semi-idiot and overeager rich bitch Janis, she noted.

Maybe it was a sign, urging her to hit Screw U for a couple hours.

She could get a brew and smother all the echoes.

Eve sat back in her chair, pressed her fingers to her eyes. 'Cock and Balls,' she said.

Roarke glanced over from his station at the auxiliary. 'Is that a request? As I'm nearly done here and happen to have those items handy.'

She lowered her hands. 'Who'd think a woman who

wears cock-and-balls earrings would come off as the least skanky and most sensible on the list so far?'

'I couldn't say. How large were they, these particular accessories?'

'Big enough. And yet she says she's only had sex with three on our list, though she "messed steamy" – her words – with two others.'

'Perhaps, though her jewelry choices belie, she's being modest and/or discreet.'

'No. She's too scared to lie about it, and is even now huddled up at her mother's place in New Jersey. Sexy Bitch, on the other hand, claims to have had sex with all of them, and some at the same time. She might be lying.'

'Sexy Bitch.'

'Tattooed,' Eve said, swiping her fingers over her chest.

'I suppose no one ever pointed out to her that if you have to announce you are, you simply aren't. But you do meet the most fascinating people in the course of your day, Lieutenant.'

'I'm going to meet more tomorrow because I'm going to have to track down and talk to all the male skanks. I'm not through my list yet and there's not one of the rockers who hasn't been done by multiples on my list. It's not the sex.'

'Well now,' Roarke began.

'No, it's the score. The act, sure, the literal bang, but it's the racking them up. And racking them up fills a void. I get sex just for the bang, and what's wrong with that?'

'I can think of literally nothing as long as it's consensual.'

'These women, Cock and Balls, the Sexy Bitch? They might hook with one of those for a short amount of time, sometimes a short and intense amount, but they'll still look for the bang with someone else. None of it's real. A few of them — Loxie, Yola, that level? It's more a roller coaster. They're hooked longer, tighter. There might actually be something there. Not necessarily a good something or a healthy something, but something. Still, they guzzle illegals and booze — another void to fill. And, like the character of Bliss Cather in the book, live in deliberate disregard for others. Fight with their chosen counterpart in public because that gets them off, too. Playing for the crowd, reading about it later, seeing vids on the gossip channels.'

'And Strongbow observes.'

'Yeah, she observes, and most likely concludes the women are — because they come off that way — interchangeable. All of them offer the wrong things, destructive things, to the man she's selected as above, as better, as one worthy of her — of the character she's living in, of the writer she believes herself to be. Remove one — one she judges as influential — and he has the chance to reach that worthy potential.

'And I'm circling,' Eve admitted. 'Because none of this points me at her.'

'Circling maybe, but you're thinking like her.'

'I'm thinking like I think she thinks,' Eve amended, 'but she's slippery. Because she's crazy.'

'You've bagged the crazy before, Lieutenant. You'll bag her.'

'Penguin coats and blue dreads, a personality so malleable

it absorbs itself into fictional characters. But I damn well will bag her. Give me what you've got so far on the rockers.'

'It's a subjective and unscientific sort of ranking.'

'I'll take what you've got. Top pick.'

'At this stage, that would be Glaze, aka Adam Glazier, lead guitar and vocals for the Glaze.'

'Loxie Flash's ex.' Swiveling toward the board, his photo, she frowned. 'I'd have slotted him in loser territory.'

'You have to dig down a bit. Financially, he's very solvent.'

'So trash rockers make big bucks. What—'

'Many blow those big bucks on illegals, overpriced homes, and vehicles. They live carelessly, engage poor management, and so on. Take Nadine's Jake as a yardstick.'

'I don't know if he's Nadine's Jake.'

'For simplicity's sake. He bought his mother a house – that qualifies him as a good and loving son, but also a man with enough brains not to buy her some flash jewelry, for instance. To think of her security, her future. While he certainly engages managers, he also remains involved and aware. Glazier hasn't bought his mother a house.'

'Okay.'

'But he has purchased a condo in New York, his base in the city. And while he tosses money about, he also culls a sensible percentage out to invest, with a reputable money manager. He hasn't, using Jake again, maintained friends and bandmates over long terms, as he's fronted two bands prior to this, but Glaze is being handled professionally. He's been dinged more than once for possession, and apparently developed a taste for Zeus in the last turbulent months of his relationship with this Loxie. While he has had court-ordered rehab, he entered, voluntarily, a facility in Zurich four months ago. And upon his return to New York, during the recording of a new album — with reportedly all of the songs written or cowritten by him during his treatment — he's continued with addiction therapy and meetings.'

'Okay, good potential here. Is he in New York now?'

'He is, recording — and in the small-world department — the Glaze is using East Side Sound — that's Jake Kincade's studio.'

'Okay, I'll talk to him in the morning.'

She grabbed her 'link when it chirped. 'Dallas.'

'She's here!' The harsh whisper hissed under a wall of noise. 'The blue dreads. Lieutenant? It's Brad Smithers. I just saw her.'

Eve was already up and moving. 'Don't approach. Tap your own security, have them block exits. I'm on my way.'

'To where?' Roarke asked as he grabbed a coat.

'A dive called Screw U, downtown. She's there.'

Roarke snagged her hat and scarf, as she was already striding out the door and calling for uniforms.

16

Before she walked into the club, Loxie popped a tab of Buzz. She had a few more tabs at home, and a decent supply of Erotica. But she'd dip on Janis for the party favors, and save her own for that trip to the islands.

Her mood bounced straight up – the Buzz and the crowds, the screaming music, the flash and swirl of lights.

People, so many people who knew her, wanted her, envied her.

She made it a point to scan for Glaze, spotted him at one of the VIP booths. Not just the hos, she noted, but his bass player, his hard-eyed manager, and a third pair of tits she didn't recognize.

The minute she saw him grin at the pair of tits, lean toward her so they could share a laugh, she decided he'd be the one to scratch her itch.

She swirled off her coat. She'd gone bare-legged with a glittery, short, snug, crotch-skimming skirt and a top that opened in a vee down to her navel. Thick chains draped into the vee and hooked to the nipple clamps clearly outlined beneath the top.

She'd damn near frozen on the trip to the club, but knew Glaze had a weakness for tits – and he'd given her the chains and clamps.

He would remember what they'd done with them.

She slithered through the crowd on chunky short boots with high, curved heels.

When he saw her, when their eyes met and held for just a couple beats, her nipples hardened against the clamps like shards of glass.

'Hey there, G-man.'

'Lox. How's it going?'

'Up, up, and away.'

She had to shout it – the music's volume demanded it. She leaned over the table, leading with that deep vee, pursed her red-to-the-edge-of-black lips in an exaggerated kiss.

'Haven't seen you around.'

'Haven't been around.'

'Yeah, another detox, right? I need a drink.' She picked up his glass, downed some. 'Jesus, WTF.'

'Mineral water, twist of lemon.' He took the glass back from her, set it aside.

'How the mighty have fallen. You get up off that fine ass and want to live again, I'm over there.'

She hip-swung her way to another booth where Janis and some of the usual crowd piled together.

'Hey, Lox. I wondered if you'd show up tonight.'

'I said I would, didn't I?' She screwed her ass between two others, slouched back, angled toward Glaze's booth. Spread her legs.

Her smug smile faded when she glanced toward his booth, saw he not only wasn't looking, he had his head together with the new tits.

In retaliation, she laid her hand on the cock of the man beside her, gave it a teasing squeeze. 'Who do I have to fuck to get a drink and a tab?'

She grabbed a drink off the table at random, downed it. And didn't see the woman with the blue dreads come out of the shadows to sit at the end of the bar.

Loxie hit the obliging Janis for another tab of Buzz, pulled the obliging cock – Bennie, she remembered, maybe Bernie – onto the dance floor. Pushed through the twisting, grinding bodies so she'd be in Glaze's line of sight.

She turned her back to her partner, ground her ass into his crotch, arched and gleamed when his hands slid over her breasts, tugged lightly at the chains.

When Glaze looked at her this time, she slithered up and down the body behind her, ran the tip of her tongue over her lips. And, lowering her hand in front of her crotch, curled her fingers in invitation.

His eyes didn't fire with lust, as they always did. Instead . . . Was that fucking pity? she thought. Enraged, she nearly leaped to his booth, vicious words ready to scream from her throat. She stoked the rage by spinning around, grinding crotch to crotch, grinding mouth to mouth, fully aware that more than one clubgoer had pulled out a 'link to record the moment.

Everyone would see – every-fucking-body would see. She was known, wanted, envied.

She listened, blood cold, as Bennie or Bernie or whoever the hell he was told her all the things he wanted to do to her.

'Later. I need that drink.'

She cast a look over her shoulder on the way back to the booth, but Glaze wasn't watching her. In fact, he signaled for the check.

Leaving, she thought. Let him. Fuck him. She nudged the hands groping and pawing all over her away.

'I said later.' Snatching up the martini glass filled with deep red, she drained it dry with a long series of swallows.

She heard the shout-out to the Glaze as the band kicked into one of their hits.

Perfect, she thought. Now she had to listen to that shit when . . .

A woman moved, just for a moment, into her field of vision. Red hair, blue side dreads. All the layers of enhancements couldn't disguise the fact she'd already hit the 4-0 mark.

Old bitch, smug smile, fucking crazy eyes. She started to shoot her the finger, started to demand another drink, another tab.

And it all came flooding back.

Poison. Pomtini. Stay out of the clubs.

'No.' She croaked it out, grabbed her dance partner, tried to scream.

He took it for an invitation, began to dry hump her while the laughter rose, the music screamed.

Her gasps for breath only made the man with his hand up her skirt moan.

Then the music faded; the lights dimmed.

When she went limp, Bennie – it was Bennie – tried to haul her up.

'Fuck, she passed out.'

He dumped her back on the booth. Unconscious, essentially already dead, she rolled onto the floor and began to seize.

The woman who currently embodied Bliss Cather's killer smiled, satisfied. Vindicated. She turned away, caught the stunned, horrified stare of the bartender.

He looked straight at her, into her. And had a 'link in his hand. When he shouted something, something drowned in the music, she snatched a coat off the back of the dead woman's booth and sprinted away.

Not toward the front. The bartender continued to shout, to gesture now. And to her own shock leaped over the bar to push through people, to push in her direction.

She turned sharply, slammed into the kitchen, ran through and out the back. Kept running, running, shot around a corner, dragged on the coat.

A coat that turned out to be a hip-length fur – mink! – with a hood.

She ran another block, turned another corner.

She dragged at the dreads, yanking them – and some of her own hair – off. She slowed her rush long enough to shove them in a recycler. And pulling the fur hood over bold red hair, shed the character.

Strongbow walked through the icy night, stroking the fur.

She thought: To the victor go the spoils.

Eve walked into chaos and knew it was too late. Just as she knew whose body she'd find. Loxie Flash had been the only one on the list who hadn't answered her 'link as Roarke raced over the icy roads downtown.

She badged the big bulk of the bouncer. 'Stay on the door,' she told him, and shoved her way to the first uniform she spotted.

'I want this scene secured.'

'We're trying, Lieutenant. We've got close to three hundred and fifty in here, and a lot of them are drunk, a lot are stoned, a lot are both. I just called for more uniforms.'

'Tap Dispatch for Officer Carmichael out of Central, and his partner.'

'Got it. We've got two men on the DB, got people moved back from there. Looks like an OD. Somebody called the MTs, but she was already gone. LT, the bartender – ah, Brad Smithers – claims you told him to BOLO for a woman with red hair, blue side dreads. Says he saw her, tagged you.'

'That's correct.'

'We've got him over there. But he stated she took off.

He'd just alerted security, and they were on the main door. She caught on to him, he thinks, and she took off the other way. He tried to pursue. She went out the kitchen – again, according to his statement. He didn't see a trace of her by the time he hit the back door.'

Eve nodded, continuing to push through. She found some relief the body had been blocked off, and two uniforms kept the area clear. Someone had covered the body with a long, black leather coat.

As it was bound to be death by poison, she opted not to grind her teeth over the possible screwing with trace and forensics.

She lifted the coat enough to verify the victim, then called it in, with a request to notify her partner.

'Your field kit, Lieutenant.' Roarke held it out to her.

'Hold on to that a minute. I need to establish some damn order in here first.'

She elbowed her way to the stage. Some guy in leather pants and nothing but tats to his waist stepped up to block her.

'You can't touch the equipment.'

She tapped her badge.

'Yeah, but still.'

'I need one of those mics. You want to get out of here sometime before dawn you can get me one, set it up.'

'I can do that.'

He got her one that curled over her ear.

'You're hot. The mic's hot, I mean,' he said quickly.

Eve stepped onto the stage, and even with the mic, had to bellow.

'I'm Lieutenant Dallas, NYPSD. I need everybody to shut the hell up. Knock it off! The sooner you cooperate, the sooner we can get your information and let you leave.'

'Fucking police state!' somebody shouted.

'It's a crime scene and, while we have adequate facilities at Cop Central, I doubt most of you want to spend the night in the tank. I doubt most of you want to submit to a personal search, then find yourselves charged with possession.'

'Narc bitch!'

'Homicide bitch,' Eve corrected. 'One who'd be happy to take each and every one of you into Interview and question you regarding the death of Loxie Flash.'

'Loxie!' Someone screamed it, then began to sob loudly enough to drown out the complaints.

Eve shifted, subtly laid a hand on her weapon when the man she recognized as Glaze from his ID shot approached.

'I might be able to help calm them down. They know me.'

He looked tired, she thought. Sad. Resigned. But not threatening.

When she nodded, he got another mic, joined her on the stage.

Inexplicably to Eve, a wild cheer erupted through the crowd.

'Don't do that.' He didn't raise his voice, but held up a hand. 'Don't do that,' he repeated. 'This isn't the time for that. Most of you knew Lox. I'm asking you to show some respect. Just chill it off, okay? Chill it off, and let's get through this.'

'I need everyone to sit down, keep it down,' Eve told them. 'Officers are going to take your information and statements. You'll be released in an orderly fashion.'

She pulled off the mic, turned to Glaze. 'Adam Glazier, right?'

'Yeah.'

'I'm going to need you to stay. I need to speak with you, but we need to move the bulk of these people out.'

'Sure.'

She gave instructions to the uniforms, then moved to where Brad Smithers sat at the end of the bar.

'I saw her – the redhead. I saw her, but it was too late.'

'You did what you could. You did right. Loxie didn't listen. Tell me how it went.'

'Okay.' He blew out a breath, sucked another in. 'I was kind of keeping an eye out, and I passed the word, like you said to. We were busy. A lot of people came in because the city asked people to stay home. It's like a red flag, you know?'

'Yeah, I know.'

'I took my break, went back to the kitchen, got some chow. Loxie must've come in when I was on break. Probably did. I didn't see her come in. I just heard a couple people talking about how she was making moves on Glaze, and he wasn't having any. Then I saw the redhead. I saw her at the end of the bar. I didn't see her before, or see her come in.'

She was just there. It was crowded, so she could've slipped by me. If I'd—'

'No ifs, Brad. You saw her, you tagged me.'

'Like, right then, I swear. It took me a minute to get to Malted – that's our bouncer. A couple minutes. And when I got back. Jesus, when I got back she – Loxie – she was on the floor. Convulsing. I was going to go over to her, like you said to, and maybe move her to my station at the bar, but . . .'

He scrubbed his hands over his face. 'I was going to tag nine-one-one when I saw Loxie on the floor. And the redhead was standing there, watching. She saw me – the redhead. She saw me seeing her, and she took off. I tried to yell for Malt, but he couldn't hear me. I tried to run after her, but I got hung up. Back door's through the kitchen, so I figured that. I asked when I ran in, and they said she'd gone straight out the back. I wasn't fast enough. I lost her.'

He swiped at his eyes. 'I've never seen anybody die before. It's bad. Man, it's bad. I couldn't even give the artist cop a decent description. But I can now.' He swiped again. 'I got a good look at her, good enough, and I've got it in my head. It's weird light in here, but I got a good look.'

'Can you come into Central, work with him tomorrow?'

'Yeah. I can come in first thing. I'm sure as hell not going to sleep tonight.'

'You go on home now. Is there anyone there?'

'Yeah, two roommates, but . . . I've got a girl. I think I'm going to her place.'

'I'm going to get you transpo.'

'You don't have to.'

'It's bad out there. We'll get you to your girl.'

She walked off to arrange it, then took the other bartenders.

And found the one, still shaking, who'd poured and shaken the base for the murder weapon. Sasha Quint, in her first month as bartender, trembled and leaked as she gave her statement.

'Brad told me, he told me about watching out for a woman with red hair and blue dreads. And to tell him if I saw her, especially if she ordered a pomtini. I wasn't paying attention, we were so busy, and I just went on auto. This guy knocked over a whole screamer, all over the bar, then got in my face about it. He was really harsh, so I was mopping it up and making him a new one, and she must've sat down.'

'She wasn't sitting there before the screamer?'

'I don't think so, I really don't. I'm not a hundred percent, okay? But I don't think so. And I'm dealing with this dickwad, and she orders the pomtini. Lays down the cash, and a solid tip. I was thinking more about the dickwad, and the tip. And Brad was on his break, I think, and people were yelling for drinks, and I had two table orders to fill, so I was just on auto.'

She snuffled back a sob. 'Am I in trouble?'

'Did she say anything else to you?'

'No. I don't think. She just said, "pomtini," put the cash down. And I finished the screamer for the dickwad, who was still giving me grief like I knocked the glass over, which I didn't, and I finished one of the table orders, mixed the pomtini, took the cash, filled the other table order. She wasn't sitting there anymore, I don't think, because Dorinda – one of the waitresses – came up and ran down another order, and I think I'd have seen her. And Brad was back, and I thought, "phew," then all hell broke loose.'

'Did you see her when all hell broke loose?'

'No. No, not really. People were yelling, and, Jesus, Brad jumped over the bar and started running. Then some people were pushing and shoving, more than usual. And then I could see something bad was happening at VIP-4, but I didn't know what. I don't understand what happened. I know the Flash died. She OD'd, right?'

'Not the way you mean. Do you have the cash for the pomtini?'

'I put it in the till. I ... I, uh, put the tip in my pocket. You're supposed to report it, but ... '

'I need that. I'm going to give you a receipt for it, and you'll get it back.'

'Okay.' She took some bills out of the bar apron pocket, drew out a fresh, lettuce-crisp five. 'It's this because it's, like, brand-new.'

Eve signaled Roarke, then programmed a receipt, printed it out, handed it over. 'You can go.'

'I'm not in trouble?'

'No.'

'I'm really sorry I made the drink.'

Not as sorry as Loxie Flash, Eve thought, and took an evidence bag from the field kit.

'Peabody just came in – with McNab.'

'Good.' She slid the five-dollar bill into the bag, marked and sealed it.

'What can I do?'

'Doubtful there are any cams in here. Take the outside surveillance, find her. I can put McNab on her personal devices. Peabody.'

Face pink from the cold, Peabody stepped up. 'Which one is it?'

'Loxie Flash. Order in a screen, then round up anyone seated near VIP-4 – Flash's table – start on statements and contacts and releases. Hold anyone who had contact with or a good line of sight on the redhead. Leave Glazier and his group – we need to interview him separately. I'm going to start with the waitstaff and her table companions.'

'Glaze is here, too?'

'Yeah. Was that a bonus, or did she manage to arrange it? McNab, the uniforms have the vic's purse, coat. Check her pocket 'link. I spoke with her earlier this evening, and left a v-mail that will likely time in after or around her TOD. See who and what else.'

'I've got it.'

Eve started on the waitstaff, got nowhere. No sightings until the dash. She walked back to the first on scene.

'Where are the people who were at the DB's table?'

'We stowed them up in a privacy room, but had to put a

man on the door. Bunch of assholes, Lieutenant, to tell the truth on it.'

'I guess they fit right in then. Names?'

He checked his notebook, and she transferred the names to hers. She started for the stairs, stopped when McNab hailed her.

He jogged over on his plaid snowboots. 'You're going to want to see her last text. It came in about twenty after your conversation with her.'

She took the 'link, read.

'Just couldn't say no and stay the fuck home.'

'It's from a Janis Dorsey.'

'One of her group. At least that keeps it simple. She's upstairs. I'll talk to her now. Roarke's got the door cams. You can help with statements and contacts. I need to clear out most of these people before I start on the DB.'

'Roger that. Screen's on the way.'

'Give me a buzz when it gets here.' She went upstairs and to the uniform on one of the privacy room doors. Saw it was Shelby from her own division.

'Stick around, Officer.'

'Yes, sir. Sir, they were half-stoned when we herded them in there.'

'Won't this be fun?'

Eve went in. Two males, three females, she noted. One of the males and one of the females were currently tongue diving each other. The male's hand squeezed the female's exposed left breast with its glitter-painted nipple.

The lot of them may have been half-stoned when they'd entered the room, but they'd crossed the finish line.

'I can see you're all grieving over the loss of your friend.'

A female with half a mile of blond hair scattered with pink braids smiled glassily. 'Loxie puked and went plop, right on the floor.'

The female beside her who'd chosen swirls of black-and-white body paint in lieu of pants giggled.

'Yeah, that's a laugh, all right. The old puke, plop, and perish.'

'Perish my left ass cheek.' The other male snorted, slouched down farther on the single bed they all shared. 'Bitch is messing around, like she does.'

Eve took out her badge, walked closer to shove it into his face. 'I'm Homicide, you fucking moron. Dead's my business. Loxie Flash is dead.'

'No serious way. I was humping her like a minute before she puked and plopped.'

'Consider it her last hump.'

'She's, like, dead?' The blonde blinked and some tiny glimmer of sanity flickered in the glassy eyes. 'Like, *dead*?'

'Yes. You two.' Eve kicked the bed to break up the tongue-diving competition. 'Knock it off, cover it up.'

'Sex is life, man.'

'If you take that pathetic replacement for your brain out, I'll haul it and you down to Central, lock you in a cage, and forget about you for the next forty-eight. Man.'

His hand paused in the act of undoing the trio of buttons

that covered the bulge of his crotch. 'Fuck, a bitch oughta lighten up.'

Eve just opened the door, finger curled to Shelby. 'Officer, take that extreme asshole into Central, book him on committing lewd acts in public, and toss him in with the other perverts.'

'Whoa, whoa.' He threw up both hands. 'Take it down, yeah? I'm chill. I be chill.'

'Stand by,' Eve told Shelby, and shut the door again. 'You be quiet until I tell you otherwise. Janis Dorsey.'

The blond raised her hand, wiggled her fingers.

'Did Loxie have plans to join your group of stupid tonight?'

'I . . . I don't know. I hadn't hooked with her for a few days.'

'You texted her this evening.'

'I did? I don't know.' She looked at the woman beside her. 'Did I?'

The woman shrugged. 'You didn't say.'

'But I . . . Uh-uh, I didn't. The G-man came in, and I thought it'd be some laughs if she came in, too, but then we wanted to dance, and I forgot. Anyway, I texted her how he was in Palisades when I went in to have dinner awhile ago, and she got super pissed. And all, like, "Why should I give a shit?" So I wasn't even sure I should because she's mean when she's pissed. Then she came anyway.'

'Let me see your 'link.'

'I don't think you hafta.' The one whose crotch had ceased bulging gave Eve the hard eye. 'She needs, like, a warrant.'

'I can get one – and you can go to Central and wait until I have one, wait until I examine your friend's cold, dead body, until she's taken to the morgue, until I finish with the crime scene. Then I'll come let you out of the holding pen.'

'You can't—'

'I warned you to stay quiet. Speak again, you're charged with obstruction, the lewd behavior, and possession of whatever's left in your pockets of what you've ingested.'

'You can see it, you can see it.' Janis opened a tiny, useless purse, pulled out her 'link. Closed the purse so fast Eve assumed some of what was left was inside the small and useless.

Eve took the 'link, called up the texts. Then turned the display screen around.

She watched Janis's face, saw the baffled shock. 'But I didn't! Hey, Dodo, look! This isn't from me. It doesn't have my sig.'

Dodo stopped examining her nails, looked at the display. 'Bogus. She, like, signs her texts. Jadar. Like radar with a *J*, right? No sig, not hers.'

'You can look, go on and look, all my texts. I can show you.'

'I can find them.' Eve called them up, ignored the gossip, the nonsense, the bullshit displayed. And saw every one with the *Jadar* signature line.

'All right, did you lend your 'link to anybody?'

'As if!'

'Was it in your possession all evening?'

306

'Right on the table.'

'Right on the table, say, when you all got up to dance.'

'Sure. Nobody's going to steal it, right? And I've got more at home anyway. Not like my hoodie. Somebody took my hoodie right off the booth, and it was my favorite mink. Anyway, I didn't text Loxie.'

'I need the 'link. I'll give you a receipt.'

Janis sighed. 'Bummed.'

'Run it through for me, from the time she came in.'

'Okay, well, I saw her over at the G-man's booth. He was there with a group, and I saw her hitting on him pretty hard, but he didn't bite, right? So she came over to hang with us, took my drink, right, Dodo?'

'Slurped it right down. You gave her a tab of— Hey,' Dodo objected when Janis jabbed her with an elbow. 'What the fuck does she care?'

'Anyway,' Janis said quickly. 'Loxie said how she needed another drink, but then she slithered up Bennie to dance some sexy, then she came back, drank her drink down. Then she . . . she fell on the floor. Plop, then puke. Everybody scrambled up because, wow. I didn't think she really died. I didn't think.'

Do you ever? Eve wondered. 'How did she get the drink, the one she had before she died?'

'Ah . . . I guess she ordered it?'

'Who served it?'

Janis shrugged, looked at Dodo. Another shrug, looked at Bennie.

'It was there when we came back to the booth.'

Eve looked at the second male, got a snarky smile.

'Speak.'

'Little tits. I notice tits.' He brushed his hand over the partially covered breast of the woman currently curled up, passed out, and snoring beside him.

'The server had small breasts.'

'Barely made bumps in her top. Like yours.'

She let that pass. 'Did you happen to notice anything else about her?'

'Some fan.' He started to reach for the unconscious woman's breast again, caught the hard glint in Eve's eyes. Laid his roaming hand back on his thigh.

'Why do you assume that?'

'I assume it wasn't a waitress because they all wear short black skirts and tight red tops, and she wasn't. Hangers-on send over drinks all the time. And other things,' he added with that smile.

'What was she wearing?'

'It wasn't that. Home dye job, red, fake side dreads, blue.'

'You noticed her tits and her hair.'

'Her tits because I have a dick. Her hair because it's what I do and am. Sylvio, hair designer to those who rock. You could use some work. Some Brimstone lowlights to add some fire.'

'I'll keep that in mind.'

17

It took her longer than she liked to pick her way through the memories and observations of the group in the privacy room. Since the one woman slept through it, Eve arranged for her transportation home, and earmarked her for later, if necessary.

At least by the time she came back down the screen closed off the body, and at least half the number of patrons had been moved out.

Eve went first to Glaze's booth. 'I'm going to ask you to wait awhile longer.'

'Not a problem, as long as you need. But could you let the others go on home?'

Before she could answer, the man to his left shook his head. 'We stick, brother. We all stick.'

'I'd appreciate it.' Eve turned away, started for the screen. Roarke intercepted her.

'I've got her coming and going. You might want to have a look.' He offered her a handheld. 'I copied the feed, just her bit. First, the arrival, front door cam. Second, exit out of the back.'

Eve studied the feed. The hat, the goggles – the same as she'd worn at the vid palace. Dark, knee-length coat with some sort of glittery braiding on the cuffs, the hem, the shoulders. Thick-heeled ankle boots – gold chains with dangling skulls draped from the top. Skin pants with a star pattern.

A shoulder bag – larger than the useless one Janis used. Big enough for a vial of poison, she assumed, and the cash needed, with room enough to stow the goggles, the gloves, the scarf, and the hat.

She noted the time stamp, calculated Strongbow had entered the club about the time Eve herself had spoken with the victim. Maybe slightly prior.

She switched to the exit. 'Got the purse,' she noted. 'Wearing it cross-body. I can see the strap across her back. Carrying a coat, but not the one she wore in.'

'No,' Roarke agreed. 'It looks like a fur of some sort, and there's a hood. It's dangling down there.'

'Yeah, I see. It's going to be mink. Damn it, she snatched the coat off the vic's booth. Had the presence of mind not to run out into the cold and wind without a coat. That's thinking on your fucking feet.'

She handed him back the device. 'Start contacting cab companies. Ten-block radius to this location. A pickup matching her description.'

'They might not cooperate, as I haven't a badge number.'

'You'll find a way.' No question of that, Eve thought. 'She probably didn't cab it. Subway maybe. Or grabbed a bus. Cab's are tough on the budget, but we'll start there.'

She scanned for Peabody, spotted McNab. 'McNab!'

'Yo.'

'Transit Authority. Start with lines going to Brooklyn. Have them scan for a woman wearing a hooded mink jacket. Add her description, though if she has brains – and she does – she'll have ditched the dreads. I want subways, and buses.'

'You got it.'

She damn well hoped so.

'Have Peabody search the club for a dark coat with glitter braiding. Probably homemade. She'll know.'

Eve stepped behind the screen. 'Okay, Loxie, you idiot, let's do what we can.'

She removed the leather coat, tossed it on the padded booth. And did what she could.

When Peabody stepped behind the screen, Eve closed her field kit. Straightened from her crouch.

'Rounding it, TOD's eighteen minutes before I got here.'

'You must've flown.'

'Roarke can drive. Strongbow sent the text from the moronic Janis Dorsey's 'link – one she conveniently left on the table when she got up to dance with her moronic friends. Sent the text – which Loxie answered in less than a minute to announce she was on her way to die – faded back, and waited. The place is full of a lot of other morons, most of them high.'

Eve looked down at the body with a combination of pity and disgust. 'She waits until Loxie comes in, and doesn't

Loxie play right into the damn script and go over to try to sex up the ex. He, by all accounts, wasn't sexed. She comes over here, drinks, takes more illegals, gets up to dance. Which presents excellent timing for Strongbow to order the drink, tip in the poison, and goddamn set it down on the table herself.'

'She served the drink. Man, that's ballsy.'

'Risk and reward,' Eve muttered. 'Nobody gave a shit that some stranger set a drink down. Nobody gave a shit what might be in it. Probably hoped it was laced with good stuff. She comes back, drinks it down, lets the guy she was dancing with paw her. And it kicks in. If, as advertised and as her color indicates, it's cyanide, she had some trouble breathing, felt off, weird.

'Did she think then?' A hint of rage leaked into Eve's voice. 'Did it even begin to occur to her then that she'd killed herself because she couldn't not be a fuckhead? Who the hell knows? She passes out, falls off the bench. Starts to seize. That cherry-red's coming up in her face. Her system revolts, tries to expel what's already killed her. The morons she's surrounded herself with squeal, scramble, and laugh. I'll bet vids of her death are already making the rounds. Meanwhile, the seriously not-moronic bartender has not only called the cops and gotten his bouncer on the front door, but after locking eyes with the killer, tries to catch her when she runs. She's smart enough to grab one of the morons' coats, which – her lucky day – is a goddamn mink hoodie. She bolts out the kitchen, and she's gone.

'So's Loxie, long before the MTs can get to her.'

'A few people caught a glimpse of her,' Peabody added. 'She knocked into a couple as she fled. The descriptions are what you'd expect given the alcohol, illegals, lighting. I've got the coat she wore to get here.'

'Score one for us.'

'McNab's getting a bag from the kitchen. We don't have any big enough. It's well made — professionally made. She's got skills, Dallas, and a professional machine. It's a cheap, blended material, but she put in a decent lining for warmth. Cheap braiding, but perfectly sewn. Nothing in the pockets.'

'She had a purse, put everything in there. Where did you find the coat?'

'She left it on the barstool. It looks to me like she hung it there when she ordered the drink. Left it there when she walked the drink to the table here.'

'But didn't go back for it. Stayed here, closer to the booth. She wanted to watch, to make sure it went according to script.'

'I guess when she saw Brad made her, she grabbed the closest coat right off the bench. Did you say mink?'

'Yeah.' Eve jammed frustrated hands in her pockets. 'If she tries to pawn it or sell it, we may be in luck. I've got the description from its idiot owner. We'll get it out. Contact the other women on the list, Peabody, contact Yola Bloomfield. She got a text from the moron's 'link, too. And the rest of the list. See if they got one from another 'link.'

'It's really late, Dallas.'

'It's a hell of a lot later for her.' Eve glanced at Loxie again. 'Let's get the dead wagon and the sweepers.'

She stepped out, moved to the only people present now besides cops – and an expert consultant, civilian.

'I'm sorry you had to wait.'

'It doesn't matter,' Glaze told her.

'If I could speak to you, Mr Glazier. Over there.'

'Glaze,' he said as he rose, laid a hand on the shoulder of the brunette sitting beside him. 'Mr Glazier's my old man.'

She took him to a table away from the body, and his friends.

'You and the deceased were involved at one time.'

'We were a lot of things at one time.' He had a compelling face, with deep, dark eyes against pale, pale skin. Hair, nearly as dark as his eyes, that shagged long around it. 'We were a lot of things, off and on, for too long a time. You never think it'll be you. That you'll be the one to play too hard, party too much, cross that line, and check out. Lox thought she was invincible. I used to think the same.'

Eve didn't disabuse him about the overdose. 'Did you know she was coming here tonight?'

'No. I guess I knew she might, that somebody might tell her I was here. The last time we ran into each other, it was pretty harsh.'

'When was that?'

'Five months, three weeks, and two days ago.'

'That's very specific.'

'Yeah. I'd been clean. For nine weeks and two days before

314

that, I'd been clean. We'd busted off again, me and Lox, a couple weeks before that, and I meant it to stay busted off. I started seeing Lauren.' He glanced in the direction of his booth.

'I met her at a frigging bookstore, do you believe it? I was trying to stay straight, and I was reading a lot. I just happened into this place — I didn't have any actual books. She did, she worked there. We started talking, and ... doesn't matter. I started seeing her, started to see how it could be. Then I got restless one night. Nine weeks and two days clean, and I got restless, decided to drop into Styx — another club, not much different than this.'

Shifting, he stared at the stage. 'Not much different,' he said again. 'I just wanted to hear some music, maybe jam in on a set. That's what I told myself. Maybe have one brew. What could one hurt? And there's Loxie. We got trashed together, went back to my place, got more trashed.

'I woke up the next afternoon sick, strung out, hating myself. Hating Loxie. We busted up again. I didn't tell Lauren. Didn't have to, as word got out. She wouldn't see me, talk to me. I begged. The next few weeks, I sent her a text every day. I'm clean, day one. Day two, like that.'

He spread his hands on the surface of the table. Two thick silver rings winked on his fingers.

'Finally, she met me for coffee. It wasn't enough, she told me, and she was right. I needed help, she said, and right again. Nobody could make me, and God, didn't I know it? I had to do it. So I did. I went to Zurich, and I got help. I wrote music. I got my shit together. I've got Lauren. No sex,' he added with a wry smile. 'I get to a year clean, we'll celebrate. We're recording. That's why we came in tonight. We had a string of really good days in the studio. I've been clean for five months, three weeks, and a day.'

He let out a long breath. 'I wanted to test myself. To see if I could sit in a club, hear music, be around people drinking and popping. And I could. I could, and that was better than any high I'd ever pumped in. Can't explain it.'

'You just did.'

He stared down at his hands. 'I needed to test myself, and I passed. And when Loxie came in, and gave me all the signals, it didn't push the buttons. Not because of Lauren — or not only. But because of me.

'I was feeling so damn good about it, about turning that corner, man. Then . . . I didn't see her hit the floor. I heard — I think, maybe Janis — scream. A kind of wild, laughing scream. I just glanced over. Then I saw. Loxie on the floor, seizing. I yelled for Kick — my bass, my friend — to call nine-one-one, to get the MTs. I got over to her, finally. People in the way, crowding in, taking fucking vids. I couldn't find a pulse. I tried CPR, like you do, for a couple minutes, but . . . She was staring up at me, just staring. There wasn't anything there. I knew before the MTs got here, before they said there wasn't anything there. Lauren brought my coat over, and we covered her up.'

He let out a breath. 'She's not the first person I've lost this way. It would've been me sooner or later. Me, lying on the floor of some club or bar or some alley after a score. I'd cut her out of my life, you know, to save my own. But I didn't want to see hers end.

'She's got a mother and a sister,' he said. 'They don't get along, but . . . If they can't or won't take care of, you know, the arrangements and all that, I can.'

'I'll contact her family, and let you know. I'm going to describe someone, and I want you to get the picture in your head, think about if you've seen her. Tonight, in here, or at any other time.'

'Okay.'

'A woman, in her forties, but maybe trying to look younger. About five-six, slim build. White. Red hair, blue side dreads. Orange dragon tat on the inside of her right wrist.'

He waited a moment. 'That's it?'

'I'll have more tomorrow, but for now.'

'I wasn't really scoping the crowd tonight. A test, right? I was sort of closed into the booth, to friends. Some people dropped by . . . I don't remember seeing a woman like that tonight.'

'Maybe around where you live, in a restaurant, around where you're recording.'

'I don't think I . . . ' As he trailed off, his eyes narrowed. 'Maybe, yeah, yeah. Outside the studio. Like last week. I went into the next room – this space where you can just sit and clear your head or have a meet. I wasn't nailing the bridge, just wanted to chill it down. I looked out the window. That redhead in the bad coat – all that glitter trim – staring at the studio. Most likely for Jake – Jake Kincade, Avenue A? It's his place, his studio. East Side Sound. But I caught her eye and waved. She ran like a rabbit.'

He laughed then, sighed out the rest. 'And I caught sight of her just this afternoon out there. Waved again. This time she blew me a kiss. I let Jake know he maybe has a stalker. He plays it low-key. I don't get how that plays into Loxie.'

'Loxie didn't OD.'

'But I saw—'

'What you saw was death by poison. The woman you saw, twice, poisoned her.'

His slumped shoulders jerked back. 'But, come on. Murder? A lot of people might have wanted to kick her ass. I did myself, plenty. But . . . ' She saw it come into his head, saw it in his eyes. 'Was she stalking me? Me, not Jake? Oh Jesus Christ, did she kill Lox because of me?'

'She killed Loxie because she's a murderer, and Loxie provided her with the target and opportunity she wanted. I don't think you'll see her again, but if you do, don't approach. Contact me.'

'Lauren.'

'She has no reason to wish any harm to Lauren. This person is delusional. She killed Loxie because Loxie fit certain characteristics. From what you've told me, Lauren doesn't have anything in common with Loxie.'

'Me. She's got me.'

'It's not you, Glaze, it's the illusion of you, and, again,

certain characteristics that no longer apply. I can almost guarantee you're not even a blip in her world now. She's finished with you, with Loxie, with this . . . scenario.'

And now she becomes someone else, Eve thought.

'Add to your security, and Lauren's if you're worried. But you, this, tonight? For her it's a closed book.'

'I will. I am.'

'I'm going to talk to the rest of your group, then you're all free to go.' Eve rose. 'You know it's a long street after that corner's turned. I hope you stay on it.'

'One step, every day, the rest of my life. I like the street. I like who I am when I'm walking it.'

Eve talked to Glaze's group, excused herself to take a frantic 'link tag from Yola Bloomfield, then finished up.

Before she could hunt down Peabody, Roarke pushed coffee into her hand.

She all but inhaled it. 'I'd grant you exotic and possibly illegal sexual favors for this alone.'

'I'll make a list.' He set a hand on her shoulder. 'You should take a moment, gather your thoughts.'

'They're gathered. Where the hell is Peabody?'

Even as she spoke, both Peabody and McNab came out of the kitchen area.

'F train, Second Avenue station,' McNab said. 'Transit copied me on the feed. I can hook it to the stage screen. Might take a minute.'

'Take the minute.'

While he went to work, Peabody added her progress.

'I gave the suspect's coat to the sweepers, told them to get Harvo on it. Any hair or fibers thereon, she'll find them and pin them down.'

'Asshole named Sylvio claims the red's a home-dye job, and the dreads are fake.'

'Sylvio? Like the hair king? He'd know. I can start running down the dreads.'

'Do that and start a search for them – focused between here and the Second Avenue subway station – also inside the station, and on the F train. If she has brains, and she does, she'd have yanked them off and ditched them on the run. We find them, and Harvo's got something else to play with.'

'All over it. The only one on the skank list who also got a text was Yola Bloomfield.'

'Culled it down to two,' Eve noted.

'Got it up, Dallas.'

Eve moved over to the stage area.

She watched the night owls, the party people, the LCs calling it a night head for the platforms. A couple of sidewalk sleepers in from the cold huddled together on the floor, begging hats displayed – and ignored.

She saw Strongbow. Mink hoodie up and buttoned to the neck, wind goggles in place. As she approached the transoms, Strongbow unbuttoned the hoodie to reach inside for her purse.

Took out a swipe.

Eve braced. Do it, do it, you crazy, murdering bitch.

But she stopped, dipped her head lower. Stepping aside, she reached in her purse again, carefully counted out cash.

She took it to the machine, paid for a new swipe.

Cash, Eve noted from the display. One ride.

'Smart enough, smart enough to be careful. Didn't use a multi-swipe – we could've tracked her movements. Didn't use an account via her 'link, and you can bet she's got those. Cheaper than a ride-by-ride.'

Strongbow pushed through, kept her head bowed as she waited on the platform. When she got on the train, McNab switched the feed. Eve saw her sit in a corner, huddle there.

'She's aware of the cameras, thinking about the cameras. Brooklyn, yeah, she's got to risk that, but you can bet your ass she won't get off at her usual stop. She'll walk, warm in a scene well written and in that damn stupid jacket. Wearing gloves, probably had them in her purse, but still she's careful not to touch things. Overcautious about prints or a germo-phobe? Can't see any hair. You ought to get a hint of the dreads from some of the angles, but nothing. She's already ditched them. Peabody, push on teams to scour the area from here to the station where she got on.'

Eve paced in front of the screen as Strongbow rode.

'Mistakes, got some mistakes now. Got spotted, had to run. What does she think of that? Is she asking herself how the bartender made her? Will she go back over the scene, looking for the mistakes? Had to leave her coat, got the better part of the deal with the mink, but we've got some pieces of her now. She didn't get away clean.'

'I kind of wonder . . .'

When Peabody trailed off, Eve turned to her. 'Finish it. Half thoughts are weak and annoying.'

'Okay, I wonder if getting spotted, running, if that added a new element for her. If she got a thrill out of it. It's attention, right? She craves it.'

'That's good,' Eve said. 'That's very good. First the shock, the fear, then the thrill. Nadine's broadcast gave her a taste of it, likely juiced her up to move on this next chapter tonight. Now she's got more. She hedged her bets,' Eve added. 'She texted Yola Bloomfield from dumb-ass Janis's 'link seconds after she texted Loxie.'

Eve jammed her hands in her pockets, rocked back on her heels. 'Yola tagged me, full panic. Word's already out on Loxie Flash – with video.'

'So it didn't matter which of them,' Peabody said.

'Glaze mattered. Loxie was likely top prize, but Yola's done the dirty with him a couple times, so she'd do. Or would have if she hadn't had the sense to stay home. She's getting off. That's . . . on Jay.'

Head down the whole way, Eve thought. Even in the expensive coat, she was a woman who barely made a ripple on the air.

'We'll check store and street cams in that area,' Eve said. 'She's going to know where they are and how to avoid them, but we have to check. I'm betting her usual stop is at least a couple stations down the line, or a transfer. But we're going to have a sketch tomorrow. Copy that transfer feed to my units, McNab. Peabody, morgue, eight hundred sharp.'

'I figured.'

'Go home, get some rack time. I'll seal up here.'

'I hear that.'

'There's transpo waiting for you outside,' Roarke told them. 'Ice has gone to snow, which means ice under snow. It's ugly out there.'

'That's even better news than "go home".' Wearily, Peabody shrugged into her coat. 'Thanks. Mega serious thanks.'

'Squared,' McNab added, then snagged Peabody's hand so they swung arms on the way out.

Eve walked back over to the booth, shook her head.

'Loxie almost had to see her. Look at the angles – booth to bar. Strongbow had to be close to the booth, maybe about here.'

Eve walked around, imagined the mink hoodie carelessly tossed over the plush back. 'Wits put vic here.'

She circled again, pointed to the curved end farthest from the bar. 'Here, Loxie's got Glaze's booth in her line of sight, and she wants that. Wants his eye on her – doesn't get it. The way the booth curves, if Strongbow's more or less where it makes sense – close enough, angled there, so she can watch Loxie drink and die – Loxie probably saw her.'

'Does it matter?' Roarke asked her.

'Just helps me get a picture. Vic here, killer there, bar there, Brad the bartender down there. People crowded around, moving through, plunked in other booths or at tables. She gets back from the dance floor – far end because she wanted Glaze to see her rubbing herself all over some guy named Bennie. Drink's sitting here because Strongbow ordered it from this end of the bar – that stool where she left her coat – and set it down in front of five oblivious idiots.'

Eve sat on the end of the booth. 'Stand over there, will you?'

Roarke moved in as surrogate for the killer.

'Lots of weird lighting, lots of people, lots of noise, but here I am, pissed and insulted because my ex doesn't have a boner for me. I pick up the drink.'

She mimed lifting it, drinking it down. 'Bennie's got his hands all over me. Maybe I'll let him do me later. Probably. Definitely want to get laid. Can't get my breath – weird. I don't feel right. Something's wrong, it's wrong. Bennie's humping me, but I can't breathe. I can't—'

Eve drew a line with her hand from where she sat to where Roarke stood. 'Almost had to see her. Not unconscious like the first vic, not in the back like the second. She wanted to be seen. She wanted to see and be seen. And that matters, because she's going to want that again.'

Heaving out a breath, Eve rose. 'Did Loxie have that moment of awareness – seeing the woman with the blue dreads, thinking about the taste of that stupid martini? Did she have enough time for that fuck-me moment?'

She shook her head again. 'Anyway. Strongbow cut

back her lag time. Cut it way back. That's the broadcast with Nadine.'

'You won't blame yourself for this.'

She turned back to Roarke. 'Damn right I won't. I laid all this out for Loxie Flash, just like the others. I warned her, showed her crime scene pictures. Hardly more than a goddamn hour before she walked in here, I talked to her again, warned her again. She had to do one fucking thing to stay alive. Stay out of the clubs. Give me a few days, and stay out of the clubs. Instead she got her slut on, walked in here. Bad enough, all that's bad enough, but I told her the drink to avoid. She drinks it anyway. Drinks what's in front of her because she was weak, stupid, and liked sticking her finger in authority's eye. She's a goddamn accessory to her own murder.'

Releasing frustration, Eve kicked the booth, twice. 'And now she's mine.'

'She's yours,' he agreed. 'And you're tired. Let's follow your own orders and go home, get some rack time.'

'Yeah. Nothing more to do here.' Looking at him, knowing he saw her, saw in her, she let the exhaustion come. 'Damn it, Roarke, goddamn it. She just had to stay home.'

'Baby.' He moved to her, drew her in. 'Some can't. For some, being alone is a kind of death.'

'She made her choice. The last shit choice in a series of shit choices. Yeah, let's go home. I need to notify her next of kin, though if Yola's anything to go by, they already know.'

18

Eve surfaced out of dreams mildly annoyed with her sub-conscious. Couldn't it give her a break once in a while, come up with some puffy white clouds for her to float on?

Why would she – or anybody – want to float around on puffy white clouds? One strong wind could knock you off, then you'd have to dream up a parachute. And for all you knew, you could end up splashing into some big dream ocean and get eaten by sharks.

Forget the damn, stupid clouds.

'You're thinking too loud.'

Eve opened her eyes, looked straight into Roarke's.

So blue, she thought. If you splashed into an ocean that blue, there wouldn't be any sharks because it would be perfect.

'What are you doing here?'

'I was sleeping until your brain woke up and started muttering.'

'Is there nothing left in the universe to buy or sell or build or invent? Have we reached critical mass?'

'Buying, selling, and so on can wait another hour.' As he spoke, his hand skimmed down her back, glided over her ass.

'Somebody told me last night that sex was life.' Since it was handy, she gave his really exceptional ass a pat. 'I wish I had time to live,' she added, rolling away from him and out of bed.

Galahad leaped off behind her, beat her to the AutoChef. Pretty much on auto herself, she programmed his kibble, and two mugs of black coffee.

The first glorious sip fired up a few circuits as she walked over to hand Roarke the other mug.

'Thanks.'

She narrowed her sleepy eyes at him. 'How can you look awake? How can anybody look awake before the coffee? It's just not right.'

'I enjoy the awake more after the coffee.'

'Not the same thing. Do you think the subconscious gets bitchy because it knows it's starting the day at the morgue?'

'It may factor. Bad dreams?'

'No, bitchy ones. As in dead Loxie Flash bitching about being dead. Everybody's fault but hers, right, until you wanted to punch her in her whiny face. But since she's dead, what's the point?'

'I'd say your subconscious recognizes your latest victim contributed to her own fate, and if personality follows into death, she'd bitch and cast the blame about.'

'Yeah. She deserved a good punch in the face, but she didn't deserve murder – or having her last moments splashed all over the Internet and gossip venues. So.' She drained her coffee where she stood. 'Morgue,' she grumbled and headed for the shower.

She'd just started to work out the basic outline of her morning when Roarke stepped in behind her, into the hot, crisscrossing jets.

His arms came around her. That hard, wet body pressed against her back, and she lost her train of thought.

'A little life to start off the day.' His hand slid down to her center. 'And to counterbalance the morgue.'

'When you put it like that.' She started to turn around, turn into him, and found herself pressed to the tiles.

'We'll just have to make it quick.'

His fingers slid into her, shot her straight to peak even as his teeth grazed over the back of her neck.

She splayed her hands on the tiles, prepared to push off, pivot somehow, and grab on to him. But he thrust inside her, destroyed her with hard, fast strokes. Her vision blurred – crazed pleasure, rising steam, the pulsing beat of water – so she closed her eyes, surrendered.

She heard the helpless sounds she made, echoing, drowning under the hot rain. And everything in her tightened, clung, hung on that sharp, stunning edge between pleasure and panic.

Then fell.

Somewhere, somehow, she felt his heart pounding against her back and his lips brushing against the side of her neck. Felt his grip become a caress before he turned her.

Once again she looked straight into his eyes, and thought she'd fallen into that perfect blue sea after all.

She skimmed her fingers through his wet hair. 'I guess the word's *wow*.'

His lips curved as she brushed hers over them. 'Something about having my naked wife serve me coffee in bed, I suppose.'

She held on to him another moment, decided dreams of the bitching dead and trips to the morgue really could be counterbalanced.

Then she nudged him away. 'Okay, that's done, now hands off, pal. I've got to move.'

She finished showering, hopped in the drying tube and, grabbing the robe off the back of the door, went out for a second hit of coffee. She'd programmed breakfast by the time he came out, a towel slung around his hips.

'Hungry, are you?'

'I am now.'

He grabbed a robe for himself so he could join her. And, after removing warming domes, sat a moment in silence.

'You programmed oatmeal.'

'Yeah, so? I . . . What? Damn it!'

He sat back, laughing at her shocked consternation.

'You've screwed with my subconscious. I should be eating waffles.'

He patted her leg. 'Tomorrow, waffles it is, whoever gets to the AC first.'

Since she just continued to scowl at the bowl, he doctored

up the oatmeal as he knew she liked – or tolerated. 'It's a good choice. We're caught in this cold snap, dipping down from Canada. We'll be lucky to hit twenty degrees today.'

'Canada's got no business dipping down here so the rest of us have to eat oatmeal.' But she ate it, and comforted herself with berries.

'What can I do to help today, if I manage to find some time for it?'

'You can let me know if you know any rich old ladies with a greedy, murderous son who plays the biddable, and a daughter who can be framed.'

He considered as he ate. 'I likely have a passing acquaintance with a few.'

'Next vic. She'll have her target selected and set up. I don't know how long she'll wait to move on it now. Whether she'll push or step back. But if the bartender comes through with Yancy, I'll have a face. And maybe Harvo finds something on the damn coat. Maybe we turn up the dreads and get something off them. Loxie made it easy for her, but she still moved too fast, and she made mistakes.

'I've got to dig deeper into Delaware,' she continued as she got up to go to her closet. 'Especially if I have a face. She had a life there. She lived somewhere, worked somewhere. Shopped, ate, has a history there. Maybe family.'

She thought it through while she dressed, came out to find Roarke knotting a wine-colored tie with thin gray stripes. The gray matched his shirt exactly and came in a few tones lighter than the suit.

As she strapped on her weapon, she saw him pick up the gray button he always carried, slide it into his pocket. And felt a stupefying wave of love.

She rubbed a hand over the diamond under her sweater. Here was the cop, sentimental over a big, fat diamond. And the kazillionaire sappy over some stray button.

What a pair they were.

'Luck's bullshit.'

He glanced over. 'Darling Eve, those are fighting words for an Irishman.'

'Luck's bullshit,' she repeated, and put a hunter green jacket over a sweater the color of Mira's tea. 'Except when it isn't. I'm feeling pretty lucky to wake up with you, then there's the whole getting nailed in the shower, even if oatmeal followed. I can't say that counterbalances Strongbow's luck last night, but it's given me a damn good start to the day.'

Eve filled her jacket pockets with her usual paraphernalia. 'She doesn't have that – not just the waking up and getting nailed. She might have a rush from the kill, but she's got to be worried. She got spotted, chased, left possessions behind. She has to worry about that. She has to worry about me.'

Now he studied her as she'd studied him. 'How will she write you in, Lieutenant?'

'Can't say, but I can guarantee her story isn't going to have a happy ending.'

Thinking of stories, of endings, she sent Feeney a long text as she drove downtown along madly slippery streets.

Attached are several writing samples from my prime suspect in the three murders associated with Blaine DeLano's Dark series. If you're not up to date, McNab can brief you. Is it possible to run an analysis of the writing, do a global search for similar styles, word uses, blah, blah, focusing on sites for writers? Wannabe types? Especially places where they can put up samples of their work for others to read?

I can have Peabody start a search on social media sites. Suspect wrote a manuscript titled *Hot Blood, Cold Mind*, but my searches for the title on self-publishing types, social media, and so forth gets bupkus.

On my way to the morgue now to see what Morris can tell me about her third vic. I'll be in Central in about an hour if you need any clarification. Appreciate it. Dallas

Long shot, Eve thought. She wasn't confident Strongbow would put her work out there for comments or criticism. But maybe, maybe, there was a hunger that needed feeding. Maybe she'd risk it.

Eve's DLE handled the ice patches with barely a shudder, and certainly better than the pair of Rapid Cabs she saw crunched together on Ninth between Thirty-fifth and Thirty-fourth.

Still, she couldn't deny relief when she could get out of the damn car, off the damn streets, and into the white tunnel of the morgue.

Halfway down she heard the unmistakable Peabody clump behind her.

She paused in the air that smelled of chemical cleaning, fake lemon, and death.

Bundled like a candied Eskimo in her pink coat, pink fuzzy-topped boots, a scarf in bleeding shades of blue with pink fringe, an earflap hat in the same pattern with bouncing pom-poms, Peabody clumped to catch up.

'I take it back about the dumb-ass wind goggles. I wish I'd had a pair just for the walk to and from the subway.'

'Blame Canada,' Eve told her. 'It's a changeup from blaming February.'

'I've been looking at gardening sites. We're going to do some window boxes, plant herbs and stuff. I shouldn't have started thinking about spring.'

'Maybe we'll blame you then.' Eve kept walking, and pushed through Morris's double doors.

He'd gone for a black turtleneck rather than a shirt and tie – and who could blame him? It gave the steel-blue suit a sort of artsy vibe. He'd wound his hair into a single, thick braid that hung down the back of his protective cloak.

'Here we are again,' he said.

'She wouldn't listen. Hit the club, drank the drink.'

'Vodka, a whiff of vermouth, pomegranate juice, and a lethal twist of cyanide. That's in addition to the Buzz, Erotica, Zoner, and the champagne cocktail – champagne, bitters, sugar substitute, and a splash of grenadine – already in her system.'

'That's fast work on the tox.'

'I started on her last night. We had several unexpected guests – weather related.'

'You've been here all night?'

'Considering the weather and the state of the roads, it seemed wiser to spend the night with the dead rather than risk joining them. I have a very comfortable sofa here. It's unfortunate my house here doesn't run to anything approaching decent coffee.'

'Peabody.'

'On it.'

'No, no.' He waved a hand in the air. 'Don't go out in this urban Arctic on my account.'

'Just to my vehicle,' Eve told him. 'I have the real deal in its AC.'

'Then I'd be grateful.'

Eve waited until Peabody scurried off. 'Plus it gets her out of this part – she hates this part.'

'Some never fully adjust.' He looked down at Loxie Flash, naked, chest still splayed open from the Y-cut. 'Here you have a young woman, only a few years over the legal age, whose body has already been ravaged by addictions. Kidneys, liver, heart, lungs all already showing signs of that abuse. If she'd continued down this path, it's unlikely she'd have seen forty. Of course, she didn't have the chance to continue or to stop.'

'She had the chance. She didn't take it. Cyanide confirmed COD?'

'Yes, and the TOD from your gauge confirmed. You see the cherry-red skin color. There are a couple of hair-line fractures on her ribs I'd speculate came from an attempt at CPR.'

'There was an attempt.'

'The lack of bruising there indicates it was already too late. The cyanide salts she ingested would have acted quickly. The tats and piercings as you see. She was a bit overweight, and considering the lack of muscle tone didn't exercise. She had breast enhancements, and was wearing nipple clamps when delivered to us. She has little else to say. A life hard lived, hard ended.'

Peabody came back with a small pot. 'I grabbed this out of your office, programmed you three cups from the DLE's AC, dumped them in.'

'You're a genius.'

'I couldn't remember how you take it.'

'At this moment? With great gratitude.'

'If anything else shows up with her,' Eve told Morris, 'let me know. Otherwise, you've given me what I expected.'

'I don't think she's holding any secrets now, but we'll finish. I haven't heard from next of kin as yet.'

'If you don't, her ex said he'd make her arrangements. Let's hit it, Peabody.'

'Be safe out there,' Morris called after them. 'And my eternal thanks for the coffee.'

'I didn't stall,' Peabody began, and Eve shook her head.

'Straightforward poisoning. No surprises. Unless you consider the fact she was slowly killing herself with alcohol, illegals, and bad choices a surprise. I don't. You can start trying to nail down where Strongbow got her hands on cyanide salts. Let's give the next of kin another twenty-four before contacting Glaze.'

Once she slid behind the wheel, Eve sat a moment, organizing her thoughts. 'We're going to focus on looking for the next target, try to get ahead of her. In the book, the vic was sixty-eight, so let's go from sixty to seventy-five. She was worth about two hundred and sixty mil. We're going to go from two mil up to four. She can be widowed or divorced – the fictional vic had been both – but she won't be currently married or cohabbing. She'll have a son and a daughter. Maybe other offspring, but she'll have to have one of each.'

'I reread parts of it last night before I got the call from Dispatch. I can start a search.'

'Okay. Unless Harvo pulled an all-nighter like Morris, she hasn't had time to get us anything yet, but we need to keep on that. I want Yancy all over the sketch. We push on the canvass for the damn dreads.'

'Can I have hot chocolate?' Peabody offered a winsome smile. 'I fantasized about it on the hike from the subway.'

'Go.' Eve flicked a hand at the in-dash.

She drove to Central, saw with some astonishment a couple of kids sliding down the sidewalk on what looked like flattened cardboard.

'Why aren't their asses frozen?'

'Probably because they're only ten-year-old asses.' She handed Eve a go-cup of coffee. 'I've been thinking about the coats – the two she made. Well, three, since one was reversible. She has to have a professional machine, like I said, something that will handle the heavier materials, the heavier thread. She probably brought it with her to Brooklyn. If she's on a budget, buying one's a big expense, so with her skill level, she probably had it before, hauled it or had it shipped up here. Maybe we can track it.'

'We need to push into Delaware. That's another angle there. If she had her own professional machine, she likely did work out of her own place. Either full- or part-time. Do you need a license for that?'

Considering, Peabody pursed her lips. 'Maybe a certification. I'll check. If she sewed under the table – I mean didn't report sales or fees – that's a harder route to follow, but she'd have had some reportable income, or big flag. She'd need a certification or a tax ID to buy supplies wholesale.'

'She'd want that,' Eve concluded. 'She'd need to maximize income. Start playing those angles back in Delaware, and we'll keep on them in Brooklyn.'

She pulled into the lot at Central, shuffling the agenda in her head.

'Start digging on the license or certification or whatever the hell for tailoring. Female, in Delaware, and cross with any lapses in the last two years. Lapses or transfers to New York. We'll look for employment, income from tailoring, seamstressing in Delaware, and again the lapse that fits our timeline.'

Eve got out, headed to the elevators. 'I'll push on Harvo, take another look at the Transit Authority feed – and see if we can track her from the stop in Brooklyn last night. Even in a stupid fur hoodie, it was freaking cold, so maybe she took a cab or a bus.'

As the elevator doors opened, something, some compact missile with arms and legs, launched out. It slammed Peabody on the fly, knocking her back and down. At the same instant Eve managed to pivot, catch the missile on her shoulder, use its momentum to flip it over.

A clatter of footsteps on the iron steps echoed with Peabody's breathless curse. Eve pivoted again, but wasn't quite quick enough to avoid one of the limbs – a foot – from glancing off her jaw, another from banging into her ribs before she dropped bodily on the now-cackling ... man, she realized. A very small man with a really long beard.

She said: 'Fuck, fuck, *fuck* me!' as she held him down, shifting to pull her restraints off her belt.

He continued to cackle, to wriggle, as Peabody gained her hands and knees and the thundering footsteps became a pair of breathless uniforms.

'Little asshole,' one of them spewed as Eve finally clamped on the restraints. 'He just all of a sudden went batshit.'

Eve sat on the little asshole, eyeing the uniforms balefully. 'What the fucking fuck?'

'Sir, he came in to report an assault, he said, and we were starting to process when he went batshit. He took off for the elevator like he had wings on his tiny little feet.'

Eve looked down at the crazed, glassy eyes of a man who looked like a creepy garden gnome. 'And neither of you could tell he's on something that makes him think he can fly? Get him in the tank. He assaulted an officer. Peabody, your status.'

'I'm, ah, okay. Rapped my head pretty good.' She reached around, probed with her fingertips. 'Ow!'

'Haul his tiny, stupid ass up the steps.' Eve dragged him up, shoved him at the uniforms. 'Two counts of assaulting an officer,' she said, rubbing her stinging jaw. 'Find out what he ingested, popped, or smoked. For Christ's sake.'

'I love you, sweet cheeks,' the tiny, wriggling man shouted at Eve. 'Wanna kiss your boobies!'

'Yeah? Well, I want to kick your tiny ass. We'll both live with the disappointment.' She gripped Peabody's arm, guided her into the elevator.

'Boobies!' he shouted before the elevator doors shut.

'I'm surrounded by boobies. Do you need medical?'

'I don't think ... Were we just slammed by a giggling, bearded dwarf?'

'You were.'

'Then I probably only need an ice pack. And a blocker.'

'Get both. Goddamn world's full of goddamn crazy people.'

The elevator doors opened; several people started to get on. Eve snarled. Several people backed off.

She repeated the process all the way to Homicide, where once again she gripped Peabody's arm and dragged her to the bullpen. 'Somebody get Peabody an ice pack and a damn blocker.'

Baxter swiveled in his chair. 'You take a hit, Peabody?'

'I got decked by a flying dwarf.'

'I can't count the times that's happened to me.' But he

rose, patted her cheek. 'I've got you covered. Let's get your coat off, sweetie.'

Across the bullpen, Santiago pulled open a drawer on his desk. 'Got your blocker, Peabody.'

Someone else came up with a tube of water, and the reliable and earnest Trueheart trotted over with an ice pack.

Satisfied her partner would live through the morning, Eve started to turn away and walk to her office. She caught the scent of fat, yeast, sugar. Narrowed her eyes as Nadine walked in with a bakery box.

And with a rock star.

The blue line dissolved in the scent of fresh donuts.

Nadine, wisely, pushed the box at Eve and avoided a stampede. 'Are you all right, Peabody?'

'I got slammed by a flying dwarf. Hit my head.'

'A flying dwarf?' Nadine repeated with a look of concern at Eve.

'It happens. What do you want, Nadine? We're a little busy.'

'I come with baked goods, and some potential information. If you aren't interested—'

'My office.' Eve set the box on Peabody's desk, gave her men the hard eye. 'She gets the first, or I hear about it.'

'Awww,' Peabody said as Eve stalked away.

'What information?' Eve demanded. 'I'm not bullshitting about the busy, and Peabody's eyes are still wheeling around in her head.'

'Um . . .' Tall, built, and handsome in a been–there–done–that sort of way, Jake glanced over his shoulder. 'Where did the flying dwarf come from?'

'The elevator.' Eve headed straight for the AutoChef, as her to-go cup of coffee had splatted on the garage floor. 'You're here because I was going to look you up later, see if you could tell me anything about Glaze and Loxie Flash.'

'Actually, that's why . . . ' Jake trailed off as he caught sight of her murder board.

Eve programmed three coffees, gave him a once-over. 'If you're sensitive, we can take this elsewhere.'

'I wouldn't have thought, but . . . that's pretty harsh. I guess usual for you, like flying dwarfs.'

She reassessed him. She'd only met him once, under tense circumstances, and had found him steady. He had that tall, dark, dangerous look she knew some women went for. She assumed he had more going for him if Nadine was flustered over him.

He turned to Eve now, gestured toward her face with a long finger. 'It looks like you took a slam, too.'

'The dwarf had feet in really hard shoes.' And her ribs ached at the moment like a bad tooth. 'Sorry, crap mood.'

'Getting kicked in the face by a dwarf's bound to sour the mood.' Jake took the coffee she offered. 'Thanks. Listen, I heard about Loxie. It's all over the everywhere. Nadine figured I should come in, talk to you.'

'Talk.' She gestured toward her visitor's chair.

He sat, winced a little. 'Does this chair have teeth?'

'Apparently. Glazier's been recording at your place.'

'Right.' Jake shoved at his long, tousled hair. 'I want to say he's turned himself around, and it's not always easy in our game. He's been an asshole, but he's young and it's almost required you're an asshole when you're young and rocking it.'

'Are you an asshole?'

'Jesus, Dallas.'

'It's fair,' Jake said to Nadine with a spark of humor in crystal blue eyes. 'I'm not so young, and while I had asshole moments, I decided early on the music was more important than the party. Even than the sex, though that can run neck and neck in some cases. Glaze took awhile to get there, made some idiot choices, but he's on the road. Loxie was a big pothole in that road.'

The humor died as he glanced down at the coffee in his hand. 'I'm sorry she's dead. I'm sorry she died like she did, but Glaze had already driven around that pothole and moved on. He wouldn't have hurt her.'

'Do you know who would have?'

Jake looked at Nadine.

'You can be straight,' Nadine said in a way that told Eve she had said the same before. 'She won't think less of you.'

'I think a little less of me for saying it, but okay. She was one prime bitch. Selfish, mean as a rattler, with no sense of loyalty. My opinion? She wanted Glaze more after he didn't want her. Dog in the manger.'

'She had a dog?'

For a moment, Jake just stared. 'It's an expression. Like, you want something more when you can't have it.'

'What does that have to do with dogs and mangers? Never mind. You knew her well?'

'Not really. I knew who and what she was. I've seen her kind plenty. Between bouts with Glaze she made moves on Rocky – our drummer. Our married drummer. He didn't move back. She made them on me, and just hell no. She just wanted to leech onto rockers. That sounds harsh.'

Apparently he did have a sensitive side, and Eve didn't have time for it.

'Does being dead make her less of a bitch while she was breathing?'

He blew out a breath, stared down into his coffee again. 'No. Nadine figured I should tell you I ran into her a few days ago, and we had some hard words.'

'When, where, what?'

'She came to my place, wanted to see Glaze. They were recording. I was going to lay some tracks with them, so I was around. I saw her on the security. I didn't say anything to Glaze – she's a distraction. Was,' he corrected. 'I went to the door, told her to blow. She told me to suck it and so on. She was high. Buzzed most likely. She offered me a bj if I'd let her in. I said, shit, I said I thought too much of my dick to have her mouth on it. She took a swing at me, missed. I told her if she came back, if she tried any of that shit again, I'd twist her up. And I shut the door on her. So, I threatened her.'

'How about you tell me where you were last night at about twenty-two hundred.'

'Is that ten in actual time? Because about then Lois and I were engaged in certain activities.'

'He was at my place from about nine o'clock last night, and we were together all night. Stop playing with him, Dallas.'

'It's routine and procedure,' Eve corrected. 'Did she try to come back?'

'No, at least not when I was around. Glaze is clean – I know when someone isn't. He's seeing a really nice woman, and he's focused on staying clean, the woman, and the music. This'll mess him up some, and I'm more sorry about that than her being dead. And that's harsh, too, but truth.'

'You're around the studio a lot?'

'I live there. I work there. So, yeah. When I'm not traveling or we're not doing a gig or promo, I'm there.'

'Did you ever notice a woman hanging around—' Before she could finish he flashed a grin, the one that told her just what flustered Nadine.

'Maybe one or two.'

'A specific woman,' Eve continued. 'About five-six, on the lean side. Red hair, blue side dreads.'

'Hitting around forty? A couple of times.'

Eve went on alert. 'Outside the studio?'

'Across the street. I nearly ran into her – I think the same day as Loxie. I was coming back from a meeting, to lay those tracks, and she must've been camped out, like, I'd seen her a couple times. She sort of bumped into me, then freaked. I started to say something, but she jerked back and took off running. Didn't think much of it. We get the type.'

'You—'

Eve jabbed a finger at Nadine to silence her. 'How good a look did you get?'

'Face-to-face is a pretty good look.'

'Off the record,' Eve snapped at Nadine. 'I need you to work with our police artist.'

Jake lifted his eyebrows. 'You think that strange, spooky woman's involved?'

'You were face-to-face with a strange, spooky woman who's killed three people. Nadine, none of this goes out.'

'I know the damn drill, Dallas. I need a one-on-one update.'

'Can't do it. Listen, if you get two from me in as many days, it'll rub too many feathers. I'm giving you an according to an NYPSD source, name withheld, as the source doesn't have authorization to discuss the investigation.'

Nadine sulked a moment, then nodded. 'That works.'

'That source indicates investigators conclude the murder of Loxie Flash is connected to two other open cases. Multiple eyewitnesses have identified a person of interest, and investigators are pursuing new leads.'

'That's a runaround,' Nadine complained.

'Those are facts. And we're going to have a likeness of that person of interest this morning. Wait – add the hair, and a mink hoodie.'

'A mink hoodie?'

'She grabbed it on the run last night. No point letting her

enjoy it. Jake, I need you to come with me. Nadine, out of my office.'

'I need to feed this to the station.'

'Not from my office.'

'Fine. Are you using Yancy?'

'Yeah.'

'I'll be there in a few minutes.' She patted Jake's arm when he rose. 'I won't be long.'

'It's okay. Weird, but okay.' Then he dipped down, kissed her. 'Do what you do, Lois.'

19

Eve led Jake out of the bullpen and toward a glide.

'There's a guy back there wearing a tie designed to fry corneas, and another guy in a cowboy hat,' Jake noted.

Eve said, 'Yes.'

'But they're cops?'

'Yes.'

'This is a really weird day.'

Eve didn't glide on glides. She moved. Jake, long legs and jump boots, kept up with her, weaving and bobbing. She noted he got a lot of double takes, chin and finger points along the way. Apparently he didn't consider being recognized every five seconds part of a weird day.

She caught a movement, glanced back to see a woman barreling up the glide with a wild look in her eyes. So Eve finger-pointed herself. 'No,' she said, firm and cool.

'But I just wanna—'

'No.'

Jake flashed a smile over his shoulder as he quickened his steps to match Eve's pace. 'Maybe later.'

'I love you, Jake!' the woman shouted – with, Eve noted, a glimmer of tears in her eyes.

'Is that usual?' she asked.

He shrugged. 'It happens. Did you really get kicked in the face by a dwarf?'

'It happens.'

When he laughed, Eve decided he was – possibly – okay.

'Since you had that face-to-face,' Eve began, 'did you notice her eye color?'

'Brown. Ah . . . maybe hazel leaning brown.'

'You pay attention.'

'I like looking at women,' he said easily. 'All kinds of women.'

'The one who just confessed her love for you. Can you describe her?'

'Ah . . . heading toward forty – not quite there yet. Pretty blue eyes, a lot of dark blond hair. Wavy, not curly. Is this a test?'

'You did okay.'

'She was wearing a wedding ring,' he added. 'Not everybody does who is – you do – but it's something I like to notice.'

'Not a bad policy. How about the redhead? Did you notice any jewelry?'

'Skull earrings, now that you mention it. She had gloves on, so I can't say if she wore a ring.'

Keeping up the pace, she wound him through to Yancy's division, and saw Brad the bartender already there.

Brad spotted her, and the initial look of relief in his exhausted eyes turned to wide-eyed stunned when he recognized Jake.

'Um, Lieutenant . . . um.'

'Dallas.'

'Right. This is so chill. I mean, it's awful. I've been trying . . . Jake Kincade. Wow. Iced.'

'Detective Yancy, Mr Kincade also got a good look at the suspect.'

'You – you were there?'

'Another time and place,' Eve said before Brad could stammer out more. 'We appreciate you coming in this morning, Brad.'

'Didn't get any sleep anyway. I got a good look at her, I did. It's just harder to, like, see her now. The lights in there are whack, on purpose, so . . . '

'We're getting there.' Yancy, only a few years Brad's senior, offered the bartender an encouraging smile.

Eve imagined Yancy looked more like an artist than a cop, with the curly dark hair, the soulful eyes. But he was damn good at both.

'Let's see what you've got so far.'

As Yancy worked both by hand and by comp, he turned his sketchbook around.

She'd worked with less, Eve thought as she studied the sketch. But she'd have judged the woman the face represented to be in her late twenties – and the hair dominated the face itself.

'We haven't been at it long,' Yancy told her. 'Just really getting down to it.'

349

'More than we had. Does this match your impression, Jake?'

'Well, she's a good ten years older than she looks here. She's got some wear – don't mean any disrespect.'

'We're not here to respect her,' Eve pointed out.

'Okay, so.' Head angled, he studied the sketch. 'She's got some wear, you know? Lines starting.' He started to reach for one of Yancy's pencils, stopped himself. 'Out from the eyes, beside the mouth.'

'Do you draw?' Yancy asked him.

'I fool around.'

'Why don't you go ahead and show me?'

'I don't want to mess it up.'

'It's already comp-logged. Go ahead.'

'Okay, so . . . ' Jake took the pencil. 'I'd say her eyes are a little rounder. More like . . . ' He rounded them subtly, smudged some lines at the corner with the side of a callused thumb. 'And maybe a little broader nose. It seemed broader because her face is narrow, and it narrows more at the chin, like . . . that. Then the expression lines here. And I want to say she looked sallow. Like somebody who doesn't get out much, in the sun.'

'That's right,' Brad murmured. 'That's really right. Her mouth's smaller than what I said, isn't it?'

'I was going to say tighter, but yeah. Her features don't really balance. It's just a click or two off. She's not—'

Jake passed the pencil back to Yancy. 'It feels wrong to diss a woman in front of a woman.'

'A cop,' Eve corrected. 'You want to say she's not attractive.'

'Not like dead ugly, but not the sort you look at twice. A fader, if you get me. The hair was all "Look at me, I'm on it," but it didn't go with the rest of her. She was trying to be what she wasn't. Trying for younger, edgier, and just missing the mark.'

'Wanted to be with,' Brad supplied, 'and she's without.'

Yancy worked on the mouth, redefined the chin.

Eve studied the sketch. heavily lined eyes, darkly dyed mouth, the dreads falling on either side of the face, closing it in.

'It's a good likeness,' Jake commented. 'It's a real skill to be able to draw a likeness that good of somebody just from other people's bits and pieces.'

'We'll run with it,' Eve said. 'Log that, copy, and send,' she told Yancy. 'And can you do another, take away the heavy makeup, the dreads? Jake says brown eyes, possibly hazel, so go with brown hair.'

'Playtime.' Yancy rolled his shoulders, swiveled to the computer, and began some tech magic.

On-screen the dreads vanished. He filled in temples, cheeks, and side jawlines. Layer by layer he brushed away the thick eyeliner, the thickened lashes, took the eyebrows from dark and bold to a calmer brown.

The lips went from hard red to pale, almost undefined.

'Yeah, a fader,' Jake murmured as her hair faded to a nondescript brown.

Before Eve could speak, Yancy held up a finger. 'Gimme a second.'

He redefined here, smudged there, deepened some of the lines. 'Naked face, they'd show more,' he muttered.

Eve leaned over his shoulder, studied the result. 'There you are, bitch. There you fucking are.'

Satisfied, Yancy nodded. 'I can start facial recognition here.'

'Do that, send it to me, and I'll back that up. Damn good work. Go home, Brad, get some sleep.'

'I helped?'

She wanted to get to it, to start this part of the hunt with the scent inside her. But she took a moment. He looked so damn young, and so damn tired.

'You helped now, you helped last night.'

'The Flash is still dead.'

'Not a damn thing you could've done to change that. There's another life on the line now, and what you did last night, what you did right here, could help save that one. Tagging me, that was smart. Chasing after her, that was brave. Coming here, that was responsible. You hit all three marks. Go home and sleep.'

'Will you let me know when you get her? I'll sure sleep better when you do.'

'I'll let you know. Do you need transpo?'

'No, no thanks. Thanks, Detective Yancy.'

'Back at you, bro.'

'I know it's whack timing and all, but, man, it's like the ult meeting you, Jake.'

'Another back at you.' Jake shook his hand and Brad walked off grinning.

'Gotta book. Again, good work, Yancy,' Eve said.

'Nice meeting you,' Jake added to Yancy.

'I'll go with whack timing, the ult, and add "Night Run" still bangs all the bells.'

'Appreciate it.' Jake had to stretch his long legs to keep up with Eve's. 'What do you do now?'

'The job. Sorry,' she said quickly. 'You were a big help, more than usual, so we got this likeness nailed fast.'

'There's another life on the line? That wasn't bullshit to make Brad feel better – because it did. The idea that he helped, I mean.'

'He did help, and no, it's not bullshit. You're in line on helping save that life, too.'

Nadine came clicking along in her high-heeled boots before Eve reached the glide. 'I got hung up,' she began. 'And you were fast. Don't tell me you got her. You got her?'

'You said don't tell you.' Eve hopped on the glide.

Nadine reversed course, hopped on behind her. 'Let me see her.'

'No.'

'Goddamn it, Dallas!'

'You can't broadcast the sketch unless the commander gives that a green. And he's not going to give it a green at this time.'

'If I broadcast it, odds are somebody's seen her, can lead you to her.'

353

'Odds are shorter she rabbits. If I don't have her in the box or a cage within thirty-six, that's another story.'

'It's *my* story.'

'My case.'

'Your case, my story. They're not opposed. I damn well helped you get this far this fast.'

'You'll get your story when I close my case.'

'Jesus, you guys are sexy. Sorry,' Jake said without a hint of remorse when they both blasted him with stares. 'Thinking out loud. But facts are facts. Sexy is sexy. Do you ever go at each other like that when you're, you know, more . . . casually attired?'

'Don't respond,' Nadine said. 'It only encourages him.'

'Run with what you've got,' Eve advised, 'and within thirty-six' – less, she thought, less – 'you'll have the rest.'

With that, she vaulted over the side of the glide, dropped down two feet, and bolted.

Nadine hissed after her.

Jake grinned. 'I like her.'

Eve double-timed it into Homicide.

'We've got a face,' she snapped at Peabody as she continued straight into her office.

She pulled up the file Yancy sent, programmed for facial recognition, then printed out hard copies.

When Peabody hustled in, Eve slapped the sketch on her board.

'That's her? She looks . . .'

'Harmless,' Eve finished. 'Part of her arsenal, looking harmless. Being so bland she can morph into anyone. A "fader," Jake said, and that's just right. She can fade into the characters she chooses. And right now she's got some rich woman in her crosshairs. We are *not* going to let her take that shot.'

'McNab tagged me, said they're working on a search for you, and have a first pass.'

'Where is it?'

'They're refining it. He says it's too broad, and they're working on narrowing it.'

'How fast will she move?' Pacing the confines of her office, Eve kept that face in her line of vision. 'That's the question. She won't be in the system, so the facial match may take longer. She won't have done anything up until now to get noticed. Maybe we'll find some mental, emotional treatments in her medicals when we nail her down, but that's no given. Nothing to stand out.'

'She's a good seamstress. Better than good.'

'Yeah, you do that alone. And to make a living, you do it for other people who get to wear what you make, or alter, right? Do they notice you? Do they give you a second thought – like the line chef in a restaurant who's sweating it out to make the meal you order? Behind the scenes, under the radar. Writing, now, you get your name out there. *Bullshit Book* by A. E. Strongbow. You get recognition, praise, maybe some fame and fortune. Here I fucking am. It's her turn, goddamn it. Finally her turn.'

Eve swung around, drilled a finger into Strongbow's face. 'How does she gain access to the rich woman? In the book, the greedy son argues with the rich mother, ends up shoving her. She falls down the stairs, breaks her neck. He manages to pin it on his sister because said sister had a public tiff with the dead mother just that afternoon. How does she get into the house?'

'Disguises herself as the son?'

Eve shook her head. 'Rich people have security. She can't get through that pretending to be a member of the household. Security, staff.'

'Delivery person,' Peabody considered. 'Part of a cleaning crew, newly hired staff.'

Eve held up a finger. 'What does she do well? Sews. Rich women hire seamstresses, right? They can have them come to their home – more private, more convenient. She's been in New York long enough to have established herself in that line of work. Has to pay the bills, and she thinks ahead. She needs a rich woman to kill.'

'Leonardo.' Peabody shrugged. 'It's a long shot, but we have a direct line to a top designer. Rich women, such as yourself, use top designers.'

'I'm not rich. Roarke's rich. Leonardo's an angle. Let's see if we can contact him, show him the sketch. Maybe it'll ring. If not, he has plenty of contacts of his own in the business. Somebody he knows might recognize her.'

'I'll tag him.' Peabody looked at the sketch again. 'She doesn't stand out. Her work might, but . . . '

'Try it. I'm going to set an alert on the search and go up to harass Feeney on his.'

She can't wait long, Eve thought as she headed up to EDD. The last chapter didn't go as she'd written. She knew she had a cop on her heels. Up until now Strongbow had hidden in plain sight, and it worked for her. But under the crazy, she had a brain, and had to know the plot had twisted on her.

So, no, she wouldn't wait long.

Eve walked into the colorful circus of EDD. She took a quick moment to look through the dancing, prancing e-geeks to see McNab hard at work at his station.

Hard at work, she judged, as his shoulders bopped, his fingers snapped, and his head did a kind of jive that had his multitude of earhoops glinting.

She dived for the sanity of Feeney's office.

He leaned on the side of his desk in his shit-brown suit. He had what might've been a coffee stain on his shit-brown tie, but it was hard to tell.

His face, like his suit, looked comfortably baggy. She figured he'd had a recent trip to his barber, as his silver-threaded ginger hair sprang out to about half of its known capacity.

He shifted his basset hound eyes from his screen to her face.

'No point pushing us, kid. We're working it.'

'I've got a face.'

'Got a name and location to go with it?'

'Not yet.'

'We'll get her. Problem on this end?' He flicked a finger at the screen. 'Her writing samples hit dead average, even some below in some of them. So we've got a hell of a lot of maybes.'

Eve glanced at the screen, saw words, phrases skimming by, along with figures that looked like code, and numbers that looked like math.

Altogether, it looked impossible. Which was why she wasn't trying to do the damn search herself.

'Average or just below is what she is, with a couple of exceptions. She can tailor, and she can kill.'

She showed Feeney the printout of the sketch.

'You got forty to forty-five, white, brown and brown. No distinguishing anything. If she's not in the system for a bump or two, you're going to be awhile on facial.'

'Yeah, I got that. Hides in plain sight. A fader. That's the best term for her. Jake called her a fader.'

'Jake? You got a new man in your division?'

'No.' Eve frowned at the sketch, trying to see *more*. 'Jake Kincade. Nadine's tangling with him.'

'Didn't know she had a . . . ' Feeney straightened, shoved a finger at Eve. 'Jake Kincade? Avenue fucking A?'

'Yeah, she met him at the Garden during the assault. I guess they hit it off.'

Feeney jabbed a finger again, this time made sharp contact. 'You had Jake fucking Kincade in the house?'

'Yeah. He'd seen—'

'In. The. House. Jake Kincade. And you don't think to

tag your old pal, your old partner? The one who pulled you off street duty and into Homicide?'

His eyes looked a little fierce, a little wild. Eve eased back a step before she got poked again. 'No. I was kind of busy trying to get the face of a serial killer so I could, you know, discourage her from killing the next person on her list. Anyway, how was I supposed to know you'd want to meet him?'

Now Feeney stepped back – almost reeled back – slapped a hand to his heart. 'Do you even know me at all? What did I have playing when I trained you on stakeouts?'

'Music. Rock music,' she muttered when he stared holes in her. 'But—'

'And who would be my favorite rock band?'

Mentally – she knew better than to try it physically with him staring at her – she rolled her eyes. 'The Stones.'

'That is correct. What did I try, and obviously fail, to teach you about music? About Jagger and Clapton, about Springsteen, about Kirkland, Dobbler, and Jake fucking Kincade?'

'They, ah, rock?'

'They are each the voice of their generation! My old man's and his, mine, yours. Jake Kincade and Avenue A followed in the footsteps of the greats, and made their own. Have you even *heard* their cover of "Paint It Black"?'

'Ah . . .'

'But he's in our house, and you don't tell me.'

'I'll get him back.'

'You'll get him back.'

'Yeah, I'll ... fix it. I've got to get back down, but I'll fix it.'

She escaped.

'"Burn It Up" is the rock anthem of your generation!' Feeney shouted after her.

She quickened her pace, grabbed her 'link on the fly. 'Nadine, I need a favor.'

Nadine's feline eyes narrowed. 'Really?'

'For Feeney,' Eve corrected before she ended up trading for an appearance on *Now*. 'A favor for Feeney.'

She fixed it, put it away, and planned to close herself in her office and will the facial recognition to hurry the hell up.

Peabody waylaid her in the bullpen. 'Leonardo's coming in.'

'In? He doesn't have to come in. Just show him the damn sketch.'

'I did, and she didn't pop for him, but he was just leaving his studio anyway, and said he'd come in, take another look. And maybe we can give him some details that could help. He'll talk to his team, and spread the word.'

'Okay, that works.'

'Everything okay? You look hassled.'

'Because I am. I am hassled. Did you know Feeney has a hard-on – musically speaking – for Jake Kincade?'

'Dallas, anybody who spins rock does, and for Feeney rock's a religion. Santiago's sulking a little bit because you pulled Jake out before he could meet him. That on top of not getting to meet DeLano has bummed him pretty wide.'

'We're cops,' Eve groaned. She turned toward the slightly sulky Santiago, then lifted her arms to the rest of the bull-pen. 'We're cops.'

'Murder cops!' Baxter called out.

'Protecting and serving,' Jenkinson added.

'Because you could get dead,' Carmichael finished.

Trueheart grinned. 'Go, team.'

'Jesus, I need coffee.' She started to stalk away, rethought. She could throw one of her men a bone and save herself a step. 'Santiago, Carmichael, you're going to take the sketch of my suspect to DeLano in Brooklyn.'

Santiago visibly perked up, actually adjusted his cowboy hat. 'Yeah?'

'I want her and her family to watch for this individual, who is known to have stalked them previously. Find out if DeLano, her mother, or her daughters have seen this woman – when and where, if so. Take another copy to the daughters' school, show it around. Issue warnings. Check in with Brooklyn PSD, leave them a sketch. Hit the neighborhood shops, restaurants, and so on. Work it. The streets, alleys, shelters, boutiques, markets, diners, LCs, sidewalk sleepers, beat droids.

'She fades, but she's not fucking invisible. If she scouts in that neighborhood, somebody's seen her. Go.'

Santiago rose. 'All over it, boss.'

'Peabody.'

'Printing out sketches now.'

Once again, Eve started toward her office, stopped when she heard a trill of crazed laughter.

Bella.

Not just Leonardo, she thought, but the whole family.

Mavis Freestone bounced in on electric-blue airboots with two-inch sparkling soles. The boots matched the current color of her hair, worn today in masses of braids. Her open coat – blue again, with thin stripes of pink and green – revealed a deep purple skin suit.

Beside her, Leonardo towered, copper skin, bronze tipped coils of hair, and a long leather coat the color of good port wine.

In his arms, Bella, blond curls falling under a hat with a puppy face and long floppy ears, waved her mittened hands and shouted, 'Das!'

'Heartbreaker in training.' Baxter got up from his desk grinning, walked over to snatch her and toss her up in a way that made Bella squeal and Eve's heart stop.

'Jesus, Baxter.'

'She's a cutie.' He set her down.

She toddled straight over to hug Eve's legs, then try to climb up them.

Left with little choice, Eve hauled her up. Bella planted a wet, sticky kiss on her cheek, bounced, babbled, with blue eyes dancing. And ended with a question. 'Ork?'

'He's not here.'

'Aw. Ove Ork.'

'Right. Listen, I appreciate you coming in.'

'We were close by,' Leonardo told her. 'Anything I can do to help.'

'Probability's high she's working as a seamstress or a tailor. Most likely out of Brooklyn, but she may commute. Peabody says she's good. Really good.'

'Design and execution,' Peabody confirmed. 'Hey, Bellamina, want to come with me?'

Bella blew Peabody a kiss, but curled into Eve. 'Das.'

'Let's take it into my office.' Because Eve couldn't quite get her head around standing in the bullpen holding a kid.

'Sure. Hey, Jenkinson.' Mavis beamed at him. 'That tie is the total ult.'

'Don't encourage him,' Eve mumbled and led the way.

'I'm running facial recognition,' she began. 'And we've got a couple other angles. Since you're in the business, maybe you know somebody who knows something. If she's as good as Peabody says, maybe she works for a top outlet or designer. We need to—'

As they stepped into the office, Bella gasped. She pointed at the board. 'Ow!'

'Oh shit.'

Leonardo grabbed Bella, turned her face into his shoulder. He went pale and glassy-eyed himself even when he deliberately looked away from the board.

Moving fast, Eve snatched up her coat, tossed it over the board to cover the crime scene photos.

'Sorry. Shit, sorry.'

'Shit,' Bella echoed against her father's broad shoulder.

'And again, sorry.'

'Hey, Bellissima.' Cool and calm, Mavis took her from

363

Leonardo and gestured toward the sketch of Eve done by a young survivor. 'Who is that?'

'Das!' Ow forgotten, Bella threw back her head, gave her big belly laugh. 'Das!'

Remembering how Leonardo reacted to the sight of blood and violence, and there'd been plenty of it on the board, Eve pulled out her desk chair.

'Thanks. I don't know how you do what you do. I don't know how anybody does.'

'Got any of Mira's tea in the AC?' Mavis asked.

'Yeah. Give me a second.'

'I'll get it. Hey, Bella, let's make Daddy some tea. Just think happy thoughts, moonpie.'

She managed them, Eve thought. Her friend, the former grifter, the woman who changed her hair color more often than some changed their socks, the music-vid star and walking rainbow, handled the big man and the little girl as naturally, as smoothly, as if she'd trained for it all her life.

With Bella on her hip, she set the tea on the desk, leaned down to kiss Leonardo's cheek. 'We're going to sit on the floor here, and play with our blocks.'

'Das!'

'Dallas has to work, my baby doll, but we get to play.'

She sat on the floor, pulled a bag of colorful blocks out of the enormous pink-and-green handbag.

'Okay then. Here's the deal.' Eve leaned on the desk, brought Leonardo's attention to her. 'She's about forty, and she relocated from Delaware about two years ago. She'd live alone, on a budget. She'd be unlikely to socialize or make an impression. With her work, yeah, but not otherwise. Not the sort that draws attention, more slides into the background. She writes. She's probably a reader. She's going to seem harmless. She's going to have her own professional machine at home. She's likely to do side work.'

'A lot of tailors do side work. Off the books. I did myself when I was just getting started.'

'Did you go to clients' homes?'

'Once you establish a relationship? That's usually what you do. If you have a place, they might come to you, but usually, you're offering them the convenience. A fitting, alterations of something they already have, sometimes an original design.'

'How do they find you?'

'Word of mouth.' He sipped tea and seemed to relax again. 'If you're working in a shop – department store, boutique – you'd slip them a card, let them know you'd be happy to come to them for a job. Big or small. If you're working for another tailor, you'd have to be really careful about that – some will fire you on the spot. If she doesn't socialize, it's harder. It might be she gets side work from having a customer approach her.'

'Okay, got that.'

'I've still got contacts from my early days. I can ask around.'

'I'm going to give you the sketch, and ask you to do

just that. If you get a hit, remember, she's not harmless. Just tag me.'

She stopped when her comp signaled. Turning to the screen, she felt the lift, the buzz as she studied the ID shot side-by-side with the sketch.

'Ann Elizabeth Smith. Average name, average face. No more fading,' she stated. 'I've got the bitch.'

'Bitch!' Bella said cheerfully, and laughed like a loon.

20

The minute she cleared her office, Eve started a run on Ann Elizabeth Smith, barked for Peabody.

Peabody came on the run. 'Mavis said you—' She caught the face on-screen. 'Yes!'

'Born and raised in Wilmington, Delaware. DOB March 14, 2018. No sibs. Parents divorced in '27. Father relocated the same year, remarried six months later. Already had a skirt on the side,' she deduced. 'Mother, a seamstress, ran her own shop. Fit for You, established 2023.'

'She learned young,' Peabody said. 'Her mother taught her to sew. That fits.'

'The mother remarried and relocated in '36. It looks like Smith took over the management of the shop. Run a side search on that, the financials. It shut down two years ago – coordinating with her move to New York. I've got a Brooklyn address, and employment at Dobb's.'

'Small, exclusive department store,' Peabody told her as she worked her PPC. 'High-end clothing and accessories.'

'Carmichael and Santiago are already in Brooklyn.' Eve

pulled out her communicator. 'We'll have them sit on her home address. Keep running that, and get us a conference room. Pull in Uniform Carmichael and . . . Officer Shelby. We're going to work out the takedown.'

While Peabody went out, PPC in hand. Eve contacted her detectives, gave the order. Then contacted Feeney.

'Told you already. It's going to take awhile,' he said stiffly.

'I may have her – don't stop what you're doing, and I don't want to pull McNab off it. I need a geek. Can you spare one?'

'You can take Callendar.' His tone stayed as frosty as the day. 'She knows how you work.'

'Perfect. I'm taking a conference room, working out the op.'

'I'll get her moving.' Though still stiff, he added, 'Good hunting.'

'One more thing. I'm sending you an address.'

He offered her a mournful stare. 'You got any detectives in your own division?'

'Non-work-related. It's Kincade's recording studio. Avenue A – the band – is having – doing? – whatever, a session. They expect to start about fifteen hundred today, go through till maybe twenty-two, twenty-three hundred. It gives you a big window. You're cleared for it.'

'Cleared for it?' Feeney said blankly.

'To, you know, go. To hang. Watch, listen. He didn't have time to come back to Central, but you can go there. If you want.'

'I'm cleared to watch Avenue A record?' The frosty tone melted into the awed.

'Yeah. I said I'd fix it.'

When he didn't speak for a full fifteen seconds, Eve worried he'd suffered a small stroke. 'Feeney?'

'You didn't fix it.' His voice came out raw, then went to booming. 'You killed it! Holy shit, holy mother of shit! Best day of my life! Don't tell my wife, my kids, my grandkids I said that. Ever. Holy hot, steaming shit.'

She wasn't sure she could tell anyone – ever – that the cop she considered to be as steady, cynical, bullshit-free as any she'd ever known currently looked just a little insane.

That there might've been a tear in his baggy eye.

'Okay. So we're good?'

'Good, my ass. Kid, this is how you rock it.'

'Okay then. I've got to get on this, you know, murder stuff.'

She clicked off fast because Feeney's face reminded her of the big, sloppy dog at the vet clinic.

Peabody clomped back. 'Conference room two. I've got some financial data. It's a little convoluted.'

'Do I need Roarke?'

'Not that convoluted. It looks like the mother retained ownership, kept Smith on salary. Decent enough, I guess, but not as much as you'd think for a daughter – only child – taking over the running of a family business. One said daughter worked in, on record, since the age of seventeen. It's, you know, stingy. No percentage, no bonuses.'

'Okay. Okay.' Eve thought it through. 'Maybe a hard relationship with the mother. Mira turf, but it may play into Smith's obsession with the female writer, the female characters, the female vics.'

'No personal female power, or female circle,' Peabody finished with a nod. 'A little more on that. The place did good business under the mother, held its own for the first couple years after she passed the management, it shows a small decline, then a big drop. The big drop's about a year before she shut the doors. The mother, from my interpretation, shut them.'

'Got it,' Eve said as she walked herself through transferring what she had to the comp in the conference room. 'Let's get set up. Walk and talk. We've got Callendar on the e-work. On her way. Patch in Santiago and Carmichael when we're ready to brief. I want a map, and whatever we can get of her residence.'

'She'd probably be at work now, right?'

'We need her direct supervisor. Let's find out.'

In the conference room, Eve immediately set up the board with Smith's ID shot front and center.

'Address is a three-story, eighteen-unit apartment building. She's on the second floor, second unit, west side.'

Eve filed it in her head, visualized it, while she worked on the board.

'We tag the store,' Eve said, thinking out loud. 'Ask for the seamstress department.'

'I think "Alterations".'

'Then that. Request Smith by name for a 'link consult. She might know your face. We get Callendar to do it. Determine whether or not she's in the store, how long she'll be there. We need a sense of the area she works in – exits, how much running room. I'd rather wait until we're there to notify store security. We don't know them.'

As she worked out those logistics, Uniform Carmichael came in with Shelby. 'Grab coffee if you want it. We're waiting for our e-person. Peabody, try Records. See if we can access a blueprint of the Dobb's store.'

'The one in Brooklyn?' Shelby asked. 'I've got a friend who works there.'

Eve stopped what she was doing, turned to Shelby. 'Is she a blabbermouth?'

'She can flap them, sir, but not if I swear her down. If I do, she'll zip it.'

'Tag her and do that. I need her to find out if a seamstress is working today. Ann Elizabeth Smith.' Eve gestured to the board. 'She's our suspect. I need to know if she's in the store, and the structure of the department where she works.'

'Jill, she'd know. She works in the fancy dress section, like formal wear and all that.'

'Just the data, and no blabbing.'

'She'll stay frosty, Lieutenant.' Shelby pulled out her 'link as Callendar came in.

She'd whacked her hair short, added blue tips. She wore the many-pocketed baggies the e-geeks seemed to love. Her multitude of pockets sported blue-and-pink polka dots over their fields of electrified green. The rest of the baggies picked up the pink while her high-top sneaks reveled in the green and blue.

The frisky puppy frolicking over her shirt – and impressive breasts – seemed at odds with the weapon clipped to her belt.

She said, 'Yo.'

'Yo. Grab coffee, I'll brief in a minute.'

'Got fizzy.' She shook the go-cup in her hand. 'Ready and able.'

'Lieutenant? The suspect isn't in today.'

'We'll focus on her residence.'

'Sir?' Shelby continued. 'She hasn't worked there in almost a year. She quit, Jill says. Handed in her notice and split.'

'Didn't update her data. Is your friend still on your 'link?'

'I've got her holding, sir.'

Eve walked over, took the 'link, flipped off the hold. 'This is Lieutenant Dallas.'

'Oh, okay.' The big-eyed blonde managed a nervous smile.

'Did you know Smith? A. E. Smith?'

'Ann? Sure. Well, I didn't know-know her. We didn't, like, hang or anything, but I used her a lot when she worked here. For fittings and alterations. She was top-notch, you know? And fast, too. A lot of my regulars requested her.'

'How did she get along there?'

'Um . . . She was really good at her job. I guess she wasn't so good with actual people. Not rude, like, just . . . Really shy maybe? She never had anything to say.'

'No friends?'

'Around here? I guess not. Ah, Mo said I wasn't supposed to blab. I've got the lock down.'

'That doesn't apply to me.'

Shelby leaned into the screen. 'Spill to the lieutenant.'

'Okay then. She was weird. Not just quiet and shy, but weird. Wouldn't look you in the eye, mumbled, spent her breaks huddled up with her PPC – that's if she took a break. Mostly she worked through. We're friendly around here, right? She just wasn't. And Dobb's throws a primo holiday party. She didn't even come when she was here. I guess she sort of creeped me. But she was really good at her job.'

'You haven't seen her since she quit?'

'No. I'm pretty sure some of my regulars use her, on the side.'

'Okay, appreciate it. Put the lock back on.'

'Could I ... Before I do that, can I ask if she did something whacked? You know how you hear people say, "Oh she was so quiet, kept to herself," and how they never thought they'd do something whacked? Well, Ann was quiet and kept to herself – mega – but I wouldn't be surprised if she did something whacked.'

'Shelby will let you know about that when our lock's off.'

Eve handed the 'link back to Shelby, made a wind–it–up signal with her finger.

'Gotta go, Jill. I'll get back to you.'

'Peabody, patch in the others.'

Eve lined up the steps in her head, got the nod from Peabody.

'The suspect is Ann Elizabeth Smith, aka A. E. Strongbow. She has, we believe, killed three people. Rosie Kent,' Eve continued, gesturing to the board, 'Chanel Rylan, and Loxie Flash. Each victim was chosen, each murder constructed, to correspond with a novel written by Blaine DeLano.'

She ran through the outline of the victims, murders, motives, and Smith's obsession with DeLano and the series.

'So not only does the whacked,' Callendar said, 'she is the whacked.'

'Legally whacked is for the courts and shrinks to say. But she's not the shy, quiet, harmless woman she appears to be. She's both dangerous and cunning. We won't underestimate her. Santiago? Any sign she's in residence?'

'Privacy screens are down, LT. We haven't sighted her going in or coming out.'

'Our e-person will determine when we get there. If she's not in residence, we wait until she comes home. Peabody and me inside, Santiago and Detective Carmichael in the vehicle with Callendar, uniforms out of sight at the rear of the building, moving in on my signal. If she's in residence, I want the uniforms on the rear, cutting off any attempt to exit. Detectives enter with me and Peabody, holding on the first floor to cut off that route. Callendar with us. You'll knock, get her to open up. She doesn't know your face, and she's not going to think "cop" seeing you.'

'Hey!'

'She won't think "murder cop",' Eve temporized.

'Accepted.'

'She opens, you step out of the way. All weapons, low stun, but we take her down fast. She's a seamstress so she's going to have sharps. We don't know if she has other weapons.'

'It's an old, low-rent, working-class building,' Peabody added. 'You should be able to get a heat signal with a portable, Callendar.'

'Copy that. I'll get eyes and ears, too, in case.'

'Gear up,' Eve said, 'and let's roll.'

Straightforward, Eve thought as she drove into Brooklyn with Callendar and her e-toys in the back. But no op, however straightforward or simple, could be taken casually.

The straightforward could become the twisty and the simple the deadly. She worked out contingencies as she drove. The uniforms followed in a black-and-white while Peabody mined for more data on the PPC.

'I've got the mother's social media pages. She's got a stepdaughter – well, two – through her second marriage. But the younger just got married last June. A lot of pictures – and commentary. Splashy white wedding in Savannah, where they're located. Gorgeous bridal gown.'

'That's of great interest because?'

'Because Smith's mother designed it with her stepdaughter, and made it. The stepdaughter's got commentary on here, refers to Smith's mother as Mom – new husband's a widower. Goes on and on about her new mom, the dress, the family. Not one mention of the stepsister she inherited. No photos of Smith anywhere I can find. I don't think she went to the wedding.'

'No family ties.'

'I'm not finding any. Her father – Smith's – has a page, too. Not as chatty as the mother's, but he has one. Photos of him and his second wife, some golf buddies. And several including his son with second wife, and his grandson. None of his daughter. Also no mention.'

'It's kind of sad,' Callendar commented. 'The old man takes off, hooks up, starts a new family, and his daughter's left out. The mother sticks till she's of age, then she books, too. New life, new family. Of course, since Smith is whack, maybe they considered it a kind of escape. But that's sad, too.'

'Family's supposed to be family.'

'That's what I say.' Callendar bopped Peabody on the shoulder. 'I mean half my family's whack. Not kill-you-in-your-sleep whack, but whack. But we stick.'

'You're assuming the parents did the booking and forgetting,' Eve pointed out. 'And not factoring in the father may have tried to keep lines open. And the mother didn't shut the doors of the shop until a couple of months after Smith walked out of it. Walked out of the family business, out of where she lived and worked her entire life. Then she walked out on her job here in New York.'

'You've got a point,' Callendar conceded.

'And whoever did the booking and forgetting? Three people who did no harm are dead by Smith's hand.'

'Yeah, that's a big factor in it. Are DeLano's books sexy? I like sexy books.'

'They've got a heat element,' Peabody told her. 'But it's more "Will they ever do it" instead of "Hey, they're doing it again."'

'We'll hold book club later,' Eve said. 'Tell the uniforms to peel off. I want them to go around the back rather than drive past and go around. No point in having her glance out the window, see an NYPSD cruiser, and panic.'

Peabody relayed as Eve made the turn onto Smith's street. She spotted her detectives' vehicle, approved they'd found a slot out of direct sight line from Smith's window, but with a good view of the building and the street.

She pulled up across the street, contacted them.

'Hold there until Callendar gets her read. Officer Carmichael?'

'Parking, Lieutenant. We'll move into position in a couple. First floor, rear door. We'll cover it until you say different.'

'Callendar?'

'Take me a sec. It's a nice old building. Could use some work, but that's good, solid brick there. And . . . crap windows with crappier screens. I got you a heat source like bang. Far side of the room, looks to be sitting down. One source, Dallas. Sitting, but active.'

'We move in. Uniforms, take the back. Detectives, wait until we enter, then take the first floor. Callendar.'

'Wait once. I can keep this running, transfer to my pocket piece, and keep an eye on her. You want the eyes and ears?'

'Shouldn't need them. Ready?'

'Set,' she said.

Peabody muttered, 'Go,' as they got out of different doors.

They moved fast, not at a run, but a quick New York walk down the sidewalk to the building entrance. Eve mastered it open, gave her detectives the signal, then went in.

She gestured up a set of narrow stairs. 'You knock, say somebody gave you her name about tailoring.'

'What do I want tailored?'

'Oooh, a wedding dress! Say a wedding dress,' Peabody urged.

'Frosty. I can play that.'

'She starts to open the door, step back.'

'I'm a real cop, you know.'

'You're a real cop, and you're coming in behind us. Draw your weapon, and keep your hands out of view.'

Eve judged the doors they passed. A couple solid kicks, she estimated. If Smith didn't open, they'd take the door down, and her with it.

'Where is she?' Eve kept her voice low as they approached the apartment.

'Same spot.'

'Peabody, take the other side of the door. Santiago?'

'Got the door and the stairs.'

'Officer Carmichael?'

'On the back, Lieutenant.'

'Stand by.' She nodded to Callendar.

Callendar put on a happy face, stepped up, weapon held low, and buzzed.

A staticky intercom clicked on. 'Yes?'

'Hey! I'm Debby! A friend of mine gave me your name. It's about my wedding. She said you're really, really good, and my mom really wants me to wear her dress, so it has to be altered before the big day.'

'Sorry? What?'

'In May. The wedding's in May. I've got a picture. Can I show you?'

'Hold on.'

A chain rattled. Callendar stepped back.

'Door's opening,' Eve murmured into her comm.

When the lock clicked and the door creaked open a crack, she shoved through, had the woman spun around against the wall.

'Oh my God, oh my God, take whatever you want!'

'We're the police.'

And though she was already cursing silently, Eve turned the woman to face her to make sure.

'It's not Smith. Where is Ann Elizabeth Smith?' Eve demanded.

'I don't know.' The woman's gaze, full of fear, bounced from face to face. 'I don't know anybody like that. Please, my kid'll be home soon. Take whatever you want.'

'NYPSD.' Eve holstered her weapon, took out her badge. 'This apartment is listed under the name I gave you.'

'I'm Gracie Lipwitch. I've got ID. I can show you.'

'No need, Ms Lipwitch, and I'm sorry we frightened you.'

'Frightened? I may have wet my pants! I'm sitting here, on my day off, icing cupcakes for my kid's scout meeting, and the next thing I know. You said wedding. I thought you were looking for a wedding cake. The damn intercom's a piece of crap.'

'Ms Lipwitch, how long have you lived in this apartment?'

'Eight months, three weeks, and two days.'

'That's very specific.'

'We moved in exactly one month after my kid's no-good father took off on us. I'm going to sit down. My legs are shaking.'

'Can I get you some water?' Peabody asked, but Lipwitch waved her off.

'You scared the life out of me.'

'I'm very sorry,' Peabody said, adding a look of concern. 'The person we're looking for lists this as her address.' She pulled up the photo on her PPC. 'This woman.'

Lipwitch looked at it. 'I'm sorry. I don't think I know her. But the way you came barging in here, she better have killed somebody.'

At the beat of silence, her face went pale. 'Oh God, you think I killed somebody.'

'No, we don't,' Eve assured her. 'Can you tell us if the previous occupant left anything behind?'

'The place was empty – and not all that clean – when me and Darby moved in. My girl. I cleaned like a maniac for a full day. A lot of, like, slivers. Of material. A lot of smudges on the wall, like from taping stuff up. That's about it. You said wedding.' Now she let out a long breath. 'I thought you wanted a wedding cake. I'm a baker. I work at a bakery a couple blocks from here, and do some cakes on the side. My day off,' she added. 'And what am I doing but making three dozen cupcakes for my kid's scout group.'

'They look really great.'

Lipwitch looked at Callendar, sighed. 'You can have one. I made a few extra.'

'Seriously? We'll split one.' Callendar chose one with a swirl of creamy white icing, broke off a chunk. 'They're terrific.'

Eve dug out a card. 'You can contact me. I'm going to make sure the address is changed so no one bothers you again.'

'Okay. Listen, did somebody who lived here really kill somebody?'

'We're looking for this individual in the course of a homicide investigation.'

'That's even scarier than having you barge in here. I don't know if it helps, but I got this place fast because one of the people who lives downstairs comes in the bakery a lot, and she knew I was looking for a place for me and my kid. It's just a one bedroom and I wanted two, but the price was right and it's close to work, and it was available. Whoever lived here before just walked out. I mean, she left the last month's rent in an envelope with the keys, took her stuff, and left. It looks like nobody knew the difference for a couple weeks.'

'That is helpful. Can you tell me the name of the person who told you about the empty apartment?'

'That's Mrs Waterstone, down in 103. She's probably home. Don't scare her.'

'We won't, and I apologize again.'

'I'm mostly over it. I might even think it's exciting later. Look, take her a cupcake.' Lipwitch transferred one onto a little paper doily. 'She's got a sweet tooth. And I guess if anybody knows anything about anybody, it's Mrs Waterstone.'

Eve started downstairs with the cupcake. 'Officers Carmichael and Shelby, mission abort. Suspect no longer lives here. Do a canvass of the neighborhood, show her photo. Maybe we'll hit something.'

At the bottom of the stairs, Detective Carmichael pointed a finger. 'That's a cupcake.'

'Excellent powers of observation, Detective.'

'You've got a cupcake.'

'No, Mrs Waterstone in 103 is getting a cupcake.'

'I got one I'm sharing because that's the kind of exceptional human being I am. Break off a bite.'

'Thanks.'

'Then head back to DeLano's neighborhood and keep at it,' Eve told them.

Santiago broke off a bite himself. 'She's slippery, boss.'

'Yeah. She's damn slippery.'

'Want, Peabody?'

Peabody eyed the chunk left in Callendar's palm. 'Half of that because loose pants.'

'Half. Dallas?'

Eve shook her head, headed to 103.

'She is Woman of Steel,' Callendar observed. 'Who says no to cupcake?' And since it was there, she popped the last bite in her mouth.

Eve buzzed at 103, got another staticky intercom.

'Yes?'

'Mrs Waterstone, I'm Lieutenant Dallas with the NYPSD.'

'You're a little out of your neighborhood, dear.'

'Yes, ma'am. Your neighbor upstairs, Ms Lipwitch, said you might be able to help us with information on a former tenant of the building. And she sent you a cupcake.'

A rattle, a click, and the door opened to a tiny black woman with a snow-white bubble of hair and a cheerful smile. 'She knows my sweet tooth. Goodness, three of you, and all girls. All girl police?'

'Yes, ma'am.'

'That's what I'm talking about. That, and that cupcake. Well, come ahead in. I just finished all my chores and was about to sit down with my book. This should be even more fun. Do you want tea?'

'No, thanks.'

If chores meant cleaning the apartment, the little woman was a champ on chores. It all but glimmered. While the furniture showed years of use, it didn't carry so much as a speck of dust.

By book, Eve realized she meant the real thing. Roarke would have approved of the shelves packed with them.

Photos tucked in here and there, a lot of kids' faces.

'Now, you girls have a seat and tell me what you want to know.'

'Did you know Ann Elizabeth Smith?'

'The little mouse who used to live upstairs? Couldn't say I knew her. Wouldn't say boo to a goose, whatever the hell that means. Why would anybody? What's she done?'

'We'd like to talk to her.'

'You can't bamboozle me, dear.' Waterstone set the chair into an easy rock. 'I was a teacher for fifty-five years. I know all, see all. I have three girl cops at my door asking about her, she did something big. Wouldn't surprise me.'

'Why do you say that?'

'Sneaky, unfriendly, unhappy. A bad combination. I never once saw her bring anybody home, or have a visitor.'

Waterstone paused to tap her finger on the arm of her rocking chair. 'That's not healthy. I did get out of her she worked as a seamstress at Dobb's. That's high society there. I like to sew a little myself, but I couldn't get her to talk to me. Asked her in a couple of times, but she scurried away. The girl up there now, with her sweet girl? Nice as they come, but the other one? She had a look about her. The word is *furtive*.

'I do recall her coming in one time – late in the day – crying. Mad crying, if you understand me, not heartbroken crying. Carrying a package. I asked what was wrong, like you do, and she yelled at me. First time she looked straight at me, first time she spoke to me above a mutter. Told me to mind my own damn business. And since she's right above me, I could hear her slamming around, stomping around for a good hour after. There's a bad temper inside that little mouse. You'll want to be careful when you find her, dear.'

'Would you have any idea where we might find her?'

'I'm sorry to say I don't. She left here in a hurry, or so it seemed. She must've had whatever furniture she had moved when I was out. I didn't know she was gone, only that I didn't hear her upstairs. I'm going to say I was worried some – and nosy – so I went up and buzzed. Then I contacted the management because, well, that kind of unhappy can come to a bad end. I thought maybe she'd killed herself. Turned out she'd just moved on. Left the rent, though, every penny. That's when I told Gracie upstairs about the apartment. It's a happier building now. That other girl, she carried a cloud with her. And sooner or later, clouds break into a storm.'

21

Eve walked fast, talked fast.

'Officer Carmichael,' she snapped into her comm. 'I want you and Shelby to hit every building, every apartment, every shop, restaurant, take-out joint, and dive on this block. Peabody, send them and the detectives the photos of all her looks. Show all of them to every resident, shopkeeper, sidewalk sleeper, and street thief.'

She got behind the wheel. 'Plug this Dobb's place in,' she told Peabody, then contacted Santiago. 'Peabody's sending you pictures. Hit every building on DeLano's block, and every building in the shopping area where the kid spotted the suspect. Somebody's seen this bitch.'

She peeled out. 'She's not far, she won't have gone far,' she stated. 'Maybe changed her look again. She's smart enough for that, but she can't change her nature. She still has to earn a living.'

As she drove, she contacted Feeney. 'Anything?'

'You're there. The addy Peabody shot to McNab.'

'She's blown.'

'Not surprised. She went dark from there about nine months ago. Nothing posted or sent from that location since. We're working through another batch. Thing is, she got into a couple of tangles on one of those writer sites – didn't take criticism very well, and she shut it down. Pulled her stuff off, from what we can see.'

'That's her break. Nobody appreciates her art. She'll show them. Not just DeLano, nobody. Keep at it.' She clicked off. 'Callendar.'

'Yo.'

'Peabody's going to send you what we've got on a search for the next target. I know you've only got your handheld, but pick it up.'

'Copy that. Does this AC back here – and that is frosty enough – have fizzies?'

'I don't know.'

'It does,' Peabody told her.

'*Excelente*. Put one on my tab. I gotta keep the sugar going.'

Time for reinforcements, Eve thought, and tagged Roarke. She expected to go through his admin, Caro, but he answered himself.

'Good afternoon, Lieutenant.'

'Yeah. Listen, have you got any time for consultant work?'

'I may. Depending on the fee.' He smiled.

'Ha. I've got EDD working two separate searches, and don't want to lay another on them. I ID'd the suspect and her location, but she poofed from there months ago. Ann Elizabeth Smith. I've got men in the field canvassing two locations, because she's damn sure still in Brooklyn. I need a deep dive into her financials, and whatever shadow accounts she might have set up.'

'Poking into other people's money is vastly entertaining. Will you work at home or Central?'

'Central, for now anyway. I'm heading for Dobb's in Brooklyn first.'

'Going shopping then?'

'Well, they're having a big shoe sale.'

'And there's nothing you'd enjoy more. I'll be at Central in an hour, an hour and a half latest.'

'Appreciate it. Gotta go.'

She spotted Dobb's – a three-story, elegantly faded brick building with big display windows and a large brass plaque embossed with its name over fancy double doors.

She considered pulling into its underground lot, thought, Fuck it, and zipped into a no-parking zone, flipped on her on duty light.

'I'll stick,' Callendar said from the back, 'keep on this, unless you need me in there.'

'Stick.'

'I've never been in here.' Peabody climbed out, studied the window display of mannequins that appeared to be strolling over the deck of a cruise ship in flowy pants, sheer dresses. Another stretched out on a lounge chair in a bathing suit that cut down to the gemstone glittering in her navel while she held a tall glass topped with a pink umbrella. Everyone's hair fluttered as if from an ocean breeze.

'It's February,' Eve commented. 'Why aren't they wearing coats, sweaters, boots?'

'It's February,' Peabody agreed. 'That's when rich people get out of the cold and go on cruises or to warm places. So cruise wear.'

'In New York, and that includes Brooklyn, it's February.' Eve pushed through the fancy doors.

She saw it coming, the three people in sharp black with maniacal smiles converging on her from three directions. Like a pincer movement on the battlefield.

All armed with spritzers.

'Any of you who sprays me with any of that crap is going to be arrested for assault.' She whipped out her badge. 'Where's Alterations?'

Two slunk away, but one stood firm – all six feet of her – in towering black heels that should have had her feet screaming in protest.

'Any of our consultants on the second or third floor can assist you with a fitting expert.'

'I don't want a fitting expert. I want Alterations.'

The woman's smile never wavered. 'Any of our consultants on the second or third—'

'Never mind.'

Eve strode toward the glide. Behind her back, Peabody stuck out her arm, turned up her wrist, invited a spritz.

She sniffed at it as she hurried after Eve. 'Too musky.'

'What?'

'Nothing.'

'I can smell you. You smell like you slept in somebody's great-grandmother's attic.'

'Yeah, too musky.' As she walked, Peabody rubbed her spritzed wrist on her thigh. 'My mistake.'

Eve glanced around the second floor. Racks and shelves of clothes, little alcoves with names of designers above the entrances full of more. A lot of frozen fake people wearing outfits. Three grouped together appeared to have a conversation as they posed.

And that was just creepy.

Eve arrowed toward an actual person, one carrying a couple pair of those flowy pants, and moving too fast to be a customer.

'Hold it.'

'Good afternoon! I'm sorry, I'm with a customer. Let me call for a consultant to assist you.'

'I need Alterations.'

'Of course. Just let me—'

'Get me, ah, Jill. Formal wear. Blond, big blue eyes.'

'I'll call for her right away. Just one moment.'

When she hurried away, Eve decided to give it exactly two minutes before she shoved her badge into someone's face.

Jill made it in about ninety seconds. When she saw Eve, her big eyes went bigger yet.

'I didn't say anything to anybody! I swear!'

'We're not here for that. I need you to take me to Alterations.'

'Oh. Gosh. Customers aren't allowed down there.'

Eve drew out her badge, but didn't shove it into Jill's face. 'This makes me a cop, not a customer.'

Behind Eve's back Peabody dropped her hand from the sweater she'd been stroking.

'Look, Jill, I'm pressed for time. I can get the store manager, go through the damn protocol, or you can just take me where I need to go.'

'I guess. Okay. I guess it's okay because you're the police. I saw the vid and everything.'

'Great. Lead the way.'

'We should take the elevator. It's in the basement, and you have to swipe to get down there. It's employees only.'

The elevator proved roomier than the ones at Central, and not as packed with bodies. But once you added the multitude of shopping bags, a baby in one of those wheeled chairs – strollers, Eve remembered – and a good-size dog in a plaid sweater, it made a decent crush.

Everybody poured off on the main floor. Jill swiped for the basement.

Given the underground location, Eve expected a sweat-shop atmosphere. Dozens of people huddled over machines, or killing their backs and feet crouched over worktables and stations. Bad lighting, chilly air.

Instead, she stepped into a brightly lit area where about a half dozen people worked on machines or with hand tools at individual stations. Some of them chatted away as they worked. Some wore headsets and bopped a bit like an e-geek.

'This is the main area,' Jill told her. 'There's like a break room and the bathrooms, and a supply area, but—'

'This works. Thanks.'

'I can go back up?'

'Yeah. Keep it zipped for now.'

'I will. I swear!' She escaped.

A woman, dark hair coiled at the nape, some sort of magnifier hanging from a fancy chain around her neck, came out of the back, started toward a station.

She spotted Eve and Peabody, shifted direction.

She looked to be about sixty, Eve judged, with perfect makeup and a trim black jacket over pegged pants.

She wore sensible shoes.

'I'm very sorry, this is an employees-only work area. Can I escort you back to the store?'

Eve drew out her badge. 'We need to speak with the supervisor.'

'You are. I'm Conchita Gomez. How can I help you?'

'Lieutenant Dallas, Detective Peabody. You once employed an Ann Elizabeth Smith.'

'That's correct. Ms Smith left Dobb's employ several months ago. May I ask what this is in reference to?'

'We're looking for Ms Smith for questioning regarding an investigation.'

Gomez kept her voice low, under the hum of machines. 'Your badge said Homicide.'

'That's correct.'

'Is Ann a suspect in a murder?'

'We need to locate Ms Smith.'

'I don't know how to help you. She did good work here, was paid well. When she handed in her notice, I was surprised, and asked her if there was a problem. She only said she had other priorities and needs. I offered to request a raise for her, but she refused, in her way.'

'Her way?'

'Head down. "Thank you, but I'll finish my current alterations before I leave." I hated to lose her, as her work was exemplary.'

'And otherwise?'

'Painfully shy, I suppose. She didn't mix well. I run an efficient department, and we can be extremely busy. But good working conditions, community, contented employees help foster that good work and efficiency. Ann was efficient and creative. I wouldn't describe her as content.'

'Any outbursts?'

'From Ann?' Gomez patted at the coil at the nape of her neck. 'Absolutely no. Although I sensed something simmering in her silence. She rarely spoke to anyone.'

'Where'd she work?'

'Last station, left. I know she did side work. Most of them do. I look the other way as long as it doesn't interfere with the work assigned here.'

'Do you know specific customers? It could be important,' Eve added when Gomez hesitated.

'I can't say I know, but I certainly have an opinion.'

'I'd like a list of your opinions.'

Dark eyes registered surprise, but the voice stayed smooth. 'All right. Let me look through my files and compile that for you. It is opinion, not concrete.'

'Understood. I'd like to talk to the other seamstresses.'

'Not all of them knew her. Ming, in Ann's former station, came on after Ann had left. And Della only last month after our cherished CeCe retired. First station, right.'

'If I could interrupt the work for just a few minutes.'

Gomez turned to the room. 'Ladies!' she called out. 'And Beau,' she added with a little smile to the only male in the room. 'This is Lieutenant Dallas with the NYPSD. She needs to speak with us.'

'Does anyone know the whereabouts of Ann Elizabeth Smith?'

Eve watched people glance at each other, a couple baffled, others fascinated or curious. Nobody spoke until Beau shrugged.

'She used to work here. Quit. She was stuck-up anyway.'

If Eve had seen him from a distance, she'd have pegged him as mid-teens. He had an explosion of curling purple hair under a knit cap, a narrow goatee with a silver stud in the center of his chin, and a slouchy posture now that he'd kicked back from his machine.

Still, he had about fifteen years on the mid-teens.

'Stuck-up.'

'Wouldn't talk to you if you were on fire. Wouldn't contribute to the pool. We do pools for birthdays and stuff. And the Secret Santa deal. Hell, I put in for that, and I'm Jewish.'

'You didn't much like her.'

'I didn't like her at all. Sorry, Cheeta,' he added with a grin to his supervisor. 'It didn't break my heart when she split.'

'Any idea where she split to?'

'Not a clue.'

In the back, across from Smith's former station, a tiny redhead raised her hand. 'Um, is she in trouble?'

'We need to speak with her,' Eve said.

'It's just, she was sort of nice to me once, and I don't like to get people in trouble.'

'Yolanda, it's very important you tell the police anything you know.'

At her supervisor's firm, quiet voice, Yolanda hunched up her shoulders. 'Once, when I was really slammed, she helped me out a little bit, and that was nice of her.'

'I think she was writing a book or something.'

Eve looked over at a sturdy blonde. 'Did she tell you that?'

'She never told anybody anything. I came in early one day to finish up some work because I was going on vacation. She was here, back in the break room. You have to pay for snacks, but the coffee and tea and water are free. She was back there with coffee, working on her tablet. She was into it because she didn't even hear me, and I looked over her shoulder like you do. She was writing stuff, and I said: "Hey, you writing a book or what?" She jumped like a mile, and grabbed her stuff. Didn't even say a word, just ran out.'

'I saw her once. After she quit,' Yolanda added.

'When?' Eve fired back. 'Where?'

'Well, gosh. A couple months ago. I was shopping for Christmas with my mom and sister. She looked a little different, but I knew it was her.'

'Different how?'

'Her hair. She'd cut it. She always wore it long, back in a tail, but she'd cut it to right above her shoulders, and dyed it really red. I thought it was a nice change for her. I guess – I don't want to be mean – but maybe she gained some weight? She had on this big coat, and she looked a little bulky in it.'

'Did it have penguins on it?'

'Yes! So I saw her, and I called out, like you would. And I waved. I was going to cross the street and say hi, see what she was doing, but when she saw me, she just kept going. Walking away fast. It hurt my feelings a little.'

'Where?'

Yolanda chewed on her lip, then her thumbnail. 'Um.'

'Just try to think back to what you were doing when you saw her. Across the street,' Eve prompted. 'In the big coat with penguins on it.'

'I think . . . I guess . . . We did a lot of shopping that day, but it was either over on Third Avenue or maybe over on Ninth Street. I mostly think Third Avenue, right after we came out of Baby Love. My brother and his wife had a baby right before Thanksgiving, so we shopped there. I think that was it. Or else it was when we were on Ninth Street. It was back in December for sure, though. The first Saturday in December, because I asked for the day off – right, Cheeta?

Cheeta can check. I asked for it off so we could go shopping as a team. And have lunch and – before lunch!'

Now Yolanda clapped her hands together, as if she'd won a prize. 'Before lunch. I'm sure it was because it hurt my feelings when she saw me and walked away, and I talked about it at lunch. So the baby store for sure.'

'That's very helpful, Yolanda.'

'I hate to get her in trouble.'

'You haven't. You may have helped others out of it. If anyone remembers anything more, I'm going to leave cards with your supervisor. Contact me, anytime. Ms Gomez, if you can compile that list.'

'I'll need about an hour. Last year's files would have been archived, as would a former employee's tickets – work tickets.'

'Send it to me the minute you have it. Thank you for your time.'

In the elevator Eve pulled out her 'link.

'That was a lucky break,' Peabody commented.

'Maybe. Time to call in the locals.' She tagged her contact. 'Lieutenant McMahon, Lieutenant Dallas. I'm still on your turf.'

By the time she got to the car she had Brooklyn ready to canvass the two areas Yolanda gave her.

'Anything?' she asked Callendar, who worked, car-seat danced, and slurped a fizzie in the back.

'Got a list started.'

'I'm going to have another coming in. We're going to

cross yours with that, see if we get any matches. Can you stick with this, Callendar?'

'You got me until the cap says different. Somebody smells like a fancy girl's gym locker, after a sweaty volleyball game.'

'I've got to get it off!' Peabody rubbed at her wrist. 'It was just a little spritz.'

'Serves you right.'

Eve took off, updated her teams – both of which currently batted zero.

'Shorter red hair,' she murmured as she wove through traffic. 'She needed that to stalk Glaze in character, to select which woman connected to him would be her primary target.'

'Probably a rinse,' Callendar murmured back.

'A what?'

'Maybe she dyed it, maybe she went with temp color. You got somebody needing the different looks to become different killers, smarter to rinse it so you can wash it out, change it back, or change it to something else.'

'Like Mavis,' Peabody explained.

'It just washes out?'

'It takes a few times – and you can seal it so it won't wash out for more than a few. Like my tips. I want to try them out for a while – not make a total commitment, right? It costs more to seal it up, but you can still do it all yourself. Home jobs.'

'Home jobs – that's what I heard before, too,' Eve remembered. 'The next killer she'll become is male. Dark brown curly hair – past the jawline. I was figuring wig, but she's on a budget. Which is cheaper, home-job curls or wig?'

'Home job,' Peabody and Callendar said together.

'Especially temp curls. You can wash them out, too,' Peabody added. 'You can get them with a hair tool and some product. If you want longer lasting, you need to do a home perm.'

'What does "perm" – whatever that is – have to do with curly hair?'

'I don't know,' Peabody realized. 'It's just called that. I'm betting the tool and product. You can use the tool for years, and the product's not that expensive. Wash or brush out your hair, you shed the character – and the disguise.'

'Yeah, that's my bet. Those areas the seamstress gave us – neither of them are close to DeLano. She wasn't out stalking DeLano. She lives or works around there. I say both. Working private now, working in her own place. As little contact with people as Smith as she can manage. She needs to keep Smith fluid and ready to absorb characters. Her priority is to live the scene, writing it her way. Her needs and priorities couldn't be met if she spent all day sewing in a basement.'

She played with angles, calculated probabilities on the drive back to Central. When traffic slowed on the bridge, she took a year or two off Peabody's life by going vertical for ten car lengths. In the back, Callendar didn't even blink.

When she pulled into her slot, Eve shoved out of the car. 'Callendar, keep at it, but send me what you've got so far.'

'Can do. Will do.'

'Peabody, contact the team, tell them to shift over to these new areas, coordinate with the locals. And add a male with dark brown curly hair to the list.'

She got on the elevator, thinking, thinking, thinking. Hopped off when it insisted on stopping on every level for others to pile on. 'Callendar, let Feeney know I'm back in the house, and need whatever he can give me.'

'Can and will. Cha.'

Eve jumped on a glide, kept moving up while Peabody hustled to match her pace.

'Slippery, she's slippery, lives in her own head most of the time, lived in the shadows all her life. Choice or circumstance, but she lived there. Writing's going to be her way into the light, then she gets shut down. DeLano won't read her work. That's the first crack. Decides DeLano's stolen from her, stolen her work, her chance. That's the next crack, and what's been simmering in there starts leaking out. She has to pay for stealing that light. And Smith has to shove everything else aside and focus. Quits her job. She can manage on the side work and whatever she's squirreled away. She can get a smaller, cheaper place. But then, she's putting her work out there, showing it off, and people – jealous fuckers – criticize it.'

'Some would be downright mean on top of it,' Peabody predicted. 'It's easy to be mean online.'

'And that's the final break. The cracks just explode. She's better than all of them. She's sure as hell better than that bitch thief DeLano. Screw the light. It's the dark that has the power. The dark that can kill and get away with it. I see her,' Eve stated. 'I see her. I'll know her when I look in her eyes.'

She headed straight to her office, pulled up short when she found Roarke working on her comp, working at her desk.

He glanced up. 'And there you are. If you want this, you'll need to give me another minute. I started here, as it's handy and in a quiet spot.'

'Keep going. I need a minute, too.'

She tossed aside her coat, contacted Yancy.

'Where are you?' she asked as the screen showed movement.

'Just heading out. End of shift.'

'I need a favor.'

'What's the favor?'

'The sketch. Can you use it to do another? She'll be going male, curly dark brown hair, about jaw length. Well groomed. Rich guy. No facial hair. Age about thirty-five.' She cast her mind back into the book for more details. 'Heavier eyebrows and blue eyes. Dark blue, almost navy.'

'I can do that. It won't take long.'

'I'll owe you. Send it to me when you've got it.'

She programmed coffee, paced, tried working on her PPC, as Roarke hogged the comp.

'Would you like to know what I've got?'

She all but pounced. 'Yes.'

'Ann E. Smith left Delaware with sixty-three thousand and change in savings. She had no income for half a year, and listed "novelist" on her tax returns, with documentation for writing supplies.'

'If she lived off her savings for six months, that sixty-three didn't go far in New York.'

'Rent and utilities ate more than half in that tax year. She sought and found employment at Dobb's, lived frugally. She paid her rent, taxes, all bills promptly and in full. I'd say she used cash for most expenses, as there is no credit or debit card in her name. Approximately nine months ago, she withdrew all funds from the local bank she used, stopped paying rent, stopped reporting income. Essentially, she's been living off the grid since that time.'

'You're confirming what I have, but giving me nothing new.'

He swiveled in his chair. 'Essentially, the *nothing* is the new. She has no bank or brokerage accounts. None. She deals in cash. This means whatever income she may receive is also cash based. It's possible to get checks cashed at some outlets, for a fee, but why would she? Cash leaves no paper trail. When she withdrew her funds, they amounted to thirty-three thousand and change. So in addition to her pay from Dobb's she likely did some side business in cash, banked it, or a portion of it. To survive on side business and those dwindling savings, her expenses have to be cut to the bone. I'd look for her in an SRO. Being off the grid, she can't apply for assistance, and would be unlikely to pass the vetting in most established rentals.'

'We had a sighting, two months ago. I need to bring up a map.'

He got up, offered her the chair. 'Have at it.'

'Brooklyn. Flatbush . . . this area. What the hell is there?'

'Let's see.' Leaning over, he manually shifted a few things. 'Working-class area – family restaurants, shops, residential, some studios. She couldn't afford to live there with what she has. If she took other employment—'

'She hasn't.'

'Well then.' He shifted things again. 'Only a few blocks south. A little rougher, certainly cheaper. More your tat parlors, dives, haunts for the street people, and your projects and SROs.'

She contacted Santiago, relayed the area. 'Push there, pass that to the other team and the locals. SROs most likely, but she could've slithered into the projects. Check private homes that take in borders. Some of them do that off the books.'

'Very good,' Roarke said when she clicked off. 'I hadn't thought of that last one. Which is why you're the cop. And one, I'll wager, who hasn't eaten since breakfast.'

'I've been busy.'

He went to the AutoChef, programmed her a slice of the pizza she'd forgotten he'd somehow stocked in there.

'Fine. Thanks.' She bit in. 'Jesus, that's good. She's likely gone off the Internet, too. Feeney found her, but she went dark the same time she quit and ditched the apartment. That's her break, that's when she got serious about killing. But not DeLano – who's responsible in her head. She has to prove something first. She's better – and the villain's superior to the hero. That's her mission. That's her new passion.'

'She's lived a lonely life.'

'Her choice, that's first. And a lot of people do who don't decide to kill strangers to prove a fucking point.'

He heard the frustration under the cool, rubbed a hand on her shoulder. 'I can't argue it.'

'I don't know when she's going to move on the next, but she won't wait long. She can't. She feels the squeeze, so she needs to finish. She's got three out of eight, not even half-way there – and don't forget DeLano for the final chapter. She has to move soon.'

She grabbed the incoming when it signaled, studied Yancy's sketch. 'This is good. It's her, but just enough like the character. This is how she'll look when she goes for the next kill. Maybe how she looks now as she gears up for it.'

She sent the sketch to Santiago and the rest of the team.

She pounced again at another incoming.

'And that?' Roarke asked.

'Head seamstress at Dobb's. Customers she thinks Smith did side work for. Good, this is good. Only fourteen names.'

Roarke lifted his eyebrows when her comp signaled again. 'Aren't you Lieutenant Busy Bee today?'

'Callendar. She's pushing through on what we started in the search for the potential target. Gonna cross-check and maybe. Son of a bitch, son of a big, beautiful bitch, we got one. Natalia Durban Berkle.'

'Ah, I know Natalia a little. She's very philanthropic if

a cause appeals. A widow now, since her husband fell off a mountain.'

That jerked Eve back. 'Fell off a mountain?'

'Attempting to climb one. Off, or it might have been into – as in crevice. Either way? Oops.'

'Huh. Does she like you?'

He smiled. 'Why wouldn't she?'

'Right. You're with me.' She grabbed her coat, calling for Peabody as she went.

22

With Roarke behind the wheel, Eve used the drive time to the Upper East Side to dig into the data on Berkle.

'She fits. Wealthy widow, late sixties, one son, one daughter. Big charitable foundation – family run – lots of committees and causes, and plenty of fancy-dress functions. She lives in a three-level penthouse rather than a freestanding mansion like the book vic, but three levels equals stairs. She fits.'

'That's good work by Callendar,' Peabody commented.

'Yeah, it is. If we connect Berkle to Smith, we'll set things up. Berkle contacts Smith. Needs some alterations, and fast. If she's already got some on the slate, we get Berkle to move up the appointment.'

'And if she's not connected?' Roarke asked.

'Berkle did some hefty shopping at Dobb's, used Smith as her fitter. Berkle fits the fictional vic profile. They're going to connect. Dobb's is a long trip from the Upper East. Why go there to shop?'

'I wondered that,' Peabody said from the back – between sips of hot chocolate. 'I played around some. It turns out her sister-in-law lives in Brooklyn. They're pretty tight. They probably go together, have lunch, that kind of thing. Girl day.'

'She's sixty-eight.'

'A girl's a girl,' Peabody said.

Eve looked at Roarke. 'Is she a sensible, steady sort of girl?'

'I don't know her particularly well, but my impression is yes. She has a reputation for being no-nonsense when it comes to business, and generous in her causes.'

'Good. Steady would be good.'

They pulled up to a pale gold tower, one that boasted a pair of doormen in dignified gray-and-silver livery.

Eve stepped out even as they marched, in tandem, toward the offending DLE.

'NYPSD.' She whipped out her badge. 'That's my ride, and it stays where it is.'

'Miss—' At her fierce stare, the doorman on the left looked at her badge again. 'Lieutenant,' he wisely corrected. 'If you could use our private garage—'

'Where it is,' Eve said and strode between them to the doors.

Behind her, Roarke pulled out a couple of bills. 'Ease the sting a bit.'

Eve strode straight to the concierge desk in a deep lobby mirrored with the pale gold. The air smelled faintly of roses, and her boots sank into the red-and-gold carpet spread over the polished floor.

At the desk, which held the roses in a fat, clear vase, a woman in a suit of bold blue smiled politely.

'Good evening. How can I help you?'

Eve held up her badge. 'Natalia Durban Berkle. Is she in?'

'Before I discuss a resident or guest, I'll need to verify your identification.'

'Do it.'

From under the desk, the woman took a scanner, ran it over the badge.

'Yes, Lieutenant, Ms Berkle is at home. Is she expecting you?'

'The badge makes that question irrelevant. Is she alone?'

'Her daughter is with her, and her staff. No other outside visitors have logged in.'

Eve lifted a hand for Peabody. Peabody handed Eve the photo of Smith.

'Has this woman visited? Ann Elizabeth Smith.'

'I believe so, but let me verify.'

She turned to her comp, went to work. 'I can verify that Ms Smith has signed in to the visitors' log. Her last visit was February third, at three in the afternoon.'

'Clear us up.'

'Lieutenant, I'm obligated to notify Ms Berkle of requests to visit her private residence. If you could . . . ' Her gaze shifted to Roarke. She blinked, twice.

'No harm in that, is there, Lieutenant?' Roarke said easily. 'If you'd let Ms Berkle know that Lieutenant Dallas, Detective Peabody, and Roarke would like a few moments of her time?'

'Of course. If you'd like to take a seat while I—'

'We're fine,' Eve snapped. 'Tag her, clear us up.'

'Absolutely.' She tapped her earpiece, waited a couple of beats. 'Yes, Earnestine, it's Paulette at the concierge desk. Would you see if Ms Berkle is home to Lieutenant Dallas, Detective Peabody, and Roarke? Yes, I'll hold.'

Eve shifted to eye the bank of three elevators – mirrored gold like the walls.

'Yes, thank you. I'll be sending them up now.'

After another earpiece tap, Paulette went back to her comp. 'Ms Berkle would be delighted to greet you. Please take Elevator Three. I'll clear it for Ms Berkle's residence. Enjoy your visit.'

Eve said nothing until they walked into the elevator and the doors shut – with soft, mindless music cuing on.

'You tipped those snooty doormen.'

'The snooty doormen were only doing their job,' Roarke responded.

'And you tipped the tight-ass concierge.'

'That I didn't.'

'With Roarke charm.'

'Ah, that. Well now, that simply exudes when it's called for, and is free for the taking.'

Peabody unsuccessfully muffled a snicker.

'But you don't own the building, or we'd already be talking to Berkle.'

'I believe Natalia owns it, or the majority portion of it. Would you like me to make her an offer?'

'I've already dealt with a tight-ass, so I don't need the smart-ass.'

'But it's such a good match with your own. Our lieu-tenant draws smart-asses like bears to honey, wouldn't you say, Peabody?'

'I don't want her boot up mine, so I'll take the Fifth.'

'Wise, as is our lieutenant, as she's already connected your suspect with Natalia.'

'Coincidence is bollocks,' Eve said as the doors opened.

A woman stood pin-neat in black pants and a creamy white sweater, her hair a short and glossy brown bob around a pleasant face.

'Good evening, please come in. I'm Earnestine, Ms Berkle's personal assistant.'

She gestured them through the private foyer decked with fresh flowers in a dozen slim vases and a tinkling wall fountain of a mermaid pouring water from a seashell into a small pool.

The New York view dominated the living area through a wall of glass doors. Inside, a long, narrow fireplace snapped with light and flame under a large painting of a poppy field.

A U-shaped sofa in pale, shimmery blue faced the fire.

More seating – chairs, sofas – arranged in conversational groups picked up that shimmery blue and the poppy-red.

More art – lilies, overblown roses, and something that speared in purple that Eve couldn't name – turned the walls into a garden. Obviously Berkle liked flowers.

A series of clear, floating shelves held what Eve assumed were expensive trinkets. In one corner stood a white piano with a trio of thick silver candlestands.

'Ms Berkle will be right down. Let me take your coats.'

'We're fine,' Eve told her.

'Please, take a seat. Be comfortable.'

Instead, Eve held out the photo. 'Do you know this woman?'

'Yes, of course. Ann. She's Ms Berkle's seamstress.'

'When did you see her last?'

'The beginning of this month when she delivered some alterations for Ms Berkle.'

'How do you contact her?'

'I ... have a 'link number.'

'I need that.'

'I, ah ... Ms Berkle.' Relief pumped off Earnestine as Berkle descended a sweep of glossy white stairs.

She didn't look sixty-eight, Eve thought, but she did look rich.

Diamond studs glittered at her ears, and a fatter diamond weighed down her left hand. She wore those flowy pants, silver gray with the sheen of silk, matched with a draping blouse that showed off the diamond heart around her neck.

Icy blond hair swept back from a face with long-lashed blue eyes, a straight sharp nose, and a wide mouth dyed as red as the poppies on the wall.

She let out a quick trill of laughter and held out both hands to Roarke.

'What a lovely surprise!' She kissed both his cheeks.

'And you, Natalia, lovely as always.'

'You should've seen me three minutes ago.' She laughed

411

again. 'But I've had decades of practice in the art of illusion. And this must be your very impressive wife.'

'Lieutenant Eve Dallas, Detective Delia Peabody, the always lovely Natalia Berkle.'

'I'm simply delighted to meet both of you. Isn't this exciting! Dru will be right down. You've met my daughter, Dru, haven't you, Roarke?'

'I have, yes.'

'Wonderful. Let's sit down, have some wine.'

'Ms Berkle,' Eve interrupted. 'This is official police business.'

'Yes, I assumed, which is part of the excitement. Oh, no wine then,' she said as she took Roarke's hand and led him to the sofa.

'I'd love some,' he told her. 'But it would be coffee for the lieutenant and detective.'

'Earnestine?'

'Yes, Marsha's already seeing to refreshments. Should I finish upstairs?'

'I need you to stay.' Eve struggled not to snap. 'I'm sorry to be abrupt, Ms Berkle, but—'

'Natalia, please. I'm sure this is all part of the official police business. And here's Dru. Dru, join us. I think we're about to be interrogated.'

She looked like her mother – a younger version in stylish street clothes. And, like her mother, she walked to Roarke as he rose, kissed his cheeks. 'So nice to see you again. And to meet you, Lieutenant Dallas, Detective Peabody. Mother and I both read Nadine Furst's book, and saw the vid. We're very big fans.'

'We're not here to interrogate you, but we do have some questions. About Ann Smith.'

'Ann? Oh, thank you, Marsha,' Berkle said as a woman in a black dress wheeled out a cart. 'That lovely Cab for the gentleman, Dru, and myself – after all, it's from the gentleman's vineyard. And coffee for the ladies.'

'That's black for you, Lieutenant Dallas?' Dru asked. 'And cream and sugar for you, Detective?'

'Thanks. Ann Smith,' Eve repeated. 'I need her contact information.'

'Certainly. Earnestine can get that for you.' Berkle fluttered a hand at her assistant. 'Ann's a genius with a needle – sewing needle. I've used her quite a lot in the past . . . I suppose it's over a year now. She worked at Dobb's in Brooklyn, but went out on her own. I hope she's not in trouble.'

'We have evidence making Ann Elizabeth Smith the prime suspect in three murders.'

'Murders? Good God.'

'Ann?' Dru lowered her wineglass. 'We couldn't be talking about the same Ann Smith. She's the sort who'd run away from a fly if one landed on her.'

'Still waters, sweetheart.' Berkle patted her daughter's hand. 'She's, as I said, a genius in tailoring. Very short on conversation and social skills. Not awkward so much as . . . closed,' Berkle decided. 'Exceedingly polite, but more

413

like a droid who's been programmed than genuine, if you understand me. I can't say I sensed any violence in her – discontent, yes, but not violence. She's been in my home many times.'

'We believe you may be her next target.'

'Me?' Berkle's eyebrows winged up, and a faint flicker of alarm rippled across her face. But her voice, and the hand that lifted the wine to her lips, stayed steady. 'Whatever for? We've never had a cross word between us.'

'You fit the profile for her next victim. A wealthy widow with a son and a daughter.'

As quickly as possible, Eve hit the salient points. The books, Smith's obsession, the sightings and stalkings, while Earnestine gave Peabody Smith's contact number.

Berkle watched Eve calmly.

'This particular book – and, Earnestine, let's get those, I want to read this series – has me representing a woman killed by her son, who then attempts to frame his sister. He pushes me down the stairs?'

'Yes.'

'I should be safe in that case, as I have no intention of letting her back in my home. Added to that, my son left with his family this morning for our estate on Kauai. I, along with Dru and her family, leave in the morning. For two and a half weeks.'

'Who knows your plans?'

'A number of people, including Ann, as she recently delivered some of my vacation wardrobe.'

'She could be waiting until you get back,' Peabody pointed out, but Eve shook her head.

'No, she has to move quickly. She can't wait that long now. She had contingencies with Loxie Flash. She'll have one here, too. Regardless, Ms Berkle—'

'Natalia,' she said again. 'We're compatriots at this point.'

'Regardless, you need to take precautions. If Smith attempts to access your home before you leave—'

'She wouldn't get past the lobby. You can be assured I'll notify building security. And I won't open that door.' The fat diamond on her finger winked light as she lifted her wine. 'I like my life.'

'Are you staying here tonight?' Eve asked Dru.

'No, actually, I'm leaving shortly.'

'I'm going to have you escorted. You'd open the door if she threatened your daughter?'

'Yes, I would.' Berkle's breath inhaled, exhaled – and shook. 'Yes, I certainly would. You do exactly what Lieutenant Dallas says, Dru.'

'We'll have you escorted home. Engage your security, and keep your family inside. I'm going to have all of you escorted to your transportation in the morning if this isn't resolved.'

'I'm grateful,' Berkle said as Eve rose.

'You don't seem shaken or surprised.'

'Truthfully, I'm a little of both. If you'd told me Ann had drowned herself in her own bathtub, I'd have been sorry, but unsurprised. This is just another way to destroy her own life.'

'Natalia.' Roarke rose, took her hand and kissed it. 'You're a wonder.'

'I'm a survivor,' she said. 'And, Dru, we're going to leave tonight. How much time do you need?'

'I can get Renaldo and the kids up and running in an hour.'

'Earnestine, change of plans.'

'I'll take care of it.'

'Good thinking,' Eve commented. 'I'll arrange for the escorts. One more thing,' she said as a switch flicked in her head. 'You said Smith is a genius – and you shopped at Dobb's with your sister-in-law. Did she also use Smith?'

'Occasionally, yes. But Sal's married – three girls, no sons. And currently is in St Kitts.'

'I imagine both you and she might have recommended Smith to others.'

'I can't speak for Sal, but I certainly have.'

'Can you think of anyone who fits the profile?'

'I haven't really thought . . . ' She lurched to her feet, all the color in her face leaching away. 'Oh my God. Oh my God, Dru!'

'Aunt Felicity! Not my actual aunt, but—'

'My oldest friend, godmother to my baby girl. Felicity Lomare. She's a widow. She lost her husband six years ago. She has a son and a daughter, the same as I do. She uses Ann. I praised her to the skies and introduced them. Oh my God.'

'The address.'

'It's—' Berkle pressed a hand to her temple. 'I can't think—'

Stepping in, Earnestine rattled off an address a few blocks away. 'It's a private home, not a building,' she added. 'It's gated.'

'I have to call her, call her right away. If anything happened to Felicity—'

'Tell her we're on our way,' Eve told Berkle as she walked to the elevator. 'If she's not at home, she should stay where she is until we get there. We'll contact her.'

Eve ordered the lobby.

'She won't be on the Dobb's list. Smarter, smarter to go for somebody she didn't work with while at Dobb's. Berkle was more likely the contingency, and Lomare the prime target.'

Her comm signaled. 'Dallas.'

'We found her hole,' Santiago told her. 'A flop in Brownsville a few blocks from that sighting. Fourth-floor unit. We're outside it now, but we don't think she's in there. Nosy guy on the first floor saw her leave about an hour ago. LT? He says he almost didn't recognize her because she'd changed her hair, gone all curly, and was wearing a man's coat and hat. But she was carrying her big sewing kit. He recognized that.'

'Get a warrant for entry, for search and seizure. Take down the door.'

'Should we wait for you to take the door?'

'Don't wait for me. I have another line on her. Take the

door, secure the flop. Record every fucking thing. Leave a watch on the street in case she comes back. If I'm wrong, take her down there.'

Eve ran across the lobby, startling the concierge, then the doormen. She jumped into the passenger seat, hit lights and sirens.

'Burn it,' she told Roarke.

'Delighted.'

As he burned it, Peabody clung to the seat with one hand, her 'link with the other. 'Straight to v-mail, Dallas. She may still be talking to Ms Berkle.'

'Try Berkle.'

As Roarke swerved around a Rapid Cab, streamed between a limo and a shiny sedan, Peabody's grip tightened.

'She says she can't get her to answer.'

Roarke screamed to a halt in front of secured gates.

'No, don't call through,' she told him. 'Just open them.'

He lowered the window, boosted himself up to sit on the frame, and pulled out some little device.

'It's a good system,' he said after a moment. 'So it'll take . . . ' The gates slid open. 'That much time.'

He dropped onto the seat again, roared through the gates, up a short, straight drive to a three-story brownstone as regal as a queen. Lights shined in every window and around a grand entrance door under a portico.

Eve jumped out, pointed at the door. 'Now that. I don't want her to know we're coming,' she said as Roarke got to work. 'The target's not answering her 'link, may already

418

be in distress. Or dead. When he gets it open, if the vic's not lying at the foot of the damn stairs, clear the first floor. Roarke, head up to three. I'll take two. Otherwise—'

The door opened into a sparkling, quietly lit foyer. With no body at the foot of the wide double staircase straight ahead.

At the sound of approaching footsteps, Eve swung her weapon toward the archway to the right.

A woman of about fifty – white apron over a black dress – squeaked, slapped both hands to her mouth.

'Stay quiet. NYPSD.' Lowering her weapon, Eve drew out her badge. 'Peabody.'

Peabody pulled out the photo. 'Is this woman in the house?'

'Y-y-yes. Upstairs, with Ms Felicity.'

'Where?' Eve demanded. 'Exactly where?'

'But-but-but—'

'Your employer's at risk. Where are they?'

'Second floor, west wing, double doors at the end of the hallway.'

'Go back into the kitchen. Stay there.'

As Eve started up the stairs, Felicity turned in front of the triple mirror. 'I'm so glad you called, Ann. Getting all these pieces fitted tonight takes the rush off, doesn't it? And it makes me think of spring.'

She turned again. 'And the fact that my new trainer's helped me take off six pounds! And I really wanted you to do the alterations. The seamstress at my boutique just doesn't have your touch.'

Well used to dominating the conversation during fittings, Felicity sipped some wine and rambled on.

'I just can't get over your new 'do. Such a bold and fun choice. I really like the new look.'

She didn't, not a bit – the curls struck her as too tight and mannish. But she wanted to be kind.

'I do wish you'd look through those clothes Marlene and I culled out of my collection. I know they'd look wonderful on you.'

And considerably better, Felicity thought, than the mannish trousers and jacket.

'We'll have a look after you've finished,' she insisted. 'We'll have some fun with it, and ... '

When Felicity saw the tall woman in the long black coat step into the dressing room doorway with a – was that a *stunner*? – in her hand, she squeaked much like her devoted housekeeper.

Ann, busy pinning, saw the reflection, too. She pulled the sheers out of her belt, dragged Felicity back against her with the keen points pressed to Felicity's throat.

'I'll slice her throat!' Her voice hit a masculine growl, suiting the trousers, the white dress shirt. 'Drop that weapon, or the bitch dies.'

'That's bad dialogue, Ann. Clichéd.'

'My name's Calvin Underwood, and my penny-pinching mother's going to get what's coming to her. Back off!'

'If you're Calvin, let's see your dick. Otherwise, Ann

Elizabeth Smith, drop those sharps. If you jab her, I take you out. If you don't jab her, I take you out. Either way, you're going down.'

'Fuck you!'

'On the contrary.' Felicity rammed back with her elbow, followed through with a vicious back fist.

The sheers clattered to the floor as Smith fell back from the double blow, smacked into the triple mirror. She went down with a crash of shattering glass.

'Twenty-one years' bad luck,' Felicity said and kicked the sheers away. 'Damn it, I really liked that mirror.'

'Excellent moves, Ms Lomare. Peabody, secure the suspect.'

'Suspect, my ass. She was going to kill me.' Wincing a little, she reached up, dabbed at the shallow cut on her throat. 'Nicked me a little, didn't she?'

'Just a little.' Roarke stepped forward with a handkerchief, dabbed at the blood.

'I know you, handsome. Roarke. I met you with my friend Natalia a few times.'

'I remember well. Let me see that very pretty hand. Yes, indeed, you'll have some bruising. You'll want an ice patch and a healing wand.'

'It's nothing. Takes me back. I was counterintelligence during the Urbans.'

Eve studied her – pretty in almost a candy-coated way. Small and slim and likely, like her best friend, pushing seventy.

'You haven't lost those moves.'

'You never do. Now who the hell is Calvin, and why does this very rude young woman think I'm her mother?'

'It's a long story.'

'Good. I dropped my wine, and I definitely want another. You can tell me that long story.'

'Where is your 'link, ma'am?'

'My 'link?' She looked distracted – and once again harmless – as she glanced blankly around the room. 'I'm always leaving it somewhere. Maybe by the bed. No! The bathroom. No, the sitting room. I think.'

'Peabody, contact Ms Berkle and let her know her friend is safe and well.'

'Natalia? What does she have to do with this?'

'I'm going to explain. Roarke, why don't you take Ms Lomare downstairs, get her that wine. I'll be down shortly.'

'One question first. Would you have fired while she had those sheers to my throat?'

'I'd have fired before she jabbed them into your throat.'

'I thought so. Good for you.' She laughed when Roarke offered her his arm. 'Such a charmer. You married a cop, didn't you? Of course you did, I remember now.' She glanced back. 'That one?'

'That's my cop.'

'Handsome, charming, and excellent taste. Let's have some wine.'

'I think she's my new hero,' Peabody said. 'Suspect is out cold.'

'Call for the wagon. Let's have her hauled down and booked. I really want her in the box.'

Eve pulled out her comm when it signaled. 'Santiago, suspect is secure.'

'Glad to hear it. We're in her place, Dallas, and I'm going to say she's going to stay secure, in a cage, for the rest of her natural life. Take a look at this.'

The screen shifted, showed her a wall, dingy behind photos of victims. And their alternates, Eve noted. The three she'd killed had blood-red X's over their faces. She'd labeled each with their fictional name, and added a picture of herself as she'd been dressed for the kill.

The victim wall panned down to Felicity, and Eve saw she'd been right about Berkle being the alternate. Four more sections revealed she had other targets selected, and alternates.

With a large photo of DeLano framed after the eight targets. And, Eve noted, not without some small satisfaction, one of herself as the final chapter.

Along with the photos were street maps, transportation routes, schedules. Sketches of outfits – the coats, trousers, hairstyles.

Interesting, Eve noted. The character written – or being written – to kill her dressed as a uniform cop. Smith had named her Officer Lucy Borgia.

'Plotting to kill a police officer.' Santiago tipped his hat. 'That's going to leave a mark. Anyway, we sent for an e-person – locals are cooperating and working with us. She's got a cheap little comp here, but it's passcoded. We figured to let the geeks take it. I don't know why she bothered, as she's got handwritten notes all over the damn place. Souvenirs, too. Looks like she has a used tube of lip dye – Carmichael's betting she took it off the first vic.'

'For Christ's sake, don't bet her. You'll be wearing that hat until spring.'

'I learned my lesson. She printed out the ticket from the vids on the second killing, took a bar coaster from the third. She's got them in this handmade box marked Treasures. It's all decorated. She's got her work stuff – actual work. The sewing machine thing and supplies, one of those dummies. Looks like she was in the middle of making some fancy dress.'

'The next killer in the series is a married socialite who killed her secret working-class lover in her workshop with a hammer after she dumped her.'

'Well, hell hath no fury, right? We got her cold, LT.'

Eve glanced back at the unconscious Smith. 'In more ways than one.'

23

Often Eve faced a suspect in the box with the goal of squeezing out a confession, tripping them up, pulling out details to polish off a case.

This time she had what she needed. But the courts liked everything spelled out, so she'd push Smith to spell it out.

And there was, in addition, the sheer satisfaction of facing off with a killer.

'I've got this,' Eve told Peabody. 'You can go home, get some sleep.'

'No way I'm missing the end of this story. We can call it *Dark Justice, The Final Chapter.*'

'You've been saving that one.'

'All damn day.'

Eve picked up files, headed out. 'Roarke's already in Observation because he feels the same.'

'Are you sure you don't want Mira here?'

'She can review the record, evaluate Smith tomorrow. No point dragging her out for this tonight. I already know Smith isn't likely to pass the legal sanity level. It doesn't matter.'

'It chaps my thighs,' Peabody complained. 'Jesus, Dallas, she was planning to go after you.'

'I like that part.' Shook her up, Eve mused, just as planned. Added to those rewrites and shook things up.

'Think of it this way,' she continued. 'There's a very interesting woman alive and well tonight because we worked the case and bagged a killer. There are four other people who won't have to worry about having a target on their backs. Add DeLano, possibly her family. And if she'd slipped through on us, she wouldn't have stopped there. I'm not talking about me.'

'I don't know if DeLano would have published the next Dark novel if Smith was at large.'

'She wouldn't have stopped,' Eve repeated. 'I think she'd have used her own failed novel. The killer hero. I think she's always been going there. And once she took on that role, she'd have had a lot of pages to fill.'

Eve paused outside the Interview door. 'Ready?'

'So ready.'

Eve stepped in. 'Dallas, Lieutenant Eve, and Peabody, Detective Delia, entering Interview with Smith, Ann Elizabeth, on the matters of . . . ' She paused as if to check her files, rattled off the case numbers.

She sat, waited for Peabody to take the other chair. 'Have you been read your rights, Ms Smith?'

When Smith didn't respond, just sat head down, shoulders hunched, arms defensively across her chest, Eve shrugged. 'I happen to know you were – once you regained consciousness and had medical treatment – as I read them to you myself. As the record will show. But we'll go over them again. We've got all the time in the world.'

Eve recited the Revised Miranda, waited. 'Do you understand your rights and obligations in this matter? If you don't, I can explain them to you point by point. Like I said, all the time in the world.'

Smith mumbled.

'Please speak up for the record.'

'I understand.'

'Good. I'm going to be straight with you, Ann. We've got you cold on three counts of murder – that's first degree – and one count of attempted murder. We've got your – let's call it your storyboard and your drafts of plotlines for future victims. We've got the ice pick you used to kill Chanel Rylan along with the printout of the vid ticket placing you in the theater that night. We've got your reversible coat – and the security feed showing you entering and exiting the theater. We have an eyewitness placing you outside the flop where Rosie Kent was strangled, and the drug you used to knock her out.'

Eve flipped through the files. 'Oh, yeah, we have the red hair dye and a couple of blue faux hairs that will match the blue dreads recovered a short distance from Screw U – you yanked out some of your own hair when you pulled them off, so we also have that. Then there's the club itself, where we have additional eyewitnesses verifying you ordered the drink you then doctored and served to Loxie Flash. Then there's the mink hoodie you stole – let's go ahead and add that charge of grand theft while we've got you here.

'Are you following me here, Ann?'

Smith shifted her eyes up for an instant. The right showed the bruising and swelling caused by a dead-on backhanded blow. Eve saw the flicker of temper before Smith lowered her gaze again.

Good. She'd fan the flames.

'I can sit here and list all the evidence we have against you, but you already know all that. You may not know that I've just gotten a report from our lab, from our expert on hair and fiber. The coat you left behind at the club? She found both hair and fiber on it – you were in a hurry, after all. A strand of hair that matches the hair taken from a brush in your apartment, and the blue dreads. Some fibers from the clothes you wore the night you killed Loxie Flash match clothes recovered from your apartment. She put a rush on that work for me, so we can wrap this up, nice and neat.

'She'll find trace on the reversible coat, too. And, you know, there's just a little bit of blood on the sleeve of the reversible coat – the dark side. You probably didn't notice, but we did. It's going to be Chanel Rylan's blood.'

Eve sat back, slid photos of the dead out of the file. 'So, sloppy work, Ann. Careless, sloppy work.'

Smith's shoulders tightened. She shook her head.

'Oh, yeah, sloppy and careless. Since we've got that in the bag, let's move on to motive. We've got that, too.

Blaine DeLano and her Dark series. We're big fans, aren't we, Peabody?'

'I love those books. Can't get enough. The way Dark hunts down the bad guys? Man, she's smart. And she's fearless.'

'She's a thief,' Smith muttered.

'Sorry, did you say something?' Peabody asked.

'She's a thief.'

'Deann Dark?'

'No! Blaine DeLano. She stole from me.'

'Oh right, right.' Eve waved a hand in the air. 'She mentioned something about some whack fan – that would be you – bitching and whining about her, DeLano, copying from the whack fan's – yours – lame-ass excuse for a book.'

'My book is groundbreaking!'

And there's a rise, Eve thought and nodded at Peabody.

Peabody reached into the satchel at her feet, pulled out the manuscript, dropped it with a *thud* on the table.

'Perfect cure for insomnia,' Peabody commented. 'I was nodding off by page two.'

That earned a dark look under stubby lashes from Smith.

'You're not wrong. Your book is bloated and self-indulgent,' Eve told Smith. 'I can say that after suffering through the first chapter.'

'You know nothing about literature. Neither of you.'

'Literature? Is that what that waste of time and paper's supposed to be?'

'More like purple pap.' Peabody snickered with it.

'Pap's accurate. Just take the opening line. What was it? Yeah, yeah,' Eve murmured as she plucked up the first page. "With skill and grace, with focus and cunning, he tracked his victim like a sleek, predatory wolf to a plump, senseless lamb, but never showed the shine and keenness of his fangs." Seriously? If I didn't get paid to do this, I'd have stopped right there. Bloated,' Eve said again. 'And what's the term — yeah, florid. DeLano writes lean and mean.'

Smith, an angry — and, yeah, sallow — face surrounded by incongruously cheery curls rapped a fist on the table.

'She took my work. My sweat and blood, and twisted it into something ordinary.'

'Your work doesn't approach the lowest level of ordinary. But let's say, for argument's sake, she did. You get pissed off about that and kill Rosie Kent, Chanel Rylan, Loxie Flash?'

'Do you understand nothing?'

'Enlighten me.'

'Amanda Young killed Pryor Carridine. Justin Werth killed Amelia Benson. Gigi Hombly killed Bliss Cather.'

'Yeah, yeah, I read the books. Those are fictional characters, Ann. Fictional characters don't bleed.'

'Of course they do.' Hazel eyes, edging toward brown — Jake had observation skills — bored into Eve's. 'You don't understand, you're incapable of understanding. You're not a writer.'

'Explain it to me,' Eve invited. 'Explain to me how and why as Young, Werth, and Hombly you killed Carridine, Benson, and Cather.'

Ann only shook her head, hunched up again.

'Come on, Ann, don't be shy. A writer has to face criticism, right? Has to stand up to it. Defend your work!'

Eve slapped her hands on the table. Ann Elizabeth Smith jumped, hunched tighter.

'You want to be somebody? You claim to be a writer, a groundbreaking writer? Your work's so superior, so fucking lofty? Prove it. Prove it to me, A. E. Strongbow. Defend your work.'

Those eyes shifted up again, the fire in them brighter. 'Art doesn't need defending.'

'Bullshit. A true artist stands by her art, stands for it, fights for it. You want attention? You've got mine. Here and now. Defend your work or go back to being nothing and nobody, sitting in the shadows, cutting and pinning and sewing for rich bitches. Bitches like Blaine DeLano.'

'She's the nothing! I've proven it already.'

'How? By killing make-believe people?'

'They're flesh and blood. They must be flesh and blood. I *made* her cardboard characters flesh and blood. I transformed them and breathed life into them. A true writer must embody the characters she creates. Must live inside them. Occupy them. Think and speak and feel as they do.'

'But you embodied and you killed DeLano's characters.'

'My characters! Mine. I made them mine, because I'm better. I showed her I'm better.'

She tapped her fisted hands on the table like beating a drum. Passion flushed the thin, sallow face.

'The villain is the key. The villain is the core. Anybody can write the expected, write the trite and tidy good overcomes evil. I showed her how much more creative, more *real*, more fascinating it is when evil triumphs. Why does Dark always win? Because DeLano has no real imagination, because she refuses to take creative risks. I showed her.'

'You didn't kill three people on the pages of a book. Three actual people are dead. People you selected only because they fit the fictional profile created by another writer.'

'A hack,' Smith said dismissively. 'I made them real.'

'You made them dead.'

'Art demands sacrifice.'

The fire burned hot now so Eve saw the fanatic. Saw Strongbow. She saw the rage, and the horrible *pride* the mousy Ann Smith concealed.

'How did you select Pryor Carridine's surrogate for sacrifice?'

'It's basic research to a serious writer. To write, you have to experience. I learned that. I'll admit Blaine DeLano taught me that. I risked everything to come to New York, to give up the ordinary, the comfortable, and strive.'

'Your mother's shop in Wilmington,' Eve prompted.

'My mother.' Smith sneered. 'She was no mother to me. Did she ever encourage me to be more? No, it was always, "Control your temper, Ann. Stop daydreaming, Ann." She wanted me to sew for the rest of my life! "Make a good living," she'd say. And never, never believed in *my* dreams. A hobby. She called my writing a hobby!'

'She left her shop, her business, in your hands.'

'I didn't want it. It only paid the bills, only trapped me inside the ordinary. Doing the ordinary while I wrote? I barely slept for months. Months. Years. It blurs.'

'You left the business, came to New York.'

'Blaine told me to.'

'She told you to come to New York?' Eve qualified.

'Yes, yes. She encouraged me to dream, and that's the same thing. I loved her for that. I believed in her, I thought she believed in me, so I risked everything. I worked for hours to pay the rent while my mind wrote and wrote and wrote.'

The hard light in her eyes softened as she pressed both hands to her heart. 'Coming home to take those scenes, those characters, out of my head and putting them on the page were the happiest hours of my life. I often wrote through the night, then went back to Dobb's or took a side job so I could support my true art.'

'You can't know the joy, the thrill, the satisfaction in the *soul* of finishing a book, that labor of sweat and blood and love.'

The rage snapped back. 'And what did she do when I sent her that labor of sweat and blood and love? She rejected me.'

'That stung.'

'It cut me to the quick. I was so angry, so disillusioned, so *wounded*. She was my mentor, my friend, my teacher, and she put lawyers between us? Agents and lawyers prevented her from reading my book? I tried to understand, to forgive. I tried. And then ...'

She lived in it now, Eve noted. Smith lived in that murky world where reality and fiction blurred. And while she did, she had to tell her story.

'*Sudden Dark*,' Eve prompted. 'You read *Sudden Dark*.'

'And I saw what she'd done, how she'd used and betrayed me. I trusted her and she murdered that trust. She killed my innocence. She crushed my dreams.'

'She had to pay.'

'She had to pay. She had to *see*. See me as I now saw her. The evil in her, the selfish, calculating evil in her. She used Deann Dark to destroy me. I would use Deann Dark to destroy her, and to show her, to show everyone duped by her how it should be done. How a real writer creates.'

'Starting with Rosie Kent.'

'Pryor Carridine,' Smith corrected.

'Pryor Carridine.' Eve nodded. 'Tell me about her – as you wrote her.'

'I knew as soon as I saw her. Young, rebellious, foolish. Trading her body for money and thrills. There were others, and I could have rewritten them, made them work and work well. But she was so perfect. She inspired me. I watched her. I did my research. I wrote, rewrote her scenes. I perfected them.'

'Yeah, we've got those, too. From your computer.'

'You can see how superior my vision is. DeLano's character grieved as she killed – grieved for the life she'd learned was a lie, for the husband who'd made that life a lie. There's your *pap*. My character didn't grieve, so she didn't make mistakes. My hands didn't shake like Amanda's because I

434

wrote them steady. My heart didn't pound in my ears as I tightened the scarf around Pryor's neck, because I wrote the quiet and the calm. I understood from creating Evan Quint a killing should be calm and controlled, a killer must consider all details. So I did.'

'Chanel Rylan.'

'Amelia Benson. I had to invest there. It's expensive to go to the vids, but the investment was necessary.'

'You had an alternate.'

'Of course. I wrote several alternate scenes for each character. In this case, it involved creating the scene at a play – even more expense. I may use that alternate scene in another book. It's good work. No work is ever wasted.'

'The reversible coat was clever.'

'Details. DeLano skimmed over them, obviously. I enjoyed designing that coat.'

'Your work, your seamstress skills,' Peabody qualified, 'are exceptional.'

'It steals time from the art, but it pays the bills. When my book's published, I'll enjoy sewing as a hobby.'

'What was your mind-set when you jammed that ice pick into the back of Chanel Rylan's neck?'

'I was inside my character. Justin Werth didn't kill only from desperation, a desperate need to see his work produced. In my character there was also greed, a stronger motivator, I believe. In my version he wasn't hired or bribed to kill. I blended him into a stronger, slyer man by merging two inferior characters.'

'The screenwriter and the boyfriend.' Eve nodded. 'So the killer became, in your version, both.'

'Yes. He knew, in my version, the part his lover and Amelia Benson competed for was a star-maker. It would make her not only famous but rich, and he'd benefit. So I imbued him with a kind of glee when he killed her.'

'Which, embodying his character, you felt. You felt glee.'

'Of course.'

'And then?'

'Then, much smarter than the original character, I slipped out before Amelia's companion returned to her seat. You know about the vet clinic.'

'Yes.'

'I liked writing that part.' She smiled a little. 'It was a kind of comic relief. The cheap clone 'link, the breathless voice babbling about the injured dog. I imagined the dog as a young German shepherd mix. I don't know why, it simply came to me. I named him Prince in my head.'

'Of course you did.'

'In any case, it went exactly as written. The recorded communication, the companion going out to take the emergency tag. When Amelia was dead, I slipped out, reversed the coat, put on the hat, and so forth, and sat in the back of the other theater. I knew it would let out shortly and I could, as written, just walk out with the others. It's all written out.'

'Yeah. Indulge me. Loxie Flash.'

'I had three choices for Bliss Cather. I disliked the one who became her the most, so it was satisfying to have her come into the club, as I hoped. I did initially plan for more time, more research, but I had to write you in.'

'Me?'

'Another inspiration. When I saw you do that interview, I realized the story had taken a turn. Now it had an element of cat and mouse.'

As Smith leaned forward, her eyes actually danced. 'But who was the cat, who was the mouse? You'd find out when your chapter came. I knew to keep up the pace, I had to move more quickly, take that risk. There are eight books, after all. And the author, before you.'

'You didn't have as much time to plan.'

'I'd done my research. And then Glazier came in. It was a sign, it was a bonus.'

The sallow skin flushed with pleasure, pride.

'It was perfect. I had to rewrite my rewrite afterward to include him, but it made the scene so much stronger. And the chase,' she added. 'That was unexpected. A good writer knows when to let the characters take over – it acknowledges they're alive. I enjoyed the chase. I hadn't known how it would feel. Running through the cold and the dark,' Smith murmured, caught up, caught in. 'The sidewalk slick with ice as I ran with my pounding heart, my pumping blood, the soft, warm fur of the mink around me like a lover's embrace. Streetlights, headlights, the rush and grind of traffic like music from another world. But only one thought echoing, echoing in my head. Escape. Escape.'

'You didn't want to get caught.'

'Of course not.'

'But here you are.' Eve sat back again. 'Caught. You bungled your attempt on Felicity Lomare. Rushed it, didn't do that research. She knocked you out, Ann. You had sharps to her throat, but she knocked you cold. She had the guts, she had the skills.'

The first tears sparkled, and spoke of self-pity.

'I would've written myself out of it. I didn't have time! You weren't supposed to be there.'

'That's called a plot twist,' Peabody commented. 'A good writer knows how to work them.'

'You ruined the pacing, the arc. I was still working on scenes with you.'

'Yeah, I read them, too.' Sitting back, amusement on her face, Eve laughed.

'You'd lure me into an abandoned warehouse, where I go in alone, without backup, without notifying anyone I'm pursuing a lead on a serial killer. Then you get the drop on me and kill me with my own weapon. Seriously? You think that plays?'

On those flushed cheeks two bright red flags burned through. 'It's a first draft.'

'Right. Well, you'll have plenty of time for a second draft, or however many it takes. You'll have the rest of your life. Ann Elizabeth Smith, you've confessed to the murders of Rosie Kent, Chanel Rylan, and Loxie Flash. You've confessed to the attempted murder of Felicity Lomare. Evidence supports you further planned and plotted several other murders, including that of a police officer.'

438

'I haven't finished polishing those scenes. I haven't finished the structure of the plotting on all of them.'

'Uh-huh.' Eve rose. 'You might want to think about writing scenes that take place in a maximum security prison, likely off-planet.'

'I don't want to go off-planet. I want to stay in New York. I want my writing tools. I want my sewing tools.'

'I don't recall any of those options included in your rights and obligations. You're a stone-cold killer, Ann. My partner and I? Our art is taking down stone-cold killers, and we sure as hell stand up for our art. You are hereby down. Officers will come shortly to escort you back to your cage. Get used to the view.'

'I don't like this scene! I'm going to rewrite it.'

'You do that.' Eve paused at the door. 'Why "Strongbow"?'

'A strong bow is a lethal weapon.'

Eve raised her eyebrows. 'That's it? Huh. Dallas and Peabody exiting. Interview end.'

'She's completely bent,' Peabody commented. 'Do you really think she'll get maximum security, off-planet?'

'I think the tenor of "completely bent" depends on Mira's and the other headshrinkers' opinions. I lean toward her getting that max security, but likely in a ward for mental defectives. Either way, she's down and she's done.'

She glanced down as Roarke stepped out of Observation.

'Get her taken to her cage, then go on home. I'll write it up.'

'I can give you a hand with it.'

'I've got it. Find McNab, he's probably lurking around here somewhere.' Even as she spoke McNab came out of Observation with Callendar. The two of them looked like the headliners for a carnival.

'Didn't want to miss the big finish,' McNab said.

'And that chick is whoa,' Callendar added, making her eyes jiggle in her head.

'She's all that and a side of fries. Thanks for your help, both of you, in bringing her down. Peabody, get her gone, then get gone yourself.'

'You off?' McNab tapped his fingertips to Peabody's. 'I could use some libations, some chow, maybe some tunes. You in, Callendar?'

'You had me at libations. We can wait for you, Dallas. Do a victory lap with brews.'

'That's okay, go ahead. I've got ends to tie yet.'

'Sucks being the boss.'

Eve glanced back at the Interview door. 'Not tonight it doesn't.'

She walked toward her office with Roarke. 'It can suck otherwise, because I'm going to be about another hour writing and wrapping this up. I can meet you at home.'

'Why don't I have dinner with my wife in her office while she works? It can be pizza.'

'You had me at pizza.'

'I always have you at pizza.'

In her office, she dropped into her chair, let him program it. 'She's fucked-up crazy, but there's a lot of sly in there.

Sly and smart in there, too. I don't know if legal crazy wins or not.'

'She'd added you to her list. You knew she would.'

'I knew she'd never get that far. Plus you should read the scene. A boneheaded first-day rookie wouldn't walk into the situation she dreamed up for my untimely death.'

'And still she managed to kill three people.'

'And still,' Eve agreed with a look at her board. 'I don't think she'd have taken Lomare, even without our arrival on the scene. That's not a woman who gets pushed down the stairs.'

'I tend to agree with you.' He set the pizza on her desk, sat on the edge of it, and took a slice.

'Did you get this tube of Pepsi from my AC?'

'You generally prefer it, when you can't have wine, with pizza.'

'Why didn't I know I have Pepsi in there? Do you know the bullshit I get at Vending?'

'I do, which is why you have Pepsi in there.'

She cracked the tube, drank deep. 'Sometimes I sort of like the challenge.'

He knew that, too.

'Well then, now you have a choice, depending on your mood. You pushed the right button when you challenged her to defend her work. At that point, and from that point forward, she wanted to confess.'

'Not confess so much as tell the stories, brag about them, hype her work and brilliance – which amounts to the same.'

She bit into pizza, took a moment to acknowledge and enjoy her own little victory lap.

Roarke, a cold tube of Pepsi, and pizza.

'You know, if we really wanted to stick it to offenders, they would never again taste the amazement of the pie.'

Smiling, Roarke brushed his fingers over her hair. 'That seems very harsh.'

'Okay, not all offenses – sliding scale. But murder? Pizza's off the menu for life. It could be a deterrent. Anyway, I'm eating this slice, then I'm giving Nadine the heads-up. She earned it. And I'll contact DeLano, tell her it's closed up. And Rylan's roommate, our cooperative bartender, the kick-ass former counterintel agent, the skanks.'

'Why don't I contact Felicity for you? She gave me her contact info.'

'She wanted contact with you, ace, full contact. That was clear.'

He smiled again, danced his fingers up Eve's arm. 'Was it then?'

Eve mulled as she finished the slice. 'I could take her. She's wily and tough, but I could take her if she moved on you.'

'My money's on you. But I might place a small side bet on her.'

Eve guzzled more Pepsi. 'I can take her, so, yeah, go ahead and let her know. She'll tag Berkle, put her mind to rest. Okay, one hour, the rest of this pizza, then home.'

'And there, I can take you.'

She glanced at him, decided she could eat another slice

while making the calls. 'Want to lay a bet on who takes who first?'

'Either way, I win.' He leaned over, kissed her. 'Good work, Lieutenant.'

'Yeah, all in all.'

All in all, she thought again as, with a slice in one hand, she swiveled her chair around to finish the job.

And close the book.

EXCLUSIVE EXTRACT

Read an extract from

Leverage in Death

The new J.D. Robb thriller

1

Thou shalt not kill.

Paul Rogan didn't consider himself a religious man, but that commandment played over and over in his head as he stepped into the lobby. As his wing tips clicked on the polished marble floor, those four words beat inside him.

As he'd done every weekday morning for eleven years – minus holidays, sick days, and vacations – he swiped his company ID at check-in.

Stu, manning security, gave him a nod. 'Monday again, huh, Mr. Rogan.'

'Monday,' Rogan muttered and turned, as he did every Monday morning, to the elevator banks.

Behind his back, Stu smirked a little. It looked like Mr. Rogan had himself a big-ass Monday morning hangover.

Rogan stepped into an elevator along with a handful of other execs, some admins, a couple of assistants. He wore a dark, pin-striped suit over an athletic frame, a crisp white shirt, and a blue-and-red-chevron-pattern tie in a single Windsor knot.

Despite his cashmere topcoat, the cold seeped into his bones as he listened to the voice in his head.

Cecily. Melody.

The voice spoke the names, again and again even as four words pounded out a rhythm.

Thou shalt not kill. Thou shalt not kill.

And yet.

He stepped out on the thirty-second floor – executive level, Quantum Air. The logo, the silver whoosh of it, streaked over the wall behind the curve of the reception counter. Already the 'links and comps beeped and hummed. The waiting area, empty at this hour, sat quiet and plush. Another wall, all tinted glass, opened the room to New York, its sky and skyline.

Blue today that sky, so blue, he thought as he stared a moment. How could it be so blue, so clear?

He turned from it and, without his usual words for the trio at reception, walked to the double glass doors.

They opened, splitting the logo's whoosh in two. He understood what it meant to be split in two.

Cecily. Melody.

Thou shalt not kill.

He passed assistants, admin stations, offices. Though it was still just shy of nine, men and women in sharp suits sat at desks, opened briefcases, sipped their fancy coffees while studying reports.

His own admin jumped up. So young, so bright, so earnest, Rogan thought. He'd been the same, just the same, once upon a time.

'Good morning, Mr. Rogan. I updated your tablet for the nine o'clock conference. It's on your desk. If you're ready to go over some of the updates—'

'Not necessary. No calls, Rudy.'

Rudy opened his mouth to speak, but Rogan closed the door to his office. Though he frowned when he heard the *click* of the lock, Rudy decided his boss just needed a few before the big meeting.

Inside his office, Rogan begged, bargained, pleaded. The voice inside his head never changed in tone. Utterly calm, utterly cold. When another voice came through, desperate and terrified, he wept.

He trembled as he removed his topcoat. Once again he stared through a glass wall at the blue sky, as he stood in an office he'd worked diligently to earn.

It all ended today, as February dribbled into March 2061. Eleven years since he'd come aboard Quantum as a junior exec.

The voice gave him only two choices, so he had no choice at all.

Surrendering, he followed the instructions inside his head and opened his briefcase.

At eight-fifty-six, he stepped out of his office. Rudy popped up again.

'Mr. Rogan, I wanted to tell you I added a few more notes, some personal data on Ms. Karson. Just chat points.'

'All right, Rudy.' He paused a moment, looking into that young, earnest face. 'You do good work. You've been an asset to me, and to Quantum Air.'

'Thanks.' Rudy brightened. 'It's a big day.'

'Yes, a big day.'

Feeling the weight of it, Rogan walked to the conference room. 'Please stop,' he murmured as his heart beat like a brutal fist inside his chest.

Inside the conference room, the blue sky, the sweep of downtown Manhattan, the glint of the river gleamed through the tinted glass. On the wall, the screen held steady and silent with the silver logo.

On the long, polished table, silver trays held glossy pastries, perfectly ripened fruit, pitchers of water – sparkling or still. China cups waited for assistants to fill them with tea or coffee.

Reps from EconoLift – one male, one female – sat studying tablets with cups and glasses at their elbows. Two of Rogan's associates did the same. Lawyers and accountants from each company filled more seats.

'There needs to be another way.'

At Rogan's murmur, Sandy Plank – senior VP, accounting – gave him a quizzical glance.

But Rogan only heard the voice in his head.

At nine sharp, the doors opened again. Derrick Pearson, Quantum's president and CEO, stood for a moment surveying the room. His black and silver mane flowing, he entered along with Willimina Karson.

In heeled boots, Karson – Econo's president – stood six foot one inch. They made an imposing pair, Pearson in his severe black suit and silver tie, Karson in her straight-line red dress and short jacket.

Everyone around the table stood.

'Good morning, everyone,' Pearson said in his lion's roar of a voice. 'Let's bring in Chicago, New LA, Atlanta, London, Rome, and Paris.'

As he rattled off cities, the screen flashed into sections, those sections flashed with other conference rooms or offices, more people in suits.

The voice in Rogan's head spoke incessantly, sharper and sharper. Then added screams.

Rogan took two staggering steps forward, interrupting Derrick's opening greeting.

'Paul.' More surprised than annoyed, Pearson touched a hand to Karson's arm. 'Willimina, you've met Paul. Paul Rogan, our VP of marketing.'

'Derrick . . . I don't have a choice. I'm sorry.'

Something in his voice, something in his eyes, had Karson stepping back even as Pearson stepped forward.

'Are you all right, Paul?' he asked, gripping Rogan's arm.

'I'm sorry. I'm so sorry.'

Rudy, dashing toward the conference room with the tablet Rogan had left on his desk, got within three strides of the doors before they blew.

Lieutenant Eve Dallas stood amid the carnage. The air stank of blood, charred flesh, piss, and vomit. Water from the sprinkler system soaked into the carpet so it squished underfoot. With her boots and hands already sealed, she studied the room.

The blast had blown off the doors, shattered most of the mega screen, blown chunks off the table, sent chairs and people flying – and some burning.

The thick carpet now bore a wide, blackened hole, and the walls as well as the floor carried spatter – blood, brains, other bodily fluids.

Lieutenant Lisbeth Salazar, heading up the Explosives and Bombs Unit, stood with her.

'Eleven dead, nine injured. The dead include the bomber. We're picking up the pieces there . . .'

Both women watched the sweepers in their protective white suits, the boomer hounds in their thick gray, comb the room.

'But we've got some wits from the other side of the room, more shaken than stirred, who state Paul Rogan, VP of marketing, revealed a suicide vest seconds before he detonated it. I can tell you from the extent of the damage, it was either designed for short-range effect, or it piffed and that's all he got. I'm estimating a range of twelve to fifteen feet.'

'You're saying it could've been worse.'

'Oh, a whole hell of a bunch worse.' Salazar – an imposing woman with skin the color of well-steeped tea, eyes of flaming green – gestured. 'He was facing away from the table, angled toward the door – toward Derrick Pearson, CEO. He blew Pearson with him, and the people at the front section of the table. It looks like some of the DBs took chunks of the table and the shrapnel as COD rather than the actual explosion.

'We've swept,' Salazar added. 'And we're sweeping again – the entire building. But I'm saying this was the only device, this was the only bomber.'

Eve noted the spears of wood and metal impaled in the walls, the webbing cracks on the wall of glass. But the bulk of the damage, the radius of the blast? Yeah, around twelve feet.

'How'd he get it in the building?'

'Briefcase – lead-lined. He breezed right through the standards, and he's worked here nearly a dozen years. Security had no reason to wand or ray him. I did a run, the guy's got no record. Married going on fourteen years. An eight-year-old daughter.'

'Where are they, the wife and kid?'

'I sent some uniforms to pick them up. You and the ME make the call, Dallas, but this looks like homicide to me. It's not terrorism, domestic or otherwise, on the face of it. Maybe the guy flipped out, who knows? Some big deal supposed to go down today – here. Maybe he didn't want it to go down. We'll pick up the pieces, and we'll tell you what kind of boomer.'

Eve stood tall and lean in the long leather coat. Her hair, short, choppy, and brown, haloed a face of angles, with a shallow dent in the chin. Her eyes, brown, sharp, and all cop, swept the room again.

'You handle your end, I'll handle mine. Let's see where we end up.'

'Works for me.' Salazar pulled out her signaling communicator. 'Salazar.'

'Lieutenant, neither Cecily Greenspan nor Melody Rogan showed up at the school this morning where the kid attends and the mother is assistant principal. The mother texted in that the kid wasn't feeling well. They don't answer their 'links.'

Salazar's brows lifted, and Eve gave her the nod.

'Officer, I'm passing you to the primary in charge. Lieutenant Dallas.'

Eve took the comm. 'Get to the residence. If there's no response, you have probable cause to enter.'

'"Probable cause"?' Salazar said as Eve passed the comm back.

'Eleven dead, nine wounded, and a missing wife and daughter. That's more than probable for me. I'll let you get back to what you do. I'll start doing what I do.'

Eve walked to the doorway. 'Peabody!'

Her partner hustled down the ruined corridor in pink cowboy boots. 'This is ours. Treat it as a homicide until it looks otherwise. Bomber, deceased, was Paul Rogan – do a run. Officers are en route to his residence to locate his wife and daughter – neither of which is where they should be this morning.'

'Devoted family man.' As she looked into the conference room, Peabody blew out a breath. 'According to one of the wits who survived that. A Sandy Plank, another VP, minor injuries, treated on-site. Hardworking, loyal, smart, and crazy in love with his wife and daughter is how she describes Rogan.'

'The loyal don't generally blow up their boss and coworkers,' Eve pointed out.

'Yeah. She's a mess – Plank, I mean. She states he didn't look well, and she heard him mumbling to himself. She thought he said: There needs to be or has to be another way. And when his boss and Willimina Karson – head of EconoLift – came into the meeting, Rogan walked over to them. Plank said she was watching Rogan because she thought he must have been feeling ill. She heard him say he didn't have a choice. He said he was sorry. He was, according to her, crying. Then he opened his suit jacket. Boom.'

'Run him, and let's find out what this meeting was about. Details. Any idea where his office is?'

'Down and left, second right. Salazar put a man on the door.'

'I'll take it.' She started down, stopped. 'Pearson, deceased, was top dog. Let's find out who's top dog now.'

The Eve Dallas series

**Eve and Roarke are back in
Leverage in Death – out September 2018**

CRIME AND THRILLER FAN?

CHECK OUT **THECRIMEVAULT.COM**

The online home of exceptional crime fiction

KEEP YOURSELF
IN SUSPENSE

Sign up to our newsletter for regular recommendations,
competitions and exclusives at **www.thecrimevault.com/connect**

Follow us

@TheCrimeVault

/TheCrimeVault

for all the latest news